W9-BZW-164

THE BOYS' CLUB

THE BOYS' CLUB

A Novel

ERICA KATZ

HARPER

An Imprint of HarperCollins*Publishers*

This is a work of fiction. Names, business names, characters, places, and incidents are products of the author's imagination or are used fictitiously and are not to be construed as real. Any resemblance to actual events, locales, organizations, or persons, living or dead, is entirely coincidental.

HarperCollins books may be purchased for educational, business, or sales promotional use. For information, please email the Special Markets Department at SPsales@harpercollins.com.

FIRST EDITION

Designed by Bonni Leon-Berman

Library of Congress Cataloging-in-Publication Data has been applied for.
ISBN 978-0-06-296148-8

20 21 22 23 24 LSC 10 9 8 7 6 5 4 3 2 1

To my mom and dad, for this amazing life and their unwavering support each and every day of it. (I'm begging you to skip over the sex scenes when you read this.)

THE BOYS' CLUB

ANATOMY OF A FAILED MERGER

1. THE TARGET LIST. A list of potential buyers and sellers of companies in the relevant market.
2. THE NONDISCLOSURE AGREEMENT (NDA). A written legal agreement between two or more parties entered into in order to protect the sensitive information each party will become privy to as negotiations are entered.
3. INDICATION OF INTEREST (IOI). An expression showing conditional and nonbinding interest in engaging in the purchase or sale of a company.
4. ATTEMPTED CLOSING. An attempt to conclude the merger process and legally transfer ownership through signing and recording of all documents.
5. BREAKUP. The termination of a deal without closing; typically, a fee is paid by the party failing to follow through with agreed-upon closing terms.
6. POSTBREAKUP MATTERS. The "cleanup" and adjustments made after a deal or breakup in order to ensure that each party to the transaction can successfully function.

PROLOGUE

SUPREME COURT OF THE STATE OF NEW YORK
COUNTY OF NEW YORK: IAS PART 29

SHEILA PLATT,
INDEX NO. 1476/46
Plaintiff,
-against-
GARY KAPLAN,
Defendant

WITNESSES:
ALEXANDRA VOGEL, WITNESS FOR PROSECUTION
MICHAEL ABRAMOWITZ, ATTORNEY FOR MS. VOGEL
EXAMINATION BEFORE TRIAL OF GARY KAPLAN,
taken by and before MARA HARVEY, a Court Reporter and Notary Public of the State of New York, held at the offices of MEYERS & COWLER, ESQS., 41 Kenmare Street, New York, New York, on Monday, June 6, 2019, commencing at 11:30 in the forenoon.

DIRECT EXAMINATION BY MR. ZEIGLER:

Q. Good morning, Ms. Vogel.
A. Good morning.
Q. My name is Avery Zeigler, I am with the law offices of Zeigler & Babchick. I represent the defendant, Gary Kaplan, in an action that was commenced against him by Ms. Sheila Platt.
I'll be asking you some questions about your professional

career and specifically your relationship with Mr. Kaplan. If you don't understand my questions, please let me know and I'll try to rephrase them.

Let's begin with some background questions. Where did you go to law school?

A. I went to Harvard Law School.

Q. And where did you work after you graduated from law school?

A. My first job out of school was as an associate at the firm of Klasko & Fitch.

Q. And what group were you in when you joined Klasko & Fitch?

A. At Klasko, you join the firm as an unassigned associate. You list your interests in a given practice area, and in April, you match into a group.

Q. How do you match? What is the process?

A. Associates state their areas of interest. They do work in those areas. And if the group likes the associate, they allow them in.

Q. Are there a limited number of spots in every group?

A. Well, there needs to be enough work for the associates who join. A practice group can't take an unlimited number.

Q. Is it a highly competitive process?

A. I would say some groups are more coveted among associates than others.

[Defense counsel confers with cocounsel]

Q. Did you ever feel the need to go beyond the call of duty? To become personally involved in a nonprofessional capacity with colleagues or clients?

I gave a slight shiver as my armor of high heels and a pristinely tailored suit began to crack. I was no longer in the overly air-conditioned boardroom of my attorney's sleek Manhattan office; there was no longer sunlight streaming in through the window in gold ribbons that curled up in my lap. My manic first months at Klasko & Fitch rushed over me, soaking every inch of my body in the competition, the exhilarating feelings of success, the frayed nerves, the fear and loathing and all-consuming intensity of being an unassigned associate, trying desperately to secure a place in a prestigious group. I wiped the sweat from my brow and closed my eyes for an extended moment.

PART I

THE TARGET LIST

A list of potential buyers and sellers of companies in the relevant market.

CHAPTER 1

"Does this look okay? Sam? Sam!"

Sam stared at the television as *Morning Joe* blared, his mouth slightly agape. I stomped the heel of my new nude pumps on our hardwood floor.

"What?" He turned to me, his dark eyes large and questioning above the lingering indentation from a peaceful sleep across his right cheek.

"Does this look okay? Does it look lawyerly?" I smoothed my blouse into my skirt and breathed in. "Jesus Christ. I'm so jumpy."

He lowered his stubbly chin as he scanned me up and down. "You look really sexy."

"Ugh!" I grunted as I turned toward the bedroom. Sam followed me sleepily, scratching at his stomach under his white undershirt, just above his flannel pajama pants.

"What? What's wrong with that? How are you supposed to look? However you're supposed to look, that's how you look."

I pulled my blouse over my head and ran to the closet. "Professional! I'm supposed to look professional on my first day as a lawyer. Obviously," I huffed, riffling through my tops.

"You do look professional! Well, you did." I was now standing in my heels, skirt, and a bra, and he slid into the space beside me and wrapped his arms around my waist.

"Really?"

He nodded and picked my white silk blouse up off the floor and handed it to me as a buzzing reverberated out into the room from the top of my dresser. I turned from him and grabbed for my phone.

I stared at the word "Home" for a moment, hovered my finger over the decline button, then thought better of it and pressed the green button as Sam took the opportunity to make his escape back to the couch.

"Hi Mom! I'm just rushing to get ready! What's up?"

"We're both on!" my mother shouted. I put my phone on speaker and pulled the blouse back over my head.

"We just called to wish you good luck!" my dad chimed in. I pictured them leaning their heads together in the kitchen and yelling into the now-yellowed receiver, the inordinately long and irreversibly twisted cord curling at their feet.

"Aw thanks, guys. I'll call you later and let you—"

"Alex?" my dad asked.

"Hello? Can you hear me?" I checked my screen to see I had four bars.

"You hung up on her!" my mother whined.

"You have me on mute!" I yelled, immediately cursing the futility of my exclamation. *I'll give it five seconds, and then I'm hanging . . .*

"Bunny?"

"Mom?"

"Hi! We thought we lost you! Are you nervous?"

"Not really!" I lied, tilting my head to the side to get a better angle to bite my thumbnail. "It's just orientation."

"We're so proud of you," she gushed. My stomach churned, and I stole a glance at the Ann Taylor suit, still with tags, hanging at the far end of my closet.

I wished I had spent one of my law school summers at Klasko. I'd know what to wear—what to expect.

"I'm wearing a skirt and top. Do you think I should wear a suit instead?" There was silence on the other end of the phone.

Why am I asking for advice on business attire from a stay-at-home mom and a guy who wears scrubs to work every day?

"I'm sure you'll look beautiful in whatever you decide!" my mother finally piped in.

I rolled my eyes. *Useless.*

"Thanks, Mom. And thanks for calling, guys. But I have to get going."

"Knock 'em dead!" my father shouted.

I felt suddenly deeply inadequate. "Relax, Dad. Not like I'm curing cancer."

"That's why I told you to knock 'em DEAD!" my dad sang proudly. I couldn't help but smile at the corniness of his dad joke.

My father was an oncologist, and while I knew he was proud of me, I always had the sneaking suspicion that he wished I had stuck it out at Sanctuary for Families, though he never said as much.

When I was a kid, my parents always told me, "You can be whatever you want to be when you grow up. A doctor, or a lawyer . . ." They always trailed off there. I couldn't recall when I decided that those were my only two options. My upper lip beaded with sweat. *How the hell did I get here? Do I even want to be a lawyer? Maybe I shouldn't have taken a job in BigLaw. Sam and I could have survived on my Sanctuary for Families salary until his company started making money . . . if his company ever started making money.* I looked at the large closet full of blouses and skirts, most with the tags still on, and I knew it wasn't true. I wanted this life, my luxurious apartment, a wardrobe full of new clothes. I chose them.

"Your mother and I are off to the farmers market. We love you! Good luck!"

My phone beeped with an incoming call, and I saw the name

Carmen Greyson on the screen. "Thanks guys! Have to run! Love you!" I picked up the new call without waiting for their last goodbye.

"Hi!" I sighed, relieved to hear from my law school classmate. "I'm so glad you—"

"What are you wearing?" Carmen demanded.

"Um, nude pumps, navy pencil skirt, white silk blouse?"

"Yes. Perfect. Totally perfect. Neat and clean and professional," Carmen assured me, and I felt my heart rate slow immediately.

While Carmen and I had never quite become close at school, the fact that we were joining the same firm made us comrades. Plus, she had spent her last summer interning at the firm, so I planned to latch on to her for social introductions and advice on navigating firm politics. Carmen was sharp, and spicy, and severe—exciting in a way that I was unaccustomed to, having grown up coddled in Connecticut.

I exhaled slowly, allowing my cheeks to puff out with the force of my relief.

"I'm wearing a skirt and top too. But I'm not sure . . ." Carmen waffled over her various outfit options as I poked my head out into the living room.

Sam was sitting on the new tufted gray sectional that I had purchased with the last pennies of my firm moving stipend. I missed him already. I wished the summer had lasted just a few months longer. After I'd taken the New York bar exam, we'd bounced around Southeast Asia with my father's credit card in hand, his all-too-generous present to me for completing law school, and a steady buzz in our heads for three weeks. I didn't feel ready for the real world just yet.

"Okay. See you soon!" Carmen's voice punctured my thoughts, and I managed a goodbye before she hung up. I walked over to Sam, who tore his gaze away from the morning news and looked up at me, grabbing my collar gently and pulling my lips down to his.

"What?" He narrowed his eyes at me as he contemplated my expression. I eased myself down beside him.

"I have no idea why I'm so nervous. It's only orientation. It's not like I'll be doing any real work today."

"You're going to be great." He squeezed my thigh dismissively and turned back to the television. I watched him for a moment longer, hoping for further encouragement. There was none.

I made my way to the mirror in our entryway, smoothing my long, toffee-colored hair and wishing my tired brown eyes looked brighter. *Relax,* I told myself. *You're going to be fine.* I stepped back, gave myself a final once-over, and ripped the tag off the chocolate-brown leather tote with clean lines and enough space for a laptop that my mother had bought me. I wasn't quite sure how my mother managed to pick out such a perfect gift—she had worn pleated pants and practical flats to volunteer at the library for as long as I could remember—but I imagined she had asked a sales assistant at her suburban Bloomingdale's for help with what "working women" carry to the office. I breathed in slowly, cautiously drew air into my lungs, pushed it out through my pursed lips, and headed for the front door.

"I'm off!" I announced.

Sam peeled himself off the couch with breathy, sputtering sound effects that he misguidedly believed combated his stiff morning muscles as he zombie-walked toward me.

"Good luck." He smiled as he leaned in to kiss my cheek.

"What are you going to do today?" I asked.

"Alex, I work. Every day." As Sam shifted his feet away from me and toward the television, I registered the dejection in his voice. "There is so much to do. The investor meetings have been going well. We still need to buy all of the actual inventory—"

"That's not what I meant," I said, cutting him off as I glanced at my watch. "I know how hard you work. I'm just nervous. And I have to go."

"Go! Good luck!" Sam attempted a reassuring smile.

"Everybody tells me this job is going to take over my life. We're going to be fine, right?"

He took my cheeks in his hands. "You're the one who said it's all totally manageable unless you match with mergers and acquisitions. Don't request work from them. Don't rank them. Don't match with them. Easy peasy," he said with a wink.

I smiled up at him and gave him a long kiss before making my way down the hallway, the nerves settling right back into the pit of my stomach as I pushed the call button for the elevator incessantly until it opened on my floor with a ding.

I arrived twenty minutes ahead of schedule at one of the hundreds of hulking office buildings lining Fifth Avenue, all of which looked exactly the same to me from street level. I'd given myself forty-five minutes to get to work, padding the twenty-three-minute subway commute from Chelsea to midtown that I'd made two dry runs of the week before. The building I now stood outside housed the American headquarters of a Japanese bank, two consulting firms, and Klasko & Fitch—the largest and one of the most prestigious law firms in the world. I pushed through the revolving door, my heels clicking in my ears inside the glass pie wedge before it spit me out into the sprawling marble lobby.

The sterile foyer was a cacophony of one-sided phone conversations and perfunctory salutations. Everybody who passed me seemed to have a purpose. Nobody dawdled, nobody chitchatted. The men and women making their way to their respective elevator banks with the polished swipes of their key cards presented themselves cleanly and confidently to the world. Following suit, I allowed myself only a sideways glance at the soothing sheet of water cascading over the white stones and the caution tape sealing off the construction around one of the far elevator banks, where building management had posted a sign politely asking me to "pardon our appearance." I did so, careful to continue at my quick clip toward the large blue sign declaring "Welcome New Klasko & Fitch Associates" at the far end of the lobby.

A man at the security desk whose name tag read "Lincoln" smiled kindly at me as I passed. I imagined he was a seasoned spotter of nervous new associates.

"Hi! Welcome to Klasko & Fitch! We're so happy to have you with us. Alexandra Vogel, yes? Sorry. You go by Alex, is that right?" A cherubic brunette who looked to be in her midforties smiled up at me warmly from the welcome table. "I'm Maura. Head of recruiting. I'm not sure if you remember . . ."

"Of course! We met at the on-campus interview. And yes. Alex. Thank you." My voice was steady, as it always was in tense moments. Some vestige of my teenage competitive swimming career allowed me to hide my nerves at performance time.

As she flipped through the stack of folders behind a small sign reading "R—Z," I glanced at my watch.

"You're right on time," she assured me, without looking up from the folders. "Not the first one here. Not the last. Right in the middle of the pack. Don't you worry at—ah! Here it is." She pulled a branded K&F folder out of the stack. "Your photo ID and keycard are in there. You'll need them to get into the elevator bank. And you'll head right over there and up to the forty-fifth floor. If you forget that, it's right on the first page in that folder. If you need anything—"

"Hi, I'm Nancy Duval." Maura and I both turned to see a

wide-eyed blonde picking at the fraying hem of her jacket. For a moment my heart sank to see that she was more formally dressed, but then I assured myself that my well-tailored skirt and top was just as appropriate as her well-worn suit. I wondered whether her interruption was the result of first-day jitters or a more general social awkwardness, the kind I'd become very familiar with in law school.

"Hi!" A tall, thin blonde appeared at Maura's side and looked at Nancy. "I'm Robin, the other recruiting manager. I can take care of you over here."

I thanked Maura for her help, slipping the folder into my tote.

She winked. "Love your bag." I smiled back at her and made my way toward the elevator bank serving floors 35 to 45, where three women in suits waited. I prayed they weren't going up to the forty-fifth floor. *I should have worn a suit. I'm going to be the only one in business casual except Carmen. All the men will be in suits. Where is Carmen, anyway? I should stand next to her so I don't stick out.*

"Alex!" the tallest of the trio sang in my direction.

I stared at her. "Carmen! Hey!"

I felt the heat rise from my chest up to my cheeks as I took in her perfectly tailored navy-blue Theory suit—one I'd tried on but decided was too expensive.

She pulled me in for a hug as I stood with my hands awkwardly plastered to my sides.

"You went with a suit," I said, forcing calm into my voice.

"I texted you! You look amazing though!" Carmen beamed. Her pale, almost clear, blue eyes scanned me up and down. I looked down at my phone and saw a text from her, from four minutes back. I guessed she'd sent it while I was in the subway. When it was already too late. I don't know why I listen to my mother, I thought. She has no idea.

Before I could respond, Carmen turned to her friends. "This is Jennifer and Roxanne. We went to undergrad together."

"Hi," Jennifer said warmly, her large brown eyes seeming to betray a certain anxiety below her chunky blond bangs.

"Hey!" Roxanne said with a wave. "I'm so nervous for some reason!" She laughed as she brushed her auburn hair away from her eyes. She was petite and adorable—like the redheaded Cabbage Patch Kids doll that sat on my bed when I was a child.

"Me too!" My shoulders dropped, grateful for her admission. Two men in suits sporting Klasko name tags approached us, laughing with one another, and warm embraces between the other five ensued while I stood off to the side, watching the poised young professionals as they caught up with one another.

"Hey! I'm Kevin," one of the guys said, turning to me as he extended his hand. I forced myself to maintain eye contact despite his prickly gelled hair. *Do men really still spike their hair?*

"Alex." I smiled, but felt envious of the summer they had spent getting to know one another, and getting to know how things worked at Klasko, all the while earning six times what I had at my nonprofit internship.

Even though twelve years had passed since seventh grade, and I now had a healthy social life, a law degree, and reasonably toned arms, I felt the same way I had when I was forced to eat turkey sandwiches on a toilet seat every lunch hour for a week in seventh grade when Sandy Cranswell, our class's queen bee, had decided she detested me because I had "man shoulders" from all of my swimming, so no one would sit with me in the cafeteria. It hadn't lasted long, since Zach Schaeffer befriended me on the coed bus to state finals, and his eighth-grade posse had quickly followed suit, putting me back into Sandy's good graces, but I still remembered the sting.

The six of us crowded into the elevator with a few others, and while the rest of them chatted excitedly, I stood in the back and allowed my eyes to close for a moment, desperately willing the bead of sweat dripping down my spine to evaporate before it bled through my blouse.

As soon as our elevator emptied onto the forty-fifth floor, we saw wide-planked oak floors supporting a modern marble reception desk surrounded by rich brown leather couches and armchairs. I remembered the space only vaguely from my call-back interview almost a year before. But I had been too nervous that day to appreciate how beautiful the office space was. Two women and one man, all seemingly in their twenties, sat behind the desk, wearing headsets. They plastered smiles on their faces when they saw us, without pausing their choruses of "How may I direct your call?" and "One moment please." A sign reading "First-Year Associate Orientation" directed us down a hallway lined with glass-walled conference rooms.

The doors to our meeting room had been propped open to welcome us, and the curtains had been pulled back to expose the south-facing view, which seemed to span all of Manhattan below Fifty-Fifth Street. The MetLife Building, front and center, relished the spotlight; the Freedom Tower stood reflective and resolute in the distance; the Empire State Building seemed to rush with impossible confidence skyward, as if challenging the Chrysler Building to a battle of wills; and off to the left, the Brooklyn Bridge yawned sleepily out over the silver waters of the East River.

A woman in a gray pantsuit stood at the podium, watching us with a small smirk as we took it all in. "Pretty impressive, right?" she announced into the microphone. Some of my fellow first-years took their seats, some chatting, and I realized that none of the others were marveling at the view. They must have become accustomed to it while they interned as summer associates. I relaxed slightly, though, as I noted with relief that several of my fifty-two new colleagues were wearing skirts with blouses, too. I surreptitiously slipped away from Carmen, Roxanne, and Jennifer so I wouldn't stick out as underdressed and took a seat between Kevin and an African American man wearing a navy suit with a red bow tie speckled with little yellow flowers.

The guy in the bow tie leaned over me and pointed to Kevin's tie, an orange number with little puppies tied in a double Windsor that made his neck appear even skinnier than it actually was. "Ferragamo?"

"I . . . um . . ." Kevin flipped over his tie and looked down at the label. "Yup! I guess I'm wearing the uniform!" He laughed and extended his hand. "I'm Kevin."

The other man shook it with a wink. "I dig your spikes, man." I cringed, though he didn't appear to be making fun of Kevin at all. "I'm Derrick. I summered last year out of the LA office, so I'm the new guy," Bow Tie explained, leaning back and putting his hand to his heart before extending it to me. He was handsome, with sharp cheekbones and a square jaw, but he also had style, and a broad smile that released the knot that had been forming between my shoulder blades.

"Alex," I said, taking his hand. "I spent last summer at Sanctuary for Families." He gave me a short nod, acknowledging our common ground as newcomers.

"Good morning, everybody." The woman in the gray pantsuit at the front of the room spoke into the microphone, and we all quieted down obediently. "I'm Eileen Kasten. I'm a litigation partner and head of your first-year training program. For your first eight months at the firm, you will have a training each Monday morning on general firm practices. We hope you spend these first months learning as much as you can about as many different practice areas as you can so that you can make an educated decision about what you'd like to work on for the rest of your career. In eight months, you will match into a practice group which will be responsible for training you on the specifics of their practice. You rank them. They rank you. You match. Everybody, all fifty-two of you, ends up happy."

Derrick snorted and rolled his eyes. "At least half of us will be disappointed," he whispered to me. "There's not enough space for everybody in the best practice groups." I hadn't realized that any of the practice groups were considered better than others, only that M&A was considered more intense.

She went on. "For today, I want you to take note of one another. Look to your right." I looked at the shiny, gelled back of Kevin's head. "That person was in the top fifteen percent of one of the top fifteen law schools in the country. Look to your left." I turned to see Derrick, his eyes crossed and his tongue stuck out just inches from my nose, and covered my mouth to keep from laughing out loud. "That person was in the top ten percent of one of the top ten law schools in the country." She gave a dramatic pause. "How do I know that to be true?"

"We're all in the top ten percent of the top ten law schools," Derrick shouted up toward the podium.

"What's your name?" the woman asked.

"Derrick Stockton," he said with a confidence I envied.

"That's exactly right, Derrick Stockton. This is not meant to intimidate any of you. Quite the contrary, it's meant to put you at ease. You belong here. But it is also a warning that you will not be differentiating yourself here on intelligence alone. Not easily, at least."

I swallowed hard and picked at my cuticle.

"What a load of horseshit. So cliché," Derrick muttered under his breath. He took a mint out of his pocket and popped it in his mouth. "Want one?"

"Oh god." I cupped my hand over my lips. "Do I need one?"
Derrick stared at me for a moment and then narrowed his eyes playfully.

"You're a little nuts, huh? I like it," he whispered. "Your breath is fine. I was just being polite."

"I'm nervous," I admitted, taking the mint.

"Who's not?" He grinned, instantaneously calming me.

". . . we will be looking for you to demonstrate work ethic. Drive." The woman at the podium moved her head mechanically from one side of the room to the other. "Tenacity. We're looking for you to be sponges. You're here because you're the best the American law school system has to offer us. The same holds true, by the way, for the local law school systems in the UK, Germany, France, Japan, Hong Kong, Brazil, and Australia that have educated your international colleagues. By the way, you'll have the opportunity to meet all of your fellow first-years at First-Year Academy in LA in early February. As you might know, we're not only the largest, but we're arguably the best law firm in the world. We are twenty-five hundred lawyers strong in thirty-seven offices across the globe. We took Facebook public. We are the firm that defended affirmative action for the University of Michigan. We . . ."

"They fucking *love* to tell everybody they defended affirmative action. Like it makes them not racist or something," Derrick whispered as he leaned into me.

As Eileen droned on at the podium, I glanced around the room, feeling the nervous energy of my new colleagues despite their placid faces. I marveled at their new ties and well-tailored suits, their shiny heels and pressed collars—the adult equivalents of sparkling white sneakers on the first day of kindergarten. I looked ahead at the Columbia girls sandwiching Carmen in their subtly different suits and instinctively smoothed my blouse in response.

I caught Derrick eyeing me knowingly. "You're lucky," he said quietly.

"Hmm?"

"Nobody really knows what 'business casual' means for girls. You can wear whatever you want. For all anybody knows, it's a fashion statement." He paused for a moment. "But for the record, you're right. Suits are business attire. You're in business casual."

"You're in a suit!"

"I'm all business all the time, baby." He winked; another laugh slipped out of my closed lips. I didn't hear the end of the simultaneously intimidating and motivational speech, but we were suddenly dismissed to the fortieth floor for technology training. As we shuffled en masse down the hallway to the elevator, we passed a glass-enclosed conference room where six white men in dark suits sat around a glossy, hulking wood table.

"Those guys are probably in M&A," Derrick said with a cock of his head.

"How can you tell?" I asked, staring through the glass.

"The way they sit. What they wear. How they look." I looked at him with a raised eyebrow. "Like total douchebags. The highest-paid, most well-respected douchebags at Klasko. It's the most competitive group to match into. It was the same in the LA office. And everywhere else, I think. What groups did you say you were interested in on the questionnaire they sent around?"

"I put real estate," I muttered, hoping that would pass muster. I looked back at the men in the conference room and the intermittent strobes of light thrown off their wrists by their watches and cuff links. They were all well groomed and well dressed. Their gazes were focused, and they seemed to be playing a part in the exact scene one might picture when asked to imagine a meeting taking place in corporate America. Perhaps because of this, they made me feel slightly starstruck.

One of them, who seemed younger than the others, still had an expertly cut suit, shiny hair, and perfectly tanned skin. I saw then that Derrick was right. It wasn't just their attire or just the intensity in their eyes or just the way their knees spread confidently apart under the table. It was the combination of it all. They somehow seemed more important than the rest of us—than me. I struggled to peel my eyes away from them as Derrick and I drifted down the hall, my neck rotating to keep them in my sightline. When I finally turned my head forward, I reminded myself of the rumored astronomical hours they billed and demanding clients they catered to. As I continued to our next session, their sheen dulled in my memory.

CHAPTER 2

The technology training room we were led into was a dimly lit interior space with at least a hundred computers and phones lined up in neat rows. Frigid air blasted down on us from overhead vents, keeping the machines cool and our bodies shivering. Derrick pulled a seat out next to his for me, and I gratefully plunked myself down into it.

A woman with a long, frizzy braid down to her waist paced the front of the room, then cleared her throat to speak. "The computers and phones at your stations are designed to look just the way the ones in your offices do. We're going to start with the phone . . ."

"Ten bucks says no other living thing has been inside her apartment this decade," Derrick whispered.

"Harsh!" I whispered through a laugh. "You're on."

". . . and believe it or not, the most common mistake people make with the phone is not hanging it up. You've been warned." She smiled broadly. "Let's start with how to place a call. It's the easiest thing we'll do today, but let's get in the habit of practicing absolutely everything. I've turned off my cell phone, and written my number on the board behind me. You dial nine for an outside line and a one, so to call me it's 9-1-9-1-7-6-1-2-3-1-4-2. Everybody practice calling it now, but do me a favor and don't leave a voice mail."

We laughed courteously as we picked up our receivers and dialed. I waited for her outgoing voice mail to come through.

"Nine-one-one emergency response, what is your emergency?" the voice on the other end asked. I looked at the receiver in horror and then slammed it down in the cradle.

"What happened?" Derrick leaned over, looking at my phone, but I was too mortified to answer.

"Very good. Okay. Let's move on to transferring calls." We all turned our attention to the front of the room. "You'll note the hold button—"

Suddenly, my phone rang, interrupting our instructor.

The entire class turned toward me; Derrick even rotated his chair to stare me down. The instructor frowned, gesturing at my ringing phone, and I grabbed the receiver.

"Hello, everything is fine . . . I'm fine . . . I just misdialed," I stammered into the phone, then hung up before the caller could say a word. I could feel my cheeks radiating, confirming that I had turned a humiliating shade of crimson.

"Who was that?" the instructor asked, sounding more curious than accusatory.

I stared at her, unable to invent a story quickly enough. "I must have dialed an extra one after the nine-one," I said quietly.

"You called nine-one-one?" Derrick hooted. There was a brief silence in the room, followed by an eruption of laughter. I looked up from my white-knuckled fists resting on my thighs and was surprised to see a roomful of sympathetic faces. Derrick threw an arm over my shoulder, and I melted into his side with a dramatic pout.

"Whatever, I just called the managing partner of the firm by accident," somebody called out from the back of the room. I looked toward the voice and met Carmen's eyes.

"You called *Mike Baccard*?" the instructor gasped.

"At least nine-one-one can't fire you!" Carmen said, and the room erupted into laughter again. I nodded gratefully at her.

The instructor smiled. "Oh, you really are a special class. But let's move things along. At this rate, we're not getting out of here before the end of the day, and I have three new kittens at home who aren't going to feed themselves!"

Derrick and I locked eyes. "I'm pretty sure pets count as living things," I said.

"You have me there, Vogel." He smiled. "I owe you a drink."

We were given offices with unobstructed views of Manhattan, firm email accounts, firm cell phones, firm laptops, firm credit cards, firm 401(k)s, firm health insurance, Equinox gym memberships, and firm gym bags to encourage us to use them. I met my secretary, Anna, who showed me the picture of her grandchildren in the locket around her neck and proudly told me that her oldest son had just joined the clergy. I liked her immediately. She asked me about my message-taking preferences, offered to turn my changes to documents, and insisted she'd keep me fed even when I thought I was too busy to eat. I didn't know what "turning changes" meant, and I couldn't fathom living in a world where work ever trumped the demands of my growling stomach, but I thanked her profusely, and silently vowed to never ask her for a single thing I could manage to do myself.

"I come in at nine each morning to get your affairs and schedule in order," she continued. "Most attorneys come in between nine thirty and ten thirty, but there's no rule for you. I leave at five thirty, and the night secretary covers you until I come back in the morning. Sound good?"

I nodded, and she returned to her cubicle outside my office to allow me to get settled.

"Let me know if you need anything, anytime!" she yelled to me. "I take care of you and the two attorneys on either side of you, but I'm never too busy, even if I seem it."

I smiled gratefully and sat back down at my desk, scanning emails from the training coordinator about our schedule for the coming week. To pass the time until our lunchtime ethics training, I called Carmen's extension to practice joining a conference call. The rest of the day flew, and when our benefits training ended at four thirty, I returned to my office, feeling it was too early to leave. Soon after five, I looked up and locked eyes with Anna, who was packing up to leave for the night just outside my office. She nodded knowingly and walked toward me, leaned her shoulder against the doorframe.

"You should go home, honey. You'll be working so hard you'll forget what your apartment looks like soon enough. I'll see you tomorrow." She ducked out of my doorway before I could say goodbye.

My phone rang, instilling a sudden panic in me that it was time to do real work, but Carmen's name was on the caller ID.

"Hi."

She laughed. "How weird is it that we have offices?"

"Right? I feel like I'm playing a lawyer on TV!"

"We're all going to the bar across the street to celebrate our first day. Come!"

"I promised my boyfriend I'd be home for dinner tonight."

"Don't be absurd," she scoffed. I glanced at my watch. Orientation had finished ahead of schedule, and Sam wasn't expecting me home for at least another hour. I thought for a moment about all the postwork happy hours I'd seen on television and in movies. I had never before had colleagues willing to spend money on overpriced midtown drinks.

"Fine. I'm in." It felt good to yield so easily, allowing me to feel like a professional for the first time in my life.

"First round is on me!" Derrick insisted as he handed the bartender his credit card, our crowd of five circling up behind him at the bar.

"No!" we protested in unison.

"It's my treat. I'll take it out of my moving stipend," he said with a smile. "What's everybody drinking?"

After we shouted our orders at the bartender in turn, I scanned the sparsely populated bar.

Kevin leaned in to me. "Just us and the trading and advertising crowds now. The lawyers and investment bankers won't get here until six thirty at the earliest."

Derrick passed me my vodka soda over Roxanne's head, and I mouthed a thank-you. "How do you know they're in advertising?" I asked Kevin.

"Their clothes. Could be just bad taste, but lack of funds is more likely," he answered before heading off to commandeer a high-top whose occupants were paying their bill. I noticed the preponderance of khakis and ill-fitting dresses around the room, then looked back at our small clan's well-tailored suits, smart skirts, and flowing tops. *And we haven't even gotten our first paychecks yet.*

Kevin waved us over to the table as the waitress was finishing clearing the glasses and wiping up whatever gummy residue of dark liquor was left on the heavily varnished wood.

"Derrick, how do you have anything left in your stipend, by the way?" Carmen asked. "My stipend barely covered my move, and I only came from Boston. Didn't you move across the country?"

Derrick shrugged. "My parents have a furnished place in the city where I'm living now, so I didn't really have anything to move. But Klasko asked if I was moving from outside New York City to inside New York City. I said yes. Because I was. And now I have ten grand to spend on you lovely folks."

We met his glass in a cheers.

"They give you ten grand to move?" Roxanne asked. "Columbia

kids weren't offered anything." She looked at Jennifer, who nodded in agreement.

"Thank god they did," I said. "It was the only way my boyfriend and I could have afforded our security deposit. We only had money left for a couch after we signed a lease."

Carmen looked at me. "You moved in with your boyfriend!? Sam, right?" I nodded, impressed she remembered his name, as they'd only met in passing in Cambridge.

"How long have you been with him?" Jennifer asked.

"Almost four years."

"What's his deal?" Roxanne asked.

I shrugged. "We met in college—I was at Harvard, and he was at MIT—and then he started his company in Boston. It's part of the reason I stayed at Harvard for law school." The group around my table nodded, and I felt a sense of comfort in knowing that they didn't think I was bragging.

"I give you six months at Klasko until you find yourself single!" Derrick teased. Everybody laughed, and so I forced one from my mouth as well, but my stomach twisted up.

"Derrick, don't be an idiot," Carmen said, giving me a reassuring nod.

"I was just messing with you," Derrick said, checking me lightly with his shoulder as I bit my lower lip.

The door to the bar was flung open, and we all turned to look as three men in suits entered purposefully, seemingly unfamiliar with both the feeling of rejection and the force of gravity. I recognized one as the young, attractive attorney I had spotted earlier in the conference room. The waiter was readying their drinks before they even reached the bar.

"Those are some of the M&A associates," Carmen said in a low voice.

"They're probably going back to work after this," Kevin said, looking at his watch. They leaned against the bar and threw back three shots in tandem, chasing them with only slight grimaces before turning to sip the amber liquid in their short, stout glasses. How could anybody do any work after a shot and a drink? I watched the handsome dark-haired associate peel a bill from his money clip and slide it across the bar toward the bartender.

"That makes me think—we need some shots!" Derrick said, commandeering our attention again.

"I should get home, actually," I said apologetically.

Carmen opened her mouth to object but then nodded. "I'll walk you out."

As we left the bar, two dapper men in suits on their way in held the door for us. Well groomed. Well mannered. Well dressed. I supposed the bankers and lawyers were now trickling in. I stepped to the curb and peered east on Fifty-First Street, scanning the street for a taxi. I could feel Carmen watching me.

"I think we can call this a successful first day!" she said cheerily. "I'm sorry that Derrick was being kind of a dick. It's only because he thinks you're cute."

"Really?" I looked back at her, and she nodded. I hadn't pegged Derrick, with his fashionable haircut, colorful bow tie, and flamboyant manner, as being interested in women.

"I asked him. You'll get to see soon how nosy I am," she admitted, picking at her fingernail. "And competitive. Supercompetitive." I had never encountered somebody so self-aware, and so forthcoming.

"I'm competitive, too," I said. "But mostly with myself, I guess."

It wasn't exactly a lie. I had been a competitive swimmer for my entire youth, and I'd held the girls' World Junior Record in both the 50- and 400-meter freestyle for ten years. (A few years back, a Russian teenager snatched my title.) I'd been recruited by the swim coach to Harvard, but halfway through my sophomore season, a badly torn rotator cuff forced me to delete "athlete" from my "student athlete" title.

"As far as I'm concerned, you and I are on the same team," Carmen said. "I'm so happy to have somebody from law school here!"

Swimming hadn't really given me the opportunity to be part of a team—I never even swam the relay—and I welcomed the idea of belonging to one, even though part of me wondered if I even knew how.

"We're on the same team for sure," I agreed.

Carmen stretched her back, hands on her hips as she leaned to look up at the sky, then straightened and looked me in the eye. "I think I only became a lawyer because my father and three brothers are. I just want to show I'm just as good as them. Or better." She grinned mischievously. "Like I said, competitive."

"That's a better reason than mine. I think I'm a lawyer because my parents just sort of suggested it."

"Only child?" Carmen asked. I nodded. "Classic. They could have guided you to worse places, I guess. Anyway, I'm glad we're in this together." She spotted a lit-up cab coming toward us and held her hand up.

I envied the way Carmen could create fact by stating it aloud. Simply because she said it, we were friends—allies—when yesterday we were only former classmates. I smiled and gave her a wave as I hopped into the cab she had hailed for me.

When I arrived home, Sam was sprawled on the couch watching *Anderson Cooper 360°*. At least he'd changed out of his pajamas. I tried to imagine what he did in the house all day without me.

He had met with potential investors for his start-up before we went to Asia, and as far as I knew, he was just waiting for their responses. He held his arms out to me, and I curled up into them.

"So?" he asked.

I frowned dramatically. "Well . . . I called the cops on myself today." He opened his mouth to ask a question, but I held up a palm to stop him. "In front of everybody."

"You need a drink." He laughed as he gave me a peck on the lips and rose.

Sam returned from the kitchen with two glasses of red wine and put one into my outstretched hand. "To my working woman." He clinked his glass against mine. "So, how were the other lawyers? Any friends? How was that Carmen girl you know from Harvard?"

"I met some really nice people. Everybody is so . . . sure of themselves. Carmen is pretty amazing. It's a shame we weren't closer in law school."

"You had me to be close to in law school."

"I know." I kissed him gently, wiggling my way into the crevice between his side and his arm.

He was right, of course. But I'd also had friends from undergrad, many of whom had stayed in Boston after we graduated, minus two LA natives who'd moved back to the West Coast. Though I'd grown up in New York's suburbs, I didn't have any real network of friends in the city. I would have gladly stayed in Boston forever, but because Sam was going to have so many more options for his start-up here, we'd decided to make the move.

"How was your day?" I asked.

"Good! Super productive." He looked at Anderson Cooper rather than at me as he spoke. "Guess what I decided today?"

I raised an eyebrow.

"I'm going to start training for the Boston marathon and run it with some MIT buddies. The company is in a bit of a holding pattern right now, and I've always wanted to run one, anyway."

I studied his profile, looking for an indication that he might be feeling inadequate. In our dimly lit apartment, I started feeling the effects of the wine on top of the vodka soda I'd consumed on an empty stomach. I contemplated reassuring him that this time spent building his company would pay off, then thought better of it, knowing it would make him feel small if he didn't already.

"Wow! Cool!" I took another sip of wine and moved thoughts of Sam's company to the periphery of my consciousness. Alcohol always had a useful way of clearing mental space for more pleasant thoughts.

CHAPTER 3

From: Caroline Meyers
To: Alexandra Vogel
Subject: First Assignment

Alexandra,

Pleased to meet you via email. As you might recall from orientation (though I'm sure all those sessions are a blur!) I will be your assigned staffing coordinator until you match. First assignments have begun rolling in, and I'm happy to report we've been able to accommodate your request to work with the real estate group. Your first assignment will be the review of leases in conjunction with an asset sale. Be in touch with Lara Maloney for details.

Best,
Caroline

I dabbed the sweat from my upper lip with my fingertips and knocked on the frame of Lara Maloney's open door. She waved me into her office and stood, extending her arm to me and shaking my hand almost too firmly. She'd paired khaki trousers that were the business-casual equivalent of mom jeans with clunky black block heels and a black collared shirt, and her dark, frizzy hair was streaked with gray. She didn't seem to wear makeup, but her bright blue eyes were alert and energetic.

I noticed that the beads of perspiration on my upper lip had replenished themselves immediately, and felt suddenly sick. I should have read up more on real estate transactions in M&A

deals prior to this meeting, I thought. I knew that first-years weren't expected to know much about the law itself, but I had the new and unwelcome feeling of being less than sufficiently prepared.

I scanned Lara's office to see if I could engage her on a personal level and camouflage my professional shortcomings, but didn't see many useful clues. A thinning brown ficus with crispy leaves blanketing its soil sat in a pot in the corner. Undergrad and law school diplomas, both from UPenn, were perched on the wall behind her guest chairs, virtually out of sight, but I spotted a painting of a turkey made out of a child's handprint hanging on the wall. I couldn't quite make sense of the woman before me. She clearly placed more value on her child's work than her own academic achievements, and the folders on her desk were meticulously stacked and labeled even as her plant cried out for water and her appearance was just this side of unkempt. I could not think of a single piece of small talk, but fortunately, she didn't seem to be one for idle chatter.

"Hi. We're happy to have you on board! Please, sit!" She gestured to the chair on the opposite side of her desk. "So, we're representing the buyer," she began. I grabbed my legal pad and began to scribble notes. "Our client, Stag River, is acquiring TO's Bakery . . . have you heard of them?"

I nodded, thinking of their delicious sticky buns.

"It's disgusting. People always talk about their sticky buns, but that's because most people have never had an actual good one. Still, I used to go to the one on Lex all the time. I used to be fat, but I got CoolSculpt. You basically freeze your fat cells and pee them out over a few weeks." I stared at her, feeling my jaw slacken, and she waved away her own tangent. "Anyway, TO's is objectively the shittiest bakery in the world, but they have about six hundred properties, and we need to make sure there are no encumbrances on any single property. It's more grueling than difficult. Does this make sense?"

I nodded as my heart skipped two beats. I hadn't written down a single thing after she'd uttered the words "fat cells." I forced myself to focus and began to write again.

Lara continued with the logistics of where I could actually locate the leases (the virtual diligence room), how I should make note of potential issues (never in email or other written communication, except on paper, to be immediately shredded after the deal closed so that if something ever came up in litigation later, the only evidence would be that we had "diligenced the company completely and satisfactorily," never that we had misjudged an issue).

"Did you ask to do real estate, or did they just give you this assignment randomly?" Lara asked suddenly.

I underlined *shred* and looked up. "No, I definitely listed it on my preference sheet," I said, finishing my note on the seller's finances as I spoke.

"What interests you about it?" she asked.

"On the most basic level, I like that there is a physical structure at the center of the deal—something to wrap my mind around."

"Me too." She nodded enthusiastically, indicating I had passed her test. "Also, real estate hours are more manageable compared to other transactional groups, but we work a lot with other groups, so you get a lot of exposure."

I nodded at the elevator pitch with a relieved smile. All of the groups at the firm except M&A boasted the same perks: work/life balance, good exposure to deals at a junior level, a clear path to partnership. Based on what Derrick and Carmen had told me, the M&A attorneys seemed to pride themselves on not sleeping and not seeing their families. And they walked the halls of the firm more proudly and arrogantly than the members of what they referred to as "support" groups.

"Okay, I'll get started on these leases right away. I'll shout out any issues I see and just update you on the progress I'm making . . . daily?"

"COB daily works for me," Lara said. "And I'll send you a calendar invite to our monthly meeting, which is next week. If you're going to be in real estate, you'll learn a lot from it."

Is that it? Am I in the real estate group now?

She dismissed me with a nod, and I went back to my desk and googled "COB."

Close of business.

"Al?" Sam opened our front door.

"I'm in the kitchen!"

Sam slid his hands around my waist from behind as I stirred the liquid dotted with bits of toasted rice. I leaned my head back into him, my work heels bringing me closer to his height. "I'm making Parmesan and black truffle risotto. And I broiled some salmon."

Sam smacked my butt. "It smells incredible." I felt him eyeing the small dark nugget on the counter. "What happened to being on a budget until your first paycheck?"

"I know," I said with a sigh. "But I walked home from work and passed Eataly, and there was a sign saying that Italian black truffle season is almost over!"

"Babe! You walked by Eataly? That's like somebody in AA walking by a liquor store! You gotta take a different route." He backed away from me and hung his coat in the closet. *He would die if he knew what the truffle cost.* Since we'd started dating, Sam had grown to appreciate good food. But he'd grown up in a warm and loving family of academics who lived frugally, and the most glowing praise I had ever heard him give to a meal was that it was a "bargain."

"I know, I know! But it's fine. Everything at work is free! The coffee, the cafeteria, the snacks," I countered. "How was your day?"

"Good, I just finished up meetings with Skylark Capital, the guys who funded that company Uno I was telling you about. They seem really interested in us." Sam sorted through the mail I had picked up.

"And? How did they go?" I added another ladleful of broth.

"Eh. Can't tell." Sam slid up behind me again, putting his hand over mine and helping me stir, but his touch felt entirely different from just the moment before. "How long do we have to stir this for?" he said into my ear.

"Until it's all absorbed," I told him, my body reacting to his. He peered over my shoulder at all the liquid and sighed dejectedly. He was adorable when he wasn't trying to be. "But I don't need to stir it the whole time."

"No?"

"Nope. Just need to stay close to stir every once in a while." I dropped the spoon and turned to him. His lips pressed into mine, and he moved his hands under my arms and hoisted me up onto the kitchen counter. He grinned hungrily and pressed himself into me, his eyes darting over to the stove for a moment.

"So glad you talked me into renter's insurance," he whispered.

***

I scanned the chafing dish, full of sorry-looking breakfast burritos oozing limp bacon and hardened cheese, in the monthly real estate group meeting. I had never been much of a breakfast person, but the smell of overheated meat and cheese made me particularly queasy. Lara and another real estate partner, Michelle O'Reilly, each took a glass of orange juice and an overstuffed burrito. Michelle was younger than Lara, taller than Lara, and more intimidating than Lara. I grabbed a black coffee.

"I envy your willpower!" Michelle glared at me, seeming to mean the opposite, and took a bite of her burrito. "Mmmm. So good."

"I woke up so early for some reason. Already ate," I lied.

"So what have you been working on besides my deal?" Lara asked, making small talk until the rest of the real estate attorneys arrived.

I smiled. "Just real estate so far!"

"What did you say you were interested in?" Michelle asked through a mouthful of burrito.

"Only real estate. I tried to learn as much about the groups at the firm as I could when they asked me to list up to three areas of interest." I paused. "But real estate was the one that appealed most to me. Maybe I should diversify my experience. I have two more weeks to add areas of interest. I'm thinking of adding M&A as well." I hadn't thought of it until that moment.

"Diversity of experience is a good idea. But M&A guys are the worst. They're a bunch of frat boys who walk around like they own this place because they have clients like Gary Kaplan." Michelle took in my lack of reaction. "You know who he is, right?" I shook my head. "He runs the private equity M&A world. He founded Stag River, which is the firm's biggest client by far. He gives us about a hundred million dollars of business each year. And he's a scumbag. Peter Dunn is his go-to guy—which makes Peter think he's God's gift to the world. Peter's an asshole. So are all the other M&A partners. And associates. They fail to realize they couldn't do anything without the rest of us." Michelle's nerves seemed to be fraying audibly.

"Yeah, and they don't let women in," Lara added. "I mean, they *say* they try to promote women, and that it's the hours that weed the women out. But it's their attitudes. Misogynists, all of them." She leaned back in her chair, resting her case along with her spine.

"Got it. No M&A," I said, though the challenge of a group where few women had succeeded oddly appealed to me. "Who's real estate's biggest client?" I asked, attempting to change the topic.

I noticed a sideways glance between the two women. "Stag River," Michelle answered. "Because we do all the real estate for the M&A and capital markets teams."

I sipped at my coffee as I listened to the other attorneys who'd trickled in discussing their deals. *Doing work for somebody else's clients all the time would certainly explain the rather large chips on their shoulders.* I smoothed the flyaway strands of hair that framed my face behind my ears and wondered if they noticed what I did during that meeting: that I didn't really seem to fit in with them.

"You missed a great happy hour last night," Carmen told me, staring at the tomatoes as we stood pensively at the cafeteria salad bar. The day after the breakfast, I'd been staffed on another real estate portion of an M&A deal, this time with Michelle, and I started to fill my days at a decently busy pace. While I didn't find the work particularly interesting, I was gratified by the thought that I was earning the same salary as the M&A

associates who were emailing us about the deal at all hours of the night.

I spooned green peas over my bed of romaine. "I know. I got staffed on this new real estate deal, and I worked late. Who was there?" The truth was, real estate work never kept me much past six, and I'd gone to see a movie with Sam, but I didn't feel great admitting that out loud.

"Monochromatic salads are so last-season," Derrick interrupted, ducking in between me and Carmen. "Saving you seats!" he declared before taking off toward the tables.

"So who went?" I turned back to Carmen.

"Usual crew—Derrick and Kevin—but then some older M&A associates," she said casually as she contemplated the protein options. I pushed down the fear that friendships and cliques were already forming without me, and that Carmen was getting a leg up.

As we made our way down the salad bar, we had to pause behind a redheaded associate who had been standing there since we got our plates. He stared ahead, unmoving, at the containers of vegetables nestled into the ice. Carmen and I glanced at each other and then back at him.

"Sorry, can I just . . ." I reached over him for the tongs in the chickpeas. He blinked and snapped back to life.

"Sorry." He looked back at me with eyes that looked bloodshot and bleary. "I just fell asleep." He looked back at the salad bar, curled his lip, and turned on his heel, leaving his empty tray on the rack.

"That guy's in M&A," Carmen said in a low voice.

I nodded but kept my eyes on him until he disappeared out of the cafeteria. There was something almost honorable about his level of exhaustion.

We took our trays into the seating area, where I followed Carmen to the table where Derrick sat with Roxanne and Jennifer. After greeting them, we placed our phones faceup on the table with all the others and took our seats. I quickly surveyed the other tables in the dining room to see that each and every attorney sat with a phone positioned just as we had ours.

"Did you guys see on *Below the Belt* that the chairman of McAllister resigned because he was sending dick pics to all the young associates?" Derrick asked.

The others nodded, but I had no idea what he was talking about. "What's *Below the Belt*?"

"You don't know it? I read it every morning—it's like *Gawker* for law firms," Carmen explained.

"It's so entertaining. Here, I'm sending you the link," Jennifer said as she reached for her phone.

"It's so nice that they give us phones so we don't need to be chained to our desks," Roxanne commented, pushing her bangs back from her eyes and scrolling through her messages.

"They don't do it to be nice." Derrick snorted. "They do it so we officially have no excuse not to work every second of the day now."

I picked up my own phone and frowned as I spotted the most recent message. "My partner mentor canceled our lunch tomorrow," I announced. "Again."

"Who is your partner mentor?" Roxanne asked.

"Vivienne White," I said.

"Wow," Carmen said, her brow raised. "She's a big deal. You must have impressed them in your interview. Somebody wants you taken care of."

"Really? I haven't laid eyes on her yet."

Derrick looked down at his phone and burst out laughing. "Check out the email Noah Gellman sent to the whole firm."

We refreshed our in-boxes.

From: Noah Gellman
To: FIRM-ALL
Subject: URGENT! DOES ANYBODY HAVE CHAPSTICK!!!!

"Somebody must have gotten to his phone or computer before it locked," Derrick explained. "All the M&A associates mess with each other like that."

Carmen didn't seem all that amused. "So, are you going to do international arbitration?" she asked Derrick, then turned to us. "Derrick was telling me last night at happy hour that his father is the Ghanaian ambassador to the US."

"Probably. What about you?" he asked Carmen.

"I put down real estate and M&A," she said.

"Shit!" Roxanne announced as she stood and, eyes still on her phone, left the table and her food behind. Nobody reacted besides Carmen, who stole a grape from Roxanne's untouched fruit cup. In the past few weeks we had become accustomed to work emergencies trumping social niceties.

"I put real estate, but I'm going to request M&A too before our deadline. I hope that we'll be working on similar stuff. I need somebody to answer all my dumb questions!" I said, turning to Carmen.

A cloud seemed to pass over Carmen's face, and her spine slumped slightly forward. Her expression remained completely placid, but her eyes grayed over. I coughed and took a sip of my water. When I looked back up at Carmen, her eyes were soft blue again. *What the hell was that? Did I imagine it?*

"Great minds." She tapped her temple. "There's more than enough work for both of us to be in real estate if we want," she went on. "If we're both trying to join M&A, we might have a problem." She wasn't lying about the competitive streak. It rang like a bit of a warning to me.

"No desire, really," I assured her. "Just want a bit of diversity in my experience." I pulled on the hem of my skirt, suppressing the urge to accept her words as a challenge. "I'm only doing real estate now. Might just stick with it." As soon as the words left my mouth, I knew I'd try to get onto M&A deals as well. I never could turn down a challenge.

Derrick's head ping-ponged between Carmen and me, a smirk playing on his lips as he watched the sparring we were desperately attempting to conceal as idle chitchat.

That evening I shut down my computer at five thirty, changed into my workout clothes in the bathroom, and ducked into the elevator, praying I could make it out into the lobby without being seen. Even though I'd finished all my work for the day, I still didn't want anyone thinking I wasn't working hard—or that I had enough time to be staffed on more real estate deals. The elevator paused on the thirty-fifth floor, and the anxious blonde I'd encountered on the first day of work entered, looking me up and down. To be fair, I did the same to her. She looked pure, somehow younger than the rest of us, with large eyes. She wore no makeup, and her long hair was pulled back into a tight bun at the nape of her neck. She wore a pearl necklace, pearl earrings, and a neat white cotton cardigan, but when she turned to push the button to her floor, I saw that her black pencil skirt had a long thread hanging down the back like a tail. As she turned to me, we locked eyes.

"Hey," I said, forcing my voice up an octave.

She stared back at me, looking puzzled. "The employee handbook says we need to wear business casual attire when we're in the office, meeting clients, or otherwise representing Klasko in an environment where business casual attire is appropriate," she recited. I examined her expression for any sign of cattiness, but came up empty.

"I know, I'm just running to the gym," I told her, shrugging. "Sometimes you have to bend a rule to stay sane."

She nodded, looking serious. "But how do you know which ones you can bend?"

I shrugged again and gave her a friendly good-night wave as the elevator opened to her floor. She exited reluctantly, as though not wanting to let me go until I answered her question.

I made it to my gym's 6:00 p.m. spin class just as it was starting, throwing my Klasko-branded bag in a locker and slipping onto my bike as the warmup was concluding. When the lights dimmed and the instructor asked us to focus on our breathing, I allowed a smile to spread across my face, a moment of private pride. *See? I'm a lawyer. And I have a life.*

Q. Miss Vogel? Are you all right?

A. Yes. Yes. Can you please repeat the question?

Q. Had you heard of Gary Kaplan prior to meeting him?

A. I had heard his name, yes.

Q. What did you hear about him? Did you have any impression of him professionally, personally, or any other way before you actually met him?

A. I'm not . . . I don't recall the specifics of my impression prior to meeting him.

Q. Do you recall the first time you heard the name Gary Kaplan? Do you recall who said it? Do you recall what they said about him?

A. I can't be certain this was the first time anybody said his name to me, but the first time I recall anybody saying his name was at the beginning of my first year. When one of the real estate partners asked me if I knew who he was, I remember them being shocked that I didn't because he was such a big name at the firm and in the finance world. But that was definitely the first time I remember hearing Gary Kaplan's name.

Q. Would you say that you first came to know Gary Kaplan through third-party accounts from the real estate lawyers you mentioned?

A. No, I wouldn't say that. You asked me the first time I heard Gary Kaplan's name, so I explained my recollection. I came to know him firsthand soon after that through working with him.

Q. How did you come to know him professionally? Is it common for real estate attorneys on a deal to develop relationships with the M&A folks at private equity firms?

A. I actually don't know what's common for them. I would assume sometimes, if real estate is a big enough component of the transaction, then yes.

Q. Let me be more direct: as only a junior associate in the real estate group, how did you come to know Gary Kaplan personally?

A. I only worked briefly in the real estate group before transitioning to working exclusively with the M&A team. Gary was the biggest client of the group.

Q. Who introduced you to Gary Kaplan?

A. Peter Dunn.

Q. Who is Peter Dunn?

CHAPTER 4

A few days after my early escape from work, I was sitting in Lara's office, as she debriefed the M&A team that was on the phone about the real estate portion of their deal before the closing. I watched her curiously as she stiffly responded to the rapid-fire questions emanating from the speaker phone from the senior associate on the M&A team, nervously pulling at a strand of her hair. It was odd to see a partner act deferentially to an associate, to somebody her junior.

"Yes. No problem in change of control," she confirmed. I furrowed my brow, wondering why she wasn't mentioning the recapture rights I had found in the leases and bolded and underlined in two separate emails I'd sent.

"Good," said the associate, who'd introduced himself as Jordan Sellar. He then paused as though he was making a note. *Should I assume that Lara didn't think the recapture rights were an issue? Or should I just play it safe and . . .*

"Oh, um, hi," I said. "Sorry. This is Alex. I don't know if this is relevant, but two of the properties have recapture rights for the landlord. And they actually stipulate that the right remains with a change of control. Sorry. I don't know if that's relevant." I winced as I heard myself repeat the apology.

There was silence on the other end of the line. I cursed myself for thinking I could say anything remotely intelligent aloud in my third week of work.

"Who was that?" Jordan's voice came through the speaker again.

"Oh, sorry. Alex Vogel. I'm a first-year—"

"That is relevant. We'll need to get that waived, Lara. Or

worst case, we can structure around it." He sounded unruffled, and I allowed myself to appreciate a small victory in adding value to the call.

"Of course, Jordan. I've already begun the process. Was just getting to that. Will keep you posted," Lara responded quickly. I looked up to see her glowering at me. *Should I not have said that? Or waited until Jordan was off the phone to tell her?*

When the call ended, Lara took a prolonged inhale. "Alex, when you disagree with somebody here at Klasko, you should do so only within the team."

"I'm so sorry," I stammered. "I thought Jordan was on our team." *Should I remind her that I did flag the issue for her? Twice?* "It won't happen again."

She nodded slowly. "Can you please resend me the information on the properties that have those clauses? I need to make some calls." She had already turned away from me and back to her computer. Apparently I was dismissed.

I walked back to my office, cringing as I replayed the encounter in my mind.

Anna looked up at me from above the top of her cubicle wall as I came in. "One moment, please. I have Jordan Sellar for you. Would you like to take it or return?"

My breaths grew shallow, but delaying the pain wasn't going to help. "I'll take it." I walked briskly into my office and closed my door, steeling myself for a takedown.

"Hey, Alex. I've been meaning to introduce myself. I'm not sure if you're at all interested in M&A, but I'm getting lunch with another first-year associate next Tuesday to talk about our group. Care to join?"

"Sure!" I was so relieved not to be in trouble that I answered even before checking my calendar. As soon as we hung up, I went to the firm's internal Facebook and pulled up Jordan's profile to see the tanned, attractive, dapper young man I'd spotted in the conference room and at the bar on my first day. *Jordan Sellar. All-star M&A associate.*

***

The nervous blond girl whose name I could never remember sat next to me, in the same white cardigan and black skirt she'd had on last week. *I might have broken the dress code,* I thought uncharitably, *but at least I change my clothes*. There was an awkward silence as we scanned the restaurant, willing our food to come. Our waiter approached the table, carrying only two plates. As soon as he placed her Caesar salad in front of her, she picked up her fork and stabbed a crouton, plopping it into her mouth. Jordan watched her carefully, his lips tight but his expression otherwise blank as his steak sat untouched before him.

I had asked around before our lunch, and it seemed that everybody at the firm knew who Jordan Sellar was. My guess was that this was due in equal parts to his attractiveness and his legal talents. He wasn't just handsome compared to Klasko's pallid pool of lawyers—he was unarguably handsome, J.Crew-model handsome, good-genes handsome, with broad shoulders and thick black hair he wore just long enough to tuck behind his ears. And he was known to be one of the most promising associates at the firm, one who exuded calm and control in a setting where others seemed to always be panicking into phone receivers and scrambling into their next meetings. And for some reason, even though I hadn't yet listed M&A as an area of interest, he had asked me to lunch.

Jordan flipped his blue tie over his right shoulder, looking for a brief moment as though he were hanging from a noose, adjusted the large face of his Rolex, rotated his bull and bear cuff links, and cracked his neck. He seemed to be making a production of waiting for me to be served before diving into his steak, and the blonde finally noticed, looking up from her plate and her eyes growing wide at the sight of his untouched meal. She placed her fork down and blushed, covering her mouth as she finished chewing.

"So sorry, I didn't realize that Alex didn't have her food!" Her voice sounded painfully saccharine.

The scarlet hue rising from her neck to her cheeks aroused my sympathy. "Oh gosh. Please! Eat," I insisted.

"You wouldn't want your salad to get cold," Jordan said with a wink, though he seemed only half kidding.

Mercifully the waiter arrived just then with my salmon, and Jordan picked up his steak knife and fork.

"So, Jordan, did you always know you wanted to be an M&A lawyer?" the blonde asked.

"Since I was in diapers," he said dryly, his mouth partially full of T-bone.

I snorted and covered my mouth. He swallowed and grinned, revealing a row of Chiclet-white teeth. I glanced at his left hand, just to confirm there was a wedding ring on it, to assure myself that he wouldn't take my laughing at his jokes as flirting. The girl whose name I couldn't remember looked as though she was about to cry, though, and I felt bad. For the first time in my entire life, I was grateful that I had grown up an only child, constantly taken to restaurants with cloth napkins and waiters in bow ties where I was bored out of my mind by adult conversation. My parents had unintentionally taught me to navigate work lunches.

"Come on! Valid question!" I said to Jordan, trying to deflect. "Did you want to be in M&A when you started at Klasko?"

"Look," he said, pointing from her to me with his fork and

leaning forward to put his elbows on the table, "this is one of the best law firms in the world. But the truth is, all of our revenue comes out of two practices. M&A and capital markets. Every other group is here for support. Litigation and bankruptcy just exist for diversification, you know?" I didn't, but I nodded anyway. "They all work for us. But we're supposed to pretend we're all equal, just to be PC."

I cocked my head to the side as I thought about my real estate assignment for Lara, and the perks of being in a "support group," as she had explained them to me, while my fellow associate busied herself with nodding enthusiastically.

"I mean, we can't say it out loud, but they compensate us accordingly," Jordan continued. "Senior partners in M&A make five to six million a year. Real estate makes one. Tops. Nobody *chooses* to do anything other than M&A around here."

What about people who want a work/life balance?

"What about people who want a work/life balance?" the blonde asked.

Jordan's eyes widened, as though the question belied her laziness and naïveté. *Thank god I didn't ask that out loud,* I thought. "We fund everybody else's 'balanced' life. Plus, nobody actually chooses free time over six million a year," he snorted.

I was trying to wrap my mind around what $6 million in my bank account would look like when Jordan pointed the tip of his knife in my direction. "What are you working on?"

"Well, I'm on that one real estate matter . . . uh, real estate portion of the M&A matter with you," I mumbled, suddenly embarrassed to be working for a support group.

Jordan stared at me with a slightly stupefied expression before he snapped himself out of it. "Who is the partner?"

He has no idea who he was on the phone with last week.

"Lara Maloney."

"Jesus." Jordan shook his head with a disgusted sneer. "That group is a mess." I thought of Lara's disheveled look and the bit of egg on Michelle's lip in the morning meeting. Still, it seemed an unnecessarily harsh assessment to me. The real estate lawyers I had met were smart and nice and valued their families . . .

"You know, you should be on an M&A deal. I'll put you on one of mine." He said it as though he was giving me a gift.

I smiled gratefully, taking in Jordan again. There was *something* about him. And it wasn't privilege—like those lazy trust-fund boys I'd known in college. Jordan had something different behind his ease: authority coupled with confidence—and the sense that he'd earned them both.

I should discuss this with Sam. I promised him . . .

"Great!" I said, with genuine enthusiasm that surprised me.

"I'm doing tax work," the blonde announced, provoking no reaction from Jordan, though she seemed to be waiting for him to tell her she should be doing M&A for him as well.

"So, what year are you now?" I asked Jordan, just to fill the silence. I already knew the answer, but I couldn't let her writhe in pain any longer.

"Sixth. Hopefully partner in two years. God, I think my wife will divorce me if I don't make partner. I'll have spent the past six years not sleeping for no reason."

"I'm sure you'll make partner!" she squeaked.

"Nothing's for sure. There are two other guys my year in M&A also up for it. Thank god though, no women—they'd promote a woman over me for sure." He paused. "They *should* promote a woman over me. We have no female partners in the group right now."

Given how rote he sounded, I almost asked him to explain why having women was a good thing, knowing he likely couldn't, but thought better of it. "Do you think it's easier for a woman to make partner than a man?" I asked instead.

Jordan took a bite of steak as if to buy himself time. "The firm recognizes that they need to encourage diversity. They're not wrong. Clients care. It's good for business."

"I heard the new elevator bank is only for the M&A group, and that it goes right to the new fifty-sixth floor," the blonde said, apropos of nothing.

Jordan smirked. "I still can't believe Mike Baccard gave in to Matt's whining to get us our own floor. And express elevator!"

Suddenly a large hand appeared on Jordan's shoulder. I followed a wedding ring choking a bloated finger up to French cuffs and a chubby, grinning face.

"Don't listen to a word this one tells you about me." I took in the interloper, who was in no way handsome—he had dark bags under his lower lashes, and his hair plugs were still growing in—but whose smile and attitude made him somehow adorable.

Jordan laughed and shook the hand over his shoulder. "This is the chair of the M&A group," he explained to me and the blonde.

"Matt Jaskel," the man announced, extending his hand toward me.

"Alex Vogel." I deliberately projected my words through the noisy restaurant.

"Alex, a pleasure." He turned and extended his hand to my dining mate. "And you are?"

"Nancy Duval," she whispered.

"Sorry?"

"Nancy Duval," she repeated, barely louder but with her shoulders back.

He nodded and dropped her hand. "Nancy and Alex, I trust you're keeping Jordan on his toes," he said, placing a hand on each of Jordan's shoulders and massaging them gruffly.

Suddenly I felt another presence approaching from behind my chair. I recognized the sensation immediately. There was never any physical similarity to the men who elicited the tingling sensation at the tip of my spine—the last one was the skinny, bespectacled teaching assistant for my sophomore Modern American Lit class—but they all shared a certain self-assuredness. I didn't turn immediately, savoring the moment of discovery.

"This is Peter Dunn, who's also an M&A partner," Matt said.

When I did turn, I met Peter's shrewd green eyes, which were set on a tanned and square-jawed face. His gray suit showed off a lean physique, and his thick honey-brown hair made him appear younger than I thought he might be, given his seniority. "How are you finding your time at Klasko so far?" he asked, a rasp in his voice giving it a surprisingly soulful quality.

"Learning a lot. Really enjoying it, thank you," I answered, keeping his gaze.

I could tell he was assessing my posture, considering my demeanor, evaluating my intellect. I performed despite myself, feeling my body angle toward him. My toes shifted toward his shiny black shoes. Italian leather. I took in his scent. Tom Ford cologne. The blood ran to my head, and my cheeks flushed. The most delicious part of the exchange was that to everybody else at the table, in the restaurant, it was a routine professional introduction.

"We're going to get Alex here on an M&A deal," Jordan said, and Peter and Matt nodded in approval as they evaluated our plates. I recalled that whenever my swim team got a new coach, I knew I was being evaluated out of the pool as well. A good coach knew who the strongest swimmers were before ever seeing them in the water.

"Fish at a steak house?" Peter asked, eyeing the bit of salmon before me, a product of my mother's repeated reminders that it was unladylike to clean my plate.

"I don't eat red meat," I said with a shrug. "Not for any reason other than I don't like the taste."

"So why'd you take her to a steak house?" Peter asked Jordan.

"Steak houses have the best fish," I answered before he could. Peter looked at me for just long enough that I wondered if I had fumbled.

Matt nodded at me and looked at Jordan. "Let's get her on the Stag River acquisition that just came in."

"And I'll think of one of mine to put you on as well," Peter agreed.

I wrapped my napkin tightly around my palm and closed my fist over the fabric. Apparently I had passed whatever test they had just given me.

"Alex is working on real estate now," Jordan said flatly as he made eye contact with the waiter and made a scribbling gesture in the air.

Matt groaned, but Peter waved him off. "Learn as much as you can about everything you can. That's the whole reason we let you choose your work the first few months. But when you do opt in, don't be an idiot. Come work for us." Peter winked, and I felt my smile spreading in response, before he and Matt turned to leave.

Was it up to me, I wondered, to remember the name of the deal I was supposed to be on? Would Jordan take care of it? Should I ask him if he needed me to do anything?

The waiter placed the check down, and I watched out of the

side of my eye as Jordan left a 30 percent tip and signed his name, adding an "esq" after. I groaned inwardly at his need to tell the waitstaff he was an attorney. I was unable to imagine a universe in which my father would sign "M.D." to a bill, but decided to dismiss it.

As soon as we were back in our lobby and had said our goodbyes, I waited with Nancy, pretending not to notice her discomfort.

"I can't believe I started eating before everybody got their food," she said, widening her eyes as though it would create more surface area for her imminent tears to evaporate.

"Oh my god, Nancy! Don't be silly. Jordan was just kidding."

"I know, but that was so stupid. I've been practicing and everything." She threw herself through the elevator doors as soon as they opened, and I followed.

"Practicing . . . lunch?" I asked. She nodded, and I bit my lip so I wouldn't smile. "You were great!"

"Ugh. M&A is such a boys' club," she whispered, even though we were alone in the elevator.

I shrugged. "I like boys." I'd always gotten along with men better than women, but I knew adding that would do me no favors.

"Well, it's tough to get in the club. I hear they only take one woman a year at most," she added.

That couldn't be an actual rule, could it? I wondered if Carmen had already been staffed on an M&A deal, though. What if there really was room for only one of us?

"That can't be true."

Nancy sighed. "They can't afford women. Women get pregnant and go on maternity leave, and the group is too busy to absorb all the work of another partner when they do. Or at least, that's what people say."

***

That evening I ordered dinner delivered to the office so I could pore over a stack of land surveys. I probably would have been home in time to eat with Sam if lunch hadn't lasted so long, but it had felt like necessary networking, and I was glad I'd gone. As I munched on a spicy tuna roll, trying to keep my eyes open and not spill soy sauce on the large map on my desk, an email pinged into my in-box.

From: Caroline Meyers
To: Alexandra Vogel
Subject: Assignment

Alex,

Matt Jaskel and Jordan Sellar have requested you on the Stag River merger. Please be in touch with Jordan for details. Peter Dunn has also put in a work request for you—more to come on that in the next week or so. Congratulations!

Best,
Caroline

Congratulations. I smiled as I read the word, feeling that I had been invited to an elite party.

I had just finished reading the email when the metallic ding signaled another new email, this one from Jordan to the entire Stag River team regarding the diligence review timeline and cc'ing all thirteen people who would work on the deal, me included.

Just as I was wondering if and how I should be starting on diligence tonight, I heard another ding.

From: Jordan Sellar
To: Alexandra Vogel
Cc: Matt Jaskel
Subject: We're just keeping you in the loop . . .

So you can get up to speed, we'll start cc'ing you on everything. Nothing to do yet. We'll get access to the online data room any day now, and I'll walk you through what to do.

I stared at my screen, feeling both exhilarated that I was significant enough to be on an email with one of the most important partners at the firm and guilty for reneging on my agreement with Sam to avoid M&A. I picked up my phone and dialed.

He answered after one ring. "Hey, babe."

"Hey!" My voice was a decibel higher than it should have been. "Worst news."

"You were asked to work on an M&A matter?" Sam snorted sarcastically. I was silent. "You're working on an M&A matter?"

"Yeah. Sometimes they just need a warm body, and I had time in my calendar. Shouldn't be too bad, but I'll be here late tonight."

"Yeah. Totally. The deal has to end sometime. Won't be forever," Sam said, his tone aiming for supportive but approaching annoyed. "Who knows, maybe you'll like it." His words rang lightly in my ears but weighed heavily in my mind.

"Maybe."

After we hung up, I sat alone in my office, avoiding the clock and trying not to think about the sleep I'd miss while learning just enough to keep from making a fool of myself tomorrow. All the while, replaying Sam's words in my mind. The tension in his tone made them sound like a warning, or maybe a threat. *Maybe you'll like it.*

CHAPTER 5

Sam's alarm went off at seven o'clock for his run, and I groaned and pulled my pillow over my head. I had left the office at three in the morning after finishing the property review and reading all the emails that Jordan and Matt had cc'ed me on, which only stopped rolling in around two, and looking up every single legal term I didn't know (about 80 percent of them).

I thought about going back to sleep, but my eyelids wouldn't settle in the morning light, and my anxious eagerness got me out of bed. I stumbled into the kitchen and rested my elbows on the cool granite countertop as I waited for my coffee to brew. The final grunt of the steam filtering through the grounds forced me upright. I poured myself a cup and made my way to the refrigerator without blinking to grab milk. I shut my eyes, inhaled, and sipped, allowing the sleep to slough off my shoulders.

"You shouldn't drink that." Sam was standing in front of me, grabbing his foot behind his backside to stretch his quad. I just stared at him.

"It's full of hormones," he said, switching feet. "I just saw this insane documentary on Netflix yesterday. I swear I might go vegan."

I wish I had time to watch Netflix documentaries, I thought, but to avoid a possible fight and a definite blow to Sam's ego, I bit my tongue.

"I'm pretty sure coffee is vegan," I said flatly.

"I mean the milk. It comes from these cows that are pumped full of—"

"Sam!" I cut him off, holding my palm up to stop him. He laughed with a conciliatory nod and continued to stretch. I turned my attention to my work phone, and blinked as I registered the one hundred and thirty-seven new emails in my in-box, spitting a mouthful of coffee onto the wood floor.

He jumped back to avoid the splatter. "Al! My god, so dramatic. I just meant try to cut it out of your diet! Have a good day," he shouted over his shoulder.

I was too busy panicking to respond. "Shit. Shit shit shit." I ran into the bedroom and threw on work clothes. Skipping a shower, I jogged to the subway in my heels, then tried and failed to apply eyeliner on the crowded subway car. I scrolled frantically through the messages, not knowing how to prioritize them, and they just kept rolling in. I raced to my office, shut the door, fumbled with the digital directory, and dialed Jordan's extension.

"Morning," he said. I paused, surprised by his lack of urgency.

"Sorry. I mean . . . sorry," I stammered. "I was sleeping."

Silence.

"As one does . . ." He trailed off as though wondering where I would be taking the conversation. There was a click as he put the phone on speaker, as if to indicate that my call wasn't worth his full attention. I could hear him typing in the background.

"I saw the emails on the diligence requests, but there were so many I figured I'd just call you."

"Oh. Okay," Jordan said, still sounding a bit confused. "There's nothing to do yet. Just a bit of back-and-forth about one of the offshore subsidiaries."

I frowned at my still-hibernating computer screen. "One hundred and fifty-two emails is just a bit of back-and-forth?"

Jordan snorted. "Welcome to M&A, Skippy." He hung up.

Had he just called me Skippy?

From that morning on, my in-box remained perpetually full. Nine weeks in at Klasko, I started sleeping with my work phone set to vibrate on my chest, to Sam's obvious displeasure. I ate dinner with it on the table. I showered with it on the toilet. "Busy" took on an entirely new meaning. I began to block out time in my calendar each day to go to the gym—an appointment I rarely kept. That block slowly became the block of time in which I tried (and sometimes failed) to fit in a shower.

"Hi, Lara," I answered my extension perkily.

"Hi."

Shit. She sounded pissed. What had I done? What had I forgotten to do? I would have forgotten I was working for her entirely if she hadn't called.

"Did you send those leases to local counsel?"

I put her on speaker as I rapidly searched my sent mail. I didn't even know which deal she was talking about. Lara. Real estate. I thought I had. Fuck. Had I forgotten to hit send? Here they were.

"Yes. I did. I sent them last night at eleven oh two."

Silence.

"Alex. You didn't cc me," Lara said, forcing calm into her voice.

My heart sank. She was right—the cc line was blank. "Oh god. I'm sorry. It won't happen again." *Please don't fire me. Please don't fire me.*

"See that it doesn't, please. If you cannot handle this in addition to your M&A matters, I can ask for alternative staffing."

I breathed in sharply. "That won't be necessary. It won't happen again."

I heard a mechanical pulse on the other end of the phone. "I have to grab this," Lara said, and the line went dead.

I dropped my head into my hands; my lunch was in my throat. I couldn't believe I had done that. I never made careless mistakes.

"Happens to the best of us." I spun around in my chair to see

Peter Dunn leaning against my doorframe, arms crossed over his chest.

Shit, I thought. *I need to start closing my door when I'm on speaker.*

"Shake it off, kiddo," he said with a smile, and I forced myself to exhale as I fought back tears. "Either you're going to be perfect or you're going to be alive. Can't be both." He watched me carefully for a moment longer before taking one step farther into my office. "When I was a second-year associate—longer ago than I care to disclose—I sent the second-to-last version of a merger agreement to be signed, instead of the final, and it had a bunch of stuff in it we had successfully negotiated out of. Basically, I undid all of our work. And our client didn't even read it. He just signed it. And obviously the other party signed it because the terms were better for them. Such a mess." He shook his head and laughed.

"What happened?" I asked, feeling both horrified and comforted.

Peter shrugged. "The partner I was working for called me into his office. He said he'd take care of it, and that I should let it be a lesson in two things: One, ATD is king. And two, there's almost no mistake a good lawyer cannot manage. Understand?"

I nodded.

"You should ask questions if you don't understand."

"I'll work on my *attention to detail,*" I said, showing that, yes, I'd understood the acronym.

Peter smiled, putting a finger to the side of his nose and then pointing it at me. "Smart," he said. "That was before everybody checked email every three seconds! Waiting it out was fucking agony. You can just email everybody again, saying, 'Inadvertently left Lara off the email. Looping her in here.' That's it." He turned on his heel to leave before pausing and looking over his shoulder. "Oh, and I'll get you on one of my deals asap. Better to diversify your experience out of real estate." Was he telling me that my mistake didn't really matter because it was for real estate? "Oh, and don't say 'sorry,'" he called over his shoulder as he was halfway out the door. "Not ever."

I stared at the empty doorframe, feeling slightly confused, then turned back to my computer.

"Yo!"

I looked up again to see Carmen, and waved her in. "Hi!" I really needed to start closing my door.

She took the seat across from me. "Was that Peter Dunn leaving your office?"

I nodded.

"You know him?"

I nodded.

"He knows you?" She raised her eyebrows. I laughed and nodded.

"He's, like, a big deal."

I laughed again, uncomfortably this time. "I'm doing M&A now. And still trying to pretend I have time for the real estate deal I'm on."

"I heard."

"How? We don't even *have* water coolers." I gestured to the large glass bottles of still and sparking water placed on my desk every morning by the food services fairies.

"Matt Jaskel is my partner mentor. He mentioned it when I last saw him."

"Wow, he's a big deal. You must have impressed somebody in your interview," I said, echoing what she had said to me about Vivienne White.

She gave a short, approving laugh. "Have you lost weight?" It didn't feel like a compliment. "How's Sam? Can we do lunch tomorrow?" She didn't wait for any answers as she took out her phone. "Noon? I figure we better start sharing our M&A war stories if we're going to survive." She smiled from ear to ear, and I noticed again how especially attractive Carmen was when she smiled; it seemed to iron out all of her sharp edges.

I opened my calendar to check whether I could have lunch, then realized that I was about to be late to my next meeting.

"Anna! Can you grab me the documents I printed?" I yelled out my door. So much for not asking her to do anything menial. I looked back at Carmen. "I can't do noon. Late lunch at two?"

"Can't. I have a call at two, and my dad is in town this weekend, so I want to try to get ahead with work. Coffee at four?"

"Done! I'll send you a calendar invite."

"Hello!?" Carmen and I both grabbed at our chests as a third voice echoed through my office. "Hello?!" We stared at my phone as Lara's voice emanated from it. "Fucking first years," she muttered before hanging up.

"Did you forget to end your last call?"

"Shit." I shook my head, panicking as I wondered just how much of our conversation Lara had heard. "Today needs to be over. I can't do anything right."

"Happens to everybody. Was that an M&A partner?" Carmen asked. I shook my head. "Whatever, then! Who cares? Gotta run, see you tomorrow," she said, ducking out of my office.

Jordan was already sitting in one of the two guest chairs when I arrived at Matt's sun-drenched corner office. I paused at the door and waited for Matt to wave me in, and as soon as he saw me, he gestured to the empty guest seat. "Give us a second. We just need to finish up on this other matter."

Jordan acknowledged me with a nod and turned back to Matt. "The calculation is kinda fucked because those figures really should have been above the line," he mused.

I knew I should have paid attention to the conversation, viewed it as a learning opportunity, but I let my gaze drift around the room. Little Lucite plaques filled every single inch of windowsill space, touting all the impressive deals Matt had done: a Newton's cradle for Criterion, Inc., a skyscraper for Upwards Partners, an oil well for EarthBound LLC.

Deal toys, one of the other first-years had told me they were called.

"I have so much on my plate. You deal with this." Matt's voice drifted into my ears, and I flashed him a grin, knowing my job would be much easier if he liked me. Matt smiled back at me. This was going to be much easier than it was with Lara. Guys are simple, I thought.

Jordan continued to brief Matt. "And the buyer sent through the target list for us to . . . "

"Do you know what a target list is?" Matt asked me, interrupting Jordan. I nodded, grateful that I had looked it up that morning after I'd been cc'ed on an email mentioning it.

"The list of potential targets in the market. Prospective acquisitions for the buyer," I answered, trying to hide my smugness.

"I see a potential issue with Tremor, Elite Metals . . . ," Jordan went on without acknowledging me.

I turned my attention back to Matt's office decor. There were classic 1990s black-and-white professional photos of Matt with his wife and three boys, all wearing jeans with white collared shirts and bare feet. There were classic 1980s portrait pictures of his family with fading oval borders, in which the youngest child was still an infant. And one of Matt being swallowed up by the poufy white sleeves of his wife's wedding dress, her with a short, feathered bob and him with thick brown locks and a full beard.

"Hard to believe I ever had that much hair," Matt said, following my gaze. He laughed and brushed his hand over his scalp gently, as though running his fingers through his hair plugs would rip them out.

I narrowed my eyes playfully at him. "Are you saying this job causes hair loss? You're making M&A sound more appealing by the second."

He looked surprised for a moment before letting out a deep belly laugh, just as my eyes settled on his whiteboard, whose right side listed the names of twenty or so deals in green dry-erase marker. On the left side was a list of what I soon gathered were last names. "Vogel" had a check mark next to it, as did a few others, including "Greyson."

"Those are the first-years who indicated an interest in M&A. Want to get them all some experience," Matt explained, following my gaze. "Checks are for those who we've staffed up on matters."

I wondered what they had Carmen working on, and if her deal was bigger or more important than mine, but I realized she had a leg up anyway, with Matt as her mentor.

"Okay," Jordan said, stretching his neck from side to side as though stretching before a workout. "Project Hat Trick. You're up."

They both turned to me, and I felt a rush of stage fright but forced my mouth to open.

"Okay. So our preliminary bid was accepted."

"I'm aware," Matt said dryly, but Jordan nodded encouragingly.

"I just gained access to the due diligence materials on Monday, so I'm not quite finished reviewing them, but I'm moving along. There's a solid nonassignment provision in one of the Freestyle contracts." As I'd learned that morning while reading Investopedia on a lurching E train, this was a problem because when our client bought the company, that contract would become void instead of being transferred to us. I'd spent hours last night coming up with three possible solutions to present. As I prepared to share my rehearsed recommendations, I reminded myself to act as though they were off the top of my head.

Matt looked at Jordan. "Get it waived," he said calmly. Jordan nodded and made a note. They looked back to me, ready to move on. It occurred to me then just how little I knew about what I was doing.

"I've already started preparing the offer letter, just so we don't get behind the eight ball," I said, regurgitating the language Jordan had used when he asked me to prepare the letter, "but I'll update it as we go, and Jordan is reviewing my changes to the purchase agreement. I noted some concerns on the balance sheet, but Jordan will discuss them if need be, I guess. Committed financing is locked up." I exhaled and looked up.

Matt looked at me seriously. "Good," he said flatly, with no hint of praise, then turned back to his computer and began typing.

I allowed my shoulders to relax and looked at Jordan, who gave me a small wink. I couldn't keep the corners of my lips from curling skyward.

"Skip, you're killing me. I can never fucking find the attachments to your emails," Matt said, not looking away from his monitor. "Attach them right below your text. Not at the bottom of a forty-email chain."

I turned around and looked over my shoulder, but when I looked back at Matt, he was staring directly at me.

"Yes. You're Skippy. Skip for short," Matt said.

I opened my mouth and shut it, deciding to stop asking questions.

"Why is this deal called Project Hat Trick anyway?" Matt muttered to himself. "Stupid name."

Because it's the third attempted acquisition for the company. I need to start taking notes in pen. My notes in pencil are smudged. Am I forgetting something?

"What?" Matt's voice broke through my thoughts.

I looked up from my notes. "Sorry?" They were both looking at me.

"What did you say?" Matt asked.

Shit. Had I just said all of that out loud? "I . . ."

"Why is this called Project Hat Trick?" he asked.

"Oh, I have no idea. I thought maybe because it's the third time they've explored acquisition of this company. I didn't realize I had—"

"Are you an athlete?" he asked.

"I was." Though since I didn't play a sport where you could have a hat trick, it didn't really seem relevant.

"Where did you go to law school?" Matt asked. *Was he asking me because that was a stupid or a smart thing to say?*

"Um . . . Harvard?"

"Are you asking me or telling me?" Matt seemed entertained by watching me squirm.

I shook my head, suddenly dizzy. "Harvard."

"Oh, that's right. I knew that." Matt waved me away. "You're from a Harvard family, right?"

"What do you mean?"

"Didn't your whole family go there? I thought there was a library or something named after you guys."

"No." I shook my head slowly, though Matt had spoken so confidently that I found myself momentarily wondering if he was correct. "Nope. I'm the only one who went there, and I can say with some degree of certainty that we didn't donate a library."

Matt and Jordan looked at one another, and Matt smirked.

"Let the games begin," Jordan muttered under his breath.

"Up?" Matt asked, pointing at Jordan.

"Nah. I'm good. I slept last night. Gonna just power through."

"Okay!" Matt said as he turned his back to us and picked up his phone. "Thanks, guys!"

We were dismissed, and we walked down the hallway together. *What the hell had just happened?* My job felt like a conversation in a familiar but somehow unintelligible tongue, like Scottish.

"You did good," Jordan said, and I looked at him, wondering where to begin.

"Skippy?" I asked.

"We think you look preppy. Like a skipper." I looked down and smoothed my white collared shirt into my lavender skirt. "It's a good thing. He doesn't think anything at all about most first-years."

I nodded. "Why does he think my whole family went to Harvard?"

"Carmen said something that we must have misunderstood. No big deal. I have to jump on a call." He ducked into his office without another word.

Hours later, I was struggling to keep my eyes open as I scanned the minutes of a board meeting for the company Stag River was acquiring, barely knowing what I was looking for but hoping I would recognize a red flag if I saw one, when my ringing phone jolted me from my trance.

"Hi Matt!" I said, forcing cheer into my voice.

"Go home, Skip. I'm going home. I told Jordan to do the same."

I looked at the lower right-hand corner of my monitor. It was only seven o'clock.

"Thanks, Matt. I'm just going to finish—"

"I'm not asking you." His words were sharp, but his tone was kind. "This deal is going to blow up in a few weeks. I'll expect you here at all hours then. For now, go home."

He hung up before I could thank him, and I grabbed my phone and texted Sam.

On my way home! Yayayayay.

The ellipses appeared immediately. I smiled as I thought of him typing.

Yaaaaaas. Hurry!!!

I was just about to shut down my computer when something from before popped into my mind. I picked up my office phone and dialed Carmen's extension.

"Hey!" she said quickly. "What's up? I'm swamped."

"I have a random question."

"Shoot."

"So, um, I know this is weird, but did you tell Jordan and Matt that my family donated a library to Harvard?" I cursed the apprehension in my voice.

"Yeah," she said without a pause. There was no surprise or apology in her tone, and I could hear her still typing in the background.

"Um . . . why? It makes me sound like I couldn't get in there on my own."

"Oh, I just know their type, and they totally have a hard-on for that New England Ivy old-money thing. I thought I was doing you a solid."

Her response sounded benevolent enough. It left me no option other than to give her the benefit of the doubt. "Thanks. I cleared it up with them."

"Okay, cool. Listen, I gotta run. Are we still on for coffee tomorrow?"

"Yup!"

"Great. See you then." She hung up.

I shook my head to shake out the bizarre conversation playing on a loop in my brain, and packed my things to go.

When I opened the door, the faint hint of humidity in the apartment indicated that Sam had just emerged from one of his marathon showers. I inhaled deeply as I made my way to the bedroom, letting the sweet floral scent of Dove soap wash over me. He poked his head out of our bathroom, towel around his waist.

"Babe! I can't believe it. You're rocking M&A and still making it home early!" He came over to me, leaving wet footprints as he went, and gave me a kiss as he lightly tapped my backside. Ducking back into the bathroom, he called out, "How was work? I jogged ten miles today, so I'm starving. Do you want to go out for dinner or order in?"

"It was good. Really good. I think the key to this job is taking advantage of the slower nights and coming home to you whenever I can."

I put my bag down on the bed, feeling the rush of control over my life as I came home from a long day of work to my boyfriend, happy to see me, in the beautiful apartment my job allowed us to rent. Sam reemerged and picked out a T-shirt from a drawer, and watching him, I felt completely at peace. I knew Sam—really knew him. I could always tell what he thought of someone new by gauging his posture when he spoke to them. I knew that his favorite meal was grilled cheese and tomato soup. I knew the face he made in the mirror when he shaved. I suddenly appreciated that with him things were almost always what they seemed, and I knew how much he adored me. At Klasko, I didn't really know my friends at all. It didn't matter at all to me that he couldn't yet pay rent or take me to nice dinners. I'd turned down a job at Sanctuary so I could do those things for myself, and for him. I knew one day soon Sam's company would be successful, that it would all even out in the end.

"What?" he asked, looking at me. I narrowed my gaze slightly. His arms were in the sleeves of his T-shirt, and he was just about to pull it over his head.

"I'm not hungry just yet," I said softly.

His eyes widened. "No?" he asked.

I shook my head once and let the right corner of my lip curl upward. His arms still in the sleeves, his strong, smooth chest still bare, he made his way over to me. He raised his arms and pushed them over my head, pulling me close with his T-shirt as a lasso. I craned my neck up to him, and he kissed me slowly. When Sam kissed me, I could feel his goodness wash over me.

"I've missed you," I whispered. He kissed me again. I placed my hands on his chest and let my fingers creep down to where his towel folded in on itself. With a little pressure to the half-knot, his towel dropped to the floor. He pulled my hips in toward him and rested his hand on my backside. I felt his shirt drop away from his hands as he undid the zipper of my skirt. It slipped down to my heels. I locked eyes with his and raised my arms above my head. He obliged my request with a boyish grin and pulled my button-down up over my head.

I shifted my weight only slightly and lifted a leg.

"Leave the heels on," he whispered. I smiled as I dropped my raised foot back to the floor. "The only thing I can stand about you working so much is how good you look in work clothes. Also, fair warning, I can't really bend at the knee—I'm so sore."

I threw my head back and laughed, feeling my hair on my

back. I expected him to pull me onto the bed, but instead he pushed me up against the wall, where my heels made me the perfect height.

I can absolutely handle this job, I thought before I allowed myself to get lost in him.

PART II

THE NONDISCLOSURE AGREEMENT (NDA)

A written legal agreement between two or more parties entered into in order to protect the sensitive information each party will become privy to as negotiations are entered.

Q. Would you say your professional relationships extend beyond the confines of the office?

A. I'm not sure I understand the question.

Q. Did or do you socialize with colleagues? Did you socialize with clients?

A. Yes. Yes.

Q. Can you please elaborate?

A. Klasko not only encourages socializing but often funds it in the form of happy hours and retreats. I didn't go to undergraduate or graduate school in New York, so many of my friendships were formed at Klasko.

Q. I see. And what about with clients?

A. Actually, a large part of the job at Klasko is entertaining clients. In a legal market like New York City, there are so many law firms with excellent reputations to choose from, and the idea is that a client hires lawyers they also enjoy spending time with, as the hours required to close a deal are quite long.

Q. How do you socialize with colleagues and clients?

A. What do you mean, "how"? What does anybody do with their friends? What do you do with your friends?

Q. Ms. Vogel, I'm not the one testifying here. What types of activities do you engage in with clients and colleagues outside of the office?

A. Anything. Lunch, dinner, bars. I don't know. Stuff friends do.

Q. Have you ever been to a strip club with a colleague or client?

A. No.

[Defense counsel confers]

Q. Is there any difference in how you socialize with your friends and with your clients?

A. Aside from the fact that the firm picks up the tab, there is a difference in general topics of conversation. Dinner with clients is professional. We often discuss work.

Q. Is that so? Topics of conversation are relegated to work? And you, what, limit your alcohol intake?

A. Not always, no.

Q. Perhaps it would help if you elaborated on client development endeavors.

CHAPTER 6

As we shuffled into our weekly Monday-morning first-year training, a bottleneck was forming at the sign-in sheet, and I heard chatter swirling around me:

Fuck! I can never remember my attorney ID number.

Just write your name, they'll fill it in.

Who is "they"?

They! The firm!

I was so drunk that I gave the cabdriver the address of the office instead of my apartment building.

I've done that. Because we fucking live here.

My girlfriend is going to break up with me if I don't come home before ten o'clock one night this week.

Tell her to chill out. We've only just started. When we get paid tonight, buy her Louboutins. The price is nothing if it means no more nagging.

I grabbed a mug, filled it with black coffee, and grabbed a seat in the back row. In our first two sessions, I had only half listened as I busied myself with the flood of Monday-morning emails streaking into my phone. I knew I wouldn't get in trouble—M&A associates were almost expected to have their phones out during these trainings—but that day my absentee partner mentor, Vivienne White, was presenting. Figuring that she deserved my full attention, I left my phone facedown on the table. Vivienne was small and severe, beautiful with a certain frost that made me want to stare at her from a distance. Everybody was supposed to have lunch with their partner mentors in the first week of work, but I had yet to meet her face-to-face and I was just entering my third month at the firm. I had, however, emailed with her—she had canceled the very lunch dates she had requested on three separate occasions.

I saw the guy to my right checking his email, and managed to resist the urge for a few moments before following suit. Project Hat Trick still hadn't quite heated to a boil, and I hoped to take full advantage of the simmer. A bunch of us were supposed to celebrate surviving the first couple months of work that Friday, and logistical emails eagerly anticipating our dinner at the end of the workweek, even though it was only Monday, had already begun.

***

"To payday!"

Derrick, Jennifer, Kevin, and I clinked the thick, ridged rims of our steins together and dropped our shots of sake into them. I reveled in the familiar sensation of malt on the back of my tongue, which tasted all the better because of my knowledge that it would barely put a dent in the $3,700 that had appeared for the fourth time now in my checking account—my biweekly take-home pay, even after the government took its share and I maxed out my savings contribution.

I wiped at my lip as the steam from the hibachi table hit my cheeks. It was my first time at Benihana, which Jennifer had insisted was the perfect place because none of the tourists infiltrating the midtown branch of the chain would bat an eye if we got too rowdy. I gazed at the couple across the table, the frames of their bodies wavy through the heat as they giggled and groped one another. Derrick followed my stare.

"We should have gone to EMP and blown it all," Derrick

groaned as he watched our chef, in an impossibly tall hat, greet us with a theatrical display of his knife skills.

"You're the most gluttonous human I've ever met!" Jennifer laughed. I had no idea what EMP was, but assumed it was some unbelievably fancy restaurant.

"Are you kidding me? I can barely afford this after taxes!" Kevin complained.

"Right!? Half our paycheck gets stolen from us to pay for a government that does almost nothing I agree with!" Jennifer pouted. To me, complaining about getting half one's paycheck stolen was an exercise reserved for those people in the highest tax brackets, a group that I was exceedingly grateful to be a member of.

"Where are Roxanne and Carmen?" Kevin asked.

"Roxanne's stuck in the office, and Carmen's father is in town," I said, then took a long sip of my beer.

"From Singapore? Or he was already in the States?" Derrick asked. I shrugged. I knew Carmen had grown up in Los Angeles, but I didn't know where her parents lived. "You know, he started the Singapore office of Travers Cullen before he moved to LA? Impressive guy. He moved back to Singapore recently. That office needs him."

Travers Cullen was one of the largest law firms in the world. I had no idea Carmen was from a family so heavily entrenched in BigLaw. But it certainly made sense that she seemed so comfortable in the environment.

"How do you know all this?" Jennifer asked.

"*Below the Belt*," Derrick said, taking a sip of his beer. "Not all legal gossip is salacious. There's plenty of innocent stuff about job moves and stuff."

Kevin was watching me intently. "What?" He pointed at my furrowed brow. I shook my head, trying to make sense of my own thoughts.

"It's so weird . . ." I took a long sip of my beer and touched my temple. "Carmen told Matt Jaskel that my whole family went to Harvard and donated a library. Meanwhile, my dad is an oncologist in a small town in Connecticut and my mom volunteers at the library but definitely never donated one. Turns out Carmen is the one with the important family. I just don't get why she'd say that."

I looked at my friends' faces for an explanation, but they all seemed to be looking beyond me.

"Alex! Hi!"

I turned to the voice over my shoulder, realizing where my friends' gazes had been directed, and looked up at Peter Dunn with a somewhat stupefied expression. "Hi! Peter! What are you doing here?"

"I'm waist-deep in ten-year-olds." He pointed across the room to a table of children in party hats. "My son's birthday. What are *you* doing here?" he asked, a playful flicker in his eye.

"We're having dinner. Actually, I don't know if you know everybody, but this is Jennifer Goodman, Kevin Barron, and Derrick Stockton. We're all first-years." Jennifer and Derrick stared up at Peter, looking slightly bewildered.

"Hysterical," Peter said. I wondered if he was referring to their expressions or the fact that we were four adults having dinner at Benihana, but I assumed the latter. The embarrassment made me start to sweat, and when Peter put a steady palm on my shoulder and turned to leave, then allowed his hand to linger for a moment behind him, my pulse almost stopped.

Derrick and Jennifer turned to me.

"What?" I leaned backward, feigning confusion as they leaned in toward me.

"You work for him?" Derrick asked.

I shook my head.

"How do you know him?"

"How does he know you?" Jennifer corrected him.

"He sits on 41 with me. So we've chatted. I haven't worked for him. Yet!"

"I'll tell you what I would *not* be doing if I worked with a guy who looked like *that*," Jennifer said. "Working! I wonder if he has any female associates working for him. Must be wildly inefficient!"

I shrugged. "I barely remember to eat at work. I'm too busy to notice anybody's looks."

Derrick smirked. "Mm-hmm. Not buying it."

The clatter of metal on metal cut their attention from me back to the chef. He chopped an onion on his board with a knife in each hand at such speed that the thin blades appeared as just vertical silver streaks in the air before he tossed the rings onto the hibachi grill with a sizzle.

I watched out of the corner of my eye as Peter took his seat next to a woman with her back to me. Her posture was perfect, and the blond hair cascading down around her shoulders was silky and straight, the kind I'd always wished for. I often was complimented on my hair, but I still often scrutinized my split ends, thinking they were broken and limp because my hair was naturally curly and I destroyed it by blow-drying and then ironing it every time I washed it. Peter placed his hand on the back of her chair as she took a video with her phone of the children at the table, clapping in delight at the spectacle of their food being cooked.

I looked around the restaurant—at the mom-jeans wearers, the underage drinkers, and the younger children with their parents. It no longer seemed an appropriate way to amuse ourselves now that we had growing bank accounts that we didn't need to watch carefully and professional reputations that we did. I stared at Jennifer as she opened her mouth and the chef flipped a piece of shrimp into it. She and Kevin giggled childishly, and I was reminded of a fourth-grade trip to SeaWorld. I took a long sip of my Sapporo, which suddenly tasted bitter.

I angled myself awkwardly toward Derrick so that I could keep Peter in my peripheral vision as Kevin recounted his conflicted feelings over his latest date.

". . . and what was I supposed to say? You know? So, I said of course she could come over. But I don't want to see her again *because* she came over on the first date."

Peter had disappeared from my view, and his wife now sat beside an empty chair. I scanned the restaurant.

"At least she's not the only girl I'm seeing," Kevin continued. "Do you know anybody for me, Alex?"

I shook my head. "Sorry, have to pee," I said, already walking toward the restroom at the front of the restaurant, my legs wobblier than they should be after a few shots of sake and a beer.

I'd lied to my friends, but I'd been suddenly overcome by the desire to be in Peter's line of vision—to remind him I existed. I placed my phone to one ear and plugged the other one with my finger as I walked up and down the dead-end corridor housing the women's and men's rooms, furrowing my brow to appear focused. My knees weakened as the door to the men's room swung open. I corrected my posture and said "Yes" into the phone, even nodding for emphasis, but it was a large man in pleated khakis and a white T-shirt who exited into the hallway.

I resumed my pacing, but as I turned for the tenth time, I realized how simultaneously pathetic and bizarre my actions were. I took my phone away from my ear without hanging up on my imaginary correspondent and noticed a hint of perspiration at the nape of my neck. It felt unbearable, and I dropped my neck forward and scratched the skin under my hair hungrily.

"Do you know why we scratch itches?" Peter appeared at the other end of the hallway by the entrance to the restaurant, slipping his phone into his breast pocket with one hand. His nose was slightly red from the breezy night air. I placed my hand as nonchalantly as possible on the wall beside me for support.

"Lots of theories. One is that we scratch at a tingle as a reflex to prevent bugs and stuff on our skin. Amazing how we know to snatch our hand away when we feel something too hot. But we scratch it when we feel a tickle. Right? Our bodies are pretty remarkable," he said, and I had to fight the urge to scratch up and down my arms and stomach. "Some nerves cannot sense itch and pain at the same time, so it relieves the itch when we scratch it. Some say pain is more tolerable than itching."

"I have a high tolerance for pain," I said, surprisingly steadily.

Peter winked. "Don't all lawyers? I think itchiness is much worse. Anyway, enjoy your dinner. I'm back to Dad duty."

I managed a wave only after he had already turned. Then I walked back and took my place between Jennifer and Derrick.

"All good?" Derrick shot a sideways glance at Peter returning to his table. "You're just a work crush wrapped up in puppy love and tied with a little obsession, aren't you?" He playfully tapped the tip of my nose.

"You're annoying." I chugged the remainder of my beer and dove into my shrimp fried rice, then forced myself to focus on the knife tricks our chef performed. I lost myself in the charade so successfully that I forgot to look at my phone for a good thirty minutes. When I finally did, my stomach sank. I had missed thirty-seven emails in that period. The Stag River deal had clearly reached boiling point, and the latest email from Jordan told me to "call as soon as you can, no matter the hour." I excused myself before dessert, leaving cash for the check and multiple apologies.

"Get out of here," Derrick said, throwing my hundred-dollar bill back at me as though it repulsed him.

"Go!" Jennifer agreed encouragingly. I guess with our new account balances, they could afford to cover me.

It was ten o'clock on a Friday, so I opted to hop in a cab home rather than to the office. Sam was already in bed, his deep snoring indicating that he had already been asleep for some time, when I got there. I logged on to my computer at our dining table and dialed Jordan's cell phone.

"Hey," he answered. "Can you call me in the office?"

"Yup." He didn't sound angry that he was in the office while I was not, but still, it worried me. I should have never left. He was going to think I was a slacker. *Should I head back there right away? But then I'd waste the commute time.* I dialed him back on his work line.

"Hey. So, we got comments from Onyx's lawyers, and they're a mess. It's like these guys have never done a merger. Which is . . . annoying. But the bad part is, their timeline is completely out of control. They just moved closing up a month. That means we need to put together the offer . . ."

Jordan instructed me to get started on the stock purchase agreement, and from the alertness of his tone, I gathered that he had no intention of leaving the office anytime soon. He didn't mention when he would need the draft, but I decided to give myself twenty-four hours, to prove my work ethic. I put my head down and worked through most of Saturday on my couch, struggling to respond politely to Sam as he came and went from our apartment. I sent the documents to Jordan just before midnight, when Sam was already asleep. I woke up Sunday morning to an email with Jordan's markup attached, his scan showing large blocks of red ink. *Does this guy sleep?* I wondered, perusing the angry red strike-throughs of the language he wanted removed and scribbles of the language he wanted to replace it with. *Did he have a scanner at home, or was he still in the office?*

"I can barely read Jordan's handwriting," I explained to Sam, who pouted as I dressed in jeans and a sweater and called a car in to the office around ten in the morning. In truth, I needed him not to distract me. The double-wide screens and high-speed printers would help too. I worked through most of the day until the agreement was in good shape.

I made sure to pop in to say hi to Jordan before I headed home that evening, though I wasn't entirely certain he even knew what day it was when I dropped off a hard copy of the updated agreement for him to review. He barely looked up at me, his fingers disappearing into his hair as he hunched over a large document, dragging a red pen across the page with his free hand. I turned to leave without a word.

"Hey!" he called after me. I spun back on my heel. "Do you get how it all works together? The Exchange Act and the Securities Laws, because the buyer is public?" I nodded slowly, having no idea what he was talking about. "And why we had to carry out the acquisition through a wholly-owned subsidiary of the bidder?" I nodded even more slowly. Jordan stared at me. "You can only do a good job for so long without knowing the substance. I bet you did everything right in this." He held up the document I had placed on his desk. "But I bet you don't know why you did any of it."

I held his gaze, hating him for a moment as I started mentally composing a text to Sam, telling him I wouldn't be home for dinner after all, but I nodded, turned on my heel and headed back to my office. I started with the original documents, getting the Exchange Act off the Klasko library's database. I pored over it, actually reading a primary legal source for the first time since I'd started this job.

I entered my apartment after eleven o'clock at night to a note from Sam.

Hey babe,

Tried to wait up but I'm exhausted. I got you a wrap if you're hungry. It's in the fridge.

Love you.

I smiled at the note and left it out on the counter, not wanting to throw it away. I was too tired to eat or to analyze why I was relieved that Sam was asleep. I slithered out of my clothes and slipped in between the sheets beside him. I breathed in deeply in an attempt to relax, and don't even recall fully exhaling as sleep swiftly overtook me.

CHAPTER 7

From: Barron, Kevin
To: Stockton, Derrick; Vogel, Alexandra; Greyson, Carmen
Subject: Date help

Guys, I have a third date tonight with a girl I actually like (new territory!). Stuck on this call so need to change in office. What am I supposed to wear??? Also, haven't had time to make a reservation anywhere. HELP!

I sat in the windowsill of Kevin's office while Carmen sat with her legs crossed atop his desk and Derrick stood leaning against the wall, his head cocked to one side, all of us staring at Kevin.

Carmen spoke first. "I like this outfit least of all three."

"Agreed," Derrick and I said in unison.

Kevin rolled his eyes.

"I think jeans and the sweater. Seriously. She knows you're a lawyer. You don't have to dress like one," I said.

"So, first outfit?" he huffed as he wiggled his arm out of his blazer and put his tie back on.

"I think so," I said.

"No suit?" Kevin confirmed.

"No suit," Carmen corroborated as I nodded.

"Okay. Sweater and jeans. Check. Derrick, where should we go?"

Derrick looked up from his phone. "Why are you asking me?"

"You're like . . . the playboy. I feel like you'd know how to impress a date. Where do you take girls on a third date?"

I winced inwardly.

"Am I?" Derrick looked at me, and I shrugged.

He stared up at the ceiling. "Umm . . . let me think."

"Do I try to take her home with me?" Kevin asked. "She's, like, wholesome. Like you, Alex."

I blushed as I watched Carmen look down at her manicure, seemingly annoyed she wasn't being asked dating advice. "I'm not that wholesome," I protested. Kevin and Derrick both groaned playfully. "And I haven't been on a third date in so long."

"Yes! Of course you do," Carmen instructed Kevin. "It will make her feel wanted. She can always turn you down. She probably should, if she wants to keep your attention. But if you don't try, she'll think you don't like her."

Kevin nodded, as though he was getting instructions from a partner about a deal.

Jesus. I'm so glad I'm not single, I thought. *So many ridiculous rules.* But beneath that voice in my head, I had the gnawing feeling of envy of those who got to experience dating in a city like New York, and with bank accounts to play with, too.

"You've got a table for two at Il Buco in my name," Derrick announced, putting his phone back in his pocket.

"Yes! I knew you'd have a hookup! You're the man. Thank you!" Kevin extended a fist to Derrick.

"I used OpenTable," he said dryly, meeting his fist.

Jordan, Matt, and I worked late into the evenings for one week straight. Saturday and Sunday were discernible from other days of the week only in that my subway car was almost empty and the office was slightly quieter. Monday came, and with it, a deep tissue ache in the small of my back and a kink in my neck. When I looked in the mirror, I saw dull and sunken eyes, and leaned in closer to confirm that they were as dreadful as they seemed. *Yup.* But I had made it through the first round of negotiations on my first merger and emerged relatively unscathed. I was salivating, thinking of how close I was to splitting a pizza with Sam and taking a warm bath all by myself when the ring of my phone snapped my neck straight. Jordan was on the line.

"Hey." I rested the receiver between my ear and shoulder while typing.

"I'm here with Matt. You're on speaker."

"Hi, Matt." I stopped typing. Multitasking while on the phone with Jordan was acceptable, but a partner demanded my full attention. I inhaled and put my phone on speaker so that I could apply pressure to my temples and hopefully prevent my brain from seeping out of my ears.

"We have a dinner with Didier and the National Bank guys tonight at Marea. Can you come?" Matt's tone was casual, but I knew Didier Laurent, the bank's managing director of M&A, was his best client.

My exhaustion was quickly replaced by a surge of adrenaline. I should say no, I thought. I should have gone home to Sam. We hadn't seen each other awake in seven days. I needed sleep. But I knew how rare it was to be invited to a client dinner as a first-year associate, and I needed to take advantage of every opportunity to get on Matt's good side if I wanted the option of a spot in M&A. Additionally, I'd already figured out that nobody senior ever actually *asked* anybody junior to do anything. Lara wasn't really asking me to get started on reviewing leases, and Jordan was never really asking me to draft an asset purchase agreement. Senior attorneys *told* juniors what to do . . . and just added a question mark to make themselves feel better.

"Sure. Count me in," I said.

"You're the best, Skippy," Jordan said. "See you downstairs at six thirty."

***

I exited the elevator just as Jordan and Matt were stepping out of the one across the bank. We all turned and looked out the lobby windows to see sheets of water flowing outside.

"Shit. It's pouring," Matt said. "Skip, can you get us umbrellas? We'll go make sure the car is here."

I walked across the lobby to the Klasko security desk. "Hey, Lincoln. Can I grab three umbrellas from you?" The guard didn't look up, his eyes fixed on the screen in front of him. "Lincoln?" I finally caught his attention. "Can I please have three umbrellas?"

"Sure, miss, no problem."

Curious as to what had distracted him, I craned my neck around the security desk. A large flat-screen monitor was split into forty or so boxes, continually rotating live-feed views of the conference rooms, common rooms, and hallways. I took a step forward, centering it in my view, as I moved toward Lincoln.

"Wow. Are these images all of Klasko?" I asked. He handed me the umbrellas, and I drifted farther behind the desk and stood behind his chair, fascinated.

"Yup. I'm always watching."

"Creepy," I joked.

Lincoln gave a short smile before it faded and his brow furrowed. "I never tell what I see. I only want to keep you safe."

"Come on, Lincoln. What's good on TV tonight?" I asked.

Lincoln pointed to the cafeteria screen, where Nancy Duval sat covering her eyes, her shoulders shaking, seemingly crying, though the image was too fuzzy to know for certain, as she spooned a pint of what appeared to be ice cream into her mouth in a banquette surrounded by dozens of completely empty tables.

"Yikes!" I leaned in closer to see the image more clearly. "I hope you're well compensated, or we're just begging you to start blackmailing us!"

"I am," he replied, his tone quite serious.

"Skippy!" Matt yelled, tapping his watch dramatically. "Our Quality is here!"

I had no idea what Matt was talking about, but I gave Lincoln a short two-finger salute. "Thanks for the umbrellas. We're outta here!"

As we approached the Escalade waiting for us, I noticed a small white printed sign reading "Quality Car Service" displayed in the passenger window. The three of us didn't say a word the entire way to the restaurant, as we composed and received a flurry of emails about our deal. "Just got an email from Didier," Jordan announced as we pulled up to the restaurant. "One of his analysts is stuck in the office. Should we invite another Klasko associate to fill the seat? Derrick?"

I hadn't known Derrick was doing M&A, since he hadn't mentioned it, nor had I seen his name on Matt's whiteboard, but I would have been thrilled to have him to insulate me from any awkward silences with the client, even if it meant I wasn't the only first-year invited.

"I just emailed him," Matt announced as he opened the car door. "He'll be here in a few."

I sighed in relief and slid out of the car.

We greeted KJ and Taylor, the younger members of the National Bank team, just inside the door of the steakhouse. They were both impeccably dressed in navy suits, distinguished only by the slight pinstripe in Taylor's and KJ's choice of a pink tie. Didier, their boss, was notably absent.

KJ and Taylor extended their arms to fist-bump Matt and

Jordan, and I noticed the flash of the silver cuff links fastening their French cuffed shirts. They looked slightly confused as to whether they should fist-bump me as well. Had these guys ever been to a work dinner with a woman before? I forced a wide smile, smoothed my silk button-down blouse into my skirt, and confidently extended my hand. "Alex Vogel."

KJ took my hand first, saying nothing but holding it just a bit too long.

"So nice to put a face to your voice!" Taylor offered as I shook his.

"I feel like I know you guys already from all the emails!" I laughed. I saw Matt relax almost imperceptibly, knowing I would charm the clients.

"I didn't think you'd look like this," KJ said, looking me up and down. My cheeks warmed immediately, and I momentarily chalked it up to embarrassment. But it was actually annoyance that settled nicely into the base of my skull.

"Oh? What did you think I'd look like?"

He was saved by Matt, slapping him on the back and asking where Didier was. Jordan gave me a slight shake of his head, telling me to let the comment go, and I obeyed.

"Stuck on a call. He said we should start without him," said KJ.

"Good, because I'm starving!" I laughed and touched KJ's arm, diffusing whatever tension lingered in the sterile air.

I followed the group to the table, taking time to marvel at the steaming white pasta blanketed in shavings of black truffle and the sea scallops perfectly seared to a golden crust on other tables. I was last to the large circular table and took the seat Matt gestured to between him and KJ, who was already mid-rant.

". . . and I could barely fucking understand what she was saying half the time. And her acne . . ." He gave a dramatic shudder of disgust, then continued to elaborate on the physical appearance of the private equity analyst they'd worked with on their last deal. He turned to me, and I laughed too loudly, to assure him there was no need to censor himself. I shoved the feeling that I was somehow betraying my own sex out of my mind. It was all too easily replaced by the sweetness of inclusion.

Matt turned to me. "I got a couple of bottles of red for the table. But I got you a glass of sauvignon blanc, figuring you'll have fish."

"Wow, I didn't know we'd be time-traveling tonight!"

He cocked his head to one side, looking puzzled.

"Straight back to the fifties! Do I get to order my own food, or no?"

"Funny girl," he said. "What will you eat?"

"Sea bass," I said, looking over the menu.

We sensed a figure standing over us and looked up to see Derrick, who sported a red-and-blue-striped bow tie and a boyish grin.

Matt stood to shake his hand. "Hey! Welcome! Glad you could make it!"

Derrick made a round of the table, greeting everybody, and I saw how his diplomatic upbringing had formed him. He was confident and controlled—polished in a way that put people at ease. When he came to the two empty seats, he took the one closest to Taylor.

"Are you kidding me?" Taylor's voice was raised in Jordan's direction. "This World Series was purchased—"

"Are YOU kidding ME? The Yankees have the best team money can buy, and they still didn't make the series. You can't buy a good team. It helps, but there's more to it." Jordan leaned backward, folding his arms over his chest to indicate that he had had the last word. KJ leaned forward, picking his opportunity to display his baseball knowledge, and I just observed this bizarre battle of manliness.

I panned over to Derrick, who I could tell was attempting to consume himself with the cocktail list until the conversation moved to a new topic. He looked up and locked eyes with mine, then straightened his spine.

"What are we drinking, boys?" he asked the table.

Matt barely looked up from the menu. "I ordered wine for the table, but get whatever you like."

As Derrick, KJ, and Taylor eagerly announced their cocktail orders to the waiter, I watched Derrick intently. It had only been a week since we'd been together in Kevin's office giving dating advice, but those days had done him no favors. His face looked puffy, from alcohol consumption, I guessed, and his eyes had the telltale bloodshot look that comes with lack of sleep.

The waiter presented the bottle Matt had ordered to the table, then poured him a taste. I took note as he stuck his nose in the glass and inhaled and then swished the wine around in his mouth after a sip. He gave a short, powerful nod to the waiter before turning his attention back to the group.

"Is this for Didier?" Derrick asked, gesturing to the empty seat next to him, and Matt nodded. "Looks like I get the ear of the boss man tonight." Derrick clucked.

I felt Matt tense slightly next to me, confirming what I had guessed about my role at dinner. A junior associate in BigLaw was expected to be a positive presence, but not the center of attention. To drink but not be drunk. To have a good sense of humor but not be funny. Being able to be the life of the party came with status—and at the partner level. Apparently, Derrick hadn't gotten the memo.

"Hope nobody minds if I kick the night off with a few shots too," he said to the table. I caught Jordan and Matt making brief eye contact, looking slightly annoyed.

"A sauvignon blanc for the lady." The waiter placed the wine in front of me and made his way around the table with the other drinks.

"And six shots of Patrón!" Derrick called to the waiter from across the table, his voice already a little too loud. I watched him intently, wondering if he was already a couple drinks deep. The waiter looked to Matt, who gave an almost imperceptible shake of his head to indicate that Derrick's order was to be ignored, which the waiter acknowledged with only the slightest squint of his eyes as he continued to pour.

"Cheers," Matt said, raising his glass, "to our favorite clients." We all raised ours, but as soon as we set them down, Jordan came up behind Matt and spoke in a hushed tone into his ear to alert him to some email he'd received. I looked to KJ and Taylor to see if they were noticing work being done at the table, but they were both staring straight down into their laps, having seized the opportunity to check their own phones.

We all turned to Derrick as he pounded his fist on the table after a long sip of his cocktail, an unnecessarily histrionic display of masculinity.

"I'd take Nancy over this d-bag any day," Jordan whispered into my ear before heading back to his seat. I let out a small snort of laughter, recalling Jordan's expression as he stared at Nancy eating her Caesar salad at our lunch. I pushed my wineglass slightly toward the center of the table and away from my hand, suddenly very aware that I should abide by the firm's suggested two-drink maximum, which I'd read in the "Client Entertainment Policy" we'd received on the first day.

I locked eyes with Derrick and gave him a warning look, but he brushed me off with a quick eye roll and patronizing flick of the wrist in my direction.

"You're all a bunch of drunks," a booming voice declared, stealing my attention from my annoyance with Derrick.

I recognized Didier's voice instantly—it was unmistakable, with the slightest guttural trace of an accent clinging to his perfectly idiomatic English. I looked up, expecting a dapper, handsome Frenchman in a slim suit, but Didier was heavy. Fat, actually. And tall. Maybe six-three. He was also red-faced, in a way that made me think it wasn't just a momentary flush, with big blue bloodshot eyes and blond, almost white, hair. He shook everybody's hand, even KJ's and Taylor's, quickly making a round of the table before stopping at my chair.

He stared at me intensely. "You must be Alexandra."

"I am! Pleasure to finally meet you." I plastered a smile on my face as I extended my hand, which he took and raised to his lips. I inwardly shuddered at the beads of sweat on his thick upper lip, but I resisted the urge to snatch my hand away with every polite and dutiful fiber of my being.

"*Enchanté,* mademoiselle," he said. Matt coughed, sounding uncomfortable. "Madame or Mademoiselle?"

I pulled my hand away with a big smile. "Mademoiselle."

"Parlez-vous français?"

"Didier, please, have a seat." Matt sounded more desperate than generous as he gestured to the empty seat across the table in an obvious attempt to end the bizarre flirtation.

"I should sit next to the one member of the Klasko team I haven't met yet," Didier insisted, nodding in my direction.

"You've met Derrick?" Matt asked, and I could hear a slight challenge in his voice.

Didier turned to Derrick. "Do you do M&A?" Derrick shook his head, and Didier turned back to me.

"I'll move," KJ offered, rising from his seat. I wasn't sure how I was going to survive an entire meal beside Didier, but I felt Matt looking at me, and as I turned to lock eyes with him, I immediately understood that I was to keep the client entertained.

The waiter started to pour Didier a glass from the table's bottle of wine, but he shook his head decisively. "I want to taste what you're tasting," he said, leaning in toward me. He smelled of cigarettes and gin. I felt my upper lip curling at the smell and coughed to mask it. KJ and Taylor laughed, apparently accustomed to their boss's antics. Derrick looked momentarily as if he was considering intervening on my behalf and then seemed to think better of it. Jordan raised his glass to me with a small smile. I couldn't tell whether he was wishing me luck, congratulating me on capturing Didier's attention, or preemptively thanking me for model behavior, but whatever he was gesturing, I took it to mean I was about to begin a test of sorts.

I sat up straighter and adjusted my expression to telegraph to my colleagues, *This is nothing I can't handle.* I noted the heightened alertness of my senses, a weaker version of what I used to feel right before a swim meet. It seemed odd for my body to be producing adrenaline in that moment, but right then I realized how much I had missed it coursing through my veins.

Didier took my wineglass, stuck his nose in it, and breathed in deeply. He took a long sip and swirled the liquid around in his mouth. I watched him carefully as his blond mop flipped forward over his eyes, marveling that he must be worth at least forty million and yet didn't get regular haircuts.

He looked at me and smiled. "Ah. Sauvignon blanc. The most wonderful hint of citrus. I love the lime. Only the French can do wine."

I turned to the waiter, who was mercifully passing by. "May I see a wine list?" I pivoted in my chair toward Didier. "I prefer a California white, actually. Please, you keep that. I'm going to order something else."

I saw Jordan looking nervous.

But Didier laughed boisterously, slapping his palms to his gut. "She knows what she likes!"

Just as I thought. A little boy in banker's clothing who only wanted somebody to stand up to him.

We were interrupted by the arrival of the appetizers, which the waiters presented with ceremony. Matt had ordered almost every starter on the menu for the table, and I watched as more sea urchin, crudos, oysters, and caviar than we could ever eat were laid down in front of us.

Jordan took the opportunity to order another round of drinks. "Skippy?" he asked in my direction. I shook my head, but he scowled and turned to the waiter. "She'll have another too."

By the time dessert finally rolled around, everyone else was on their fourth or fifth round of drinks, and in no rush to leave with the rain still pounding outside. I pretended to sip my wine, grateful nobody had noticed that my glass remained almost full. KJ and Didier wanted all of us to take them out to a bar after dinner, and Taylor was easily convinced to join. Matt scribbled in the air to ask for the check. I watched as he signed the $3,200 dinner bill without flinching, also signing an "esq" after his name, a ridiculous affectation.

"Skippy! Drink!" Jordan pointed at my wineglass from across the table.

"Why do you guys sign 'esquire' after your names?" I asked, making sure everybody else was engrossed in their own conversations.

"We do what now?" He furrowed his brow and leaned closer to me.

"You sign 'esq' after your names."

Jordan took a look at Matt's bill and laughed. "No, we don't." Apparently finished with the conversation, he leaned away from me, and since the meal was over, I took a large gulp of wine to wash down the procession of uncomfortable conversations that I had just endured.

As Didier, KJ, and Taylor huddled at one end of the table, looking at a new email that had just come in, Derrick was eagerly rattling off the names of all the clubs he could get us into. ". . . Goldbar or Death & Co. or Acme. I can absolutely get us in to Acme," he was saying. Matt and Jordan stared at him, slack-jawed, but he didn't seem to notice.

Matt cleared his throat and spoke in a low voice. "Derrick, you're a guest here. Act accordingly."

The energy around the table dropped off a cliff. I checked to confirm the clients hadn't heard and was relieved to see that they were still huddled in their own conversation.

Derrick's face fell, and I wanted to defend him, but couldn't figure out how to do it without overstepping myself, or embarrassing him even more.

KJ broke the silence. "Let's get out of here!" he said, loosening his tie as he rejoined the rest of us.

Derrick politely indicated that he needed to get home, making eye contact with the napkin in his lap, and nobody argued with him.

"Same—I need to wake up early to wrap up some postclosing matters for all of you on Hat Trick," I said, scanning the table with an apologetic smile, grateful to have a legit excuse.

No! Come! Skippy, you can't leave! the rest of the table chorused.

I squirmed at the stark contrast between the responses to my excuses and Derrick's, and went on slightly too long about the closing checklist and the documents I needed to send to firm records for posterity, and then added a lie about a 7:00 a.m. spin class.

When Derrick and I stepped outside, it had stopped raining. He continued forward on the sidewalk, which was still covered in puddles, looking down the street for an available cab and ignoring me.

I stood still for a moment, uncertain whether I should say anything.

"D? What was that in there?"

"What?" He stuck out his hand to hail a cab, barely acknowledging me.

"I just mean . . . are you okay?"

He didn't look back at me. I stood by his side and watched the back of his head as he looked west on Central Park South.

"I'm fine. I guess it was a mistake to put my own spin on 'black man at dinner' tonight. I'm sorry if not everybody enjoyed the performance."

"Jeez. What are you even talking about? You were—"

"What am I talking about? I was only at that dinner to be the black guy. Don't be so naive, Alex. I don't even do M&A."

"Don't be so self-deprecating, Derrick," I snapped. "You were invited because people like you."

Derrick whipped his head around and stared at me. "I'm not only *self*-deprecating. You were there because you're a woman. An attractive, well-behaved, goody-two-shoes woman. You think they always invite first-years to these dinners?"

I narrowed my eyes at him before my heart sank. *Oh god. He's totally right.*

"It's the same shit all over again. It happened when I was a summer associate in LA too, but I just hoped when I was an *actual* employee they might treat me like everybody else. Especially in New York City. But no. Whatever! I just forgot which black guy I was playing tonight. All the associates expect me to be the black playboy. Partners expect me to be the black intellectual."

"Nobody expects you to be anything," I argued half-heartedly.

"Doesn't matter anyway, 'cause I can't get fired. Guess that's the upside to being their black poster boy." He spun back toward the street, formed a circle with his thumb and index finger, and whistled, and a cab screeched to a halt. "Get home safe, Skippy," he said, my nickname sounding like an insult. He lived in the West Village, and though he knew I was on his way home, he didn't offer me a ride.

I stood for a moment staring after Derrick's cab before snapping out of it to hail my own.

"Skippy! Join us!" Matt and Didier were leading the pack out of the restaurant. A sense of sadness nestled into my throat. Derrick had shattered any illusion that tonight's invitation was a result of them actually enjoying my company. It was all about optics, I understood that now. "Wasn't a question," Matt continued, smiling broadly. Maybe they did actually want my company, even if it was just so I could entertain Didier. And I really did want to see what it was like to party without thinking about the tab. How would somebody with no budget spend an evening in New York City?

"But hey, remember, what happens out with clients, stays out with clients," he warned, putting a finger to his lips.

I nodded in total understanding.

Two hours later we were in a dark corner of the Boom Boom Room in the Standard Hotel. When Matt had flashed his black AmEx to the bouncer, we'd been ushered past the line and up to the fourteenth floor, where we were shown to the plush red couches around a corner table—the only suits in a sea of skinny jeans, short dresses, and silicone cleavage. By the time I'd taken my third shot at Jordan's command, I was struggling to hold my head upright on my neck, which had dissolved to putty in the grip of vodka. The two-drink-maximum warning played on a loop in my pulsating eardrums.

"I bet it's hard for you at work, getting hit on all the time," KJ slurred, leaning over Jordan to talk to me. I shook my head playfully, hating that I was flattered. The offense I might have taken when sober to not being treated professionally dissolved and was replaced by some shallowly buried middle school complex about being the broad-shouldered girl when skinniness was in and the outspoken one when guys liked passive girls.

"I really don't."

"Tell her," Taylor growled at Jordan.

"Tell her what?" Jordan asked dryly, staring straight ahead.

"Carmen does!" I insisted, trying to turn the attention from myself.

"Does what? Who is Carmen?" Taylor asked Jordan with a nudge, but Jordan ended the conversation with an almost imperceptible shake of his head. I looked at Jordan's complete composure with envy. *How does he do it? He's been pounding wine and shots all night.* Matt leaned his head against the armrest on the opposite end of the couch as a scantily clad cocktail waitress refilled the drink in his almost lifeless hand, and Didier plunked his massive frame down beside me, resting the edge of his left leg atop my right. He snorted and then hacked back up whatever had been pushed down from his nose, only to swallow it back down again. Unwilling to catch the Plague, I tried to wriggle out from under him without success.

"Have you met this Carmen girl?" Taylor asked Didier.

Didier nodded. "She's on the Trinity acquisition."

My neck suddenly felt solid, and I snapped up my head. *She is? She didn't tell me that.*

"Is she hot?" KJ prodded. I looked for Didier's response, feeling slightly slimy for wanting to know what he thought.

"Yeah. But in a way that makes you want to treat her like shit." Didier's voice was clear, and he seemed more sober than just a few moments ago. He let out a burp under his breath, and I smelled rancid chemical waste. "You're hot in a way that makes everybody want to take care of you," he yelled, barely audible over the music.

"You have issues," I mumbled.

"You have no idea." His shoulder bounced as he laughed. "But you know, I don't give a fuck how hot you are. None of us do. You get good deals because you do good work. If you were just hot, I'd just hit on you. Not work with you."

I didn't know what to say. Part of me wanted to tell him he couldn't speak to me that way—that it was harassment. But it didn't feel like harassment. It felt like a compliment. I wasn't even certain if a client *could* harass me—he wasn't my employer, after all. I struggled to see the downside to having a client express interest in me, and although my vision was cloudy from alcohol, I could see what lay ahead: staffing on the best deals, positive performance reviews, a smoother path to success than I would have if Didier never knew my name or wanted me to like him back. The drinks suddenly hit me again, and I closed my eyes for a moment.

"Up or down?" Didier asked me.

I looked at him blankly. "What?"

He laughed. "You're cute."

This is flirting. Granted, flirting with a fat, old Frenchman I'd never consider touching. But still. I rolled my eyes at him but was smiling as he took out a travel-size Advil bottle from his suit pocket and a small glass vial from his pants pocket.

"Up?" he said, holding up the vial, which was filled with white powder. "Or down?" He held up the Advil bottle.

I stared at the vial. "What is it?"

"What the fuck, Didier?" Jordan was suddenly leaning over me, his speech deliberate and irritated. "She doesn't need that shit."

"What is it?" I pouted.

"She's so cute," Didier whined to Jordan, but Jordan took my arm and pulled me up off the couch, freeing my skirt from Didier's leg as he did so. Didier was already focused on the breasts of the waitress refilling our ice bucket.

"That wasn't Advil," Jordan yelled over his shoulder as he forged a path toward the bar through the swaying figures surrounding us on all sides. "It was Xanax. And coke. And you don't need either."

"Oh." As I allowed Jordan to lead me through the crowd, the bass from the speakers rattled my chest. I stared up at the short-haired singer in the band, kicking her fishnet-covered legs out from under her flapper dress as a brassy trumpet blared. "I don't do drugs," I said, almost apologetic. I'd never expected the most successful lawyers in Manhattan to unwind with anything but alcohol. Bankers, yes. But lawyers surprised me. It can't be all that bad for you, I thought, if all these guys do it on a random Tuesday and go home to their young children and houses in Westchester after.

"I know, I know, Skip. Drugs are frowned upon at the country club," he said with a smirk. My parents weren't country-club people, but I didn't have the chance to correct him before he pushed through to the bar and ordered us two waters. We put our lips to the large glasses dripping with condensation and tilted our heads skyward. I sucked hungrily at an ice cube, then spit it back into my glass, not worrying about seeming ladylike in the moment.

"Do you and Matt do coke?"

"Next question." Jordan smiled. I rolled my eyes, annoyed I had broken down and finally asked to clarify what the "up" that people were always offering each other actually was.

"You and Matt are like . . ." I intertwined my fingers and held them up.

Jordan laughed and nodded. "You get it. I didn't know you got it." I stared back at him, inviting him to continue. "You understand client development. You made Didier like you. And it's Matt's job to keep Didier happy."

"I have a question," I mumbled.

"Shoot."

"Remember when . . . Why do you think Carmen told you guys my whole family went to Harvard? And like . . . donated a library?"

"Hmm. Did you ask Carmen?"

"Yeah. She said it was to make me look good."

Jordan nodded, as though he assumed she'd have said as much. "Look, Skip. The worst thing you can be when you're in this business is somebody who was given what everybody else needed to earn. Makes people think you're not as smart or as hardworking as the rest of us. Look at Peter. That's why . . ."

Jordan registered the confusion in my eyes and trailed off. "Shots!" he declared, attempting to change the subject.

"What about Peter?"

"Never mind, Skip. Shots."

I rolled my eyes in reluctant capitulation.

"You never answer my questions. And no shots. We're not supposed to do shots. And we're only supposed to have two drinks! That's what they told us ten times in our business development training."

"There are rules for everybody else, and then there are rules for M&A. Matt brings in more business than anybody else at the firm. We have a different set of rules." Jordan signaled the bartender. "Two shots of Casamigos, por favor."

"Didier said I do good work," I said defensively.

"You do. Stop fishing," Jordan said and handed me a shot. "Usually first-years are just the people who schedule our meetings and do our slides. You do real work. I mean, we let you do real work. Because you're good." He remembered himself and repeated, "Stop fishing."

Q. Based on what you heard about Gary Kaplan, what preconceived notions did you have before meeting him?

A. I cannot say that I had any preconceived notions about him personally. I really didn't. I did have preconceived notions of how he would be professionally: highly successful and intelligent and somebody I should try my best to do good work for if ever given the opportunity. I thought that somebody in Gary's position could make or break a person's career at a law firm.

Q. Would you say that your preconceived notions of Gary Kaplan would have influenced how you perceived him?

A. Again, I didn't have any idea what he would be like or how he would act. I just knew he was an important client.

Q. But you said you had heard about his reputation. Did you simply disregard this information while considering his professional reputation?

A. No. I wouldn't say that. I would say that I heard things about him, all of which could have been dispelled or corroborated upon meeting him. I try to reserve judgment before meeting somebody. I hope we all do.

Q. You went in to your first meeting with Mr. Kaplan with no preconceived notions of who he was or how to behave toward him?

A. I've answered this. [*Pause.*] I knew he was an important client of the firm, and perhaps that made me slightly more . . . accommodating than I would have otherwise been.

Q. Was anybody else present the first time you met him?

A. Yes. Peter Dunn.

Q. Please describe your first meeting with Gary Kaplan.

[Let the record show Witness is conferring with her attorney.]

A. My answer will be altered to honor anything privileged by nature of the attorney-client privilege.

Q. I will remind you that privilege only extends to communications related to the purposes of giving or obtaining legal advice that are intended to be confidential.

A. Thank you. I am aware of what privilege covers.

Q. Could you please recount that initial meeting for us, as well as your impressions?

CHAPTER 8

I walked down the hallway to Peter's office and was about to give a courtesy knock on the closed door before entering for our scheduled call regarding the merger he'd staffed me on when I heard another male voice emanating from his office. Maybe his secretary had double-booked him? I almost welcomed the excuse to turn and leave. Each assignment working for a new partner was both an opportunity to prove myself and an opportunity to mess up. Matt and Jordan now knew I was sharp and hardworking, whereas Peter knew nothing about me. Instead, I knocked lightly on the door.

"Come on in!" Peter shouted from beyond the door. I cracked it open, and he waved me in. As I opened the door farther, I saw another man in Peter's guest chair.

"Gary Kaplan, this is Alex Vogel," Peter offered, gesturing for me to take the seat next to a dark-haired man wearing a tailored charcoal suit, white shirt, and baby-blue tie. *The famous Gary Kaplan. Founder and general partner of Stag River, the firm's largest client. Don't say anything stupid.* As I took him in, I was surprised to see that Gary didn't look powerful. He appeared to me meek, almost ill, with dark, sunken eyes and a sallow complexion. His suit looked expensive, but his skinny frame did it no favors.

"I'll have a coffee. Black. Please," Gary said curtly, not acknowledging me in any other way.

I stared at him for a prolonged moment and then looked to Peter to make sure I'd heard correctly.

"Oh. Alex is an associate. She's not . . ."

I looked down at the dark gray Theory suit I had splurged on at Saks after my first paycheck and wondered what about my general demeanor screamed "assistant."

"Apologies," Gary said without a trace of contrition. "But I'd still like that coffee." He looked over to Peter, whose discomfort was apparent.

"Actually, I could use one too," I said brightly. "Glad to get you one while I'm there."

Peter smiled gratefully. "And Alex? I pushed our call back by thirty minutes, so we have time."

I made myself a decaf and Gary a black coffee in the kitchenette across from Peter's office and returned moments later with both in hand. Gary took his drink and set it on the table in front of him without thanking me.

"I have dinner with my family downtown, so I need to run soon," Gary said, then paused. "Can you print me an NDA before I leave?"

"At the Nomad?" Peter asked.

"The only place I'll dine below Fifty-Seventh Street," Gary snorted.

"Alex, would you mind printing an NDA for Gary?" Peter asked. "It's on the system."

Relieved to be out of that room, I ran down the hall to my office and opened the online library of firm documents. I searched for "Stag River" and "NDA." Nothing. I searched for "Stag River." Nope. "Nondisclosure" and "Stag." Three results. *Boom.* I printed the one labeled "FORM" without any of the details filled in and returned to Peter's office triumphantly, where I handed it to Gary.

"Thanks, but could you be a doll and print a few?" He didn't look up at me. "This isn't right. An NDA for me. Personally. Not for Stag River."

I turned and headed back to my office without a word.

"I'm in a bit of a rush," he yelled after me. I rolled my eyes with my back to him but still quickened my pace. I attempted to visualize my possible reactions on the runway of gray hallway carpet before me. He was the most powerful man in finance, and he was Klasko's client. I could either accept Gary's behavior as an insult or accept it as a challenge. But either way, I had to accept it.

I took a seat at my desk and quickly found "Gary R. Kaplan NDA" in the library, then printed five and walked once more to Peter's office.

Gary flipped to the signature page and nodded. "A few is three," he commented under his breath before he got up, shook hands with Peter, and brushed past me and out the door.

"Thanks, Alex. He's a peculiar guy," Peter offered once Gary was out of earshot. *He's an asshole.* "I appreciate how you handled that. He's an important client. He gives us more than a hundred—"

I didn't want to make excuses for Gary, but I didn't want Peter to think I hadn't noticed his behavior. "Yep, I get it. That's why I didn't say anything."

Just then Peter's calendar alarm dinged, and he gestured for me to take a seat for our call.

The call with our client led to a call with the investment bankers, which led to a call with the target company's counsel. Almost four hours later, I was struggling to keep my lids open as our third call droned on.

Peter nodded at the grated speaker on his phone. "That's our understanding as well." I combed through my greasy hair with my nails, then wiped my finger under my eyes and looked at the smudged eyeliner I had just cleared. I couldn't imagine what I looked like to Peter, whose perfectly unwrinkled shirt made me wonder if he could have changed clothes in the last hour without me noticing.

David Ramirez, the company's lawyer, launched into another five-minute monologue about noncompetition restrictions potentially triggering antitrust violation issues.

"Sure, we can run that by our client, but between you and me, I think it's not happening." Peter gave a small smile as if we shared a secret, and I smiled back, though not understanding what it might be. He sat up suddenly and scratched under his collarbone, and I allowed my eyes to graze his chest and then rest on his bicep—at the brim of his white undershirt—noting how it clung closely to the muscle below it.

"I gotta tell you, David, you know I'm fair, but this is just a nonstarter. Gary will never ever agree to this. I'm not trying to be a dick. It's just the truth," Peter said calmly. He mouthed "I'm sorry" to me at the use of his language, then muted the phone. "What time is it?"

"Nine."

"Have you eaten?" He looked concerned.

How could I have eaten? I haven't left your office since five.

"I'm okay," I mouthed, even though we were on mute.

David was rambling on, and while I was failing to catch anything he said, Peter appeared to have entirely forgotten he was still on the line.

"You're not hungry?"

I shrugged.

"We'll get food." He clicked the mute button off. "Good. Glad to hear that. Alex will send the updated draft tomorrow morning. Nothing will move before Monday, so no sense in us losing more sleep before then. Good night," Peter said, and clicked off the call.

I felt like I'd just missed something crucial. What had David just agreed to? Why was it good?

"No steak, right?" Peter said.

How could I update the draft if I had no idea what had just happened? Why wouldn't anything move before Monday? It was only Thursday.

"Alex?"

"I'm sorry, I . . ."

"You don't eat steak, right?" I nodded, but looked back down at my notepad. "Meet you in the lobby in ten," he said. "We'll discuss the changes over dinner."

I buried my chin farther into my coat, hiding from the unseasonable November wind as we made our way to our Quality car. Once we were inside it, Peter alternated between typing carefully and scrolling furiously, interrupting the silence only once. "Hey, can you just call a Quality car to do a pickup at the Starlight Diner on Seventy-Second between Park and Madison? You can bill it to Stag River."

I nodded and began to type the request into my phone.

"Call. Don't email," he clarified. I picked up my phone, calling the Klasko operator to be connected to our car service, slightly confused as to why somebody from Stag River would call their attorney for a ride home.

"Who do I say the car is for?" I asked as the line rang. Peter continued to type without a response. *Shit. Did I piss him off?* He didn't look upset, though, more like he hadn't heard me.

The ringing stopped as the operator's voice piped into my ear. "Good evening. Klasko & Fitch, how can I help you?" I ordered the car, and as soon as the operator heard the Stag River billing number, she bypassed the usual step of asking for passenger name and destination. I hung up and gazed out the window at the intersection of Fiftieth Street and Park Avenue, where a young couple made out passionately as they waited for the light to change.

"That's good," Peter said. I looked over at him to see that he was finally off the phone. "When you stop taking joy in the happiness of others, just do everybody a favor and end it." I realized there'd been a sleepy smile on my lips, and I straightened them. "Did you have a moment to review the teaser language I sent you for our sell-side?"

"I did. Should I be diligencing the actual revenue numbers to confirm that they're accurate?"

"The whole point of a teaser is for the company to garner interest from the market. If the document isn't accurate, even by a little, it can destroy any potential interest—out of mistrust for the seller. It's our job to make sure the deal goes through. And companies need to know exactly who they're getting into bed with."

I nodded slowly while still mulling over his words, thinking how much the merger of companies paralleled the merger of people.

As we walked through Grand Central Terminal, the stores and restaurants were rapidly shutting down for the evening and I was growing increasingly annoyed that our dinner was really just me accompanying him on the first leg of his trip home to Westchester. The "Hours of Operation" on the glass doors of the Oyster Bar indicated that there were only three minutes left of service, but they'd already been bolted shut. Peter knocked on the glass, and one of the servers wagged his finger at us before spinning around to hear something being shouted at him by the bartender.

"Ever been here?" Peter asked as he loosened his tie. I gave a small shake of my head and peered inside at the bone-colored rectangular tile ceiling that arched cavernously and continuously in a way I thought only churches or caves did. The air looked warm behind the closed glass door, glowing with an auburn light that I much preferred to the contrived fluorescent white of the office. It was casual. Charming. No pomp or circumstance. Its confidence was raw, nothing like the places I had been to for other work dinners. My annoyance at his choice of location melted into a sort of calm awe at the grandeur of the iconic restaurant, which until that moment, I'd had no idea was actually located within the terminal.

A young waiter scurried to the door and unlocked the deadbolt. "Didn't recognize you, Mr. Dunn. Apologies," he said, looking nervous. Peter shook him off genially and pointed to the bar. The waiter nodded, and Peter led me into the restaurant, which was nearly empty. I spotted one couple finishing their wine at a table, but busboys were sweeping up around them while a few servers were gathered in the corner, counting their tips.

"Don't even worry! We're the ones here past closing!" I said to the waiter, enjoying the power of being able to calm him, and he seemed to exhale.

Peter chatted with the silver-haired bartender, whose porcelain skin and lack of facial hair made it impossible to tell whether he was gray at thirty-five or aging extremely well at sixty, and I hoisted myself onto the barstool beside Peter. I pulled my skirt down below my knees and retucked my shirt in the back as nonchalantly as possible.

"Do you do oysters?" Peter asked.

I nodded, wondering if the bartender was too polite or professional to rush us to place our orders.

"Dominic," Peter said, turning toward the bartender, "two

dozen. One from the gulf or whatever is meaty, and one of the smaller. The young lady thinks she likes oysters. But she's never been here before." He looked over at me. "We're going to show her how good they can be."

Dominic smiled at me, and I grinned back, unable to contain the thrill of being there after hours. I had never witnessed a man as in control as Peter was—people did exactly as he instructed them to.

"What'll you be drinking?" Dominic asked me, his voice and demeanor leading me to believe he was an older man who aged well.

"Rosé and oysters is my favorite summer meal," I announced, striving to sound casually sophisticated, but Peter and Dominic glanced at one another with wry smiles. I had somehow revealed my naïveté, though I had no idea how.

"Would you be open to trying it with a white?" Dominic suggested. "We have a Poulsard and a sauvignon blanc that are drinking so nicely right now."

I quickly conjured up the scene from the dinner with National Bank. What had Didier said with his nose shoved in the sauvignon blanc? Lime?

"I'd imagine the Poulsard is drinking well this year, but I love the idea of the citrus from a sauvignon blanc with oysters. Is that okay?" I asked Peter, the words falling clumsily out of my mouth.

Dominic's lip curl indicated amusement, but Peter simply said "Your world," locking his green eyes with mine. His were no longer tired and were now bright and full of mischief. The sense that he was looking straight through me was more unsettling than gratifying. "We'll have a bottle, Dom," he said, turning from me.

"So, maybe you know wine," Peter said. I didn't. "But you

don't know oysters. Dom here has taught me everything I know about them."

I became painfully aware of my feet dangling from the barstool, and placed them firmly on the crossbar between the stool legs to repress the feeling that I was just a stupid child playing at being a grown-up.

"Are you doing only oysters tonight?" Dom called over his shoulder.

"Yes! Send the kitchen home, for God's sake!" Peter said, taking off his jacket. His arm brushed mine as he twisted it out of the sleeve. "Pardon me." He touched my arm, on purpose this time. "I just want to call my wife. I'll be right back."

I took out my phone and texted Sam.

Alex: Quitting Klasko and playing the lottery aggressively starting tomorrow.

Sam: Ha! Stuck?

Alex: Home by 11. Love you.

Peter was back at my side just as Dominic put two glasses down in front of us. He presented the bottle to Peter and chatted about the Mets as he took out a knife and worked open the foil in a fluid sweep.

"Cheers." Peter held out his glass, and we clinked.

I inhaled perfunctorily before taking a long sip. "Good?" Peter asked. "I have no idea what I'm supposed to smell when I smell wine."

The oysters were placed before us, lining the perimeter of a circular tray of ice.

"Moving from west to east in doubles." Dominic pointed with two fingers, his palm upturned. "Deer Creek. Humboldt . . ."

I stared at them as the next ten types of oysters played in the background. I took in the gray of their flesh—the sheen of their brine.

Naked. Naked? Had somebody just said the word *naked*? I needed sleep. I didn't even know why I was at dinner right now. I should be working. Or sleeping.

I looked up at Peter.

"Okay? Just for the first one. Just to get the taste." He held an oyster with no cocktail sauce or horseradish up in the air. I nodded and lifted its counterpart from the ice. We loosened the meat with the tiny forks in silent synchronicity and tipped our heads backward, shells to our lips.

"What do you think?" Peter asked.

"Yum!" I blurted out, blushing at my choice of words.

"I know. The liquor is so creamy. So is the flesh. And they burst so nicely with just a bit of a chew."

I leaned forward, taking copious mental notes. It was proper to chew them slightly. I always just swallowed them. I felt the first gulps of wine work their magic on my empty stomach. The warmth spread down from my abdomen to my legs and up to my chest.

"How are we doing?" Dominic's voice slowed my blood flow.

"Excellent. Just what we needed after a long day at the office. Grab us a few shrimp cocktails too, please. Will you eat New England clam chowder?" Peter turned to me. I shook my head and wrinkled my nose, just tired and just buzzed enough to not be completely amenable. "Fried calamari?" I smiled and nodded. Dominic turned and made his way to the kitchen.

Hadn't he just told them we weren't eating, and the kitchen staff should go home? Did anybody ever say no to this man?

I took another sip of the wine, tasting the citrus mingling with the milky residue of the oyster on my tongue, and felt Peter watching me.

"Oysters are best in the winter. The whole month with an *r* thing is true, you know," he said.

"A very smart man once told me that I could be perfect or I could be alive. I think that gives me license to eat oysters in summer." I cocked my head playfully.

Peter leaned back and laughed freely, as though I had released something chaining him down. He had the confident, windblown quality of somebody who had been on adventures in foreign lands, gotten in a fair bit of trouble, and had never experienced darkness or loneliness. It made me want to be close to him, to steal it from him when his head was turned.

"You're different from the other first-years," Peter said, then shook his head, as if remembering himself. "You know, the first job I ever had was shucking oysters at this fish shack in the town where I grew up."

I couldn't picture him wearing anything but a suit. "Where did you grow up?"

"Boston. You know, prep school and lobster rolls. My old man made me work on the dock to learn the value of a dollar. Came in handy for summers on the Cape. Embarrassingly cliché." He held out his hands and pointed to the small white lines of faded scars on his large palms. "As you can see, I wasn't very good at first."

I had the overwhelming urge to trace his scars with my finger, but instead pressed my knees tighter together and took a long sip of wine.

"So," Peter said, and cleared his throat, indicating that the social portion of the evening was concluding. "The real issue with valuing a private company is that there is no market value for the equity. And the financials tend to be messier, and not as robust. So, you need to find the right metrics or comparable companies to base valuation off . . ."

I listened intently, in awe of his depth of knowledge, and trying to catch every word.

"And when it was suggested that our operating margins were . . . Eat!" he commanded, gesturing to the calamari that had appeared in front of us. I took a glistening golden ring and popped it into my mouth absentmindedly, still focused on his commentary on our valuation analysis. I wished I had a notebook to write everything down, but instead I tried to clear a path in my head for his words.

"Use sauce!" He shoved the dish toward me, and I complied. "Anyway, they were way off when they said the operating margins . . ."

When he had finished his explanation, I excused myself to the ladies' room and slipped down off my stool.

"Restroom is that way." Peter pointed over my right shoulder. "Enjoy those lips!"

I felt my cheeks flush. *Do I have something on my mouth?* I wiped at my face. *Did I wipe my lips with my napkin in a sexual way? Do I need to apologize?*

I fell through the door to the bathroom and leaned my head back on the closed door with my eyes shut. I opened them and laughed out loud in relief.

Directly in front of me in the ladies' room was a red leather lounging couch shaped like an enormous pair of lips. I ran the water until it was ice cold and wet a paper towel. I slipped it under my hair and over the nape of my neck, shutting my eyes as I impatiently waited for my body to cool down.

When I exited the bathroom, Dominic was sitting at an empty table with a stack of bills and receipts and his notebook, one hand holding a pencil and the other buried in his hair. He looked up at me over his half-glasses, which rested low on the bridge of his nose.

"Thank you for staying open for us," I said as I passed. "It's my first time here. Everything was delicious."

"So glad you enjoyed." He looked at me curiously for a moment and then added, "He's one of the best."

I nodded in implicit agreement as I turned and walked back to our seats.

"Shall we?" Peter asked, taking his coat.

I stared at him.

"What?"

"Do you own this place?"

He snorted, surprised. "No. No. Not at all." He paused and then coughed, looking embarrassed. "I'm an investor. Did Dom tell you that?" I shook my head. "Well, why did you think that?"

"We're here after closing, and we're leaving without paying a bill. When I thanked Dom for staying open for us, he looked at me the way I look at Matt when he thanks me for pulling an all-nighter. Like it's not really a choice."

Peter put a finger to his nose and pointed it at me. "Sharp girl."

I laughed up at him as I slipped my arms into my coat and braced myself for the cold night air.

Q. After you met Gary, what was your impression of him?

A. That he was powerful. And that he didn't seem to notice me at all.

Q. How did that make you feel?

A. Not great. But motivated to work for his acknowledgment, I suppose.

Q. Did it make you dislike him?

A. No, I wouldn't say the initial encounter made me dislike him especially. I would say that all my encounters with him after that made me dislike him.

Q. I was asking about your first encounter. Please focus your responses on the questions asked. Now, I'd like to ask how this dislike came to manifest itself—what exactly did Gary do to cause you to seek vengeance against him?

[objection] [stricken from record]

Q. Where did this dislike come from, if not from the first encounter?

A. If you had let me simply elaborate rather than explaining I should only answer within the scope of the question, I'd have gotten to that.

CHAPTER 9

I glanced at the time in the lower right-hand corner of my computer screen.

3:07 AM

I tried Jordan. No answer. I hung up the phone and rubbed my eyes with my fists.

Even before my deal with Peter had closed, I was staffed on a new deal, Project Duke, for National Bank with Matt and Jordan that would close on an accelerated timeline. The days leading up to Project Duke's closing were a mess of greasy hair and stacks upon stacks of paper teetering like the tower at the penultimate move of a Jenga game on my desk. I had closed the blackout curtain to my office because I found that the rise and fall of the sun messed with my brain, signaling that I should be going to bed when work commanded otherwise. I had no idea whether I was supposed to send the term sheet I had spent the last three hours on out myself, or whether Jordan wanted to review it again.

I tried Jordan again. No answer. Why wasn't he answering? I knew he was there. His firm instant messenger light was still green. Maybe he just went to take a nap. I could use one myself.

I looked at the other names on my instant messenger. The circle next to Derrick's name was green too. I dialed his extension.

Derrick picked up halfway through the first ring. "I was just about to call you!"

"I'm dying. I'm so tired."

"Come down to my office! I have coke!" he sang.

I paused, providing him with a beat to see if he was kidding.

"Pass. I was more thinking a walk around the block to wake myself up."

"Uh, pass. I can't take a real break. I have to get something out."

"Okay, talk soon." I aimed for cheery, but heard the worry deepen my voice.

"Yes. Soon. Call you tomorrow," Derrick assured me.

I slumped forward, resting my cheek on my desk, where it met the cold, smooth wood, and slid my palms under my face. I was exhausted, anxious, and uncomfortable, and I couldn't stop wondering if I should pop into Derrick's office to ask him how he was doing. Instead, I stumbled out of my door and down the hallway to the "restoration room." The thought of collapsing onto the cool leather cot and snuggling up under one of the fleece blankets was so delicious that I was almost salivating, but when I reached the door I saw the red "Occupied" indicator in the half-moon above the lock. I wilted in disappointment; the idea of traveling to another floor to lie down felt so burdensome that I nearly collapsed. But I was only a first-year associate, and I felt certain that whoever was sleeping in the room needed it more than I did. He or she had probably been tired for the better part of a decade, whereas I only had a few months of late nights under my belt.

I leaned sideways into the door until it touched my ear, only to be greeted by the sound of male and female grunts and moans coming from within. I slammed my fist on the door. I might have been willing to forgo horizontal, comfortable sleep for somebody who needed it more than I did, but not just so two associates could get laid.

"I'll be back in twenty! I need sleep!" I announced through the door, feeling slightly out of line, but emboldened by the thought that my colleagues wouldn't want to be found out and would make themselves scarce before I returned.

When I returned, the room smelled of Clorox and the linens looked fresh, but I changed them and wiped everything down again anyway, then fell asleep immediately, jerking my eyes open at the hum of a vacuum outside the door the next morning.

I looked at my phone to see that Jordan had responded to emails while I was sleeping, sent the term sheet out himself when I hadn't done it within an hour of him telling me to, and instructed me to sleep a few hours and call him as soon as I woke up. I dialed his number.

"I just want to make sure nothing can hold up closing," he said without so much as a hello. "It cannot slip past today because then we need to wait for all the funds to transfer until Monday. Disaster. Have you confirmed with the real estate team that they've filed . . ." I could hear the stress in his voice as he rattled off the laundry list of administrative details I needed to take care of.

A preview of a new email from Carmen popped up in the lower right-hand corner of my screen as I struggled to write down everything Jordan was saying, and I glanced briefly at it.

I signed you in. Saving you a seat in the back.

"Shit," I whispered to myself as I continued to write. When Jordan finished, I cleared my throat. "So . . . I completely forgot we have the mandatory monthly business development training right now, and—"

"Skip it," he said tersely.

"Matt is doing the training, and . . ." I knew I wouldn't need to say more. Supporting Matt in any and every capacity trumped anything and everything else.

"Oh. Okay. Yeah. Go. I got you covered for the next hour. You've done all this anyway, I'm just paranoid the day a deal closes. But be on email. If this deal doesn't sign by this afternoon, I'm jumping out of my fucking window."

"Why do you think our windows don't open, genius?" I asked dryly, the auto-generated response he had come to expect from me during Project Hat Trick.

He snorted. "Keep it up, Skip, and I'm requesting Carmen on my next deal."

"You suck." I hung up.

I raised my chin toward the ceiling with my palm and felt the pleasant pop of a joint somewhere at the base of my skull. I stacked the six empty coffee cups on my desk into one another and threw them into the bin below my desk. I made my way slowly to the elevator and rubbed my finger under my eyes. I felt like a fraud. It was the first true all-nighter I had ever tried to pull, and I couldn't even make it the whole night without passing out in the restoration room.

I let my back rest against the wall of the elevator until the mechanical ding of the doors opening on the conference room on the forty-fifth floor yanked me from my half sleep. A woman with a binder was staring at me, and I gave a small, embarrassed laugh as I brushed by her. I opened the door to the conference room as quietly as possible and slipped inside. Fortunately Matt was speaking, and all eyes remained on him as I let the door ease closed behind me and made my way to the open seat next to Carmen, who looked up at me with concern on her face.

"Skippy! Nice of you to grace us with your presence!" Matt called out.

All fifty-two of my fellow first-years turned to look to me.

I felt the blood rising up from my neck, but I could register that they were more envious of than disgusted by my rapport with the co-head of M&A.

"Your deals don't close themselves, boss," I said with a two-finger salute, and slid into the seat next to Carmen, embracing my greasy hair and my wrinkled shirt as a badge of honor. Matt cackled before continuing with his due diligence training, clicking through slides.

Carmen leaned in to me as if to tell me something, then recoiled. "Oh my god, Alex, you need to shower." She blocked her nostrils with her fist. "No joke."

"I'm fully aware," I whispered back. I took out my phone and continued to answer emails about Matt's deal as he lectured the group on how the firm encourages a healthy work/life balance.

As the presentation was wrapping up, I saw an email from Jordan, subject: "One Yard Line." Everything was set, and we had a closing call at four o'clock.

From: Alexandra Vogel
To: Jordan Sellar
Subject: Re: One Yard Line

I'll tell maintenance they don't need to figure out how to open your window.

Our closing call came and went that afternoon without my having to utter a single word—a reminder that no matter how hard I worked, I was still the lowest attorney on the totem pole, and another silent first-year could have easily stepped in for me. And then we were done. Closed. It was over. I spent the next six minutes making sure I hadn't missed any urgent emails while I'd been under siege, then shut down my computer and leaned back in my chair. It was four fifteen on Friday afternoon. The sun was shining. I couldn't wait to crawl into bed for the next forty-eight hours.

"Anna," I called toward my open door. She craned her neck up over her cubicle. "Can you order me a car home, please? I need to sleep immediately." She furrowed her brow. "Don't worry, I'll pay for it!"

She appeared in my doorway, looking apologetic. *Just fucking DO it,* I wanted to say. But instead I smiled. "What's up?"

"Last week you asked me to book dinner for four at the Nomad for tonight. Should I cancel that?"

Fuck. My parents were coming into the city for dinner.

They had insisted on taking me and Sam out to celebrate my deal closing. My lower lip quivered, and I shook my head.

"Can you shut the door?" I asked softly, afraid speaking louder would scare the tears out of me, then remembered my manners and added, "Please?"

Anna looked at me with pity and shut the door behind her, and the tears started—I was simply too tired to hold them in.

I woke up with my face resting on my hands, flat out on my belly in the middle of my office floor. I stayed there for a moment before sitting up and wiping the drool from the side of my mouth with the back of my hand. I was really starting to understand why people did coke. I looked at my watch. Six thirty. I grabbed my cell phone and texted my parents and Sam all on the same thread.

So excited for tonight! Meet you at the Nomad at 8! ☺

I checked my work email. Only sixteen messages, none of them pressing, and a nice thank-you from Matt to me and Jordan. I responded quickly, then grabbed my bag, popped two Advil, ushered them down my throat with a dry gulp, and walked out the door. I headed straight to the Equinox by my office, stripped immediately upon entering the locker room, wrapped myself in a towel, and pushed myself into the thick fog of the steam room, relieved to see I was alone. My pores surrendered with little resistance, anxious for release. I could taste the sour stress in my sweat. It was all leaving me—dripping deliciously down my spine. I rubbed my shoulders, letting my fingers drift over my now-slimy skin. I let my towel drop. I touched my breasts, and I thought of Peter Dunn. I thought of the way his belt buckle sat on his completely flat abdomen, the way his skin was always clean shaven.

I opened my eyes and wrapped myself in the towel again, pulling my legs up on the tile bench to sit cross-legged and forcing myself to focus on my breath. I made my way to the shower and took my work clothes into the stall, where I turned the knob as hot as it would go and let the wrinkles in the silk rise to meet the steam. I scrubbed at myself vigorously, as though I could exfoliate away the exhaustion.

I walked into the Nomad right at eight to find my characteristically early parents speaking to the maître d'.

"Hi guys!" I announced loudly. They spun around. My mom held a bouquet of white roses.

"My little Bunny!" my mom squeaked. I placed my head in between the two of them and fell into their joint embrace.

"You look wonderful! Too thin, but wonderful! Is this what you wear to work? Stunning," she said, nodding approvingly.

"You do look great," my dad said.

"I showered at the gym and came right here. It's been a rough month. Hopefully it'll be a little slower now."

"These are for you," my mother said, thrusting the roses at me.

"Why?" I asked cautiously.

"Because you've been working so hard, and we're so proud," my mother said, and I made desperate eye contact with the maître d', who beamed back at me.

"We're under Vogel," I called over my father's shoulder to

him. I turned back to my parents. "They're gorgeous. Thanks, guys. Do you have any Advil?" My mother dug in her purse and handed me two pills, which I swallowed without water.

Just as the maître d' beckoned us to follow him, Sam arrived.

"Perfect timing!" my mother said, pulling him close. My father shook his hand. I went to give him a real kiss, but he pecked my cheek gruffly. My brain spiraled, praying his awkward greeting was because my parents were present and not because he was angry at me.

As my father ordered the wine and we listened patiently to the specials, I noticed that Sam seemed to be purposefully ignoring me. He hadn't shaved for dinner. He didn't turn to me when the waiter listed a black truffle risotto addition to the menu, even though he knew I would want it. My mind raced. I didn't know what I had done or forgotten to do, but I felt utterly defeated. A fugitive tear escaped my duct; I quickly excused myself to the restroom, knowing more would follow once the seal was broken.

I put my palms on the cool porcelain sides of the sink and inhaled deeply. I'd read once that the inner wrists were a temperature control center for the body, so I pushed up my sleeves and ran cold water over my hands, waiting.

"Hi there."

I stared into the mirror to see Gary Kaplan standing next to me, smiling at my reflection in the mirror. I turned to my left so I wasn't looking at him in the mirror, to confirm I wasn't hallucinating. I blinked twice. He was still there, beside me, in the ladies' room, at the Nomad Hotel.

"Hi!" I forced the word as my mind searched for something clever to say about the continued scaling of the private equity market. Or maybe I should ask him about his family? Or talk about the food? He had said it was the only restaurant he came to downtown.

"Can I buy you a drink?" A toothy grin spread his lips wide, but his gaze remained steady. I felt fairly certain he didn't recognize me from the way he was taking in my body, but I needed to extricate myself from the situation politely on the off chance he could place me the next time he saw me in the office. All I needed was to be blacklisted from deals with our biggest client in my first year at the firm.

I turned back to the mirror to see a dark-haired, especially tanned, incredibly toned woman, probably in her late twenties, exit the bathroom stall, pulling her tight, nude Hervé Leger dress down just far enough to cover things that shouldn't be uncovered in public. I exhaled, grateful to have somebody else there to defuse the situation, but she sidled up to Gary and threw an arm over his shoulder, nuzzling into his neck.

"Hi," she breathed into the mirror in my direction. I glanced quickly at Gary's hand to see if his wedding ring was on, and it was. The woman wasn't wearing one.

"I've asked this young lady to join us for a drink," Gary said, his eyes still glued to me.

"Fun!" The woman's eyes lit up mischievously as she looked me up and down in the mirror. I smoothed my blouse, my stomach churning. Though the encounter was completely unlike any I had ever had, their intentions were obvious.

"Oh. No thank you. I'm here with my family," I stammered.

Their faces fell. "Not fun," the woman said with a pout.

"Enjoy your night," I said with an awkward wave, exiting without drying my hands. Back at the table, I plopped down and found myself in a trance, looking at my silverware, playing the scene over in my mind as my father discussed his and my mother's February travel plans to Brazil.

"You okay?" Sam leaned in to me quietly, touching my hand under the table as his annoyance seemed to yield to concern.

"Yup! All good." I smiled broadly at him and my parents, trying desperately to stop my skin from crawling. Gary Kaplan was a man who cheated on his wife, propositioned young women, infiltrated the wrong side of same-sex restrooms, and generally chilled my spine upon every interaction. But he was unarguably the firm's best client. How could I build a career on representing such morally reprehensible characters? I supposed Stag River was the client, though. Not Gary. It wasn't as bad as . . .

"So, did you win the trial? Is it over?" my mother asked.

"She does deals, not trials," my father corrected her, probably not understanding the difference either but knowing enough to distinguish the two.

"Okay, okay. Did you win your deal?" she asked. I was too tired to explain that everybody wins a deal when we do our jobs correctly, so I just smiled and nodded.

"So how late have you had to stay at work? Seriously," my father said.

"She didn't come home two nights in a row," Sam answered flatly before I could. We all looked at him.

"One night," I said, rolling my eyes to indicate he was being dramatic.

He looked at me fiercely for a moment, and then I saw something that looked like worry cross his face again. "Two," he insisted.

Six eyes turned to me.

"Oh my gosh. Two. You're right." My mother's shoulders relaxed. I sipped my wine, trying to uncover memories of the lost night. It was Friday. I slept in the office last night. I remembered the accounting call, late Wednesday. Didn't I go home after that? I remembered sending emails from the apartment. Or was that Tuesday? I guess I can pull an all-nighter, I thought. Just not two in a row. That's good!

I felt a smile on my lips but wiped it away. Something had shifted in the energy at the table; the silence was pregnant with expectation.

"What?"

"Do you sleep at all when you stay in the office?" my father asked, for what I assumed was the second time.

"Yeah. Yeah. Yes," I said, shaking my head though stating the affirmative.

"No," Sam said angrily. "A couple hours, tops, in what they call the 'restoration room,' which is just a place people catch a few hours when they're working too much."

I looked over at him. "My Sammy baby misses me," I teased. He tried to stay flat, but he cracked a smile.

"It's like your ER shifts back in med school," my mom said, looking at my dad, who nodded.

"But you're happy, right?" my father asked, so hopeful that I had to avert my eyes.

"Loving it," I assured him.

"It's an actual crime for them to charge this much for chicken," my mother said as she looked over the menu, clearly searching for a new topic.

"It's chicken for two," I pointed out. Shit. This place was really expensive. It had been inconsiderate of me to make a reservation here. I hadn't been out with nonwork people in so long, I'd forgotten to consider the prices.

"I know!" my mother said. "Still!"

"It has foie gras under the skin." I defended the dish as though I'd made it myself as I scanned the room for Gary, who I hadn't seen come out of the bathroom yet.

"I'll split it with you!" my dad offered.

"Tell us about work, Sam. How is it? We don't totally understand what it is," my mother said, ignoring my dad's suggestion.

"It's hard. Harder than I thought. And I have yet to pay myself, which is really hard." I saw my mother straighten her spine, and my father looked slightly nervous.

"Tell them again what it is," I said as I leaned into him encouragingly. "It's a brilliant concept." Sam squeezed my knee gratefully under the table.

"It's basically a service—a website and an app—for sharing the cost and use of big-price-tag items. Like a time share, but for cars, parking spots, condos, bikes, and so on. We match customers based on location and do the credit checks, background checks, personality profiles. And our company is actually the one buying the item and leasing it indefinitely to both parties for a profit, but they're splitting the cost of the lease with a stranger, so it works for everybody. Like, if you travel a lot for work, you share your car with a neighbor when you're gone. Think, Rent the Runway, but . . . own the runway, and not for clothes."

"Wow!" my mother said, her voice rising with feigned enthusiasm. I knew she was skeptical about the idea, probably for the exact reasons I was—that people don't like to share big items with strangers, and they're okay with spending more not to. I took a long, thirsty sip of wine to drown out that voice in my head.

"Yeah," Sam said, and took my hand tenderly. "I think it's going to be really great. And I couldn't have done it without Alex. She was such a trooper while I was building the company in Cambridge. All while she was in law school." I thought back to our cramped second-floor studio and found it hard to believe I had lived in it so happily. Sam had had no money to take me on dates or go on vacation, and so I learned to cook and pretended I had learned to love Boston in the dead of winter. I wondered if I could ever handle living like that again. I plastered a smile on my face and gently pulled my hand from his.

"So, we hear you're running the marathon," my father's voice piped in through my thoughts, and I took a long drink. The wine was so light, I could barely taste it.

I swatted at the tickling feeling on my nose and hit Sam's hand. I opened my eyes to see Sam sitting next to me on the bed, holding one of my makeup compacts in his hand.

"What are you doing?" I asked groggily.

Sam snapped the compact shut. "I was holding the mirror under your nose to see if you were breathing," he said. I smiled. He didn't.

"I'm alive," I sang, holding up my hands and wiggling my fingers, but he didn't look amused.

"It's three in the afternoon," he said, getting up. He was fully dressed. I peeked under the sheets to see that I was wearing my bra and underwear from the night before.

"What happened?" I managed.

Sam shrugged. "You got really fucking drunk."

I put my palm to my head. I didn't feel hungover. Just groggy. "Did I?"

"Yup!" Sam said, his voice dripping with derision. "Off of two and a half fucking glasses of wine. Your father guessed it was a mixture of alcohol, exhaustion, and Advil that did it."

Jesus. Why couldn't I remember anything after we ordered? Why couldn't I forget the look in Gary's eyes, and that demented half grin on his face?

"Don't curse," was all I managed to say before plopping my head back down on the pillow and shutting my eyes.

"Sam!" I peeled my eyes open and sprang up. "We missed Lucas's birthday!"

"No, *you* missed Lucas's birthday," he said dryly. "I had a blast."

"Why didn't you wake me?" I had promised Sam's nephew I would be there, and I had sent Anna to four different toy stores to pick out his present.

"I assure you, I tried." He looked at me. "I saved you a fucking slice of cake." I had two choices, I realized then. I could ignore him and weather his mood for the next however many hours or days. Or I could change his mood entirely.

My lips curled into a smile. "You think you're the only one who can curse?" I asked. I bit my lower lip. He watched me, taking in my tone, his body tensing as he registered it. Even after all our years together, he always wanted me. Always. No matter how mad he was. I let the sheets fall farther down my body.

"What are you talking about?" he said mechanically.

"I can curse," I said. I stood up on the bed, fanning my fingers out to steady myself and counterbalance the wooziness. I towered over him, and he looked up at me. My thighs didn't touch each other now when I stood with my feet together. As much as I had him pegged as somebody who cared less about physical appearance than most men, Sam seemed to appreciate the view of my shrinking frame. He tugged at the inseam of his pants as he shifted his stance to make room.

"I want you to fuck the shit out of me," I said, and his jaw dropped slightly. I laughed from my belly, and before I knew it, he had tackled me onto the bed. He flipped me over in one fluid motion and tore my underwear down. He was on top of me before I figured out exactly where the ceiling and floor were.

I embraced my luscious lightheadedness and the grogginess from the fifteen hours of sleep. It felt like drunk sex, the kind we had when we first met, and it was exactly what I wanted. He yanked at my hair and bit my upper back below my shoulder. As the shock of it dissolved, the pleasure returned, not in place of the pain but right alongside it. I whimpered, encouraging him, and he clamped his hand over my lips to silence me. When he lost his grip on my face to his own pleasure, I managed to get one of his fingers into my mouth. He moaned again despite himself.

We stared up at the ceiling, breathing heavily, before I burst out laughing again.

"Holy shit," Sam breathed as he patted my thigh. I rolled into him and nuzzled into his neck.

"I'm so mad I blacked out my chicken!" I said, staring at the ceiling.

"Don't be. You kept saying it tasted like nothing. You kept shaking your head and salting it and saying it had no flavor. You announced it to the people at the next table. You told the waiter it was a rip-off."

I searched his face to see if he was joking. He wasn't.

I arched my back and laughed again, and he joined me this time, letting go of our argument.

My spine relaxed into the plush mattress. "Last night when I went to the bathroom I ran into a client," I said, staring up at the ceiling. "He didn't even recognize me. And he hit on me. It was so weird."

Sam turned to me, and I saw a flash of jealousy darken his eyes before he shrugged. "Can't blame the guy." He smiled and kissed my cheek. I shivered slightly at the memory of Gary's face and turned into Sam, resting my head on his shoulder and my hand on his chest, relishing his warmth.

"Let's just stay here awhile," he whispered.

"Where?"

"Here." He looked over at me. "In bed."

As soon as he said it, I thought of everything I had to do, and my heart quickened. *I have a job. I can't spend entire days in bed anymore.* I forced a smile back his way and nodded, trying to deny the tingling in my fingertips. *I just closed a deal. It's fine. It's Saturday. Nobody is emailing me anything urgent today.* My mind flashed with the thought of an email from Matt in my in-box going unanswered.

"Babe?" I said, forcing sleepiness into my voice despite the tension in my throat. "I need coffee."

"I'll make you some." He kissed the top of my head and rolled away from me.

As soon as he exited the room I lunged for my phone, which was mercifully next to the bed. It was on 2 percent battery, so I plugged it in and scanned my in-box frantically, knowing I didn't have much time.

None of them were urgent, but I chimed in on a chain with Matt and Jordan just to indicate that I was diligently checking in on a weekend. My phone was facedown by the time Sam handed me a cup of coffee, and I sipped slowly at the warm energy rush, light with the milk I knew he objected to, exactly how I wanted it.

"How do you feel about my eating cake for breakfast?" I asked sheepishly.

Sam smiled broadly as he drew his other hand from behind his back and revealed a plate of pillowy white cake with a thick brim of white frosting, dotted with something bright green and black with brown lines. He had gotten me a good piece even though he was mad. I put my coffee on the nightstand and reached for the plate.

"Ninja Turtles?" I asked, shoving a large forkful of icing into my mouth.

Sam slid back into bed beside me. "Yeah! I got you Donatello."

"Aw babe! You spoil me."

"Let me see your tongue," he said, sounding serious.

I stuck it out at him. "Green?" I managed and suddenly felt his tongue on mine. I put down the plate and fell into his kiss.

PART III

INDICATION OF INTEREST (IOI)

An expression showing conditional and nonbinding interest in engaging in the purchase or sale of a company.

Q. I'd like to backtrack to your relationships with colleagues to get a sense of your working relationships more generally.

A. I don't see how my relationships with other people are relevant here. I already explained that at Klasko, socializing is common with both colleagues and clients. My colleagues at Klasko were also my friends.

Q. You're right that it wouldn't be relevant at trial, but it's helpful for us in figuring out what information to gather from whom.

A. Fair enough. What do you want to know?

Q. Please expound on both your professional and personal relationships with your colleagues Matt Jaskel, Jordan Sellar, Peter Dunn, and Vivienne White, as well as your client Didier Laurent. Please focus on encounters outside of the office, while observing your obligations of privilege, of course.

A. Life as a young associate is all-consuming. Often my personal life bled into my professional life in the areas of client events and entertainment.

Q. That's precisely what we're interested in.

CHAPTER 10

I walked through the parting automatic doors of the twenty-four-hour Duane Reade right next to my apartment, took a few steps onto the white linoleum floor, squinted into the fluorescent lights that stung the backs of my eyes, and stopped in my tracks. Why was I even there? I had headed there on a mission, but the errand I needed to do had left my brain entirely. It was already eleven at night, but it was my first time leaving the office before midnight in the past ten days.

I walked up and down the aisles, trying to jog my memory, before buying a pack of gum and walking the fifty yards to my apartment building. Sam was already asleep when I crept into the bathroom, and as I plunked down on the toilet, the cool porcelain shocked the back of my thighs. I placed my elbows on my kneecaps and my head in my hands to rest for a moment, then reached for the toilet paper to find only an empty cardboard roll.

Fuck.

I found myself continually forgetting things like what I'd run to the drugstore to buy, whether I'd showered the previous morning, and any and all plans I made that weren't reflected in a calendar invitation. I thought about running back to the drugstore, just to avoid Sam's judgmental stare when he woke to realize I'd failed to run the one domestic errand he had asked me to do in over a month. But instead I put some takeout napkins on top of the cistern and crawled under the covers beside him, promising myself I would be more present in my personal life, beginning in the morning.

When just a few nights later I woke up from a nap on the floor of my office to a string of angry texts from Sam that he was waiting at the restaurant, that he couldn't believe how late I was, that he was irate that I wasn't responding, and that he was eating alone and going home, I made the decision to take a break from killing myself to get into M&A.

Come mid-November, I'd stopped asking Matt and Peter for more work, I'd told the staffing partner I needed to lighten my load, and I found myself staffed on just one active M&A matter. I knew I'd soon have to fill my plate again to maintain my competitive position in the running for an M&A match, so I took full advantage of the downtime before it disappeared. I went to Bloomingdale's with Carmen during a long lunch break, and for the very first time in my life, I didn't head straight to the sale rack. I made dinner plans with Sam that I actually kept. I took his nephew Lucas on a date to Ninja—a subpar sushi restaurant in Tribeca with above-average prices where the waiters dress and act like ninjas. I gave him second and third birthday presents to apologize, and reapologize, for sleeping through his party. "You made his year," Sam's sister had told me. "Miss his birthday anytime."

The strangest part of working so hard the past few months was that long days had quickly become my baseline. I felt as though I was somehow cheating when I "only" worked from ten in the morning to eight at night. I began to remember the parts of myself that got lost in the endless markups and interminable exhibits to our agreements, like the physical grooming rituals in which many human women partake, such as eyebrow plucking and haircuts. But I also noticed that I quickly became present again during social interactions, and that I wasn't nearly as forgetful.

It seemed I wasn't the only attorney in the office who was working at a slower-than-usual pace. Vivienne had rescheduled our mentor/mentee lunch—and this time she hadn't canceled. I sipped my water as she put her personal phone facedown on the white tablecloth and turned her attention to her work phone. I stared at her phone case, which featured a photo of her and her very attractive husband and three boys at the beach. Their hair blew to the left and their smiles curved slightly right as they braced themselves against a breeze.

"So, where were you in law school?" she asked abruptly.

"Harvard," I said, and she nodded dismissively, keeping one eye on her work phone. Her platinum hair was pin-straight and tied into a short ponytail at the nape of her neck. Her nails were long and painted white. She wore a white silk blouse with a thick red pinstripe tucked into a navy pencil skirt with four-inch nude heels, which only made her about five-four. Her skin was perfectly pale and flawless. *I need to stay out of the sun,* I thought. Her makeup was minimal. *I wonder if my eyeliner is smudged. My eyeliner is always smudged.* She couldn't have weighed more than a hundred pounds soaking wet. *I need to stop eating carbs.* If I hadn't known her name, I might have guessed it was Vivienne. It suited her.

"Did you enjoy your time there?"

"I loved it."

She looked up at me skeptically, and I realized my mistake. We were supposed to portray an unruffled, contemplative, skeptical, calm-in-the-face-of-chaos persona at all times.

"It was a great education," I said, correcting myself. She clicked one more button and then put her work phone facedown next to her personal cell. She looked as though she was momentarily contemplating dislocating her jaw and devouring me.

"That was schooling. This is an education," she said, her attention now fully on me. I thought for a moment she was referring to our lunch. I suppose she might have been. But I thought it more likely that she meant working life more generally. "Anyway, I'm glad we finally got to do this. Sorry for the delay. I'm a crappy mentor, but they keep giving me mentees."

I laughed politely, at a loss for a more appropriate reaction.

"What have you been working on?" she asked, picking up her phone. "I'm listening."

"I'm doing almost all M&A these days. I did a few real estate deals when I first arrived." I was talking to fill the silence, quite certain she wasn't hearing a word I was saying. "I like M&A. I think it's more my speed than real estate."

"What do you mean?" She looked at me squarely, her hands still.

My heart rate increased. I felt my knees go slightly rubbery. "Oh. I just felt like I was more on the periphery of deal-making or -breaking decisions when I worked in real estate."

Fuck. Is she a real estate lawyer? No. Capital markets. I'm sure of it. Shit. Am I offending her?

"But then again, the deal I was on was an acquisition, so obviously I wasn't part of the core team doing real estate," I blabbered on. "Anyway, I enjoy the more centralized vantage point I have from the M&A platform."

She looked back down at her phone and resumed typing. I had the sense that she not only resented having to be my mentor but also simply didn't care for me at all.

"I totally get that. I feel the same way. That's why I do capital markets," she said without looking up. "I see a lot of myself in you, actually. So sorry. After this, I'm done. I swear."

I wondered just how I was presenting myself if she thought we were similar, but I reassured her as best I could. "Please. Don't apologize. I get it. Maybe a couple months ago, I didn't, but now I do."

"You think you do."

Her condescending tone knocked me off balance yet again,

and two simultaneous but disparate emotions cropped up in my chest: terror that if I continued in BigLaw, I'd inevitably become cold and rigid like Vivienne, and exhilaration that if I continued in BigLaw, I'd become a fashionable, beautiful, intelligent, and successful partner like Vivienne.

"Okay. I'm back." She looked up at me and set down her phone again. "By the way, nobody outside BigLaw will ever get it. Maybe investment bankers. But they're the client. They have the luxury of not responding. We don't. Doctors keep horrendous hours, but they at least know when they're going to be on call. There's no predictability with us. No ability to unplug. Do you know how many vacations I've taken where I haven't left my hotel room? I haven't been anywhere without an internet connection in sixteen years. Planes used to be the only time I really slept, and then the airlines went and got fucking Wi-Fi. The ironic part is, I did the IPO for Leopard—the company that delivers it to them." She smacked her head dramatically. "If anybody tells you they 'get it,' they're lying. And they probably hate you for being on your phone so much."

I pointed to her phone cover. "You seem to have it figured out," I said, laying it on as thickly as I dared.

She sucked air in sharply, and I wondered if I'd made a misstep. But she looked at the picture on her phone case wistfully for only a moment before smiling and then motioning to the waiter with one hand while slipping her phone into her purse with the other.

"We can order," she snapped at a server rushing by, even though he wasn't the one assigned to our table. I reached for the menu and scanned it frantically.

"I'll start with a Caesar salad. And the chicken paillard," she said, handing him her menu as he and I scrambled to catch up.

"I'll have the caprese to start," I said, trying to pick something different from what she'd ordered. "And the scallops, please."

"May I interest you ladies in some of our house-made bread?" A second server came over with a bread basket and tongs.

No way she eats carbs.

"One olive and one whole wheat, please," Vivienne barked. "And can you bring the good butter they have in the back? The whipped kind?" She looked back to me. "Something about the foil makes it taste metallic, you know?"

I didn't, but I nodded.

"Multigrain, please," I said, craning my neck over the basket. The roll was warm, and the steam escaped in tiny curls when I broke through its crusty exterior.

"Are you looking forward to First-Year Academy?" Vivienne asked, breaking her bread as well. "I think they schedule the retreat for somewhere warm in February to try to compensate for the fact that first-year associates are expected to work through Christmas and New Year's."

Well, that put an end to the conversations I'd been having with Sam about where to go for Christmas vacation.

"Definitely," I said. Oddly enough, it wasn't a lie. In theory, spending time in a hotel conference room while the California sun blazed outside didn't sound all that fun. But in reality, I wasn't yet comfortable enough in my new financial reality to not be thrilled by an all-expenses-paid trip across the country, a luxury hotel room all to myself, complete with slippers and robes and Egyptian cotton sheets, and unlimited alcohol.

Vivienne was back to reading her emails. "Great," she muttered under her breath sarcastically as she typed a quick reply. "I have to lead a training this year, so I'll see you there. Don't wear a bikini."

I swallowed before I had fully chewed my roll. "Sorry?"

"Don't wear a bikini. When you have free time at the pool," she said, looking at me, her eyes suddenly brighter and her voice lighter. "Your male colleagues see you in a bathing suit once, and they'll picture you in a bathing suit in every single meeting for the rest of your life." She must have seen the skepticism on my face. "Trust me on this one."

I nodded, but felt eager to change the subject. "So, you were a partner at Gifford before coming to Klasko?"

"Yep. It was no cakewalk being the new kid. I found I needed to prove myself. And look the part. You're lucky, you got in on the ground floor. And you already look the part." She gave me a small smile to let me know it was a compliment, and I sensed she was suddenly enjoying my company.

I tried to picture Vivienne in anything but perfectly tailored, stylish business attire and wondered what she could have worn before she "looked the part."

The busboy cleared my plate of crumbs and her plate of two whole rolls, torn apart but still there in their entirety, as well as her untouched ramekin of butter. I felt that she somehow had just purposefully tricked me into eating carbs.

She told me about capital markets work over salads and offered to get me on one of her deals over entrées. I grinned obsequiously and thanked her, despite being terrified at the prospect of working for her. She handed the waiter her credit card as she asked for the bill and signed without reviewing the check and, I was pretty sure, without the addition of "esq."

We walked back to the office in silence as she typed away on her work phone, and in the lobby we passed Carmen and Roxanne, who seemed to be on their way to grab lunch. Carmen waved and Roxanne gave me a high five, then they went through the revolving door without a word.

Vivienne looked up from her phone. "Your friends?"

I nodded. "My class is great. It's been really nice to have actual friends as I adjust to life at a big firm."

Vivienne looked at me intently. "Hmm." She finally released her grip on her phone and tossed it into her purse. "Erich Fromm once said that intelligence is a man's instrument for manipulating the world more successfully. You know what I mean?"

I began to nod slowly before I allowed my head to shake instead.

She laughed as though she'd guessed as much. "I'm just saying, be careful. You put a bunch of smart, hungry people in competition for the same prize, and the result is . . . well, people are almost never what they seem around here." She broke into a large smile. "This was lovely, Alex! Looking forward to doing it again soon."

I fumbled slightly. "Thank you for lunch. I had such a nice time."

I didn't actually know what kind of a time I'd had. It wasn't a bad time. I felt a bit like I had just lost a game of chicken, but I had never felt like Vivienne was coming at me at all. I exhaled as she waved lightly, almost brushing the air away from behind her head, and started off toward the far elevator bank.

From: Peter Dunn
To: Alexandra Vogel
Subject: FW: Goldshore

Hi Alex,

See below. The kickoff meeting for Goldshore will be tomorrow. Please schedule. The timeline will be tight, and due to some scheduled vacation time by the senior associate on the deal, you will be the only associate on it for the next few weeks. I know this deal will cut in a bit to Thanksgiving time, but we'll do our level best to make sure you can enjoy at least Thursday. Should be a great opportunity. And a lot of work. I trust you are equal to the task!
—Peter

From: Alexandra Vogel
To: Peter Dunn
Subject: Re: FW: Goldshore

Hi Peter,

Thanks. I'll schedule the meeting asap. I'm definitely equal to the task! Looking forward to it.

Best,
Alex

CHAPTER 11

"Babe, honestly, it's enough. It's Thanksgiving," Sam said, a slight whine in his voice.

He was driving our rental car to my parents' house in Connecticut, flashing his brights every so often to illuminate the murky suburban road winding before us in the moonless night. I typed furiously at my phone with my computer on my lap, making changes I could save to the system as soon as I got onto Wi-Fi. My plan to float under the staffing partner's radar hadn't lasted more than a week. More senior associates had started to travel home for Thanksgiving, and first-years were required to pick up the slack. I found myself heading into the four-day weekend on three deals, the one for Peter and two new ones for Matt.

"I know I know I know! Sorry! I just want to do this now so I can really spend time with you and our families when we get there."

Sam nodded, but I could tell he wasn't convinced.

"I'm sorry!" I begged.

"I know."

"Sorry," I repeated, defeated.

He put his right hand on my knee, and when I contorted my arm at the elbow so that I didn't hit his hand on my lap as I typed, I felt him roll his eyes at me and move his palm back onto the wheel.

"Bunny! My Bunny is home!" My mom ran into the front hall as soon as we opened the door. A savory waft of a roast in the oven and the smell of something sweet with cinnamon reached me even before she did. They immediately calmed me, and I put my bags down and leaned into her embrace.

"The house smells amazing!" I shut my eyes as I breathed in. When I opened my eyes, my heart sank. Absolutely nothing had changed in the house I grew up in. The same floral tablecloth was draped over the Formica table. The same crocheted pillow declaring "Home Is Where the Heart Is" occupied the best seat on the reclining chair. I suppose I had never noticed how outdated the decor was until I had my own adult apartment to decorate. And somehow the house felt as though it had shrunk, the walls closing in on me.

I started to feel warm and pulled at my collar. "Is it hot in here?" I tugged at the bottom of my shirt to fan my torso.

"Probably a little, because of the oven. I'll open a window." My mother continued to chatter as she made her way to the window and allowed a bit of cold air in. "I'm making Brussels sprouts, jalapeño cheddar corn bread, green bean casserole, cranberry orange chutney, ham, and turkey, of course. Sam, your mom is bringing a vegetable tartlet and two pies. Aunt Sue is bringing the salad and fruit salad. What am I missing?"

"How should I know?" I said, more sharply than I'd intended.

My mom's face fell, and she dropped her hands to her sides.

I was struck by a feeling of guilt. "I mean, I just got here! Can I just do a little work, and then we'll do a full rundown of the menu?"

"Sure! The computer is all set up for you in the basement."

"I have mine." I slid my Klasko laptop out of its cover.

"The Wi-Fi is down, actually. The last storm knocked it out. We've been meaning to fix it, but they keep giving us a six-hour window for an appointment! Who has that kind of time to sit around? Just use ours." I stared at my mother. I certainly didn't have that kind of time, but I didn't quite know what else she was doing with her days.

"Mom, I need *my* computer to be on the internet. I have files saved locally—" I breathed in sharply and put my forefinger to my temple. "Does your computer have an LAN connection? Is it only the wireless that's down? I guess I can use yours if it's connected," I said, figuring that I would only need to redo the work I'd done in the car if I couldn't connect my laptop.

"There's no internet," she repeated robotically.

I looked to Sam for help. "Maybe there's a twenty-four-hour Starbucks," he offered. I cocked my head to the side, waiting to see if he'd laugh. He wasn't joking. I had grown accustomed to high-speed printers, double-wide computer screens, and ergonomic office chairs. Working from my parents' home was bad enough. I refused to be punished by sitting in some random Starbucks in the Connecticut suburbs because my parents had yet to enter the twenty-first century. There had to be a solution, but obviously I would need to come up with it myself.

"Jesus Christ." I took out my phone and walked into the house, leaving them by the door. I began to compose a mental list of everything I'd need internet for over the weekend. *Item 1: Everything.* "I don't even know how you people function," I grumbled.

My mother followed me as I paced around the house, looking up the number for our corporate help desk.

"Klasko & Fitch technology help center. This is Arthur. How may I help you?"

"Hi, Arthur. This is Alex Vogel in the New York office. I'm in Connecticut, a couple hours outside the city, for the holiday, and I don't have Wi-Fi."

"What are they going to do about it?" Sam asked, more to my mother than to me, and she nodded, as if I was being ridiculous.

"Oh, you're able to send a messenger with a Myfi? By eleven is perfect." I gave Sam an exaggerated wink.

"No. I didn't know that was possible . . . Yes, I have it here . . . No, I'm calling you from my personal device, my work phone is in my hand . . . okay . . . okay . . . okay. Now what? . . . Really!? I had no idea. You're a genius. Hold on, let me see if it works." I opened my computer and put my phone next to it.

"What are you doing?" my mother whispered. I hated when she whispered just because I was on the phone, as though her question was less intrusive that way.

"I'm using my work phone as a personal hotspot. I didn't realize I could do that." My mom nodded, pretending to understand, then busied herself offering Sam food.

"I'm in! Four bars. Thanks again. You're the greatest. Have a very happy holiday." I hung up with a smile.

"Phew!" My mother sighed. "What can I fix you for dinner? Sam's going to have salad and chicken."

"I'm not hungry," I said, not looking up from my screen. In truth, I was starving, but few things gave my mother as much pleasure as feeding people, and denying her that pleasure was a way of punishing her for my own frustration about the internet. "Where's Dad?"

"He's in the cellar, picking some bottles for the weekend. He'll be up in—"

As if on cue, my father entered the room carrying a crate of wine, which he shoved onto the kitchen island before enveloping me in his arms. I buried my head in his chest and took a deep breath.

"What is it?" My father pried me off of him and looked at me. I immediately noticed the fraying of his collar, as well as his ill-fitting jeans and mismatched socks. Though I wished they didn't bother me, I cringed slightly.

"Nothing! I'm just tired. My brain hurts."

Back at my laptop, I kept my eyes laser-focused on my work

so I didn't have to see the sideways glances Sam and my parents exchanged as my mom threw together dinner from a mixture of leftovers and whatever she had on hand. I wanted a fresh salad, something light so I wouldn't get sleepy while working, or maybe a piece of fish, but she placed store-bought chicken cutlets and lettuce drenched in ranch dressing before us. Sam and my father's forks nearly collided as they both reached for the chicken, but I excused myself from the table without having any.

"I'll make you whatever you like!" my mother called after me. "I just didn't have the energy to cook another whole meal with thirty people coming tomorrow!"

"I said, I'm just not hungry," I called over my shoulder. I needed to make an excuse to get back to the city, to civilization, after dinner tomorrow. I could not possibly spend the weekend there. How had I ever spent eighteen years there? The lively conversation between Sam and my parents tapered off to faint whispers, undoubtedly about me. When I logged on to the Klasko system, I had forty-one missed emails, all of them regarding Peter's deal.

I closed my computer at a decent hour—midnight, I think, though I had forgotten to look at the clock on my screen. Ever since I'd moved out for college, I could never remember which clocks in my parents' house were set to which time. Some of them hadn't been turned back an hour for daylight savings, some were set fifteen minutes ahead to encourage my mother to be on time, and some seemed to run slow. When I wrapped up for the evening, all I knew was that it was late enough that Sam had already gone to bed in my old room. I made my way quietly up the staircase in the dark house, avoiding the creaky step with the graceful hop-over I had perfected so beautifully in high school that no amount of beer consumption would cause me to land on it. Nonetheless, my father came out of the master bedroom and met me at the top of the stairs.

"Hey, Dad."

"Give your ol' man a sec." He pointed at the stairs, and I followed him down and toward the kitchen table. "How're you doing, sweetheart?" He watched me closely, looking protective. The Klasko & Fitch T-shirt I'd given him when I got my offer hung loosely around his neck above the hospital scrub pants he always wore to bed.

"I'm good! I was just stressed that you didn't have internet." I looked around the kitchen, at the outdated cabinets and the slightly peeling paint that I had never taken note of before. I suddenly wanted to cry, not so much because those things were there, but because I saw them, and cared about them now. I picked at an imaginary hangnail. "You don't have to wear that shirt just because it was free."

My father looked down at his chest. "I don't wear this because it's free. I wear it because I'm proud of you." I really didn't want to cry, but my eyes welled slightly. "We know you're working so hard. And stressed." My dad put his hand on mine. I looked at his thick palm and then up to his warm brown eyes.

My tears spilled out from the outer corners of my eyes and down my face. Was I losing myself to this job?

"I'm just stressed. Not sad," I attempted to assure him, wiping at my chin and steadying my breath. My palm was dripping wet. Maybe I was sad. "I'm looking forward to not working tomorrow."

"We love you, and we're so proud of you. And worried about you! Go get some sleep." He leaned over and kissed the top of my head, and I ran upstairs again and crawled under the covers beside Sam. The mattress below me felt lumpy and old, and I missed my bed in the city—the one I had picked out with the plush pillow top. I could tell by Sam's breathing that he was still awake, and I sighed contentedly, indicating that I was on the verge of sleep to end-run any desire he had to talk to me.

"Babe?"

Shit.

"Hi love." I snuggled up to him, hoping he would appreciate the sweetness in my voice enough to leave me alone. He inhaled deeply. *Please don't start a fight right now. Please.* I suddenly remembered I had something to distract him, and hopped out of bed. "I have a surprise!" I turned on a light and riffled through my weekend bag, pulling out a small square baby blue box.

"I almost forgot about it. It's nothing. It's small. But I saw them and thought of you." I handed Sam the Tiffany's box, and he sat up in bed, confused but smiling, and opened it. His smile faded and his brow furrowed.

"They're cuff links!" I explained, then added, "They're returnable."

Sam plastered a smile on his face and nodded. "I'm not returning them! I love them. Thank you." I could hear the forced enthusiasm in his tone. My throat closed a bit. He'd never wear cuff links. It was a stupid gift. He never even wore collared shirts. I turned off the light so he wouldn't see my expression, and stood for a moment with my hand on the switch, allowing my eyes to adjust to the darkness, before making my way to the bed.

It occurred to me, there in the quiet, warm blackness of suburbia, that I was less disappointed by the fact that he didn't like my gift than by the fact that he wasn't the type of man who wore cuff links. I knew it was a ridiculous feeling, but I felt it. I wanted him to have important meetings, and to care about looking good for them. And it had nothing to do with success; it had to do with the fact that I was surrounded by people who wore them, who cared to wear them. The start-up and tech worlds frowned upon suits and shoe shines and designer labels and everything I had begun to feel familiar around and drawn toward.

I allowed myself to stand next to the bed a moment longer, then finally crawled in next to him again.

"Thank you for the cuff links," he tried to reassure me. I put my head on his shoulder. Even if he hated the gift, I was hoping I'd been successful in waylaying a conversation about my recent schedule.

"We have to get better at this," he whispered.

No such luck.

He stared at the ceiling, with his arm around me, his thumb drawing a circle on my shoulder.

At what? "I know," I said, even though I didn't. "I'm so sorry I had to work tonight. But now I'm free tomorrow!" I forced a yawn.

"It's not fair to me or your family or anybody that you're in the office so much, and when you're not in the office, you're either working or worrying that you should be working."

It's fair to my clients. "Sam, this was sort of the deal. Remember? A few years of hard work—"

"This isn't hard work. This is madness."

I sat up, my legs still under the covers, and opened my mouth, ready to ask him how he thought we could afford the apartment we lived in or the thousands of dollars he put on my credit card at JackRabbit for marathon gear and renting WeWork meeting space every month. But instead I forced myself to clench, then release, my jaw.

"It's not madness. It's BigLaw. It's what I signed up for. Our relationship just can't be all about you right now." The quilt felt heavy around my legs, and I kicked it off onto the floor.

"That's so unfair, Alex. You know it is. It doesn't need to be all about me. Nor has it been in the past, for the record. It needs to be half about me. That's how relationships work."

"Yes. Agreed. But on average. Not every day. I was patient when you were starting your company, off at tech conferences and meeting with investors seven nights a week. You went on coding binges for days at a time. And I never once complained when we were in Cambridge about cleaning up after you or doing the dishes or cooking dinner every night because we had no money to go out. And all while I was studying my butt off. And do you know why?" He was silent, and I opted to gloss over the fact that I hadn't complained because I actually hadn't been unhappy at all. "Because I love you, and people who love each other support each other. And give more when the other person needs more. Because it all evens out over time."

I put my head back on the pillow, and heard him breathing angrily.

"Jesus, you really argue like a lawyer now."

I whipped my head around toward him, and then I opened my mouth and closed it. "You're right, honey. I'll make sure to tell my clients that I can't work past five because you need dinner and a foot rub. They'll understand. And I'll want to quit as soon as we have kids, so what's the point of working so hard anyway?"

"Jesus Christ, Alex," Sam growled, then rolled his body away from me.

I didn't say anything, and a few minutes later, when I felt Sam's breathing deepen, I seethed at the fact that he'd been able to drift off in the middle of a fight. I wriggled around next to him in a futile attempt to make his night as sleepless as I knew mine would be.

Though I'd only had a few hours' sleep, the soothing morning light helped to calm my frayed nerves. It was Thanksgiving, our families would be together, and we could leave the argument in the past. As I washed my face, feeling ready to accept Sam's apology, he entered the bathroom across the hall from my room, brushed past me, turned on the shower, and stepped in without a word.

Fine. If this is how he wants it. Fine.

We put on our best faces for our families, circling the same area like two magnetic norths, never drifting too close to one another. I busied myself offering his family beverages, smiling at their stories. Lucas had taken up karate, and I laughed too loudly as he showed me the roundhouse kick he had learned to make, certain nobody in the room noticed the tension.

Our families had met a couple of times over the years, but this was the first holiday we were all spending together, and everybody else seemed to be enjoying one another's company. It wasn't surprising—we both came from northeastern suburban households that valued academic achievement. I used to take comfort in the similarities in our backgrounds, but sitting around that table on that Thanksgiving, it struck me that choosing someone so similar to me somehow indicated the narrowness of my worldview. I'd become friends with the son of a diplomat, a woman who'd grown up in Singapore, and some of the highest-powered attorneys in Manhattan. I couldn't help but imagine their Thanksgiving conversations to be far more interesting and enlightened.

I was snapped out of my thoughts by Sari, Sam's eight-year-old niece, asking if all twenty-two of us would go around the table and say what we were thankful for and what we wished for the coming year. The request was so sweet that my brain stopped spinning for a moment. I listened to my father say that he was thankful for my mother's cooking and he wished she'd stop making him diet. My mother was grateful that my father had finally lost ten pounds and had stopped snoring as a result; she wished that meant she'd sleep more in the coming year.

Sam was next. "I'm thankful for Alex, and for how hard she works every day to let me pursue my dream of starting a company." He put his hand on my knee under the table, and I looked up to see somehow expectant expressions on every face around the table. What were they waiting for? *Oh god. Please don't propose. Please don't propose.* I suddenly felt like I was in a cage, trapped hopelessly and perpetually in the world of chipped paint and crocheted pillows and spotty internet connections. *Oh god. Please don't do this to me.*

"That's it," Sam said cheerily. "Let's eat!"

I felt the blood draining from the vein above my right temple and releasing a bit of the pressure. I exhaled slowly, my heart still thudding at warp speed but the tension in my neck dissipating nonetheless.

Everybody continued to stare at Sam, but my father finally broke the silence. "Okay!" he announced, sounding almost reluctant. "I'll get the bird." Anxious chatter commenced around the room, and I met Sam's eyes and forced a smile onto my face. My turn was skipped entirely. I never got my chance to say what I was grateful for or what I wished, which was a good thing because I truly had no idea what I would have said.

When we got back to the city Sunday evening, I waited until Sam was in the bathroom and riffled through his bag. I easily found what I was looking for: a small black velvet box. My stomach churned as I held it up to my face and snapped it open.

The ring was stunning—emerald-cut with tapered baguettes—and I realized that my mother must have helped pick it out. It was huge—and it occurred to me that my father must have helped him buy it.

All the qualities I'd once loved about Sam came to the forefront of my mind. I focused on his kindness, his morality, his honesty. When I didn't think about the future, I didn't mind that he had no money and that he very well might never have any. I could care less that he wouldn't fit in with my Klasko friends and that he hadn't ever planned a fun dinner out for us. I attempted to steady my racing mind. I closed my eyes as the events from the Thanksgiving meal rushed back in on me, wincing at the memory of those expectant faces.

Why *didn't* I want Sam to propose? He was kind. And smart. And we still had great sex. Don't most girls want to get married?

I didn't need to analyze my feelings any longer. He hadn't proposed, and so I didn't need to think about it right now. I reached for my work phone as though it were a stiff drink and read through my new emails quickly, until I noticed a warm liquid underneath my fingers. I stared down, horrified, at the red streaks on my forearm, just beginning to leak drops of blood, and the bits of skin beneath my fingernails. I considered my arm in detached disbelief for a moment before I made my way to the kitchen to wash up. The sting of the soap was delicious.

***

"Holy shit." Carmen put her hand to her forehead as I finished my story, which I'd rushed through before our morning emails began to pour in on the Monday after Thanksgiving. "This is big."

"Literally. The ring was huge," I agreed.

She got up from her chair and began to pace the length of my office, though she was only able to take a few steps before having to double back.

"So, the real question is, do you think you'll *ever* want to marry him?"

"Is that really the question? Isn't the question why I don't want to marry him *right now*?"

Carmen stopped and looked at me. "Because you don't think he's the one for you. Not now, at least," she said, a hint of apology for her honesty in her tone. I slumped down in my chair, realizing she was correct. "And the question isn't whether you love him, because we both know the answer is yes," she said softly.

She was right, of course. I leaned my head back and stared at the ceiling. "I just don't know. We used to be so good. I used to want to marry him so badly. Or maybe I liked the comfort of knowing that was the plan. But since I started working here—" I pressed my palms together and then pushed them out from my chest in opposite directions. "But maybe it's just an adjustment period."

"Maybe."

"Sometimes I don't feel like he fits in this world," I said, gesturing around my office. "And I think I like this world."

A metallic ding from my computer reminded me I was due in Peter's office in five minutes.

"To be continued," Carmen assured me.

A few days later, I made my way back into my office at five o'clock, seeing it for the first time since I had left to go to back-to-back meetings on the forty-fifth floor that morning. "Jordan called. Three times," Anna announced from her cubicle. I nodded as I ducked into my office and closed the door behind me.

I dialed his number before even sitting down at my desk.

"How's your deal with Peter going?" Jordan asked in place of a greeting.

"Good." I called my computer to life and entered my password, smirking at how territorial he and Matt had become over me. I hoped it meant they'd rank me at the top of their list come Match Day. "What's up?"

"We're having a party in my mother's basement tonight," Jordan announced.

"What?"

"On the fifty-sixth floor. 'Mom's basement' is the theme of the party. A keg, beer pong, and nineties hip-hop. It's our last hurrah before they install security cameras tomorrow."

I thought for a moment about the blasting of the soundtrack to my middle school years in a space that was about to be reserved for corporate lunches and high-stakes conference calls. "Genius. I love this idea."

"I'm heading up there now! Come."

"I can't. I slept here last night. I'm exhausted, and I'm supposed to cook dinner for Sam tonight." I disliked the words as they rolled off my tongue. I would have rather been upstairs having a few drinks with Biggie and Tupac playing. The idea of sitting quietly at home with Sam, eating a meal I'd prepared and listening to his latest roadblock to funding for his company, seemed impossibly tedious in that moment. But I'd promised him I'd be home.

"Invite your boyfriend. We'll order food at some point, I'm sure."

I inwardly balked at the image of Sam in ill-fitting jeans and a worn sweater standing next to Jordan in his perfectly tailored suit. They would have absolutely nothing to talk about. "Beer pong in my office is not Sam's idea of fun."

"Fine. Not my problem if he doesn't know what fun is," Jordan said. "I gotta run. Peter and Matt are already up there with Carmen and like twenty other people." He let the last sentence sink in, making it clear to me that Carmen would be bonding with the partners who were the gatekeepers to our career, in M&A.

"Carmen's up there?" I asked, too tired not to take his bait.

He laughed sadistically. "She's up there securing her spot on the fifty-sixth floor. The whole team is going to be up there as soon as it's finished."

"I hate you."

"You love me. See you up there in ten." He hung up.

I sent Sam an apologetic text saying that my deal had blown up and I was stuck in the office, promising I'd make it up to him. I pulled at the collar of my shirt and bent my head to see how bad I smelled. I couldn't recall the last time I had taken the time away from work to shower, but it certainly wasn't within the past forty-eight hours. I looked at my clock: 8:00 p.m. I closed the door and stripped down, changing into the last of the clean blouses I'd started to keep in my office and stuffing my dirty clothes into the Klasko dry-cleaning bag marked with my employee ID number. I darted out of my office just as the stout man with the thick mustache from Paradigm Cleaning I'd seen on many evenings was finishing his last rounds of the floor.

"Excuse me! Can you add this to the twenty-four-hour service?" I shouted, running after him. He turned to me, scanned me up and down, and dropped his jaw. I straightened my spine, attempting to appear more composed. He continued to look at me with a slightly stupefied glaze over his eyes, and I opted to return to my office with a curt "Thank you." I threw on my winter coat, fairly certain the unoccupied floor's heat wouldn't be turned on yet, and headed to the party.

The floor was still bare concrete, with tape outlining where the glass office walls would be installed, but the ceiling had been finished and the windows sealed and uncovered, allowing for a spectacular 360-degree view of Manhattan. "No Diggity" blared from a set of speakers as twenty or so associates, along with Matt and Peter, stood around a keg, and Jordan arranged red Solo cups into perfect triangles on either side of the Ping-Pong table. There was a draft, but it wasn't nearly cold enough for my down coat, so I started to unzip my jacket.

Suddenly I caught sight of Carmen in a full sprint toward me. As soon as she reached me, she wrapped me in a ferocious, tight hug as I stood, frozen, palms against my thighs. "Leave your coat on," she ordered quietly, zipping me up as she backed away a few inches.

I looked at her, slightly annoyed. "What is wrong with you?"

She looked over her shoulder, then turned back to me and allowed a smile to spread across her face.

"What the fuck is wrong with you?" I demanded again.

"You're not wearing a skirt," she whispered, trying desperately to hold back laughter with a fist to her lips.

I shoved my hands in the pockets of my coat and felt at my hips, grasping wildly to try to prove her wrong, but felt only the top of my stockings. She had started to cackle wildly, and I giggled too, then winced as I recalled the expression on the dry cleaner's face and my short reaction to him.

"Oh my god. I don't have any other clothes! I just gave them all to dry cleaning."

Carmen wiped at the corners of her eyes. "My office," she managed.

I left Carmen, still doubled over, and headed for the elevator, where I held the call button down until the elevator doors opened.

"Thank you!" I called back to her from the safety of the elevator cab, and she held up a palm to me, unable to respond further. I smiled to myself, impressed that girl code had trumped any sense of competition Carmen might have been feeling. I wondered momentarily whether I'd have done the same for her before convincing myself that I would have.

The elevator doors opened on the thirtieth floor and Kevin entered, wearing his coat and looking done for the night.

"Hey! Where are you off to?" he asked.

"Just grabbing something from Carmen's office. A bunch of M&A people are playing beer pong on the new fifty-sixth floor," I told him, more than a little proud to have been included.

Kevin snorted. "Drinking the Kool-Aid, I see." I frowned at him as the elevator let me out on Carmen's floor. "Take care of yourself, Alex." He gave me a friendly wave good night, but his words felt like a warning.

Five minutes later, I reemerged from the elevator on 56 wearing one of Carmen's skirts. The hem hit my shins when I recalled it only hitting her knee, but otherwise it fit perfectly. I headed straight for the keg.

"Beer?" The redheaded associate I'd seen asleep at the salad bar offered me a Solo cup.

"Thanks. Cheers." I extended my plastic cup to him.

"Cheers," he said, hands at his sides. "I'm not drinking. I have a call in thirty minutes." I nodded at his responsible decision, then watched as he rolled a dollar bill into a tube and did a line of cocaine off the folding table. I scanned the room, but nobody else seemed to have noticed.

"Skippy! It's you and Peter against me and Carmen," Jordan yelled over to me. I nodded, looking back at the redhead, who was now staring up at the ceiling and rubbing his lips together, before I made my way to Jordan.

Carmen winked approvingly at my skirt. "You look fab."

"Winner gets the last office on 56 for the girl on his team," Peter said to Jordan with a smirk. Was there really only one office left unclaimed on the M&A floor? And could a drinking game really determine who took it? Carmen and I stared at each other, our expressions morphing into competition mode.

"I'm just kidding," Peter said, and laughed. "You should see your faces."

Carmen and I smiled, attempting to ignore the looks we'd just given each other, as "Mo' Money, Mo' Problems" blared from the speakers. Matt ambled to the middle of the table to serve as referee, his plastic cup dimpling slightly beneath his short, chubby fingers. I took my spot at the far side of the table next to Peter and glanced at the small orange cones running the length of the concrete floor behind me.

"What's with these?" I asked him, but Matt piped in before he could answer.

"They were the only way Jordan could get me to agree to a party up here. I said no one could even get near the half of the floor with the exposed elevator shaft. Nobody crosses that line. Danger zone." Matt shook his head in slow motion, already finished with the beer I'd just seen him refill. Past the cones, I saw an expanse of raw, industrially lit space, and in its center, a square hole in the floor with caution tape around it. Even though I was a few dozen yards from the shaft, the idea that a fifty-six-story drop was that close made me queasy.

"I literally went to every single hardware store in the city to find the cones," Jordan said.

"Your admin went," Peter corrected.

"Whatever. I supervised via email, right?" Jordan laughed.

Matt flipped a coin up in the air. "Heads or tails?"

"Heads!" I shouted without thinking.

Matt checked the coin on his palm and threw the Ping-Pong balls over to me.

"My lucky charm," Peter said and beamed, throwing his arm around my shoulder. Carmen glared at me, and I didn't know if it was the competition over the office or the attention from a senior partner that had annoyed her, but her eyes threw darts at me as Peter handed me a Ping-Pong ball.

Peter and I each hit our first shots, and I hit the third when we got our balls back.

"Holy shit! This girl can play!" Peter yelled, finally missing and breaking our streak. We stood shoulder to shoulder, our sleeves touching, willing Jordan to miss his first shot, but he sunk it.

"That's okay. We got this," Peter said to me. He leaned into me as a pulse of electricity transferred from his arm to mine. The combination of the beer in my veins and the high school anthems ringing in my ears amplified what was just a regular work crush when we were down on the forty-first floor. I forced myself to speak so I could focus on anything besides the energy between us.

"This floor is huge. And it seems so much bigger with no walls dividing the offices."

"This floor is five hundred square feet *smaller* than Gary Kaplan's apartment," Peter said. I looked up to him to confirm that he was serious. He raised one eyebrow to let me know he was.

Carmen's face grew increasingly flushed, though I couldn't determine if it was from frustration that she couldn't hit a shot, or the fact that she couldn't catch a break from drinking as we hit ours. I saw her teeth pressing down on her lower lip in a way that almost hurt to look at. She stared at my skirt, and I wondered if she felt any regret that she hadn't let me embarrass myself. The game continued until Matt spilled a full beer on Jordan's phone and the music cut out. I waited for the inevitable meltdown from Jordan, but he barely reacted, sinking one last shot before going to hook his old "spare phone" up to the music while Matt emailed tech support to have a new phone waiting on Jordan's desk at 9:00 a.m. I picked up the cup Jordan's ball had disappeared into, handing the ball in it to Peter, then looked up at him.

"There's too much foam," I whined before plunging my index finger into the beer and scooping up the white froth. I knew my tone was flirtier than was remotely professional. But Peter grinned back at me, encouraging me to continue. Our eyes collided, and I heard the Ping-Pong ball drop out of his hand and bounce behind us. I smiled devilishly as I went to chase after it, the beer sloshing in my stomach.

"I saw that!" Matt exclaimed. I whipped around to find him pointing at me. "You crossed the line." He smirked. I couldn't believe I'd been such an idiot. Flirting with a partner in public! A married partner! Then he pointed to my feet, and as I looked down, I realized I was past the cones. I picked up Peter's ball, exhaled deeply, and took a large swig of beer.

As soon as the game ended, Matt and Peter started putting on their coats, both looking longingly at the scene they were about to leave. I noticed that each of them called a car home, even though I was fairly certain they lived in the same town in Westchester.

"Take company cars home," Peter yelled at us over the music. "And clean up after yourselves."

"And order some food, for god's sake," Matt added as they got into the elevator. With the partners gone, the bass got louder, the lights got softer, the senior associates began pulling tiny bags of white powder out of the breast pockets of their suits, and I started to feel sleepy. As Jordan politely formed a small line with his platinum Amex for Carmen on the Ping-Pong table, I noticed that she and I were the only women left—the two others had disappeared long before. She bent low to sniff it in and rose quickly, a contented look on her face.

"I should text Derrick," I said, mostly to myself, taking out my phone.

"Do not invite him," Jordan said, almost spitting the command. "I heard from litigation that he was beyond fucked up at a client dinner last night. Not a good look."

I nodded. *Not a good look at all.* I'd call him in the morning instead.

"Want some?" the same associate who had offered me a beer asked me, as casually as boys used to offer me gum in middle school, holding out a baggie.

I shook my head. "How'd your call go?"

"It went. Want a beer?" he tried again. I shook my head again and looked at my phone in an effort to distract my brain from worrying about Derrick. I had a string of texts over the past two hours from Sam:

How's work?
Are you okay?
You are either getting crushed or you fell asleep.
I miss you.
I'm going to bed.

I looked up from my phone. "Actually, sure," I said to the associate. He shut his eyes and rubbed his finger on his upper gum.

I thought for a moment that he hadn't heard me, but a full fifteen seconds later, he said "Here" and handed me a rolled dollar bill as he carefully formed me a line. I paused for a moment, wondering if I should tell him I had never done cocaine before, wondering if I needed specific instructions. But instead, embarrassed by my naïveté, I bent low and put the bill in one nostril, sealing the opposite one with a press of my finger, and inhaled sharply, trying to mimic Carmen's glamorous motions.

It stung for a moment before tingling. I was too drunk to know if what I was feeling was the cocaine, but I felt suddenly sharper, soberer, sexier. I leaned back and smiled at the numb euphoria spreading from my nose up to my brain and down to the base of my skull. I righted my head and locked eyes with Jordan, who gave me a small, approving grin.

"Let's order Wolfgang's! Steaks for everybody?" the associate who'd given me coke yelled.

"This is my mother's basement! Let's order Domino's!" Jordan yelled, and was met with resounding cheers and applause. Jordan sauntered over to me as he placed the order, squinting to read the menu on his spare phone's cracked screen. "Slumming it is the best. Only when it's a choice, of course," he added seriously.

Three hours later, I poured myself into one of the black Quality cars lined up for us on Fifth Avenue and spit my address out at the driver. My knees bounced in the back seat of the car as I grabbed for my phone and typed "Gray Kaplwe Sag Rider NYC apt" at record speed. Google politely asked me if I meant "Gary Kaplan Stag River NYC Apt."

I scanned the hits before clicking on the second, entitled "Where to Live When Money Is No Object." In third place behind Jay-Z and Beyoncé's Bahamian island and Elton John's Beverly Hills estate was Gary R. Kaplan's $38.4 million Manhattan penthouse. I clicked through picture after picture of the dark wood floors and modern art on the walls before pausing on a shot of the building's facade, where a relatively unassuming navy-blue awning with the street numbers blurred jutted out onto the sidewalk. Something on the side caught my eye, and

I spread the picture apart with my thumb and index finger to zoom in on the sign reading "Starlight Diner" just east of the awning. I stared for a moment at it, trying to figure out how the fuzzy puzzle pieces in my mind fit together, before leaning my head back on the black leather seat as the car sped through the empty streets.

Q. Did you often have to travel for work?

A. Not often. A few times a quarter.

Q. Did you travel alone during your first year?

A. Almost never. No. Never, actually.

Q. Did the same levels of decorum exist when traveling outside of the office with clients and colleagues?

A. Yes.

Q. You behaved the same way when in different cities and countries as you did while you were in New York?

A. Perhaps clothing is more casual. Yes, I would say because there is travel and leisure time spent with one another, the attire is more casual. But other than that, behavior was largely the same.

Q. Can you please tell us about your first experience traveling in your capacity as an attorney at Klasko?

CHAPTER 12

When I entered Matt's office, he was sitting at his desk and Jordan was holding a green marker up to the whiteboard. He'd called me there to discuss the annual Lionhead Mergers & Acquisitions Conference in Miami, held in mid-December, which was only two weeks away. Jordan had asked that I assume the classic first-year-associate position of drafting their slide presentation and remain in New York while they presented my materials as their own.

"Deborah Tate?" Matt asked.

"Ew. No." Jordan shook his head.

"Avery Klein?" Matt asked.

Jordan leafed through the papers in his hand, then nodded and wrote her last name on a growing list on his whiteboard. "She's hot," he said.

As I scanned the names, a sinking feeling forced me to sit down on the couch. I'd seen that list before, and thought it was a list of associates interested in M&A. It had never occurred to me that it was made up entirely of female first-years.

I had been on that whiteboard list.

"Almost done, Skip. We just need to choose which summer associates we want to try to recruit," Matt said.

I stared at the board. "I was on that list when you did it for associates."

"We've never had a girl here for the process!" Matt laughed, as though I should be flattered. "Feel free to pick a guy you want to work with, Skip."

"Why the fuck would I want to pick a guy to work with based

on his picture?" I could hear my voice going into a shrill register, and touched my cheeks to confirm I was burning up.

The two of them stared at me, utterly dumbfounded.

"I didn't realize . . ." Matt trailed off and thought for a moment. "You know, female partners do the same thing." I gave him a skeptical look. "Or they would, if there were more of them. Power corrupts."

"I'm pretty sure power just gives you license to be whoever you really are," I snapped.

"Erase it," Matt said to Jordan, to my surprise, and gave me a small wink that he might have meant as a half-assed apology. "When you're right, you're right."

I nodded at him gratefully, even though I was pretty certain they'd have the list back up as soon as I left the room.

"Didier will be there with us. He wants us to make the plans for Thursday night in Miami," Matt said, seeming eager to move on.

I forced calm into my voice. "I can handle that."

They exchanged skeptical looks.

"What?" I asked defensively. "I know Miami." They looked at each other again. "Ohh. I get it. You guys want to go to a strip club."

"You would never come to a strip club with us, would you?" Matt asked, looking nervous. "Even at Didier's request?"

Why does he even care whether I would go? This didn't concern me. First-years were never invited to Miami. We did the slides, and that's it. But still, I had to ask, "Am I *invited* to the strip club?"

Matt looked at Jordan, who nodded at me.

"You're invited to the whole conference," Matt said, and grinned. "We registered you. You deserve to be there with us. And Didier likes you. He never likes anybody."

A smile spread rapidly across my face, my cheeks pushing their way up into my eyes. All my banter with Didier had paid off, even if I'd felt slightly icky. And more importantly, it dawned on me, the invitation to Miami almost certainly meant I had secured a space in M&A.

"Thank you! Thank you so much. I'll be there! I'll even be at the strip club, if you want me to be!" I heard my own words and paused. "But seriously, can I skip that part?"

They burst out laughing. "Yes," Matt assured me.

"We don't even want to go, Skip! It's all Didier," Jordan insisted.

"No need to lie to me. I'm not your wife." I winked.

Matt clapped his hands together. "My admin is just grabbing Didier now. We can discuss more when he gets here."

"He's in the office?" I asked Matt just as Didier burst in with a thunderous thanks to Matt's admin who had brought him down from reception on the forty-fifth floor. He gracelessly slammed the door behind him and collapsed into the spare chair. Matt and Jordan fawned over him, chatting about the week of debauchery lying ahead, but then I saw Jordan check his phone and slump in his seat.

"My wife is dying to co—" he muttered.

"No wives," Matt interrupted. Jordan nodded without looking up, and Matt looked at me. "Or boyfriends. My wife tries to come every year. It's just the four of us."

"You're in, Skippy?" Didier beamed at me.

"I'm in," I confirmed, allowing myself a moment to relish having earned a spot, wanting to share the news. Carmen was the one person who would understand just how big a deal the invitation was, but she was also the person who would be the most jealous that I was invited while she wasn't. I paused. Maybe they hadn't invited her because she would have never indulged the idea of a strip club. Maybe she was more professional than I was—more confident she could earn a spot in M&A on merit alone. A sense of embarrassment mingled with my excitement, but couldn't quite hamper it.

***

I was poring over the presentation I was preparing for the conference when I was interrupted by a cheerful "Hey, kiddo!" Peter was leaning against my doorframe, his arms folded over the front of his crisp blue shirt, one leg bent over the other.

"Hi!" I looked up from the stack of papers now forming a fort around me. I had just closed a deal for Matt and Jordan—only two hours behind our slated closing time. As soon as I had placed the receiver down from the closing call, my body shut down. The presentation for Miami could wait until after I slept. It was only five o'clock, but my lids drooped low, nausea overtook hunger, and my limbs were slow to obey my brain. Seeing the state I was in, Anna had already called a car for me to go home and sleep.

Peter stepped past the threshold of my office, where the carpet changed from the gray of the hallway to dusty blue.

"You'll be at the Stag River party tonight, right?"

I jerked my head over to him and called my Outlook calendar to life. I had forgotten to put it in my calendar, and therefore I had forgotten about it entirely.

"I forgot," I said apologetically. "I'm so busy . . ."

"Look. I know you've been getting killed lately, but everybody who does work for them shows up. That's you now. Of course, it's your decision in the end, but I'm just letting you know that it's an important event for you to attend. I'll owe you one." It was as close as Peter Dunn would ever come to asking, rather than telling, an associate to do something. "Six thirty at the

Rainbow Room." He turned to leave, pausing in my doorway. "You look . . . stressed."

"Thanks," I muttered.

"You know what I mean."

"Yes," I said sleepily, and wrapped my arm around my far shoulder in a half hug, attempting to counteract the feeling that I was about to unravel.

"Look, my wife and I are going to her sister's wedding this weekend in Mexico. She's on her fourth marriage . . . don't get me started. Anyway, our ski house in Killington is free. You're welcome to take it for a long weekend with your boyfriend. Duck out after work Thursday, and the house is all set up to work from Friday. Wi-Fi, printer, everything." He waited for my reaction.

Say no. It's an empty gesture. He's just being nice.

"Thanks so much, Peter. That's really kind. But we have First-Year Academy in LA in February, so I'm sure I'll get some rest there."

"Are you kidding? Sitting in trainings with colleagues is not relaxing. You can even bring friends to my place if you want—there are five bedrooms. There's no food in the fridge, but there's everything else you need. It's right on the mountain. And if the snow's no good, there's a spa and a jacuzzi. What do you think?"

Maybe this was exactly what Sam and I needed to get back on track, to reconnect.

"Alex?"

"Yes." I looked up at Peter. "Yes. That sounds so amazing. I could really use a break. I cannot thank you enough."

Peter reached into his pocket and fiddled with his key ring, prying one loose. He tossed me a key and fob.

"Fob is for the house. Key is for the ski locker just outside. Enjoy!"

"Peter, this is so generous . . ."

"It's a pleasure, kiddo. You've been doing great work. It doesn't go unnoticed or unappreciated. Consider this a token of gratitude."

I smiled. "I thought that's what a paycheck was."

He laughed. "Alex, if you break down your salary by the hours you work, it's a lot closer to minimum wage than you realize." I groaned. "See you at the party."

I turned back to work but couldn't focus. What if a weekend away with Sam just proved how far we had drifted apart? No. It would be great. I would make it great. I checked my personal email in-box, which was filled with all junk, except for one email from Sam with Christmas vacation suggestions. I wrote him back that, bad news, I wasn't allowed to take vacation this year, but that I'd be making it up to him with a long weekend in Vermont.

Growing annoyed at the presumption behind his email—was I supposed to pay for both of us to go to some Caribbean island?—and trying to put myself in the best possible frame of mind about Vermont, I distracted myself further by logging in to my checking account. I stared at the balance, which steadily climbed regardless of how much I put toward retirement, saved in my Roth IRA, and flushed down the toilet paying our astronomical New York City rent. I looked at the clock again and smiled slightly to myself as I realized I had just enough time to get a new outfit for the night.

After shoving my brown paper Bloomingdale's bags into the trash can nearest the Rainbow Room entrance, and running my hands down the sides of my white-and-red organza Alice and Olivia dress to make sure I had removed all the tags, I glided into the Stag River cocktail party only thirty minutes late. I had never spent more than a few hundred dollars on an item of clothing, but I had just blown upward of $600 in under forty-five minutes, and the rush of it made me feel not only beautiful but that I *belonged* in this room full of real estate titans and Wall Street tycoons.

"Wow. Skip!" Jordan fell into step beside me as I made my way to the bar. "You look really nice." He coughed awkwardly, as if he was unsure of what he should and shouldn't say after the whiteboard incident.

I smiled to let him know all was forgiven. "Not so bad yourself," I said, straightening his tie.

A jazz band comprised of musicians dressed like the Rat Pack filled the air with a 1950s vibe as the dim rainbowed lighting made everybody appear as though they were draped in swirling cotton candy. As Jordan pointed out the heads of banks and private equity firms to me, I waved to Vivienne White across the room. She smiled coolly but didn't seem to miss a beat in her conversation with a stout Asian man.

Peter slid into place next to us. "So, what do you think of your first Stag River event?" he asked me.

"Great," I told him, and meant it. It was the most beautiful room I had ever seen. The city skyline twinkled out the windows, none of the grit and grime showing and all of the magic.

"A little tame," Jordan joked.

"Dunn! Glad you made it!" Gary Kaplan slapped Peter on the back, nearly knocking the drink out of his hand, looking animated, exuberant, and far from sober. He turned his attention to me. "Well, aren't you beautiful." He took my hand and held it in his moist palm.

"You've met Alex. She's one of our associates," Peter announced, a protective overlay in his tone. "And this is Jordan Sellar, a senior associate. He mostly does your deals with Jaskel."

Gary continued to stare at me, making no attempt to avert his eyes from my body, but I finally wiggled my hand out from his grip.

"Excuse me while I get some food. Can I grab anything for any of you?" I asked the group, but before they could answer, I made my way to the display of oysters and shrimp cocktail on the far side of the room. I took a final sip of my wine as I waited for the server to place the shrimp on my plate. I was reaching for the horseradish and cocktail sauce when I suddenly felt an arm graze my breast. I snapped my back straight and stared over at Gary, mortified that I must have pushed my chest against his arm when I bent to reach the condiments.

"I'm sorry," I stammered, desperately trying to shrug off possibly the most awkward encounter I could imagine with the firm's most important client. He smiled, looking completely unruffled, the pools of black where his eyes were meant to be making me slightly queasy. It hadn't been my mistake. And it wasn't his either. The pervert touched me on purpose.

"Please, Alex." Gary gave me a reassuring wink. "Don't be sorry," he said, reaching toward me and gently placing his palm over my heart, his pinkie finger dipping low to search for my nipple.

I froze. The timpani faded, and I heard only the beating of my heart in my ears. He took his hand away and grabbed an oyster. I couldn't manage to move my legs to escape. When he turned back toward me, his eyes focused over my shoulder and his voice lightened.

"Peter! Alex and I have been chatting. She's quite ambitious! I'd love you both to be my special guests at the Private Equity Fights Hunger gala I'm chairing at the Met this spring. I'll have my assistant send you all the details."

I felt Peter next to me, but I continued to stare at Gary, trying to discern whether he'd intended the invitation as payment for his transgression or, even worse, license for future ones. As Peter responded to Gary in a pleasant tone, I did my best to compose myself, and as soon as my legs would move, I put down my plate and returned to Jordan.

"Peter told me that Japanese businessman over there with his wife just fucked his assistant in the bathroom!" Jordan cackled. I stared forward, shivering. "Skip? You okay?" Jordan bent low, his head cocked, and shoved his face into my line of vision.

I frowned. "Gary just grabbed my boob. Breast. Whatever. He felt me up. Right in the middle of this party." I didn't know how to say it, never having had to say anything like it before. It was the most unexpected, most disturbing thing to happen to me, and the fact that it happened so flagrantly, with my colleagues all around, made me question whether it had actually happened at all. "And then he invited me to the PE Fights Hunger gala at the Met."

"Fuck! Skip!" Jordan's jaw dropped. "Everybody goes. Or everybody wants to go. For somebody gunning for partner like me, it's the single most important business development event I can attend. If I had tits, I'd let him grab them both to cop an invite!" He shook his head and made his way to the bar to refill his scotch, leaving me stunned.

I made my way to the ladies' room, where I sat on the tufted circular ottoman and smoothed the fabric of my dress over my thighs. I'd thought the dress was modest. Did it make me look like a slut? I shouldn't have worn lip gloss. Or maybe my eyeliner was too heavy. I wiped my finger under my eyes to lighten it.

"Hey, you okay?" Vivienne White sat down next to me as I nodded robotically. "I love these shoes, but they are the most uncomfortable, impractical things in the world." She removed her feet from gorgeous black satin pumps with crystal-embellished straps to reveal a Giuseppe Zanotti label, then applied pressure to the arch of each foot and closed her eyes. "You sure you're okay?"

I breathed in and forced myself to speak again. "Gary Kaplan sort of . . . grabbed at my chest. And then invited me to the PE Fights Hunger gala . . . like as payment for letting him feel me up."

Vivienne sighed and rolled her eyes. "He's so grabby." I waited a moment for more—for a display of anger from her, a sign that she was horrified by what had happened. But it didn't come. "That gala is a good opportunity for you. You should go. It'll show your status in the M&A group. After Match Day, you can decline these invites. Just stick it out until then." She slapped my knee and slipped her shoe back on. "Look, he doesn't work for the firm. It's sort of . . ." She held up her palms as if to say, *Out of my hands.* She clicked her tongue against the top of her mouth and walked out the door.

I sat there for a moment longer as two blondes with impossibly long legs and absurdly short skirts emerged from a single bathroom stall, one of them rubbing her upper gums with her index finger. I stared at them as they put their drinks down to wash their hands, each adorned with nearly identical and blinding engagement rings.

"Oh! Miss! You have a little . . . ," I said to the taller one, wiping at my own nose to signal her to do the same to the white powder on hers.

"Whoopsies!" She giggled. "Better?" She bent over and leaned her face close to mine so I could judge, and I suddenly felt wetness on my leg as she emptied her glass of red wine onto my new dress.

"Oh my god. I'm so, so sorry!" she wailed as I jumped up. Her friend covered her mouth with her palm, laughing from behind it. "I'm so sorry." The girl grabbed my arm as she repeated her apology. The bathroom attendant rushed over. "Here. Let me." The girl grabbed the towel from the attendant and went to the sink to wet it. She returned and rubbed at my thigh, which only worked the red liquid deeper into the white fabric, making me look like a murder victim.

"Don't. It's fine," I said, gripping her wrist before the towel did any more damage and moving it away from my waist.

"I have to pay you! I feel awful! And it's so beautiful!" She spoke quickly, clearly feeling the effects of the cocaine. "Is it last season's Marchesa Notte? Or is it Oscar? Oh god, please don't be Oscar de la Renta!"

"No. It's Alice and Olivia," I said, staring down dejectedly at it.

"Oh, thank god. I thought it was couture." She placed her hand over her heart and breathed. "I'm sorry again! But at least it wasn't expensive," she called over her shoulder as she and her friend burst back out into the cocktail hour, the jazz sax seeping in behind her for a moment before the door shut and muffled it.

I burst into tears and called a car to take me home, slipping easily out of the party without being seen by my colleagues, who busied themselves chatting with their clients. When I arrived back at the apartment, Sam was already asleep. I contemplated waking him, knowing he'd hold me close to comfort me and find my encounter with Gary appropriately appalling. But he looked so peaceful. I'd bring it up in Vermont, I decided. I suddenly couldn't wait for a weekend alone with Sam—away from work and the city, with nothing to do but remember all the reasons I loved him.

CHAPTER 13

I did exactly as Peter had suggested, and went right to his ski house Thursday afternoon after an almost full and luckily slow workday. The house was as magnificent as I'd expected—the quintessential ski chalet punctuated with oriental carpets and chocolate leather, the plush carpeting offsetting the grandiose scale of the rooms. A gaping stone fireplace beckoned us into the great room, where 180-degree views of the mountain awaited us. I had been asleep for four of the five and a half hours that Sam drove, and was still groggy as I explored.

"No way. It's too weird," I said, standing in the doorway to the master bedroom, staring at a picture of Peter and his beautiful blond wife on the nightstand next to the California king. "We have four other rooms to choose from!"

"Are you saying you want to sleep in bunk beds?" Sam smiled.

"Fine, three other rooms," I said, and rolled my eyes sleepily.

Sam pushed a button on the wall, and the windows let out a soft groan as the blackout shades recoiled, revealing a huge screened-in balcony with heat lamps, oversize chairs, and a glass table. Beyond that, Killington Mountain was streaked with moonlight bouncing off the snow-covered trails. I put my bag down and slid open the balcony door while Sam clicked on the heat lamps, and then he slipped his arms around my stomach and leaned his chin on my shoulder from behind.

"Can we stay in this room? Pretty please?" he whined. I laughed and turned to him.

"Sam?" I said into his chest. "What if this job is changing me?" The question surprised me as I spoke.

He kissed my cheek. "I loved you before this job. I love you now. And I'll love you after," he said, making a sweeping, circular gesture around my body. "In the meantime, I'll just have to grin and bear the perks of your career."

I breathed in, believing his words and allowing myself to appreciate his goodness for the first time in too long, allowing myself to see all the things that had made me fall in love with him. I looked into his kind eyes and knew that he'd never grope a woman in public, he'd never cheat on me. I pulled him onto Peter's bed.

Eventually the animalistic need for sustenance trumped the one for sex, so we dressed quickly and got into the car. Aware that all the restaurants in the village closed at ten thirty, we walked into the first cozy Italian joint we spotted. As we waited for the maître d', Sam pressed his stomach to my spine. I slipped my hand around the back of his thigh to pull him closer.

"How many will you be tonight?" the maître d' asked politely. I felt Sam lean into me, and I turned to him.

"Should we just take our food to go?" I asked, giving him a wink.

We were on our second bottle of red wine, and the pizza was nearly frozen as we bobbed our shoulders out of the hot tub to steal bites of it before resubmerging ourselves. I thought momentarily about telling him what had happened at the Stag River Christmas party, but the night was so perfect I didn't want to derail it, so I rambled to him about interoffice politics instead.

". . . and all the first-years only hang out with each other. It's totally bizarre. And they all know everything about each other."

"How do they know?" Sam was drunk, but he looked entertained.

I was drunker. "I have no idea. I only know because Carmen tells me."

"Carmen," Sam repeated.

"She's only terrifying before you get to know her. You'll meet her at the Klasko holiday party!"

I took another sip of wine and slid next to Sam, who craned his neck to look up at the stars. "You hate that I work at a BigLaw firm," I said poutily, running my fingers over the jet by my hips.

Sam continued to look at the sky. "You're becoming an Icarus," he mumbled.

"What?" I furrowed my brow and took another long sip.

Sam lifted his head. "You're being ridiculous!" he enunciated. "I don't hate that you work at a big firm! I just hate that you're so stressed." He looked at the house hulking over us. "How much do you think Peter makes a year?"

I contemplated lying for a moment before yielding to the desire to see Sam's reaction to the truth. "Four to six. Depending on how good of a year he has."

"Million?" Sam asked, but he knew the answer. He inhaled the cold air sharply and groaned. "Who needs that much money, honestly? It's like . . . absurd. You can live well off of so much less." *If you think that's a lot, you should see what our* clients *take home each year.* "And it doesn't buy you happiness, obviously. He said he never uses this place. Bet he doesn't want to be stranded on a mountain with his family." Sam snorted. "Six million a year. Fuck me."

And so I did. Partially because he asked me to. Partially to prove to him that he turned me on without a penny to his name. Partially to prove it to myself.

That first night in Vermont was like magic—like we had been transported back to those early days in Cambridge when we delighted in discovering each other. When Sam awoke the next morning, I saw a lust and love in his eyes that I only then realized had been lacking in the past month. I hated myself for the victory of winning him over in only a day after months of neglect. I knew with such an easy victory, I would grow tired of making things right between us.

With Friday stretching out long before us with little on the agenda, Sam pulled me close while still under the covers. I indulged him out of obligation, but it made my skin itch slightly. I already knew how the remainder of the weekend would go. I knew it would feel like an eternity. He didn't want to go through the process of renting ski equipment for only a weekend. He thought massages were too expensive. He took my Thursday takeout suggestion to mean that I was content to hang out in bathrobes and eat pizza on the couch for the next forty-eight hours as well. I started growing antsy inside, rationing the time I spent on the *New York Times* crossword puzzle so it would last me the whole car ride home. I missed the grind of constant work I had become so accustomed to and comfortable with.

Sam enthusiastically took to binge-watching *Breaking Bad*, which neither of us had watched when it originally aired, while I worked on the slides for Miami for a bit on Friday and a large portion of Saturday and drafted some postclosing cleanup emails for the deal we had just signed.

"Al, this show is insane! Come watch!" Sam was practically giddy as he refilled his water glass in between episodes.

"I wish," I said, gesturing to my computer, though I knew I probably could have carved out some time to watch with him. *Miami will be fun.* I tried to force myself to relax and enjoy the slow workweek while I had it.

***

"Just a quick round, and then we'll meet Didier out front and head to dinner," Jordan said, pressing L as the doors closed to join the two halves of the Fontainebleau F inside the leather-walled elevator.

"Where's dinner?" Matt asked, not looking up.

"Joe's," I said, one hand on my phone, the other pulling at the red dress I had carefully chosen because it was both conservative and lightweight, a rarer combination than one might think, and just cute enough for going out after the corporate cocktail hour.

The elevator jolted at the end of its descent, and the automated voice announced that we were in the lobby. We all typed furiously for our last moments in the iron cage before putting our phones away.

"Game faces, people," Matt said, stretching his neck.

The chrome doors disappeared fluidly into the elevator walls, releasing us into a sea of men, drinks in hands, and a very few women, most of them waitresses. New York City's Ferragamo ties and Zegna suits were replaced by Miami's Tod's loafers and Ralph Lauren linen pants—it was like Wall Street: The Resort Wear Collection. The air conditioning pumped ferociously, almost allowing us to forget the sticky evening outside our protective cocoon. A woman with an iPad said something to Matt and then handed us all name tags, which Matt and Jordan slapped across their chests. I hesitated for a minute, then fastened mine awkwardly under my collar, just south of my neck, so as not to encourage any inappropriate eye wandering.

"Vodka rocks. Scotch neat," Jordan confirmed, pointing from Matt to me. "Skip?"

"Um, I'll do a vodka cranberry."

Jordan shook his head. "We do clear drinks." I waited to see if he was kidding. "Vodka soda?" he asked. I shrugged and nodded as we stepped out into the pit. Jordan grabbed the first waitress he saw and ordered for us.

"Watch and learn," Jordan said, leaning into my ear. "Matt's a master. He becomes exactly who the person he's speaking to wants him to be."

"Mr. Jaskel!" A booming voice erupted from our left. Matt shook a large man's hand firmly, never breaking eye contact. "Great presentation today," the man said earnestly.

"I hadn't even seen the slides until I got up there. It was all these guys." Matt pointed to me and Jordan—"Alex Vogel, Jordan Sellar"—and then to the man—"John Dornan." I looked at his name tag: "Managing Director and Co-Head of M&A at J.P. Morgan."

"Jaskel!" the managing partner of Cresthill Private Equity cut in just as the waitress returned with our drinks. We all sipped at them hungrily, in need of liquid lubrication, and I absorbed the chatter surrounding me.

"His policies will be fine for the big banks."

"Interest rates are going to climb. I'd never vote for him, but part of me is hoping he gets elected."

"It's barbell investing."

"Oh, I'm fine, thanks. This is just water. I don't drink too much. And my wife prefers it that way." Matt flashed a subservient smile to Maggie Schwartz, head of M&A at Wells Fargo, as he took a swig of vodka on the rocks. *Hence the clear drinks.* Jordan and I smiled broadly at her as well.

"Smart woman," she said.

"I'm surrounded by them. Have you met Alex Vogel?" Matt asked, thrusting me toward my comrade in genitals. I smiled politely and made small talk about Boston, Maggie's hometown.

"Would love to get lunch when we're back in the city," she said to me with an approving nod, and we exchanged business cards before she moved on. I breathed a sigh of relief, tired of pretending to be sober. Matt and Jordan took turns replenishing my drink in between making small talk with all the people we seemed to know.

"Join us on the yacht tomorrow."

"Stay with us through the weekend."

"Come to Prime 112 tonight," a balding man offered.

"We have a reservation at Joe's or we'd love to," Jordan politely declined.

"Joe's doesn't let you make reservations," the guy said, straightening his cuff links.

"Joe's doesn't let *you* make reservations," Matt corrected him, to which the guy laughed and shook Matt's hand. "Let's do lunch back in New York."

"We've done more mergers in the past three years than any other law firm in the world. Here's my card."

Jordan smiled apologetically. "I don't think any of us are in any position to party tonight. We have a flight out first thing in the morning. Let's get lunch back in New York." The thin, dark-skinned man looked dubiously at me, and I nodded.

"This is water," I assured him.

Jordan gave me a wink. "You're a quick study," he whispered to me after the man had left. I beamed. I was loving every second of the conference.

"I will send my wife your regards. And you do the same. I would have brought her, but she hates Miami," Matt said to a petite woman, looking sincerely dejected.

"It's just water for me tonight," Jordan said, pointing to his glass as he spoke to the treasury secretary's wife.

"My kids are my whole world. I miss them even when I'm away for these long weekends!" Matt showed the petite woman pictures on his phone.

"I think I've reached my bullshit threshold," Jordan finally whispered to me and Matt.

"Did anybody see Gary Kaplan?" Matt asked. Every hair on my neck stood on end. Jordan shook his head, and I forced the slightest shake of my own. "Skippy, order us a car. I've seen everybody I need to except the CFO of Oculus."

I turned to Jordan. "It bothered me when Gary touched me at the Stag River party," I said, emboldened by the four vodka sodas I'd consumed.

Jordan watched me carefully. "Look around, Skip. Do you see any young women? No. Not many of them are invited. Every young guy in this room is getting his boss a drink. Most didn't get invited at all. When you're a boss, you can make your own rules. For now, all the young people, men and women, just need to take the shit they're given." His tone was easy enough, but his words were harsh in my ears. I clenched my jaw, hailed a passing waitress, and asked her to arrange a car to Joe's Stone Crab. She started to direct me toward the concierge desk before seeming to think better of it.

"Room number?" she asked. I knew it wasn't her job to arrange transportation, but since joining Klasko I had come to expect service professionals, any service professionals, to accommodate my requests.

"Fourteen thirteen."

"Ah. Ms. Vogel," she said after inputting my number into an iPad. "We'll have the house car brought around for you right away. Much faster than calling a car. You can head outside at your convenience."

I'd never before stayed in a hotel where they'd looked me up and given me better treatment because of my name. I wanted so badly to be above it all, to resist falling for everything about the beautiful hotel and the look of deference the waitress gave me. I wanted to be blasé about the name tags of the people who passed. But as I stood in the middle of the cocktail party, I couldn't wipe the grin from my face.

***

I sat sandwiched between Didier and Jordan in the back of the hotel's house Rolls-Royce Phantom as we waited for Matt, who'd spotted the CFO of Oculus and gone to say hello. I could tell that Didier had been pregaming with more than booze—he alternated between rubbing his pant leg and wiping sweat from his upper lip as he stared out at the driveway, ogling the unsuspecting women passing by our tinted windows. Meanwhile, Jordan scowled at his phone screen. The vodka I'd consumed gave me the feeling of belonging with them. Even if they were a cokehead and a workaholic, respectively, we understood each other professionally and enjoyed each other personally. Just as I turned and looked out the back windshield for Matt, the front door opened and he slid in next to the driver. "Joe's Stone, good sir." The driver nodded, and we rolled away.

"Where the fuck have you been?" Didier thundered.

Matt turned back to us and rolled his eyes at Didier's outburst. "I have bad news and good news," he announced. Jordan stopped typing and looked up. "The bad news is, we're not going to the strip club after dinner." I breathed a sigh of relief.

"I'm going, so fuck you," Didier spit out, his French accent thicker than when he was sober.

"That's fine," Matt said. "We're not going because the good news is that Doug Capshaw is coming out with us tonight, and I'm not taking him to a strip club."

Everyone snapped to attention.

"The CEO of Oculus?" Jordan asked, staring at Matt.

"That's the one." I could only see the back of his head, but I could tell he was smiling. "CFO is an old buddy of mine. He introduced me."

Didier sprang up and grabbed Matt's shoulders from the back seat. "You are going to make me rich! Richer!" he bellowed.

"Let's show him a great night first," Matt said calmly.

"Is he cool? Should we take him to a bar? Or just meet at the hotel bar?" I asked excitedly, knowing that as the most junior person on the totem pole, it would be up to me to plan the social events for the evening.

"He's cool. He's young. Let's get a table somewhere," Matt directed me.

"On it." I was already emailing the concierge. "It's going to be a long night!" As though I had asked for it, Didier took a small Ziploc out of his breast pocket and placed some coke in a line on the flat part of his huge hand, between his thumb and forefinger, and offered it to me. I shook my head politely, and he shrugged and hoovered it up himself.

"I want," Matt said, turning to Didier, who handed him the small bag in the front seat. Matt poured a bit onto his hand. The driver had no visible reaction at all. "Jordan?"

"I have," Jordan responded without looking up, reaching into his own pocket. The driver stared directly ahead as the car plugged forward along Collins Avenue, choked with the traffic of partygoers.

"I can't believe people wait hours to eat here," Matt said, looking at the tourists milling around outside the window by our table. "I don't even think the food is that great. I only come here because I like getting to cut the line."

Jordan snorted in agreement, but I just sucked determinedly at the white-and-black shell of my stone crab claws, trying desperately to jostle loose the sweet sinew from the crevice. Didier was staring at me droopily over his scotch. I wondered if my face was slipping down toward my chin as much as I felt it was and speculated that the other tables were beginning to take note of our less-than-sober condition.

"What I wouldn't give to be that crab claw," Didier slurred at me.

"I find you repulsive," I said dryly, giving him an almost imperceptible smile as I pried off a shard of shell.

"You know the female stone crab has to shed her exoskeleton before the male can mate with her? She's prickly at first, but it all comes off in the end. It's nature. And that's what's happening here. Just waiting for you to give in to nature and stop being so prickly."

I looked up at him. "Is that true?"

"Just because I'm an idiot doesn't mean I'm an idiot."

"You *are* an idiot," I said, and rolled my eyes.

Matt and Jordan laughed, but Didier looked distressed. "My wife certainly thinks so. And she definitely finds me repulsive," he said. We all looked over at him. He looked at us and shook his head with a smile. "We're getting a divorce."

I looked at Matt and Jordan, trying to gauge whether they had known, but their faces registered the same confusion as mine. We searched Didier's face, hoping for an outburst of laughter. None came.

"Shit," Matt said, taking a drink.

"Are you okay?" I placed a hand on Didier's forearm. He was quiet as he placed his paw of a hand over mine.

"Happy to be out here with you guys," he said. "It's a good distraction."

"Can I . . . ?" The waitress appeared.

"Another round," Jordan said quickly.

"When?" Matt asked Didier.

"What happened?" I asked, a question that I never would have asked if my lips hadn't been loosened by vodka.

"A few weeks ago. Right after the Falcon closing," Didier said, looking at Matt. "I was never there," he continued, looking at me.

"Did you have a prenup?" Jordan asked.

Didier nodded, and my colleagues exhaled in unison.

"Doesn't matter. I'll give her whatever she wants," Didier muttered. My throat caught, seeing him in this vulnerable state.

"Look, let's blow off this Oculus guy and go out," Matt offered. "Anywhere you want. Just us."

Didier shook his head as our next round of drinks arrived. "Nah. This is a huge opportunity. Making money makes me happy. It's one of the few things left that I . . ." He trailed off, staring into space.

I squeezed his arm. "I'm sorry," I whispered.

"Thanks, Skip." He smiled back at me. "Let's just have a great night. I really need it."

"Yes." "Yeah." "Done," Jordan, Matt, and I responded simultaneously.

"I'm going to go get myself together," Didier said, pushing out of his chair.

"As in . . . up?" Jordan asked. Didier nodded, and Jordan followed him into the men's room, and Matt and I were left staring at one another across the table.

"Shame," I said, taking a long swig of my vodka. "I didn't even know he was married."

"Me neither!"

I gave Matt a look.

"I'm kidding. I knew. But only because it came up once. He never talks about her, and he doesn't wear a ring. I'm emailing Doug Capshaw now. Where should I tell him to meet us?"

"Basement at the Edition Hotel. We have a table in your name.

He won't have a problem," I said, taking another long drink, relishing the burn of the vodka on the way down.

"This place is connected to a bowling alley and ice-skating rink!" Doug yelled over the music as he leaned into me, his blond curls accidentally brushing my cheek. He wore light jeans, a thin heather-gray hooded sweatshirt, and sneakers. His skin was studded with pockmarks, presumably residue from teenage acne, which suited him the way a five o'clock shadow suits some men. He handed me a glass of clear liquid that I lifted to my nose.

"Tequila?" I yelled.

"Mezcal. Tequila is only made in Jalisco. All tequila is mezcal, but not all mezcal is tequila." As he recited these facts, I pictured him raising his hand in third grade and using the same tone. He kept his body angled away from me at a safe distance. There was something charming about his awkwardness and lack of sleaziness.

"Like Champagne and sparkling wine," I yelled. He nodded enthusiastically. I put the glass to my lips and threw my head back, then slammed it down on our table, which was sticky with juice and liquor. I wiped at the mezcal dribbling down my chin with the back of my hand as I sucked at the lime in my mouth and waited impatiently for it to drown out the smoky flavor.

Doug was staring at me, wide-eyed.

"What?" I yelled as soon as I pulled out the lime.

"That wasn't a shot! It's a sixty-dollar glass of tequila!" he yelled back.

"It's mezcal!" I stuck my tongue out at him and he laughed. "But it tastes like tequila. And I hate tequila! Needed to get it down fast," I told him, feeling the warmth spread throughout my chest and abdomen. "And we're paying anyway, so who cares how quickly I drink it?"

"Why did you drink it if you hate it?" He was screaming into my ear, and I could still barely hear him.

I stared at him. *Because it's my job to keep you happy.*

"Because you ordered it!" I said, smiling broadly. He looked over my shoulder at Matt, Jordan, and Didier, who were now talking to our cocktail waitress, and I followed his gaze.

"Impressive crew you roll with."

"The best in the business," I said. "They just let me tag along."

"You know Matt is considered one of the best M&A lawyers in the country?" Doug asked.

I put my finger to my lips to shush him, then pointed at Matt and put my hands to my head and fanned out my fingers, as though his head would explode if he heard such a compliment.

Doug laughed and nodded. He wasn't nearly as drunk as the rest of us. "You don't seem surprised that I've researched M&A lawyers."

"Part of our job is to know the prospective market," I added seriously, even as I bopped my head to the music. "We would love the opportunity to represent Oculus."

He nodded. "I'm going over to get to know these dudes you vouch for." I watched as he made his way over to Matt, who was sitting on the cushioned stool on the opposite side of our table; he looked over at me with a smile as Doug clearly said something complimentary about me.

I took a spot on the couch next to Didier, who was staring out at the light show bouncing up from the DJ booth, but he didn't seem to register my presence. I got up and was pouring myself another vodka cranberry when I felt a tap on my shoulder.

"Hey, hon." A voluptuous waitress with long, silky blond hair stood next to me with a petite little pixie of a woman with a tight jet-black bun atop her head next to her. They wore short, tight black dresses, their cleavage almost spilling out from the tops.

"Oh, we're okay," I told them, gesturing to the assortment of mixers on our table.

"Who are the guys you're with?" the dark-haired one asked, nodding at our group.

"What's their deal?" the blonde asked, sounding a little giddy.

I poured myself a water to coat my throat, sore from all the screaming over the music. "How do you mean?" I yelled.

"Are they single?" "Are you with them?" They spoke at the same time.

I nodded before clarifying. "No. Like, I'm here with them. We all work together. Kinda."

"What do you do?"

My throat was still raw. "We're lawyers. He's a banker." I pointed to my right at Didier, who sat staring at the dance floor.

"No shit! Good for you, girl!" the tall one said, slapping my shoulder.

"The balding one and the one with good hair are married. I'm not sure what that guy's deal is, but I get the sense that he's in a relationship," I said, pointing discreetly at Doug, and then indicating Didier. "That one is single." I figured a little poetic license was called for.

They both seemed discouraged to hear that Jordan was married, but I cocked my head toward Didier. "This banker is the best catch. His ex-wife is an idiot. He spoiled her rotten. And he's the nicest . . ."

They left my side without so much as a word and slipped over to Didier. I turned and battled my way through the crowd toward the ladies' room.

"Hey there," a tall blond man with a deep sunburn said as he stepped into my path, and I stumbled into him before I could stop myself. He put his drink up to his lips and the light caught his wristwatch. I grabbed his hand and pulled it to my face, closing one eye and frowning.

"Is that the right time?!"

He tried his best not to laugh at me as he nodded.

"Shit." I raced back to our table. "Our flight's in three hours!" I whined, pulling on Matt's arm as he ignored me entirely and snorted a line up his nose from the table, leaving a layer of white residue behind. I looked to Jordan for help. Doug Capshaw had his arm around Didier and was speaking to him while Didier nodded, his eyes trained on the waitresses I'd spoken to about him earlier, dancing close to one another right in front of him.

"Guys! Hello? We have to go!" I yelled over the music. They all looked up for a quick moment before ignoring me again. "This isn't funny. We're going to miss our flights." I had never missed a flight in my life.

"My assistant will rebook us," Matt said without looking at me, the red lights emanating from the DJ booth lighting up his face.

"Wait—I have a plane!" Doug announced, as though it had just occurred to him.

All of the guys stopped what they were doing and looked at him for a moment before diving on top of him with back pats and sloppy kisses. I exhaled. It was amazing how small your list of worries became when money was no longer an issue.

I made my way over to Didier. "Up," I ordered, and he enthusiastically cut me a line with his credit card. I remember nothing after that.

I awoke in my apartment to the whisper of running shower water and the sound of Sam clattering around in the bathroom.

I was lying on top of the covers, wearing only a pair of black underwear. I felt as though I had been in some sort of accident. I wiped the drool pooling around my lower cheek. *I should get up,* I told myself, but I couldn't move.

Sam came out of the bathroom in a cloud of fragrant steam, a towel around his waist.

"Hey," he said, rubbing his wet hair with another towel. I grunted a good morning as I cursed myself for not being able to remember my first, and probably only, trip on a private plane. I drifted back to sleep.

I opened my eyes again to find myself lying on my stomach, cheek flush against our bed, and Sam standing over me with a mug of coffee in his hand, now fully dressed in jeans, a blue button-down, and a blazer, presumably for a meeting. I closed one eye so I could see him more clearly, then opened both.

"What?"

"How was Miami?" he asked, a challenge in his tone.

"Good. I'm so tired," I said, closing my eyes again.

"I bet you had fun." He was angry about something, but I was vacillating wildly between still-drunk and hungover and couldn't worry too much about what it was. Flashes of deplaning, an Uber SUV, and fiddling with the key in my apartment door bounced around my brain. I remembered tiptoeing into the bedroom and stripping down before falling into bed next to Sam. I didn't wake him when I came home, I thought. I could pretend the trip was all work. No fun. He couldn't be mad at me for that.

"Not really. It was a ton of work. I'm exhausted." I prayed that he would let me go back to sleep and cupped my forehead in my palm, feeling like my brain might explode if I didn't. "How was work for you while I was gone?" I mentally pleaded with him to focus on anything but how banged-up I must have looked. I breathed into the pillow and caught a whiff of my own breath as I inhaled. It didn't smell like morning breath. It smelled like vodka. I cringed and began breathing through my nose.

"Good. I need to prepare for the final investors meeting next week. I have to brief everybody on potential VC funding and equity dilution, which is obviously a good discussion to need to have. It's a really big . . ." I needed to shut my eyes for just a moment, hoping he would simply continue speaking, but he didn't. I peeled my lids apart to prove to him that I was still listening. He shook his head with a disappointed laugh and walked out of the bedroom.

Just as I was about to close my eyes again, he popped his head back into our bedroom doorway.

"Oh, it says 'I'm the worst' with a fairly detailed drawing of a penis and balls in black marker across your back." With that, he turned and left the room, and I heard the front door close a minute later.

"Shit," I whispered. *Jordan.* I let my head sink farther into the pillow. Despite the sensation that a metal rod was splitting the two lobes of my brain apart, I burst out laughing. I put my palms to my abdomen and felt my muscles convulsing, before letting out a large sigh to calm myself.

There was the briefest moment of panic as I wondered if my phone had made it home with me from Miami, but it was responsibly plugged in on my nightstand. I grabbed it and dialed Jordan.

"Skippyyyyyyyyy," he croaked into the phone.

"Uhhhhh." We groaned at each other for a few minutes. "You're an asshole, you know? You drew on my back in permanent marker."

He paused. "I refuse to apologize for things I have no recollection of doing."

"It says 'I'm the worst' with a picture of a penis across my back."

Jordan burst out laughing. "Oh my god. I totally remember doing that. I'm sorry, Skip."

"Sam saw it this morning," I told him, laughing now too.

"Sucks for you, dude! I have Jessica thinking I worked the whole time."

"Are you making it in to the office today?" I asked, hoping the answer was no and I could spend the Friday in bed. I knew that there was no way Matt would be making the trek in from Westchester.

"Zero chance. Can you just look at the term sheet Matt sent around this morning?"

"Yup, will do," I said and hung up. I spent two hours on it before sending it back to Jordan, then stared at my in-box, which was reasonably quiet today. I turned on my side to go back to sleep for a bit, but the adrenaline from the weekend got me up and into the shower. I emerged clean and dizzy from the heat and checked my email again to see that only a few administrative emails from the firm had dripped in. Matt and Jordan had probably gone back to sleep as well.

The day stretched out like an impossibly long blank canvas before me. As I sat on the corner of the bed, I searched the plank wood floors for dust and the ceilings for cobwebs, but saw none. The cleaning lady we had once a week would be in Monday anyway, and she'd also do all my laundry from the Miami trip. Food shopping was pointless because I'd inevitably eat at my desk all week, and Sam liked to buy his own food. I was too hungover for the gym. I opened my phone to review my texts—the first twenty text conversations were all to and from Sam, my parents, and Klasko people. My friends from college hadn't been in touch in weeks—they had grown tired of my delayed responses.

It was just too easy not to respond to people in different cities, especially when their questions weren't time-sensitive like the ones from work. I breathed in deeply, trying to suppress the uncomfortable feeling that I had no life outside of the office, and refreshed my work email again.

This time, I was relieved to see a few new messages from Matt asking for some follow-up items to send to clients we'd seen and potential clients we'd met in Miami. The tightness in my chest dissipated as I opened my laptop and dove into the tasks at hand, welcoming the calm of purpose and productivity.

PART IV

ATTEMPTED CLOSING

An attempt to conclude the merger process and legally transfer ownership through signing and recording of all documents.

Q. Was your relationship with any of your colleagues ever sexual in nature?

A. [Mr. Abramowitz] That is beyond the scope of the trial. My client's relationship with Gary Kaplan is the only relevant relationship here.

Q. The question of your actions with clients and colleagues is highly relevant to the scope of the trial and provides valuable insight to the veracity of your accusations as well as motivation for truthfulness or lack thereof.

A. Klasko, like all large law firms, is a high-stress environment. When attorneys aren't working, they often find outlets for their stress. Often in substances. Sometimes in one another.

Q. Could you please be more specific?

A. My relationships with many of my colleagues changed over the course of my first several months at the firm, be it through regular evolution of a friendship or a rumored sexual relationship or, in one case, an actual one.

Q. Could you please provide some specific examples of the latter two? The rumored sexual relationship and the actual one?

CHAPTER 14

"Come to the associate happy hour tonight! It'll be fun!" Carmen stood in my office, arms folded over her chest. I readied my polite excuse. "Free booze! You can't turn that down." The firm believed that we needed to know each other personally to work well together, and so our bar tab was picked up each Thursday at the bar across the street to encourage us to get drunk with one another. "Plus, the older associates are really cool. You should meet them! The ones you haven't already gallivanted around Miami with." She overshot her attempt at a smile, and bared her teeth ever so slightly for just a moment. I should have told her I was going to Miami, I thought, so she didn't have to hear it from somebody else.

"I was going to tell you—"

Carmen shook her head to stop me. "I'm happy for you," she assured me, sounding convincing. "Come tonight!" I found it remarkable how quickly people forgave me when I didn't apologize. Her placid face no longer betrayed underlying resentment. Perhaps she was angrier that I hadn't told her than jealous that I'd gone. I watched her, trying to trust her. But on some level, I knew that Carmen was masterful at presenting herself exactly as she intended to.

"I'll come to the first one in the new year. Seriously, I'll kick my year off right and start showing up to these things. But we have the holiday party at the end of the week, and I cannot . . ."

"Don't be ridiculous. Who knows how busy you'll be next week, let alone next year!"

I pulled up my Outlook calendar and looked up at Carmen with a confirmatory grin. "Fine."

***

I squeezed in between two large men in suits standing right in the entrance to the bar, who were too engaged in a heated conversation about a potential trade war to pay me much attention.

"Ahhhh! You're here!" Carmen said, hugging me. She was standing with Kevin and two men I'd seen around the office. "I totally thought you were going to bail." She turned back to the men around her. "Guys, this is Alex—I was just telling you about her." She looked at me. "I told them you were my best friend at the firm!" I smiled back at her and then at them.

The two guys, who I guessed were fourth-year associates, maybe, looked like twins whose mother dressed them in different-colored shirts to help tell them apart. One wore a blue collared shirt, the other a pink collared shirt. Other than that, they looked identical: pale-skinned, with chests indicating long hours at the gym (*where did they find the time?*), close-cropped dark hair, and smooth, clean-shaven faces. They were good-looking, but in a completely unremarkable way—barely distinguishable from the other men in the bar.

As I took them in, they both scanned me up and down. I squirmed under their gaze, but smiled.

I then turned my attention to Kevin, who now blended in too. His no-longer-gelled hair now fell easily over his brow and into his cartoonishly—but like one of those very attractive male cartoon characters from Disney movies—large brown eyes. His loosely knotted pink tie rested easily on his chest, which was far more defined than it had been in September. I didn't know when he had found time for the gym either, but he looked good.

"Hi!" I hugged him. Seeing him had spurred nostalgia for my first-day jitters, which now seemed so very long ago.

A warm smile spread across his face as we released from the hug. "Hey."

"So, you're working for Jaskel?" Pink Shirt asked, while Blue Shirt gulped at his drink. I felt an odd vibe coming from them.

Why were they staring at me? Were they trying to flirt? Or had Carmen told them that Matt had invited me to Miami? I couldn't even tell if they were impressed or judging me. *Or is it that I have something stuck between my teeth?* The tiny hairs on the back of my neck stood up as I ran my tongue along my teeth.

"Yup!" Screw it. It didn't matter what they thought of me—I knew how to deal with these kinds of guys, how to win them over. The past few months had taught me nothing if not that. "Guys, I have some catching up to do. Let's get me drunk!" I commanded, pointing a finger in the air.

"Yaaaaaaas." Carmen threw a solitary fist toward the ceiling, and the three boys grinned. I peered into their short glasses. "What are we drinking?"

"Johnnie Walker Blue," Pink Shirt responded.

"Oh no no no," I said, then shook my head and pursed my lips. "Gross. I'm going to stick to vodka."

Blue Shirt protested. "It's good! Try it!" he said, shoving his glass at me and looking briefly down at my chest, which was luckily covered by a collared shirt I'd buttoned right up to the neck.

I felt Kevin tense, about to interject on my behalf, but I leaned into Blue Shirt's glass playfully, inhaled, and then scrunched up my nose. "No way. That smells like battery acid."

The Shirts both laughed as Kevin relaxed back on his barstool. "The most delicious battery acid in the world," Pink Shirt said, holding his glass up to me and taking a long sip.

"I didn't get your names."

"Scott."

"James."

"Scott. James," I repeated as I pointed, knowing I wouldn't remember them.

"Excuse me!" Kevin said as he hailed a passing waitress. "Can we get my friend here a drink?"

"I'll have a vodka rocks, please," I said. She looked at my wrist.

"Are you with Klasko?" I nodded. "You'll need a wristband, honey. I'll bring you one with your drink. What kinda vodka?"

"Tito's, please."

She took off toward the bar as I looked around the room.

The bar was clean and casual, with dark wood floors and deep red leather booths, high-top bar tables, and steel stools. Other than a male bartender, the staff was entirely female, and all dressed in black Lycra. I scanned the crowd of maybe forty people, vaguely recognizing most of the faces—though I had never exchanged words with the vast majority of them. There were a few exceptions. I spotted Derrick, who stood heads above his shorter comrades, taking shots at the bar, and Jordan perched on a barstool, surrounded by his fellow senior M&A associates. As usual, he was typing furiously on his phone, brow furrowed.

When the waitress reappeared with my drink, it shifted my attention back to my immediate surroundings.

"Cheers," Kevin said, extending his glass. I clinked with the other four glasses, then took a long, slow sip with my eyes closed. When I opened them, they were all watching me, probably stupefied by the length of my first swig.

I grinned sheepishly. "Here we go, boys," I said, and laughed.

"I like this one," Blue Shirt said to no one in particular. *That's because you like anything that flirts with you.* I felt the warm liquor hitting my empty stomach—I hadn't had time to eat since breakfast—and attempted to will it into my bloodstream. I pulled out my phone to check my work email one last time, sensing

I'd be committing malpractice if I answered any messages once I'd chugged this drink, and saw a text from Sam on my home screen.

Hey babe! Working late?

"Should I invite Sam?" I asked Carmen.

She frowned. "No boyfriends allowed!"

Just finished! But got roped into work drinks. Kill me! See you soon!

"You have a boyfriend?" Pink Shirt asked. I looked up from my phone and nodded, noting an almost imperceptible sideways glance between the three boys.

They were rapidly losing interest. The problem with flirting to connect with men was that they assumed it meant I was available. But why did I even care? It wasn't like they were clients.

I took another, longer swig of my drink and slammed it down on the table.

"So much for not drinking tonight!" Carmen threw an arm around my shoulder and leaned into me. I was already feeling the liquor, but I ordered another drink, and by the time I was halfway through my third, Carmen and I were leaning into one another, somehow remaining vertical. "You're totally gonna be a partner," she slurred, her shoulder pressing into mine. The boys had turned their attention to the basketball game on the television above us.

"Nooooo." I shook my head vehemently, thus concluding my opposing argument. I turned my head to the bar to see that Derrick hadn't moved but was now chatting to the bartender. Jordan's facial features had started drooping, and his drunk eyes were fixed on somebody across the bar, whom he winked at. I followed his gaze. Nancy. Nancy? When had they done any work together? She returned his look with an expression I couldn't quite identify.

I suddenly had to use the restroom, so I gently pushed Carmen's weight off mine, making certain her hand was firmly on our bar table before drifting away. I wavered slightly on the waxed wood floor as I made my way through the room. There were fingers shoved into one ear canal while cell phone receivers blared into the other. There were iPads open on tables as people screamed into the air with little white buds in their ears. Suits. And knee-length pencil skirts. And the occasional too-short, too-tight, too-colorful, not-from-corporate-America dress. I passed the not-so-occasional date a male associate from Klasko had invited to happy hour; the three I saw glowed with the honor of having been invited. My colleagues who brought dates looked pleased that the firm was paying for the drinks they'd otherwise have had to buy. Knees were being slapped and bills being peeled out from silver money clips. Ferragamo ties with dogs. Ferragamo ties with flowers. Ferragamo ties with elephants. Debates over the best bespoke tailor from Hong Kong, and when he'd make his annual visit to NYC. The inevitable ragging on the guy whose suits were off-the-rack.

I burst into the tiny ladies' room and nearly slipped on the tiles, which were slick with what I hoped was sink water. I pulled up my skirt and collapsed onto the cracked toilet seat as the main door opened and I heard a few women enter.

"I don't even get her appeal."

My ears perked up, and I leaned farther over my knees and toward the stall door.

"Me neither. But guys love her. She's busted. She's like a five in the real world but an eight in BigLaw. And she's totally in love with Jordan, but he'd never touch her."

They must be talking about Nancy. I actually felt a little sorry for her.

"It's pathetic how she hangs out only with male attorneys. I don't know how she lives with herself, sleeping her way to partner." Nancy's voice. If she was there, then who were they talking about?!

"Uh, yes. And she thinks she's so cool with the nickname Jaskel gave her."

I sat frozen on the seat, leaning my elbows on my shaking knees. I stared down at my black patent pumps and my pencil skirt and suddenly felt entirely too old and too accomplished to be intimidated or upset. I got up, tucked in my shirt again, and exited the stall to a view of gaping mouths and wide eyes.

"Alex . . . we . . . ," Nancy stammered.

"Please, call me Skippy. Because I think it's so sooooo fucking cool." I washed my hands quickly and left them staring in my wake. I marched directly to Jordan's high-top, where he stood with a few people I didn't know, and glared at him.

He hugged me, not picking up on my expression. "Look who made it!"

I smiled tightly, wanting to unload to him, but I curbed the urge.

"Darren, Sarah, Charles. Alex." He motioned around the table, and I forgot their names immediately.

"Are you doing M&A?" the girl asked.

"Yeah. I really like it."

"Who are you working with now?"

"Ugh! No work talk!" one of the associates said.

"I've been here for three hours, so I'm due for some shop talk," I said as lightly as I could manage, turning back to the girl. "Mostly with this one." I chucked a thumb in Jordan's direction.

"I need a cigarette," Jordan said. "Skippy?"

"I'll join you for some air," I said.

"You're Skippy?" one of the guys asked, but I didn't answer. I forced another smile and turned to follow Jordan out of the bar before I could see any looks they might be giving each other. I'm being paranoid, I thought. They are being completely normal.

The winter chill hit my cheeks, and I realized my jacket was still warming a barstool inside, but my senses had been too numbed by alcohol to truly register the cold. I leaned against a brick wall next to the bar and shut my eyes for just a moment as Jordan lit his cigarette. I sensed him watching me, and opened them.

He blew a cloud of smoke out of his mouth away from me as he shook his head. "You're drunk, Skip."

The wail of a siren grew louder, and Jordan's face strobed with the red flashing lights for a moment before all evidence of emergency faded up Madison Avenue and it was quiet again.

"You are," I retorted, not caring that I sounded childish.

He looked at me. "*I'm* allowed to be drunk. My wife used the d-word yesterday." He was almost whispering.

I felt my jaw slacken and searched his eyes, hoping he was making a bad joke. He wasn't.

"Shit. I'm so sorry."

"Thanks." His shoulders slumped.

"Does Matt know?"

"Of course he knows. Matt's my first phone call."

"What does that even mean?"

Jordan smirked. "It means that at some point or another, everybody wakes up in the driver's seat of a crashed car, next to a dead hooker, with no recollection of how he got there. Hypothetically, of course," he added. "You gotta have someone to call in that situation." He dropped his cigarette to the ground and stepped on it. "Who would you call?"

I stared back up at the night sky and opened my mouth to answer.

"You're an idiot if you say somebody you're sleeping with. Or used to sleep with. Or want to," he challenged. I closed my mouth and tried to think, my angst growing with each moment that my mental Rolodex came up blank.

How was it possible that I didn't have anybody to call? I could call my mom. Or my dad. Who was I kidding? No, I couldn't. They'd never done anything wrong in their lives. My mother once wrote "It won't happen again" with a smiley face in the memo line of the check paying a parking ticket. I should have a friend to call. Not Sam. I was sleeping with him. But also, he'd judge me. A friend. Carmen would be good to call. She could probably talk her way out of anything. But I didn't really trust her.

I watched Jordan for a moment as it dawned on me that I'd actually call *him*. He was composed, brilliant, and always available. But it seemed too weird to tell him that.

"I think I'm just not the kind of person who would be in that situation," I said, shrugging.

"That's your problem." Jordan pointed at me with one eye closed, sharp-shooting in my direction with his index finger.

"What is? That I'm a good person?" My voice came out at a higher pitch than I'd intended.

"That you're self-righteous."

My throat caught, and I looked at him. He wasn't being cruel, or at least not intentionally so.

"I wanna be on your call list," I said, pouting.

"You have to earn that spot, Skippy. But you're getting there." He sucked in the cold air. "You know, Carmen is really doing an amazing job on our deals since we got back from Miami. She's really going for it."

I felt the vein on my temple filling, but I refused to exhibit the outward sign of jealousy he was probably trying to inspire. "Carmen's great. She's really smart," I said, my tone even.

"So, I heard you're working for Peter a lot lately," he said, changing the subject. "When you're still junior, it's good to work for different partners. But you should be careful there. You'll have to choose a side eventually."

"What do you mean? Don't you need to prove yourself to as many partners as possible?"

"Not Peter and Matt. They never share senior associates. But you have a few years before you have to choose."

I stared at him. "Why don't they?"

"Honestly, they just don't like each other. It goes way back. They were at Yale together for law school. I think Matt sort of resents the fact that he worked hard and was smart and Peter just . . . married a Fitch."

"Peter just what?"

"His wife is a Fitch. As in Klasko & Fitch," Jordan explained. "Didn't you know?" I shook my head. "Well, Matt and I hope you join the light side with us. Carmen is working on a deal for me now that closes in three days. She's good. But she's not as good as you. Peter can have Carmen. We want you."

I knew I should have taken it as a compliment, but I couldn't contain the rush of jealousy that she and Jordan were now working so closely. I suddenly felt the alcohol circle back on my brain and felt an urgent need to change the subject.

"Do you get drunk linearly? I get drunk like this," I said, sticking out my index finger and bouncing it up and down.

He just smiled at me.

"What the fuck is the word? Jesus. My brain isn't . . . oscillating!" I yelled. Jordan let out a grunt of laughter. "You don't get it!"

"I get it, I get it," he assured me. "I get drunk like this." He stuck out his pointer finger and traced a steady horizontal line followed by a steep upward curve. "Not for seven drinks, and then it hits me all at once."

"Exponentially." I suddenly found the word incredibly hilarious, doubling over laughing, then catching my breath as somberness overtook me. "I used to think people fell in love the way that you get drunk." I swept my finger slowly through the cool night air before scooping it skyward. "Now I think they fall in love the way I do," I continued, bouncing my finger. A pang of guilt that Sam was home alone and I'd left my phone inside the bar had started to nag at me.

"Let's go back in, Skip, and grab your stuff, okay?" Jordan said gently. "I'll grab you a cab or an Uber."

Before I knew it, the word was out of my mouth. "Up!" I demanded.

Jordan shook his head. "Let's call it a night."

"But I need to get it together before I go home and talk to Sam!"

"Just a tiny bit, Skip," he said, relenting. "And only because I don't feel like listening to you bitch and moan." He backed up behind the bouncer at the door and pushed his back against the wall. I moved closer to him as he took a vial out of the breast pocket of his suit and spilled a small mound of powder onto the back of his hand.

I dipped my head and put one finger to my nostril and snorted in with the other, then put my head back. As I did, I felt the tip of my nose tingle and then go completely numb. I felt the coke much more immediately and powerfully this time. A metallic sludge dripped down my throat and attacked the base of my tongue, but I swallowed it back down. A euphoric detachment spread over my body, and I understood in that moment how people could become addicted to this. My mind felt sober and clear and my body more responsive to my will.

"Jesus, Skip." He rolled his eyes, watching my demeanor change.

"How many have you had?" I asked, trying to sound serious. "Drinks!" I clarified.

"Six," he said.

"One more, then!" I announced.

Jordan laughed and gestured for me to lead him back inside. "Carmen is hot, by the way," he said into my back. I whipped around. "Just saying," he laughed, holding up his palms.

"You're a pig," I grumbled, leading the way into the bar.

"I need a wet nap!" I whined loudly to no one in particular. Carmen nodded, chewing. Jordan laughed in slow motion, his arm around her shoulder, as I glared at them. I looked down at the chicken wings I didn't remember ordering or consuming. There was another glass on the table in front of me, empty besides a few half-melted ice cubes. I pressed the home button on my phone, leaving unctuous orange residue on the screen, and closed one eye so I could read the time.

One a.m. And seven texts from Sam. Fuck.

I needed to call him. But I needed a wet nap first. I made my way to the bar and leaned over its shiny mahogany surface to get the bartender's attention.

"Well, well, well. Look who graced us with her presence." I looked up to see Derrick grinning at me from a barstool.

"Another drink, milady?" he offered. "Everybody's been talking about Skippy from M&A tonight. You're the toast of the town. First first-year ever to cop an invite to Miami. However did you manage that?"

I ignored him.

"Excuse me, please, I need a wet nap," I said to the bartender, hearing the slur in my words.

"What would Matt say if he saw you like this?" Derrick's tone had turned almost hostile.

"Sam," I corrected him.

"What?"

"My girlfriend's name is Sam, not Matt. Excuse me! Can I have a wet nap?" I yelled at the bartender, holding up my buffalo-stained fingertips.

"Girlfriend? What would Matt say to THAT?" he laughed. I eyed the empty shot glasses lined up in front of him, counting six. I looked back at Derrick, realizing he must be drunker than I was.

The bartender handed me a foil packet, which I tore open with my teeth after thanking him. I scrubbed my fingertips, watching the moist lemon-scented towelette turn sunburn orange, then stuffed it into one of the empty shot glasses.

The meaning of Derrick's question finally dawned on me. "Jaskel? Why would Matt care?"

Derrick took a sip of his drink. "Because you're fucking him." My body stiffened. "Come on, don't act like it's not true. And here I thought we were friends! You should have told me!" He put his hand over his heart in feigned offense.

I stared at Derrick, hoping he would crack a smile to let me know that he was joking, but he didn't. My knees went rubbery as all the sideways glances in my direction throughout the evening formed a montage in my mind.

"I'm not," I whispered, shaking my head.

"Are you okay? Shit, Alex. I was messing around. I'm an asshole. You look really pale. Al? Hello?" He squeezed my arm, but I shrugged away and then ran past him and into the bathroom, where I vomited fatty orange chicken skin and straight vodka into the sink. The spice of the buffalo sauce on its way up stung my raw nostrils and then my brain. I gagged and vomited again, then looked into the mirror at the auburn goop dripping down my chin. I ran the water in the other sink to clean up, leaving the first sink to bubble and belch as it slowly drained the vomit.

"Ew. Get your shit together," a woman said as she exited the stall, brushing past me and out into the bar.

Please, God, let me not remember this in the morning.

***

When Sam's alarm went off at six thirty, he let the beeping continue long after his eyes were open, probably just to annoy me. As I lay perfectly still with my eyes closed, refusing to play his game, last evening rushed in on me, and I felt tears spilling out of the corners of my closed eyes. He finally pounded the button on the top of his alarm with his fist and stumbled into the bathroom. My head wasn't pounding with a hangover just yet, but my brain was moving sluggishly—which meant I was probably still drunk. I tried desperately to fall back asleep, but the image of Derrick waiting for me outside the bathroom and putting me in a car poked at my mind. I couldn't remember coming home or waving to our doorman or getting undressed, though. I smelled my hair and breathed into my palm. It smelled fine. *At least I brushed my teeth.* My heart began to race. *I'm going to puke.* I dismissed the option of running to the kitchen sink—we didn't have a garbage disposal, and also, it was too pathetic to vomit in a sink twice in fewer than six hours. I took a small sip of water from the glass on my nightstand and a deep breath, hoping I could wait out Sam's shower. He finally emerged in a towel and stared at me, as if he was struggling to choose his words.

I spoke before he could. "I'm going to work from home today. So, if you get out early . . ." I trailed off, keeping my voice sweet.

Sam's arms dropped to his sides, the bathroom light illuminating his frame, and he grinned. "I thought you forgot!" He looked so touched, I thought he might cry.

I was glad the room was dark enough to obscure my confusion. *Forgot what?* "You don't have to," he went on. "I have a really good feeling about this meeting. But that is seriously like . . . so . . . nice."

Meeting. Shit. The final investors meeting. That is today. I can't believe I came home so late last night.

"I have a good feeling too. But I'll be here. And we can have dinner in or out, whatever you want. We can just hang out and be together."

"I really appreciate it," Sam said, making his way to my bedside and bending low to kiss me goodbye. "Wish me luck," he whispered, lips still so close to mine that I could smell his toothpaste.

"Good luck! I love you!" I called after him, hearing a bit of desperation seasoning my tone.

I threw off the covers before the front door even clicked shut, and made it to the bathroom, but not all the way to the toilet, where I vomited up the bile in my stomach. I lay crumpled on the bathroom floor for a few moments before trusting myself to get up. I Cloroxed the tiles, scrubbing to get the grout back to white, catching glimpses of my slightly green face in the mirror, and lay back down to nap while intermittently answering emails.

By ten o'clock, I thought Jordan might be at his desk, and I grabbed my phone to call him.

He picked up after one ring. "Skippyyyyy!"

A salty tear slipped into the side of my parted lips from my cheek. "I'm working from home" was the only declarative statement I could manage.

"I figured! Heard you puked. All-star happy hour showing, Skippy."

I started to cry silently.

"Skip? You okay?" I couldn't speak. "Hello?" I could hear a hint of concern in his voice.

"Does everybody think I'm sleeping with Matt?" I whispered.

Silence. More silence.

"Let me close my door. Okay. Hi. Um . . . why?"

My heart squeezed its way into my throat. "Who did you hear it from?"

"Doesn't matter. I can't remember."

He was lying. I stood frozen in the middle of my bedroom floor, attempting to discern whether I'd need to run to the toilet again. I breathed in, swallowed, and relaxed.

Jordan finally spoke. "I think maybe Nancy. I told her it wasn't true. And, seriously—nobody who knows you would ever believe that."

"There are only like five people at this firm who actually know me!" My voice was almost a shriek, an entirely new register for me.

"Look, Skip, I don't mean to sound harsh here, but you gotta toughen up. When rumors fly, you're doing something right. Who cares what these other people think? You're part of our crew. That means you're going to get a lot of shade thrown your way."

I allowed myself a small smile, not that he could see it. "Yeah," I sniffled.

"Throw yourself into work. This place is a prison, but sometimes you want to be locked away from everything else. That's what I always do when my life is shit. And it's gotten me this far."

"Yeah," I said, and steadied my breath. "It's a good distraction." I hung up, took a shower, and called my email to life again, feeling somewhat ready to face the day.

From: Peter Dunn
To: Alexandra Vogel
Subject: FW: Stag River

Alex, see below. Gary Kaplan specifically requested you on the acquisition of Tremor Inc. That's something to be proud of!
—Peter

My heart sank. I contemplated saying I was already staffed too heavily for the next month, but all first-year staffing went through Caroline, the staffing partner, so she'd know exactly what my capacity for new work was, and Peter could easily find out. All I could hope was that there wouldn't be any face-to-face meetings for the deal. I shivered in disgust and shoved the feeling down so far I barely registered it.

From: Alexandra Vogel
To: Peter Dunn
Subject: Re: FW: Stag River

Peter,
I'm flattered! Please let me know when I can get started.
—Alex

I watched as my in-box began to flood: Anna reminding me that I was delinquent in recording my time; Mike Baccard announcing that Klasko had been honored with yet another humanitarian award; Zachary Kennedy, the head of PR, warning us not to answer calls from any reporters asking for comment on a partner's son allegedly paying another student to take his SATs; dozens of emails between me and Jordan, hypothesizing which partner the email was referring to; and all the while, hundreds of messages regarding my active deals devoured my attention. The deluge mercifully squeezed the anxiety from my consciousness, and after a few hours, my small laptop screen was straining my vision. I arched my back, stretched my arms, and turned on the cold water in the shower.

I stuck a Post-it to the refrigerator:

Had to just head in for a few. Be back no later than 6. I'll be sending you good vibes all day. Can't wait to hear about it.
X, A

I headed to midtown, and didn't leave the office again for seventy-two hours.

CHAPTER 15

Three days later, I finally caught a break from the onslaught, and the brief lull in a morning of back-to-back calls allowed my brain to wander back to the events of the last happy hour. I needed to figure out who had started this rumor. I shot Carmen a message, even though I knew she had a closing the next day for Jordan's deal.

From: Alexandra Vogel
To: Carmen Greyson
Subject: HUGE Favor

I really need to chat. Are you around? Know you're swamped. But, PLEASE. I'm in my office for the next few hours.

Carmen breezed into my office three minutes after I had hit send, her skin clear and taut and her bright blue eyes alert despite the stress I would have imagined she was under, shut the door, and took a seat.

"You look amazing for having a closing tomorrow," I said, then realized how it sounded. "I mean, you look really good, period. Which is impressive considering you have a closing tomorrow!"

She smiled with a slight bow of her head. Something was different. She really did look . . . She had to be dating somebody. Everybody looks better when there is somebody to look better for. But she was looking better in the office! Was she dating somebody at work?

"I'm hiding the stress well, I guess. Actually, Jordan is making this closing really smooth for me. It's sort of a complicated deal, so Jordan's holding my hand a bit." She had said his name twice in three sentences, but moreover, she'd said it as though she loved saying it, and was itching to say it a thousand more times. It's Jordan she's been looking so good for lately, I thought. I wondered if he was reciprocating. "But I have to get back to it soon. What's up?"

I shook the thoughts of her and Jordan away, knowing I didn't have much time, and launched into my deposition. "Have you heard a rumor about me?"

Her eyes widened in what resembled panic before her face settled into her classically inscrutable expression, and she gave a slight shake of her head. "What? No. Why? Have you heard one about me?"

I couldn't tell if she was expertly deflecting or legitimately wondering, but she looked genuinely worried. "No. Why would I have heard one about you?" *She's definitely sleeping with Jordan, then.* I didn't wait for her to respond. "Everybody was looking at me funny at happy hour."

She scoffed. "That's all? That's just how lawyers look. We're all socially awkward! You're being silly."

"And then Derrick accused me of sleeping with Matt."

Carmen coughed on my last word. "What? Matt Jaskel?" She glanced over her shoulder to confirm that my door was closed. "Are you?" she whispered, even though it was. She was either a very good actress, or completely shocked.

"No! Jesus. No."

"I'm just confirming before I say what I was about to, which is that that is *absurd*! Nobody is saying that." She was almost laughing.

"Everybody is saying it! Nancy, Derrick, Jordan. And I'm not being paranoid. Everybody was looking at me suspiciously. I want to die. But honestly, between Stag River and National, I'm way too busy to buy arsenic. Tell me the truth—do I need to switch firms?"

"Al, don't even kid about that. You can't leave Klasko. I need you here. And nobody would ever believe that. Ever. I trust that Nancy girl as far as I can throw her. She's so weird, and definitely has a thing for Jordan." Despite the fact that her response was a classic deflection, she also had a point. I watched as her expression clouded over. "Would you ever sleep with somebody at work?"

"I don't think so. Why?" I asked gently, trying not to scare her off.

"You know what, never mind! Don't pay attention to people. And I'm so sorry, but I really have to go. I have a closing!" She was out of her seat before I could say another word.

Carmen was right. Nobody actually believed the rumor. Plus, screw them! They were probably just jealous because I was making inroads with the M&A team. I was certain the hostility would dissipate after we were all placed into groups. I could handle the cattiness for a few more months.

***

Just before Klasko partners migrated south to St. Barth's or east to Chamonix, the firm held its annual Winter Ball. As Jordan explained, it was formerly known as a Christmas party, and then a holiday party, until the idea of offending anybody who did not observe a winter holiday overwhelmed firm management to such an extent that they created a Winter Ball instead. The entire firm and our plus-ones descended on the Pierre Hotel like a plague, a swarm just shy of a thousand. Everybody was invited. The mailroom. The librarians. Secretaries. Lawyers. Plus-ones.

Carmen, Kevin, and Derrick left without me, since I'd been

stuck on a call with Stag River, so I hurried over to the Pierre solo, trying to beat Sam there so he didn't have to navigate the party alone. As I entered the ballroom, my eyes were pulled skyward by the ornate crystal chandeliers hanging from the ceiling, and then down to take in the rich red carpeting, dotted with male attorneys wearing exactly what they wore to the office and female attorneys taking a few fashion liberties they might not otherwise—skirts a few inches higher and blouses a few lower. Their dates stood out more because they wore nonbusiness clothing than because I didn't recognize their faces from around the office. I was wearing a new high-waisted burgundy skirt from Aritzia with a white silk blouse from Intermix, an outfit I hoped was just conservative enough to be appropriate and just playful enough to be considered "festive" attire.

"Love your skirt," Mike Baccard's wife mouthed at me as he led her past me into the crowd. The compliment lightened and straightened me. I entered with my shoulders back, my neck stretched long. I was going to present myself as above it all, blissfully above the rumors and politics swirling around my ankles.

I accepted a glass of white wine from a passing server as I scanned the crowd for Sam, not able to spot him at first but taking in the scene on the dance floor. Almost no attorneys danced—I guessed they were not drunk enough yet—but Darlene from the mailroom, who always moved my documents to the top of her printing queue, was grinding against Isaac from accounting, who never bothered Jordan about our expenses, with little regard for the gawking onlookers.

I spotted Jordan and his wife, Jessica, looking the picture of marital bliss as they chatted with another couple. I hoped people would notice that Sam and I fit together as well, quashing the Matt Jaskel rumors once and for all. As I looked at the bar in the far corner, I saw Carmen ordering a drink, but just as I started off toward her, a hand slipped around my waist and I smiled. *Sam.* As soon as I turned to face him, though, my smile faded. I took in his vintage-style maroon velvet blazer, blue button-down, and the ill-fitting black jeans he'd chosen to complete the look.

"Holy shit, this is a classy affair! Is this okay?" he asked, fastening his one jacket button—the other was missing, but had left hanging thread behind as a parting gift.

I searched his face, wondering if he was deliberately attempting to embarrass me with this absurd outfit—was it a prank?

"What happened to the clothes I left on the bed?" I asked through a clenched smile. I'd laid out the tweed blazer and white French-cuff shirt I'd gotten him to wear with his cuff links, plus a smart blue tie. It would read start-up, tech nerd, cool and chic.

"I'm not a child, Alex. I can dress myself."

I shot him a look. All evidence was to the contrary, but there was nothing I could do about it right now. I took a long swig of oaky chardonnay and searched for a way to get him away from the ballroom entrance, where a number of the partners were congregating to meet their wives.

"I want you to say hi to Carmen," I said as cheerily as possible, and led him farther into the ballroom to the bar. They greeted each other warmly, having already met a few times in Cambridge, as I glanced around the room.

"Is it open bar?" Sam whispered into my ear. I nodded, relieved nobody else had heard him. I was fairly sure the Pierre didn't offer a cash bar option. "Shots?" he asked eagerly.

"Don't you have to run early tomorrow? Are shots a good idea?" I asked gently.

"I don't think I can train for the marathon anymore. Work is ramping up, and I don't have the time."

As he spoke, I wondered if this was true or if he felt the need to overstate how busy he was, in this ballroom dripping with industriousness and capitalism.

"I definitely get that," Carmen said. "But the training is just such a great way to stay in shape, so it's cool you've been doing it, even if you don't end up running the race."

I relaxed; I had almost forgotten how charming she could be with new people.

It took only one round of champagne for Sam to convince Carmen that Patrón wouldn't be a bad idea at all, but I opted out. As they ordered the shots from the bartender, I saw Peter guiding his rail-thin platinum-blond wife through the crowd. I willed myself not to stare, but my eyes would not oblige. She was even more striking than when I had seen her at Benihana. I took in the red soles of her black patent pumps and the indented delineation of muscle between her calf and shin along her outer leg—the line I'd never been able to achieve even when I'd worked out a few times a week. She's perfect, I thought. They're the perfect couple.

"Wait!" I yelled. Sam and Carmen stopped mid-cheers. "Sam, just come meet Peter and his wife so we can thank them for the ski weekend, and then I promise you can drink whatever you want."

Sam nodded, and I watched him make an effort to look sincere. I beckoned for Carmen to come with us, but she vehemently shook her head.

"I'll be here," she said, turning back to the bar.

"We'll be just a minute," I promised Carmen as I pulled Sam behind me by the wrist and we caught up to the Dunns.

"Peter, I wanted you to meet my boyfriend, Sam."

"Hi there!" Peter extended his hand, and I cringed as I watched him take in Sam's blazer. "And this is my wife, Marcie." We all shook hands, Marcie meeting my enthusiastic grin with a wan smile.

"Mini brie and fig tartlet?" A tray was thrust into the middle of our foursome.

Sam popped one in his mouth, and I politely declined. Peter took one, but his wife gave a small shake of her head, her thick blond hair sweeping her shoulders. She was exactly what I thought of when I heard the word *statuesque*: beautiful but frigid. Her skin was impossibly taut. Her nose, delicate. Her lips, plump. She wasn't a natural beauty and had certainly been nipped and tucked over the years, but she was unarguably beautiful. The quintessential wife of a partner—plastic, but perfect.

"So nice to meet both of you. And we just wanted to say thank you again for lending us your Killington house. It was the nicest getaway." I nudged Sam.

"Yes, thanks!" he added, swallowing the last bit of tartlet as he spoke.

"You have the loveliest home," I said to Marcie. She smiled graciously but said nothing, the way only truly rich and elegant women can do without seeming rude.

Another tray appeared. "Shrimp cocktail?" I felt the wine resting in my stomach, so I took two shrimp, and Peter and Sam followed my lead.

"Excuse me just a moment," Marcie said. "Pleasure to meet you both." Then she turned away, her eyes focused on something at the far end of the ballroom.

"I'm so glad you enjoyed the house," Peter said. "We never get up there, so somebody might as well use it."

"Yeah, it's a great spot," Sam said flatly, fidgeting with his lone blazer button, now looking uncomfortable with his choice of attire.

"Did you ski?" Peter asked, taking a sip of the auburn liquid in his stout crystal glass.

"I was so tired after that closing that we did almost nothing. We totally wasted the weekend," I answered. *Because Sam didn't want to do anything fun,* I refrained from adding. *He just wanted to talk and eat and stay in pajamas. No nice dinners out. No good wine. No skiing.*

"I aspire to waste a weekend someday," Peter said, then patted the puffy half-moon under his right eye with a fingertip. "Wait to have kids," he said to us with a short laugh. For the first time, I wondered if he was happy in his perfect-looking life.

"Hey, Skippy!" Matt had suddenly joined our group, given me a side hug, and slapped Peter's back. I saw Peter tense his shoulders, but his face remained placid.

"Matt, this is my boyfriend, Sam. Sam, Matt Jaskel."

"Nice to finally meet you," Matt slurred, shaking his hand. "Skippy, you excited for tomorrow?"

"What's tomorrow? Aside from a hangover on a Friday?" I sipped at my drink.

"So, just a normal Friday?" Peter smirked, and we clinked glasses.

"Bonus day!" Matt cheered. "The firm never announces it in advance, so people don't complain if it's a day late or something."

"Holy shit! I figured we wouldn't get them until January!" I exclaimed.

"I'm going to get a refill," Sam announced, taking off toward the bar.

"Where's Marcie?" Matt panned the room in slow motion.

"Off doing what she does best—hobnobbing with management." Peter cocked his head toward his wife, chatting with Mike Baccard, who was wearing a double-breasted pinstripe suit and horn-rimmed glasses. I had only seen his picture on the bottom of press releases and in the firm Facebook, but never seen him in person. He had classic male-pattern baldness and, at well over six feet tall, a commanding presence, in a room full of people with presence.

"Can I give you a piece of advice?" Matt asked. I nodded. "You and Sam have a joint checking account, right?"

Peter coughed, looking uncomfortable, and I shook my head. "Why would you think that we do?"

"Because his eyes lit up when I mentioned your bonus."

Had they? That didn't seem like him. I bit my lower lip. "So what's your advice?"

"Take half your bonus and be practical. Pay off loans, put it in savings, pay your bills. Whatever. Take a quarter and leave it in your checking account." He paused and smiled at me. "And take a quarter and blow it on yourself. Only yourself."

"That's good advice," Peter agreed stiffly. My eyes bounced from Peter to Matt. Remembering what Jordan had mentioned about their personal relationship, the tension between them was suddenly obvious to me.

"I want those," Matt announced as he left us and stalked over to a server balancing a silver platter on his palm.

Watching Matt throw his drink down his throat before taking a lamb chop, Peter and I stood in silence, but I felt his energy pulling at me. I had spent so much time around him and on the phone with him lately that I'd assumed my attraction to him must have dissipated, but I realized then that it had only been hidden temporarily by documents and deadlines. *I just met his wife!* I reminded myself. *I should not be thinking about him like this.* But without the pressure of an immediate deal-related deadline, the tension and the tingling had reappeared at the base of my spine.

"Matt's enjoying himself," I said, trying desperately to distract myself from the warmth spreading through my abdomen.

Peter shrugged. "Matt never used to drink. This place is

strange. You develop a reputation, right or wrong, and then people sort of make you into it. Everybody now expects Matt to party. He's like a caricature of himself. I guess we all are."

I watched a group of my fellow junior associates surround Matt, who gesticulated wildly while he narrated whatever story he was telling and they all threw their heads back in laughter.

"All of us?" I asked Peter.

He locked his eyes with mine, throwing me off balance again.

"Carmen's the tough one, Kevin is the sweet one, Derrick is the out-of-control one. All the partners identify you guys by an adjective for convenience's sake. But it's a self-fulfilling prophecy."

I opened my mouth to speak but closed it, needing to swallow down the anxiety that came from knowing I was about to train Peter's discerning eye on myself.

"Which one am I?" I asked.

"Skippy," Peter answered, as though it were obvious.

"No. I mean, what's my adjective?"

"That is your adjective. Prissy, proper, perfect, ready for the country club," he goaded, allowing a smile to creep into the corners of his mouth.

"That's not me at all!" I protested.

"No?" He raised an eyebrow.

"What are you?" I asked.

Peter thought for a moment. "Happy," he said flatly, draining his scotch. "I need air. Come." He didn't look at me, just turned and walked toward the exit. My heart thudded as I scanned the ballroom. Carmen was watching me intently as Sam ordered another drink at the bar. He must be at least four drinks in by now, I thought. I held up one finger to her, indicating I'd be right back, as I followed Peter down the plush carpeted hallway. There was a brief moment of silence, with nobody in front of me to navigate past, when I contemplated running back into the safe cacophony of the ballroom, with its deal talk, small talk, and slurred words.

"I need something from my car." Peter's voice pulled me back to the hotel corridor. He still wasn't looking at me, but the hairs on the back of my neck stood on end. I continued to lag behind him, my legs fighting me. I stared at the back of his pants, snug around his upper thighs. He turned to me, finally meeting my gaze. "It'll only take a moment."

I managed an affirmative blink and took a large gulp of wine. My heart rate increased as I attempted to convince myself that I didn't know what was happening. I took another, longer pull of my drink, trying to create an excuse for what I was about to do. The voice telling me that it was inappropriate to get into Peter's corporate car was drowned out by the luscious adrenaline of misbehaving, of being bad, of escaping the boring ballroom and the buzzing cell phone in my purse. I suddenly had the urge to blow up the life I had carved out for myself, and join the ranks of those to whom the rules did not apply. I drained my glass and placed it on a table in the lobby, then followed Peter through the main doors.

The air outside the Pierre was biting, and Fifth Avenue was completely desolate except for the line of black cars and the drivers leaning against them, curls of smoke billowing up from the lit ends of their cigarettes into the winter air. I smiled politely at the driver as he quickly stepped on his cigarette and opened the door of a black Quality SUV with a "Dunn" placard in the front window, and held his palm out to help me climb in. I searched his face for judgment, for recognition that I wasn't supposed to be climbing into the back of his car with Peter, that I wasn't wearing a wedding ring while Peter was. But his eyes were a blank, professional kind of polite. They seemed to barely register me at all. I crossed my legs to make myself feel more in control, continuing the charade of propriety. If I did this, I was no better than the rumors. *Fuck the rumors. Fuck the people who spread them. They don't matter.* Peter slipped smoothly into the seat next to me and put a hand on my leg as the driver closed the door with a soft thud, sealing us inside the car. Peter's hand, just above my knee, shattered the thin facade to which I had been clinging. I squirmed slightly, and there was a fleeting moment when I considered pulling back—pretending that he had somehow misread the situation and that I'd thought we were going to discuss the letter of intent on the Stag River deal.

But he took the back of my head in his palm and pulled my lips to his, and electricity shot through me.

His breath was smoky with scotch and slightly sweet, like a burned orange. Something on his skin smelled spicy as I breathed him in. He smelled so different from, so much better than, Sam.

I melted into him as my other senses sprang to life. His lips were soft and inviting. I half expected somebody of his age to kiss differently. But he didn't. I put my hand on his chest and moaned slightly in protest as I pushed him ever so slightly away, sensing that I was supposed to do so to make certain he knew I was struggling with my conscience. He played his part deftly, pushing the back of my head a bit harder, then pulling away from me and looking curiously into my eyes. He said nothing, but he cupped my face in his hand and drew me to him again. He placed his lips on my forehead, and all of my anxieties evaporated as the tip of my nose explored the cavity of his neck. He backed away again and smiled wistfully, making me blush. And then this time, I kissed him. His tongue explored mine with such gentleness that I gave up all control, sucking hungrily at the power I felt charging through his body into mine.

When it was over and the world rushed back in on me, we

locked eyes. I suppose it should have been a romantic moment, but I felt a surge of nausea. I wanted to think it was the result of too many drinks, but I knew it was from the guilt squeezing my stomach lining together and forcing it up into my throat.

"Shit," I whispered as I pulled my bra back over my breasts, struggling with the clasp in my trembling hands. Peter was saying something, but I wasn't hearing him as I shoved my blouse into my skirt and untwisted my necklace so it lay flat. I shook my head repeatedly as though arguing with the part of myself that told me I had just committed an unforgivable transgression that would alter the course of my life. I slid out of the car and shut the door behind me, desperate now to return to the party I'd longed to escape. I stole a glimpse of myself in the mirrored hallway wall and saw that I looked normal, and felt almost resentful that I hadn't been physically branded. I wiped at the corners of my mouth and under my eyes and then walked into the ballroom, plastered a smile on my face, and slid up to Sam, who was still at the bar with Carmen. He kissed the top of my head.

Did he smell Peter?

"Where were you and Peter?" Carmen asked intently.

"Peter went to find his wife. I took a call," I said, meeting her gaze steadily. "I've made my necessary rounds. Officially time to hang with you guys," I told them, realizing I was disturbingly adept at appearing calm even while my heart felt like it was about to burst through my rib cage.

"We're taking another shot," Sam said, looking as if he was bracing himself for a judgmental look from me. He didn't get one. I wanted him to be drunk enough not to notice if my sheen of composure didn't last.

"I'm in!" I ordered three shots of Casa Dragones as bits of my encounter with Peter flashed before my eyes.

We continued to drink and talk to other first-years while I

obsessively kept Peter in the periphery of my vision so I could maintain a safe distance at all times.

Carmen seemed to be keeping an eye on someone as well. "Who are we scoping out, lady?" I asked as she craned her neck out over the crowd.

"Peter's wife is super thin," she said, unintentionally answering my question.

I shrugged, unable to bring myself to speak badly about a woman whose marriage I had just compromised. The alcohol overtook the adrenaline in my system and I became exceedingly drunk in what seemed like an instant. I nuzzled Sam's shoulder, indicating I was ready to head home, and he went to get our coats. I was left with Carmen, who turned away from me without a word and made her way to the far end of the bar.

I smelled Peter before I saw him, his scent triggering the image of him unfastening my bra. I touched my temple in embarrassment and looked up to see him before me.

"Just wanted to say goodbye," he said. My breath caught, and I looked over his shoulder to see Marcie, who waved pleasantly enough from a couple feet behind him.

I gave her a broad smile, and she flashed a confident and careless one in return. She definitely doesn't suspect anything, I thought. I looked back at Peter, focusing more on his forehead than his eyes, terrified of what I might see in them.

"Good night," I said, striving for a professional tone but bordering on cold.

He leaned in slightly closer. "Great night," he said with a tiny wink—or maybe it was a squint. Either way, it sent my stomach into somersaults. He turned, placed a hand on the small of his wife's back, and guided her out of the ballroom, toward the Quality car I had just been in. I crossed my right arm to my opposite shoulder and rubbed it for comfort.

When Sam and I arrived home, I walked directly into the bathroom and stripped down, tossing my clothes onto the floor. As I did, I saw a spot of red on the inside of the right cup of my white bra. I looked at my right nipple in the mirror, or rather the tiny, perfect bite mark just north of it. I shut my eyes and stepped into the hot shower, where I leaned my back against the wall and let it slip down the cool tiles until I was sitting on the floor. I curled my knees up to my chest as the water pushed down on my hair and formed a curtain around my face.

As the water flowed, I tried to remember more about the night—what Peter was saying to me as I left his car, the look on the driver's face. But it was all too foggy. I didn't know if the memories had disappeared because of the alcohol or my own shame, and whether I'd ever recover them—or if I even wanted to. Then suddenly the image of me straddling Peter, his lips on my breasts, came into my mind. My hands instinctively flew to my face as my insides twisted in simultaneous pleasure and pain.

I stood and soaped up the loofah, taking it to my arms and chest.

"Babe? You okay?" Sam shouted from the other side of the bathroom door. "Trying to set a new record for shower length?"

I looked down at my skin, which was now red and raw.

"Out in a sec!" I yelled back, jumping out from under the now-painful hot water and blotting my body as gently as possible with a plush towel.

I applied lotion, gritting my teeth at the sting, then slipped into silk pajamas and slid under the covers next to Sam.

"Carmen is great, really fun. Glad I met her. She had the nicest things to say about you," he said, and patted my thigh and sighed, the way he always did when he had had too much to drink.

"Did she?" I ignored the sting of his touch and pretended to be on the edge of sleep as my mind raced.

"You have a whole work life I never knew about," Sam whispered, touching my waist softly.

In his unwitting acknowledgment that I was leading a double life, the rush of keeping a secret from the man who thought he knew me so well almost made me convulse in pleasure. Something was really wrong with me. I knew I should have felt guilty, but I was too keyed up from the evening to feel anything but mouthwateringly, imperfectly human. I could only respond, "I know."

Sam's breath deepened as he drifted off, while I stared up at the ceiling, my heart beating wildly, willing myself to remain still for the remainder of the night.

Q. What do you think most motivated you to want to be a partner in the M&A group?

A. I don't think I really thought about becoming a partner at Klasko when I was a first-year.

Q. What motivated you to want to join M&A as an associate, then, if the hours were worse than those in other groups?

A. I think I was probably most motivated by the prestige. M&A was the most well respected group at the firm. I think I've always been driven to be the best at whatever it is I do.

Q. Did you have law school loans?

A. No, I was fortunate enough not to.

Q. Did financial compensation motivate you to want to join M&A?

A. Not initially, no. I don't think so.

Q. But eventually?

A. I think M&A attorneys are better compensated because they bring in more revenue. They work longer hours. Their work is more difficult. So the compensation is all wrapped up in the question of prestige, in my mind.

CHAPTER 16

The morning after the Winter Ball, I opened my eyes when I felt the room brighten in the sun. Though I hadn't actually slept, I welcomed the morning, feeling firm in my conviction that what had happened between Peter and me could never and would never be repeated, and that I would never, ever tell Sam about it. It would serve no purpose but to hurt him. It seemed fair that I be the only one to suffer.

"That party was amazing. What do you think it cost? I can't even imagine, with the open bar and all that food. Must have been fifty thousand." Sam turned over to me, still under the covers. I stared back at him and nodded. He has absolutely zero idea what things cost, I thought. It was at least five times that.

"It was really nice," I agreed.

"Nice? It was awesome!? I had no idea it was going to be like that when you invited me." Sam paused. "I could get used to being your hot date at all the firm functions."

I reached for my phone and scanned my in-box. When I reached the bottom of my unread messages I scrolled up yet again, hoping I had missed one from Peter, but I didn't have a single email from him, not even one about our deal. Hurt and relief crashed into each other inside my chest. *Was it a onetime thing for him? That's good. It can't happen again anyway. It's best that we don't acknowledge it and move on.*

Sam suddenly sat up next to me. "Hey, it's bonus day!" I watched him carefully, his newfound exuberance for the finer things in life exacerbating my headache. *Suddenly, you don't hate my job so much, do you?*

I grabbed my phone and logged on to my checking account.

"Holy shit," I whispered, my hangover dissolving instantly.

"Good?"

I nodded over at him, wide-eyed. I couldn't push away the feeling that the universe had not only let me escape the repercussions of my mistake but had actually rewarded me for it. My checking balance seemed like a justification of everything I had done while at Klasko so far. Everything.

"Good. You've been working so hard. You deserve it."

I had been working hard, but I didn't think that alone was enough to warrant $50,000. After taxes! As I stared again at the number, the screen went blank and flashed "Carmen Greyson."

"Hi!"

"Hi!" We both burst out laughing. "Holy shit!" I threw off the covers and hoisted myself out of bed.

"Right? Holy shit! I love M&A!" Carmen yelled, and we dissolved into giggles again.

"Are you busy today?" Carmen asked.

"I feel like it's all died down pre-Christmas. I'm pretty slow," I said, scanning through my emails to confirm that no meeting requests or emergencies had come in overnight.

"Me too! So slow." She paused. "Are you thinking what I'm thinking?"

I'm thinking that I'm going to take Matt's advice and go on a $12,500 shopping spree.

"Bloomingdale's?" I asked.

"Fuck Bloomingdale's. We're going to Bergdorf's!" she squealed.

As I stood on Fifth Avenue, I had to fight the urge to grab the door handle from the suited doorman just inside the building and fling it open before he could.

"Welcome to Bergdorf's. Can I direct—"

"ALEX!" Carmen sprang out from behind a wall of sunglasses. I darted past the doorman and into her embrace. "Can you believe how generous they were? Thirty thousand dollars!" she whispered into my ear. I felt a pang of guilt, but a surge of pride. I got a better bonus than Carmen. Unless she was lying about her number. She pulled away from me, and I saw her wild grin. I'd gotten a bigger bonus. For sure.

I drifted toward a gray crocodile satchel sitting on the display counter and picked it up with both hands. "This bag is amazing."

"It's to die for!" she exclaimed.

"I'm going to get it!" I peeped inside the bag, pulled out the price tag, and gasped, my resolve vanishing instantly. "Um, it's twenty-four thousand dollars." I looked up, expecting to see my shock mirrored in Carmen's face.

"Of course it is. It's a Moreau." My stomach sank. I'd never imagined I wouldn't be able to afford anything I wanted on this day. "Oh, cheer up. We can do bags next year!"

I placed it gently back down on the counter. "I'm never spending that much on a bag!"

Carmen shrugged. "This year's bonus was our first. And it was prorated for a third of the year! You might be singing a different tune when you see next year's. Never say never, young one!" It hadn't occurred to me that the enormous bonus I had just received was only a fraction of what I'd receive in years to come if I continued to do M&A, and do it well. "I want to start with makeup!" she declared. "You can choose the next department."

"You need to try this. It's like butter." Carmen met my gaze in the mirror she was staring into, her skin smooth and supple, with a dewiness maintaining a careful distance from shine. "It's life-changing."

"Wow. Your skin looks amazing. But I already have foundation."

"Uh! Please!" She turned back to the mirror and patted her cheekbone with her finger. "What kind?" I refreshed my email for the fifth time since we'd hit the cosmetics department. Still nothing from Peter. Despite the Christmas music, the counter associate's elf hat, and the bulging balance in my bank account, I couldn't shake the feeling that I had been used—dismissed by somebody whose attention I wasn't even sure I wanted.

"Neutrogena. It matches my tone."

Carmen shook her head. "Miss! Can you please find a foundation for my friend here?" From behind the glass-topped counter, a woman wearing elegant black eyeliner and peach lip gloss sprang to action, contemplating me briefly before giving a resolute nod and bending down to open a drawer. "This is Chanel!" Carmen stage-whispered at me. "Our hardworking skin deserves Chanel!"

My mind drifted back to the night before, grazing over the ballroom and the tartlets and stopping at following Peter out to his car. I knew, unequivocally, that I had made a mistake, but there was something about the ability to take money and make myself into an elegant, high-fashion version of myself that convinced me that money could cover up just about any error. I hoisted my Longchamp up on my shoulder. Peter's wife was the type of woman who bought Moreaus—she probably had dozens of them in every color in clear drawers in a walk-in closet. I suddenly envied her. I envisioned her hosting dinner parties with Peter and their snobby friends at their house in Westchester. I pictured their quiet candlelit dinners at home, and the two of them sipping champagne in first class on a transatlantic flight. As I sat with these images going through my mind, I found myself wanting her life. Her rich, easy, sophisticated life.

The woman behind the counter reached toward me with a small beige cylinder boasting interlocking Cs. "Here, if you'd like to try it." I blinked myself back to reality as she pumped a bit onto the back of my hand. I rubbed the silky flesh-toned liquid between my fingers before applying it to my cheeks, where it blended in effortlessly, obliterating any appearance of pores and giving me a sun-kissed glow even though I hadn't seen the light of day in four months. I stared at my younger, healthier-looking self in the mirror.

"Okay. I need this!" I breathed in and felt suddenly calmer. "And new eyeliner. And maybe a new matte lipstick."

Carmen was gleeful, and I felt a rush as the saleswoman swiped my credit card, realizing that $200 worth of makeup wouldn't put a dent in my bank account. I signed my name to the receipt and took the sleek small black bag with my wares from the woman behind the counter. Shopping with funds to spare was a new high. *Whoever said money couldn't buy happiness had never been to Barneys after bonus day.*

We hit the third floor next, and I wanted all the clothes I saw—and not because I recognized a single one of the names on the labels, because I didn't. But they made me feel like I'd somehow penetrated the world whose perimeter I'd been walking. I felt suddenly that I was the young woman these designers designed their clothes for. I felt that in them, I belonged in the boardrooms and marble lobbies. A designer called Proenza Schouler cut skirts that hugged my hips but allowed my thighs to breathe. Isabel Marant's fabric was so sheer and light I barely felt it on my skin. A.L.C. dresses flattered my curves in a way that made me feel like I could wear them from work to a dark dinner date. I wanted to wear everything immediately.

I wanted to show it off, strutting down Madison Avenue . . . *I needed shoes.*

On the second floor, Carmen found a pair of nude Louboutin pumps that I slipped right into.

"You need them," she insisted. "They make your legs look amazing, and they're impossibly chic."

I looked at her for a moment, my thoughts racing—*I should tell her about last night. She would have good advice. She wouldn't judge me. But can she keep it a secret? Can I trust her?*—then down at my feet.

"Oh my god, I forgot to say, Sam is so fun," she gushed. "I'm mad we didn't hang out more in law school. He's awesome."

I immediately shelved the idea of telling her about Peter and looked back down at my shoes, eager to change the subject.

"They're amazing, but I literally cannot walk. I look like I threw out my back!" I wobbled across the carpeted floor to the couch and plopped into it, momentarily contemplating whether to buy them just to sit with them on my feet.

The salesman, a tall, thin, handsome guy with highlighted cheekbones, burst out laughing.

"Try these," he said, and extended a pair of nude snakeskin Jimmy Choo pumps. "They'll look fierce."

I slipped my foot into them, and Carmen nodded approvingly. "Obsessed." She slipped a pair of funky spiked Versace pumps onto her own feet.

"Let's just see if I can walk." I stood up uncertainly and floated a few paces to the full-length mirror. I lifted my pant leg a bit higher and marveled at the definition they created in my calves, the way they elongated my legs.

I turned around eagerly. "Totally obsessed! Thank you!" I squinted at the man's name tag. "James. Thank you, James!"

James grinned as he scanned our mess of shopping bags and placed a hand on his hip.

"Either somebody died and put you in the will, or you two just robbed a bank!" He shook his head as we giggled. "Either way, you have to try the silver open-toed Jimmy Choos from this summer. They're on sale for five hundred or something stupid like that. I won't let you walk out of here without them!" He turned on his heel and disappeared.

Carmen and I sat in a mess of shoes and shoeboxes. "I want everything!" she whined.

James plopped down on the couch next to me and let out a sigh of exhaustion as I contemplated my feet in the silver Jimmy Choos.

"Girl, you better be taking everything. You think I was going back and forth so you could take one pair of shoes? No, ma'am!" I leaned back into the sofa and laughed, utterly spent from my hangover and my day of dressing and undressing. "I'm messing with you. This is the most fun I've had at work in a while. Most of these Upper East Side ladies who come in will only look at Manolos and don't ask my opinion about anything!"

"We live downtown," I said proudly. "Chelsea"—I pointed to my chest, then to Carmen's—"and Union Square."

"But seriously. What's your deal?" James prodded. "Rich daddy? Sugar daddy?"

Carmen beamed. "Putting our Christmas bonuses to good use."

"No shit! Good for you. How messed up is it that it didn't even occur to me that you were spending your own money?" James shook his head. "What do you guys do?"

"We're lawyers," I told him, sitting up straighter.

"My ex was a lawyer. Looks like I should have held on to him!" James laughed. Carmen was still scanning the shoes. "Okay, I'm taking the nude and navy Louboutins and the black Alexander Wang ankle boots," she finally said.

James looked to me.

"Just the nude Jimmy Choos for me." He cocked his head to the side.

"Fiiiiiine. And the Stuart Weitzman boots!"

He nodded and began to clean up the shoes we weren't taking. "Where do you ladies work?"

"Klasko & Fitch," I said, placing the two pairs I wanted back in their boxes.

"No shit! Small world. That's where my ex was! Last I heard, anyway. We don't speak anymore. Ever heard the name Derrick Stockton?"

***

The week after the holiday party, the office was half full, populated by those of us who weren't lucky enough to have left for the holiday yet. Those of us who remained (all the first-years, who were required to stay, plus the unlucky second-, third-, and fourth-years who had had to cancel their plans entirely and submit their holiday reimbursements to the firm) worked at a ferocious pace, compensating for the absence of their coworkers who were smart enough to have already put their out-of-office replies on and jump on planes. Come the following Friday, I still hadn't heard a word from Peter, besides a bunch of group emails about Stag River. It was December 23, and the last workday he might possibly be in the office. I tried to brainstorm any and all tasks—

deal-related, administrative, housekeeping—to keep my anxious mind occupied.

The maroon skirt I'd bought at Bergdorf's and cut the tags from that morning, on the off chance I ran into Peter, went from snug to tight after lunch. Each time the seams of the leather dug into my hips, it felt like a harsh reminder that Peter had moved on. *I'm probably too fat for him. He's grossed out by my body because his wife is so thin.* By six o'clock I'd kicked off my black pumps and begun disposing of the clutter on my desk. I tied my hair into a bun and reached for the Windex that I kept on my top shelf. I flipped my keyboard upside down and slammed it onto my desk, watching the debris of countless meals eaten there release.

"Easy! What did that poor computer ever do to you?" I jerked my head up to see Peter at my door. I didn't have time to put on my shoes or take down my hair, but I blew a stray strand out of my eye with the side of my mouth and elongated my spine. "Can I come in?" he asked casually.

I gestured to my spare chair as professionally as I could, mimicking the motion Matt had made to me on several occasions. He entered without shutting the door behind him, and a wave of disappointment swept over me despite myself. My brain flashed again to the back seat of his car, and I became acutely aware of the tiny scab forming on my breast. He looked good, despite the late hour. His tie knot was faultless, his hair flawless.

I sat in my chair as he did in his. I willed my gaze to steady, but it refused to oblige my wishes. I turned to my monitor instead.

"When are you leaving for the holiday?" I asked, looking sideways at the screen and touching my mouse to wake it up, trying to sound nonchalant.

He looked around my office. "How do you find anything in here?"

From the corner of my eye, I saw Anna crane her neck toward my office. I shot her a sideways look and she ducked back down into her cubicle, but I could feel her listening.

"It's all junk. I just finished filing everything I need," I said, loudly enough so that Anna would grow bored with our conversation. "A wise man once told me not to save paper you don't want dug up twenty years later in litigation."

Peter let out one short laugh toward the ceiling before he lowered his gaze to meet mine.

He sat still for a moment before leaning back on the two legs of his chair and smoothing his hair. I watched it fall over his eyes. It was a little game: *Does he or doesn't he? Is he just trying to figure out what I'm thinking as well?*

I looked past him at a figure in my doorway. "Hey," I said as Matt poked his head in, eyes darting between Peter and me. They nodded mechanically at one another.

"Did you send the comments out?" Matt asked me.

"About an hour ago. I cc'ed you."

"Good. I must have missed it."

"Probably not the most important email you got today. How did it go with Didier?"

"Fine. Yeah. Long day, Skip. Go home. You're going to be holding down the fort for the whole holiday, so you better get some sleep while you can. See you in the New Year." He gave us both a short wave.

"Thanks. Have a great holiday! Safe travels." I started to organize the papers on my desk as though I was preparing to go home, not stopping until I was certain he was gone.

Peter looked at me, cocked his head to the side, and relaxed his body. The green in his eyes darkened to hazel as I felt a tension creeping toward me and then flooding me.

"It's late," I said, craning my neck to stay above the rising tide.

"Yes," he said, unblinking.

I watched as Anna packed up her things and gave me a wave as she headed toward the elevator. Then I gave Peter a slight nod to indicate he should shut the door, which he did before sitting again with a smirk.

I crossed my legs and leaned back in my chair as though stretching before calling it quits for the night, looking at him as neutrally as possible, almost begging him to leave. But he didn't. Nor did he move toward me. He was smarter than I was, more controlled, more evolved. He just sat there, legs slightly spread apart, his white shirt impossibly crisp under his blazer. I bit at my lower lip and felt his eyes on my mouth. I pretended to ignore him and look at my computer for a moment before turning back to him. And still, he sat. I felt a stirring below my stomach.

"It's late," I repeated.

He just looked back at me. I stood up, my head light and my legs shaking. As I walked toward Peter, it occurred to me that my brain had just capitulated to my body. I made my way slowly around my desk and stood directly in front of him, inches away but not touching. I leaned against the desk and rested on it.

For a moment I feared that he wouldn't do anything, but he reached for me, placing one hand on each of my hips so gently he was barely touching me. His thumbs rested on my stomach, right where my skirt met my blouse, and his other fingers wrapped around to my back. I felt that he had complete control over me, that he could will me into any position or direction he liked, but he wielded this power so subtly, exploring rather than commanding, feeling rather than forcing. In that moment, I realized the futility of pretending I didn't want him.

His fingers tightened, coaxing me into him, almost in between his knees, and he finally leaned into me. I was shocked by the intimacy of it, of how I felt him need me as his cheek rested on my stomach, his arms around my waist. I reached down and touched his hair, combing through the thick strands, then pulled slightly at the electricity that passed between us.

He stood slowly—painfully slowly—his hands still at my waist, his face inching up my torso toward my mouth. His lips passed my breasts and brushed them. Everything in me came alive—too alive. I felt as though I would crumble. He came to eye level with me, and then his lips passed mine as he stood straight. I couldn't bear to look up at him just yet, but I placed my hands on his chest and slid my fingers between his shirt and his blazer. I pushed the blazer over his shoulders and down his arms. He let it fall onto the chair behind him.

I put my hands back on his chest and fingered his top button, feeling the charge from his heart course through me but still not looking up at him. I undid the next button. And then the next. I let my hand rest on the brass buckle of his belt. I stopped there, too afraid of where it might lead. He ran his hands slowly down the sides of my arms, letting them slip over my silk shirt, then started back up.

I finally looked up at him then, unable to help myself, begging him with my eyes to kiss me. He didn't obey, though he knew precisely what I wanted. He put his hands back around my waist, lifted my feet off the ground and dropped me onto my desk, where my feet dangled off the floor. I stole a glance at the closed door. He saw my gaze. He registered the fear of being caught, of the affair, of what I felt for him, in my eyes. I shut my eyes and breathed as he finally kissed me. He pulled his lips away and locked eyes with me. I gave him a short, sad smile—a silent apology to Sam, to the world, for escaping into him. He worked my skirt up to my waist and I took a sharp breath in.

He pushed my head down toward my desk so my back was flat

against my mess of papers, then dropped to his knees and put his mouth on me.

I clamped my hand over my own mouth. Just as my back relaxed out of its arch and the world formed definite shapes around me again, he was on top of me. He smiled, taking a piece of paper from next to my head, crumpling it up and shoving it in my mouth. I let the paper muffle my cry of pleasure.

We lay on my office floor, the rough industrial carpeting scratching deliciously at my back. I clasped his hand in mine, staring at our intertwined fingers. I ran the index finger from my free hand over the small lines of his scars, recalling that first meal we had had together, contentedly imagining little Peter shucking oysters, basking in the New England sun. We looked up at the ceiling and out at the other lit-up Manhattan buildings. I wondered how many other interoffice affairs were happening in those little cubes of light, and how many of them had just watched ours. He rolled away from me and began plucking up his clothes from around my office.

"I leave for Hawaii tomorrow," he said, buttoning his shirt. "Catch you in the New Year, kiddo." He winked at me. I had known he was leaving for vacation before I slept with him, but it somehow now felt like he was getting on a plane to leave me personally. I forced a smile through the mental images of him with his wife and kids on a beach in paradise. I wanted him to tell me that he'd miss me. I wanted him to tell me he didn't want to go. But he touched my chin and lifted it to him, giving me a short kiss, and left me seemingly without hesitation. I felt suddenly that I might cry.

Alone in the room, I set out to destroy all evidence of the encounter in an effort to wrest control of my emotions. I swept every piece of paper on my desk into the bin with one arm, gasping to see that the wrinkled statement of intent was now streaked with blood. I got a tissue and slipped it up my skirt to see if it was coming from me. It wasn't.

I grabbed the Windex again and scrubbed the surface of my desk until it shone, then called reception to order me a car home. On the way out, I ran to the restroom, where I brushed my teeth and spit out a bit of blood. I inspected my tongue and found a raw paper cut on the tip. I used mouthwash and relished the sting—as though it were my punishment for the transgression. As I walked through the lobby, I gave Lincoln a friendly wave, searching his expression for evidence that he was aware of my indiscretion. If he was, he didn't let on, smiling warmly as usual. I slipped into the black town car that was waiting for me.

"You're Alex Vogel?" The driver eyed me cautiously in his rearview mirror as he pulled away.

My heart sank. Did all our company drivers talk to one another? Had Peter's driver told everybody about the night at the Pierre? "Yup," I said and nodded, making brief eye contact. As we drove on, I noticed him looking back at me every couple of minutes. I attempted to move closer to the window and out of his view, but the mirror seemed to follow me.

"You're a girl."

Relax, I told myself. He's not going to do anything to you. Klasko has his name, and his employee ID, and they know you're in the car. "Yup," I said again, staring out the window. I took my phone out and unlocked it, ready to use it in case of emergency. My legs shook wildly. Was this my punishment for cheating? I had only ten blocks to go. I began to pray.

"Look, I'm just saying, as a *woman* you gotta check yourself."

"Excuse me?" I allowed my eyes to meet his.

"I didn't know you was a woman. That's just . . . I got daughters.

And I would. I think you need to look in the mirror and check yourself."

"I think you have me confused—"

"I can't wait to tell everybody back at dispatch that you're a woman. Pinky is going to FREAK out. He hates that diner run."

My mind raced. I had absolutely no idea what the man was talking about, but he seemed angry, and I didn't think it would help my case to ask any questions. I unfocused my gaze, willing the car ride to be over, and when he finally pulled up in front of my building, I exited and slammed the door without saying another word to him. I guess if that was my punishment, I thought, it wasn't so bad.

CHAPTER 17

Sam and I spent a cozy Christmas Eve with my parents in Connecticut before driving to New Jersey to spend Christmas Day with his. My parents weren't religious and cared more that we spent time with them than which day we chose. We took a midnight drive on Christmas Eve to Sam's parents' house and slept in Sam's childhood bedroom, which still had his old wooden desk with etched pen carvings on its surface and high school textbooks between ceramic baseball bookends. I woke up on Christmas morning with a kink in my neck from his extra-firm twin-size mattress but couldn't complain—he'd slept on the floor beside me rather than taking the couch in the living room.

I had insisted that Sam and I skip Christmas presents to one another that year, and we'd agreed to plan a vacation for the spring instead. I knew Sam was in no position to spend, and I had no time to shop for anything but children's gifts online. We watched his niece and nephew tear into their presents while sipping our coffee, then sat down to an elaborate brunch his mother prepared, all while still in pajamas. I peeled myself off the couch after a family viewing of *It's a Wonderful Life* and *White Christmas* and called a car to take me back to the city before they started *Miracle on 34th Street.* Sam's parents handed me a large bag of Tupperware filled with leftovers, and offered sympathetic pouts for the fact that I had to work. I encouraged Sam to stay there, but he insisted on coming back to the city with me, and I appreciated the gesture more than I'd appreciated anything he'd done in a while. We were seemingly back on the track of a normal, happy couplehood.

On the first Monday morning after Christmas, the bright chill brought with it a sense of calm. It was now clear to me that my Christmas gift to myself and everyone I loved was a self-imposed moratorium on Peter and all the partying I'd been doing. I imagined that my behavior was an addiction of sorts, and that withdrawal symptoms would subside after a few days. The universe had stopped me from doing what I couldn't quite seem to end myself. I headed into a sleepy office with a sense of peace I hadn't felt in weeks and logged on to my computer.

From: Jordan Sellar
To: Alexandra Vogel
Cc: Matt Jaskel
Subject: We're staffing you on a cool deal.

Matt and I are away through the 1st so can you man the emails? Came in through Didier he's in town working so you'll be fine.

From: Alexandra Vogel
To: Jordan Sellar
Cc: Matt Jaskel
Subject: Re: We're staffing you on a cool deal.

Great! I got this. Enjoy vacation!

Within a day or two, though, something about the bustle of the city around me and being back in the office made me think about Peter constantly. I checked my phone incessantly to see if he'd emailed me, but his messages were always about work and work exclusively. I tried to occupy my brain by working from home with Sam, cooking dinner with Sam, seeing movies with Sam, and making love to Sam. Still, I was bored with Sam. On New Year's Eve, we ordered in Chinese food and watched *Trading Places.* When we got into bed just after midnight, Sam turned to me and whispered, "This was my favorite New Year's ever," just before falling into a deep slumber, and I was struck by the terrifying thought that this would be every New Year's Eve for the rest of my life. I got out of bed, brought my laptop into the living room, and stayed up till three doing all the busywork I had neglected since the Winter Ball.

Come the second day of January, Jordan emailed me that I was billing at the top of my class—fifty-five hours in the past week, and that was during the slowest time of the year. I could barely keep all my deals straight; I was on four active matters with slated closing dates within a month of one another. The office had buzzed back to life seemingly in an instant. Whatever sense of Zen my colleagues had found on their beach or mountain escapes instantly vaporized when they returned to the cold, wet New York winter. I still hadn't heard anything from Peter that wasn't about work. *He's only been back in the office one day,* I reminded myself every time I refreshed my in-box.

I shuffled frantically through the binders and papers on my desk to find my ringing office phone, and grabbed the receiver just before the call went to voice mail.

"Hi!" I said, out of breath.

"Let's do the call in my office. Matt is home for the night, but he'll dial in," Jordan said with no preamble. He and I had fallen back into our comfortable routine immediately, speaking at least ten times a day, and I kept taking care of his requests long before he ever thought to check in. I actually felt myself getting better and better at my job, having handled everything on various deals myself while my colleagues were on vacation.

"Yup," I said and hung up.

I looked at the clock in the lower right-hand corner of my computer screen. It was just past ten. I touched my cell phone to bring it to life, and the screen filled with the calls and texts I had missed from my parents and Sam. I panicked momentarily that there was an emergency, but after glancing briefly over the emoticons and how-are-yous, I opted to open Spotify instead. But I couldn't focus. My legs were shaking under my desk. I'd started to feel confined, almost suffocated, so I got up and made my way to the pantry, almost crashing into Nancy, who was exiting with a tea.

"Oh my god! I'm so sorry," she said, meeting my eyes sheepishly, clearly embarrassed about more than our near collision. "So, so sorry." I noted her sheer pink blouse with white tank. Nancy was dressing much better these days, apparently taking a note from those around her.

"No worries." I brushed past her, and I could feel her watching me as I grabbed a soda from the fridge. *She said some terrible things. You should call her out, make her feel even worse. No. Be the bigger person.* "Glad you didn't spill on yourself. That top is too cute to ruin," I called over my shoulder.

I returned to my office, opened my soda, and bopped my head to my playlist as I checked the clock and opened *Below the Belt*, the site Carmen had introduced me to, to catch up on the latest gossip in BigLaw. I perused the headlines: "Inebriated Davis & Gilroy Associate Topples Display at MOMA Gala," "Record-High Bonuses Rumored This Christmas," "Is BigLaw Going the Way of the Dodo?"

I looked back at my clock. Only three minutes had passed since I had last checked it. I turned my music off and tried to breathe to steady the thudding in my chest. My office felt suddenly tiny, as though the walls were slowly closing in on me, and I suddenly needed to get out. I dialed Derrick's extension, hoping he was free for a walk around the block.

No answer.

I texted him.

Alex: You around? Need a break.

Derrick: Litigation settled today so hopped on a flight to Vegas. Back tomorrow.

Who goes to Vegas for a night? I yanked at the collar of my shirt. Was this claustrophobia?

Was that even possible, given the view of the entirety of downtown Manhattan outside my window?

There were still twenty-three minutes before our status call. Antsy, I walked into the hallway, where a couple of still-lit offices and the hum of a vacuum from somewhere behind me were the only evidence of life in the building. My eye caught on the reflective sign hanging from the ceiling of a stick figure taking a flight of stairs, and it gave me an idea. I went back to my office, kicked off my heels, and laced up the nearly unused gym shoes I kept under my desk. I returned to the stairwell, opened the door, and breathed in the musk of dusty, industrial concrete, then hiked up my skirt and started to climb slowly, savoring the tightening in my calves and feeling my thighs start to burn from the rare physical exertion.

And then I heard a soft whimper, and stopped short. I couldn't hear anything but silence for a moment, yet I felt another presence in the stairwell, and then I registered another faint feminine whine. I silently continued upward, wondering if I should offer comfort to a colleague who was clearly having a tough time, or just retreat and leave her in peace.

Then I heard a grunt.

A distinctly male grunt.

I instinctively covered my mouth and lowered myself to sit on a step. I glided slowly upward using both my hands and feet, craning my neck slightly, too curious not to look but terrified I'd spot somebody who I definitely did not want to see me. What if it was Mike Baccard? Or any partner? He'd never be able to look me in the eye again. My career would be over! But I couldn't help myself. I crawled one step higher, and one body came into view, long blond hair on a head bobbing back and forth at the waist level of a man who was standing, his head thankfully just out of range, his white button-down untucked, his navy pinstripe jacket still on. His pants, I imagined, lay crumpled around his ankles. I watched for longer than I should have. I knew it was somehow depraved, but I couldn't tear myself away. I craned my neck again, bringing the girl's gossamer pink shirt further into view. Nancy!

I retreated back down the stairs as quietly as I could, but I dropped my phone on the concrete. A sound like china plates shattering on a restaurant floor echoed off the unforgiving surface. I stood frozen for a moment, and felt the two bodies above me tense. There was whispering. And then movement. I was certain they'd run away up the stairs, but I heard them thudding down them instead. I snapped into action, grabbing my phone and darting out of the door on the first landing I came to. I let the door close behind me, then leaned back against it for a moment, shutting my eyes. It occurred to me then that they needed to know who I was so that they could determine just how much trouble they would be in with the firm, if I was somebody who would talk. They might still be following me.

I sprinted to the elevator bank and pressed the down button frantically, then dove into the elevator. But before the doors could close all the way, Nancy appeared on the other side. We stared at each other, dumbfounded, as the steel doors sealed me in and shoved me downward. I looked up at the camera in the corner of the elevator. Lincoln must be getting quite the show tonight.

Jordan was going to find it absolutely hilarious that annoying, judgmental little Nancy was giving head in a dirty stairwell. As I walked to his office, I practiced how I'd begin the story, but when I arrived, Jordan looked stressed. He beckoned me in impatiently and immediately dialed the conference line. Hold music came on. I wiped the shit-eating grin from my face. Something must have gone south with the deal. Shit.

He opened his mouth to speak just as the voice on the line announced that the conference would begin.

Despite his seeming anxiety, the call was going according to script—which I'd learned was the absolute best-case scenario in the legal world. We had already signed up the deal, and everybody had agreed to the terms, but we had bifurcated closing, meaning that all that needed to happen was for the funds to transfer from the buyer's account to the seller's—save our $2 million worth of legal fees, of course. The closing call was scheduled for nine tomorrow morning, and with any luck, I could be home in bed by eleven a.m.

As we were wrapping up, the opposing counsel said he had one more thing to add. "Lastly, we need to disclose that there appears to have been a small breach by the buyer in the confidentiality agreement. The news of the asset purchase seems to have been announced at the annual shareholders meeting."

I lifted my head up from my pad and turned wide-eyed to Jordan. I opened my mouth to whisper a question, and he silenced me with a quick shake of his head.

"Jordan?" the opposing counsel asked. "Did I lose you?"

"No," he said.

"Look, Jordan, I don't think there is actually any effect on the company, or—" He stopped himself. "It could have been an agreement only for the seller to sign to begin with. There was no reason for the buyer to remain hush-hush. But I will have all answers by nine a.m."

Jordan sat there without speaking.

"I know this could potentially unravel the deal, but it won't," the opposing counsel stammered, filling the silence.

Matt's voice came through the phone. "That's for our client to say, not yours, John." Jordan and I breathed a sigh of relief. "And going forward, I'd appreciate you not waiting until the end of a call to tell us something that could kill the deal. It's irrelevant whether the confidentiality agreement could have been one-sided. It is, in fact, reciprocal. We'll get back to you once we confer with our client." There was a beep, and the automated voice let us know Matt had left the conference, so we hung up, too.

"I have to call Didier and tell him what's going on," Jordan said. "But I need to know all scenarios. Call Taylor now and have them run valuations now and at nine in the morning based on market rumors affecting revenue by fifteen percent going forward. I need an answer by two a.m." He glanced at his open door to dismiss me. "I'm going to circle back with Matt. It's going to be a long night."

I nodded, and was almost out the door when he spoke again.

"Alex." I turned around to see him staring at me. "Did you see how I kept my mouth shut on that call?" I gave a hesitant nod. "It's important to know when not to speak."

I nodded again, more than slightly confused. Did I speak too much on client calls?

"Am I being clear?"

He had never taken this particular tone with me—condescending and formal—and it infuriated me. I looked from his white shirt to his navy pinstripe suit jacket. I felt my eyes widen despite my attempt to maintain a poker face. I felt my gaze drift down to his wedding ring as he clasped his hands together, and then I locked eyes with him and nodded. My heart sank as I realized that the possibility that he and Nancy had gotten together for the first time tonight was remote at best.

"I didn't see any . . . yes. Clear." I forced my rubbery legs out of his office, then returned to my desk and tried to figure out how I had missed what had been happening right in front of my face.

"Hello?" I heard Taylor from National's voice through the receiver before realizing that I had called his cell.

"Hey. It's Alex from Klasko. Did I wake you?"

"I wish. I'm actually still in the office. What's up?"

"DuVont disclosed the asset sale at their shareholder meeting today," I told him.

"Fuck. It's always the ones you file as 'closed' in your brain." He sounded calm enough, though, I noted with relief.

"Yeah, so we need to rerun the valuations by one a.m." I gave myself an hour cushion in case he was late getting me the projections. "Two scenarios . . ."

I slept in the office the next two nights, and we ended up closing the deal on Friday morning instead of Wednesday. The moment we did, there was a flurry of emails from National thanking our team for its diligence and efficiency in the face of complications, and I replied-all with a quick email telling them they were my favorite client before hopping in a Quality car home. As soon as I was in the car, I recalled my last bizarre encounter and stiffened. My eyes went to the rearview mirror, where I was relieved to see an unfamiliar face. He barely looked back at me as he started down Fifth Avenue.

***

I returned to the office on Monday after a weekend of sleep, having decided I'd reach out to Jordan first thing and smooth over any awkwardness, letting him know that as far as I was concerned, the incident never happened. Little did he know, I was in no position to judge. Before I could dial his number, though, he called me.

"Hey." I tried to sound nonchalant, but overshot a bit.

"Hey, Alex."

Why was he using my real name? He hadn't called me anything but Skippy in months.

"Matt just got off the phone with the National crew. They are so happy with how the deal turned out and the job we did for them that they want to celebrate with a night out. Tonight is the only night they can do in the next few weeks. We're going to take them for dinner at The Grill. So . . . yeah . . . you're coming."

"Okay!" I said, feeling the tension through the phone and wondering for a moment whether I should say something about the stairwell to try to dispel it before thinking better of the idea. "Sounds fun!"

"K, bye." He hung up, and I winced at his abruptness.

I pulled up the collar of my shirt to just below my eyes, as if it could hide me from the awkwardness I felt, then popped my head back out and dialed his number.

"Hello?" He sounded confused.

"Hey. So, do you want to meet me at the bar in The Grill at like seven and grab a drink before we meet up with everybody else?" I squinted as I waited for his response, imagining that it was exactly how it must feel to ask somebody out on a date.

"Yeah." He sounded relieved. "Yeah, I would. Good call, Skip."

Dreading a sober walk with Jordan over to The Grill, I told him I needed to run a quick errand and would meet him there. When he arrived, I was already at the bar sipping a martini. I didn't know how to greet him, but he plunked himself down on the stool next to mine and ordered a drink before even saying hello. We made small talk about his Christmas vacation until the bartender finally gave him his scotch neat.

I waited until he took his first sip. "What happened never happened as far as I'm concerned," I began. "We never need to talk about it."

Jordan nodded slowly and then looked up at me. "But what if . . ." He paused. "*Can* we talk about it?" I nodded gently. "It's happened three times. But now it's over."

"That's good. I mean, that it's over. Not that it happened," I stammered, and we both smiled at my nervous chatter.

"But she still calls me like . . . all the time. It's a mess. Look, I know I never should have done it. But when it first happened, I hadn't slept with my wife in like five months. I was losing my mind."

I coughed as I took a sip of vodka. "Wow. I mean . . . why?"

"She wants a baby. I want to make partner first. She wouldn't use protection. It turned into a fight every time we were about to have sex, so we just stopped having it. And stopped talking about babies. And finally, stopped talking. And then we were just—"

"Roommates," I finished his sentence, wondering if Sam and I would still be sleeping together if my guilty conscience wasn't driving me toward it.

"Roommates," Jordan confirmed. "But I love her. So much. And I don't know why I feel the need to wait to bring a kid into the world until I'm fully secure. Maybe because I grew up with no money and around people with money. And I still wake up sweating, feeling like somebody could take it away any second."

He took a long sip of his scotch, leaving only a thin amber layer at the base of his glass. "I'm a shitty person."

"You're not." I meant it. I was certain of it. "If you want to be with your wife, continue to ignore Nancy. She'll leave you alone eventually. Tell your wife you want to make it work. She doesn't want a divorce. She wants a baby. And it sounds like you do, too. You can figure it out. Okay?"

He nodded.

"Everybody will be here soon. Are you good? Should we blow everybody off?"

"I'm good. I just want to get really drunk right now."

"I'm in!" I signaled to the bartender for the bill, then grabbed it before Jordan had a chance. "My treat."

Jordan watched me sign my name, then took the pen from me and added three letters after my signature.

"Expense this. You're in the club now," he said with a smile.

I rolled my eyes. "You don't need to write 'esquire' to expense something. Accounting knows we're all lawyers."

"No. But if you write 'est,' they'll know that you work for Matt, and you will never, ever get questioned about an expense, no matter how big, and you'll get the money in your checking account within forty-eight hours. That's a *t*, by the way, not a *q*." He pointed at the last letter. "Seriously, I mean, don't test the boundaries, but I once took five clients to Vegas for a night to watch a fight. It cost about six grand a person, all in. The money was back in my account before we landed the next morning."

"What does 'est' stand for?"

"The partner Matt used to work for invented it like forty years ago. Just means we work the hard*est* and long*est* and we should be entitled to the b*est* when we go out. It's corny, but it's tradition."

Even beyond the Miami invitation, and the steady staffing on their deals, this was the moment when I felt completely accepted into their group. Already a little buzzed, I threw my arms around Jordan's neck, completely unconcerned with the propriety of the gesture.

He patted me on the back. "Easy, Skip. Let's go get me drunk."

"Drunk*est*," I said with a wink.

The morning light filtered into the bedroom, even though I'd asked Sam to install blackout shades months ago, rousing me painfully from sleep. I winced before I even opened my eyes and then popped them open.

Sam stirred slightly next to me, but I lay perfectly still, my eyes glued to the ceiling, for a few moments before starting my day, a trick I had learned to help combat a hangover.

"What's going on in there?" Sam asked as I felt him watching me.

"Just thinking," I said.

"About what?"

My hangover. My colleague's adulterous relationship. How I'm pathetically obsessed with a man I cheated on you with, who clearly has forgotten I'm alive. "That my head hurts," I said, and laughed.

"Well, maybe you should drink less." He turned away from me and pulled up the covers. He'd seemed annoyed after our time together over Christmas had come to an end, but it wasn't realistic that I could continue working from home, cooking dinner every night, and sleeping with him more than usual to try to deflect my guilt.

"It has nothing to do with how much I drink," I snapped. "It has to do with the fact that I don't sleep because the ONE thing I have asked you to do around our apartment has not been done!"

He turned back to me. "What are you talking about?"

"I asked you to install blackout shades months ago!" How could he not find the time to do that? What did he even do all day?

"You mentioned once, at brunch, that we should research brands of blackout shades. That was you asking me to order them and hire somebody to install them?" Sam sat up in bed. "Maybe if you stopped waking up so hungover, you could sleep through the slightest bit of sunlight creeping through."

He threw off the covers, slid out of bed, and stalked into the bathroom.

"I don't have a headache because I'm hungover!" As I stared up at the ceiling, though, I knew he was right. I shut my eyes, trying to escape the feeling that I was spinning out of control.

PART V

BREAKUP

The termination of a deal without closing; typically, a fee is paid by the party failing to follow through with agreed-upon closing terms.

Q. You stated earlier that the nonsexual relationships you described with colleagues evolved from your initial friendly encounters. How, when, and why did these relationships change?

A. Should I focus on my relationship with Gary Kaplan?

Q. No, we'd like to hear a fuller account of the weeks before you matched with a practice group.

CHAPTER 18

I sat cross-legged on the plush beige textured carpet in my room at the Beverly Hills Hotel, refolding the clothes from my suitcase and putting them in drawers. Carmen lay belly-down on my bed, her elbows pressing into the luxurious mattress as she typed on her phone. Her nails were painted a vibrant pink, and her hair was glossy and full.

"You are looking extra good these days at work, miss," I told her. She stopped typing and looked over at me, her head cocked to the side, looking slightly confused. "Thank you."

I took a beat before continuing.

"Are you like . . . seeing somebody at work? Just wondering what's inspiring you to look so hot lately."

She blinked twice, gave me a small smile, and looked away. "Nope," she said, then looked down at her screen and then back at me. "Leave me alone!" she said, laughing, before averting her eyes yet again.

"Shaaaaady," I sang.

Carmen moved her phone closer to her face. "Derrick missed his flight. He only landed an hour ago." I glanced at the agenda to see that we had three hours before our welcome meeting. He wouldn't miss anything. "He's really out of control these days."

"Really? How do you know?"

She ignored me. Derrick had been looking increasingly worn since starting work, though it was no surprise, given that he'd assumed the role of client entertainer and seemed to be out with clients at least four nights a week. Jordan had told me a rumor that he was on track to have the largest client development spend at the firm that year, which was absolutely unheard of and totally inappropriate at our level.

"How do you know about Derrick?" I pressed.

"Information just comes to me," she said. "Like with Derrick's ex in Bergdorf's. Like, what are the chances that we met that guy?"

"You didn't tell anybody about that, right? About Derrick being gay?" I prodded, hoping that word of the private life he kept very close to the vest hadn't slipped out and somehow caused him to unravel.

"No way. Information is power, but only if not everybody has it," she said dismissively, eyes still on her phone. I stared at the creature before me, alarmed by her Machiavellian comment, but opted to appreciate her rare display of transparency rather than analyze what it said about her. She finally looked up. "Kevin was just on his way to the pool and saw Derrick checking in. He was upgrading to the presidential suite."

I knew this was completely out of line for him to do, but I couldn't help but be curious. "I want to see the suite! Should I text Derrick to see if we can stop by?"

"Kevin just said they're all at the pool. Let's go!"

"You go," I insisted, turning to my closet. "I didn't bring a suit." Vivienne's words echoed in my head: *Don't wear a bikini.*

"You can borrow one of mine," Carmen offered.

"Nah, thanks though. But I'll get a drink and put my feet in."

As we approached the crowded pool, it was obvious who the Klasko first-years were. It was almost comforting to see that first-years from all the offices around the world looked similarly stressed-out and sleep-deprived, in stark contrast to the tanned and beautiful tourists in the pool. Kevin introduced us to three male associates from LA, who stood in the pool with their elbows resting on the ledge, typing furiously into their phones, two women from Hamburg, and another from our Tokyo office. Ten or so others smiled at us with no introduction.

I took a seat on a lounge chair while Carmen pulled off her gauzy cover-up. Everybody stared at her. The LA boys stopped typing. Her breasts spilled out to the sides of her tiny black bikini top before she submerged them underwater, at which point the guys turned back to their phones.

Derrick made his way over to me. "You're begging to get tossed in," he said, eyeing my shorts and T-shirt.

"You wouldn't dare." I narrowed my eyes at him. Though he was smiling, there was something different about him, a darkness in his mood. I held my hand up to the glare of the sun to see him more clearly, but he turned to a waitress, ordered another drink, and dove into the water.

"This firm was founded in 1918 on the principles that unparalleled excellence and creative thought are paramount in the practice of law . . ." At our introductory meeting in the late afternoon, a young black female partner who was head of Klasko's Diversity Initiative spoke passionately while a photograph of the two dead white male founders was projected onto the screen behind her. I looked around the dark hotel ballroom, which was filled with roughly four hundred first-year associates trying to stay awake. One of the double doors in the back of the room opened. Derrick sauntered in and took the only free seat, which happened to be at my table. He didn't acknowledge me, his eyes never leaving the screen.

"Twenty-seven percent of our associates are diverse." I looked back at the projection and attempted to imagine the feeling of being in the numerator of the screen boasting our diversity ratio.

The next slide popped up, featuring a map of the world. The green areas were financial centers, both established and potential, and we had office locations in each of them.

"We here at Klasko & Fitch believe very strongly that in order to be a truly global firm, seamlessly servicing our clients across jurisdictions, we must know one another. I'm proud to report that all three hundred and eighty-nine of our first-year associates from our thirty-seven offices across the globe are here today. You are what we are investing in. You are our future. Please take time to get to know . . ."

I looked at the tall blond man next to me. His name tag indicated that he was Cedric Schmidt from our Hamburg office, and that he was one of eight siblings. I looked down at my own: "Alexandra Vogel, New York Office, Holder of the Girls' World Junior Record in both the 50 Freestyle and 400 Freestyle from 2009 to 2019." I blushed, thinking how boastful the "fun fact" I'd given to HR a few weeks ago must seem to Cedric from Hamburg.

"Cool!" he whispered in a strong German accent as he leaned into me.

When the screen went blank, the presenter wrapped up. "Please enjoy your free time for the next two hours. Dinner will be at seven thirty right back in this room. Jeans are more than acceptable. At nine thirty, buses will leave for bumper cars if you'd like to go. And remember, try not to work too much." Everybody laughed politely. On cue, the six waiters standing in the back of the ballroom swung the doors open in unison to reveal a full bar waiting for us just outside, and we all erupted into applause.

I grabbed two beers and headed toward my room to wait for Jordan to call me to discuss edits to the merger agreement draft I had sent him. As soon as I slipped away from the crowd at the bar and into the lobby, I spotted a blond woman in an armchair, strikingly beautiful though heavily made up. *Hooker or socialite?* She sat with her legs crossed, her legs so long that her knees nearly reached to her chest. *Socialite.* Her strappy heels looked worn. Her hair changed texture just below her neckline. *Hooker.* The handle of her Chanel bag was carefully hung from her chair arm. *Socialite. If it's real.*

As I waited at the elevator bank, I tried not to stare.

"Alex!"

Vivienne White had exited an elevator and paused in front of me, radiating a warmth I had never gotten from her in New York. The tan, silver-haired man with her stopped as well.

"Hi! I didn't realize you'd be here. So good to see you," I said as I extended my hand.

"I'm doing your ethics presentation tomorrow with George here. George, this is my all-too-neglected associate mentee, Alex Vogel. She's quickly becoming a rock star of the M&A group without any help from me, though, so don't feel too bad for her. Alex, George Jacobson."

Managing partner of our Washington, DC, office. Big deal.

George Jacobson shook my hand firmly, and I tried to maintain eye contact, but I was distracted again by the long-legged woman in the lobby. Was that Derrick talking to her now? Can't be . . .

"Pleasure." I looked again at George and then back over his shoulder.

That was Derrick. He was taking out his wallet. What was he . . .

"I'm horrible. No more canceling from me, Alex," Vivienne said, a little too sweetly. "I'll see you tomorrow, but we need to have a proper lunch when I get back."

I nodded and tried to focus, but I couldn't keep my eyes off Derrick. Vivienne turned to see where I was looking.

"Oh my gosh. Is that a prostitute?" she asked, giggling as she covered her mouth.

"For sure," George confirmed. "And in broad daylight."

My heart beat more quickly. "No, I don't think so," I said, shaking my head vigorously.

"Isn't that one of our associates with her?" Vivienne asked, suddenly serious.

"I'm not . . . I don't know," I stammered.

"That's a Klasko name tag on him!" George said.

I was saved by the ding of another elevator arriving. "Looking forward to the presentation!" I yelled after them as the doors closed me in.

I sat in my hotel room and stared at my blank computer screen. Had I just gotten Derrick into trouble? Would they even say anything to him? I bet they wouldn't. It didn't even make any sense that he'd be with a female prostitute. Wasn't he gay?

The trill of my hotel room phone sent me flying out of my seat in terror. "Hello?"

"Hey, Skip. How is it?" I could hear Jordan flipping through papers on his desk. "Do you have my markup in front of you?"

Shit shit shit. If I hadn't been staring, they would have never noticed Derrick. I scrolled past an email from Carmen telling me to call her and one from Kevin about where they'd be drinking after dinner, and opened the email with Jordan's markup. "Got it."

Turning changes took longer than I had expected, and by ten I noted with relief that I had missed an awkward associates' dinner. I ordered room service.

At midnight I finally got around to calling Carmen, who answered after one ring and with no preamble. "Where have you BEEN? Derrick got caught with hookers and coke!"

"What? What happened?!"

"I mean, he had hookers and coke in his hotel room! George Jacobson from the DC office knocked on his door and apparently saw everything."

"They were in his room? Multiple? Female? How do you know? Is he in jail?"

"No, he's not in jail! He's a Klasko associate. Could you even imagine the field day the press would have if he went to jail?"

"Seriously, how do you know all this?"

"One of the girls from the Houston office got upgraded to the suite floor, in the room next to his. She stuck her head out of her door and heard the whole thing go down. And yes. Female hookers. That's the weirdest part."

"Jesus!" I closed my eyes. "What do you think is going to happen?"

"I have no fucking idea! But seriously, you miss all the good scandals by working too much, Alex."

I closed my eyes, guilt draining the energy from my body. *I knew something was going on with him.*

"Questions?" Vivienne asked at the end of the last slide of her ethics presentation. Hands shot up. I'd searched the crowd for Derrick when I arrived, but hadn't seen him then, and I didn't see any sign of him now. I hadn't yet heard any word as to his fate, and I didn't want to reach out and embarrass him. I looked at my phone, refreshed my in-box again, and immediately spotted an email from Peter.

From: Peter Dunn
To: Alexandra Vogel
Subject: How is Academy?

From: Alexandra Vogel
To: Peter Dunn
Subject: Re: How is Academy?

More interesting than I thought it would be. Let's leave it at that.

From: Peter Dunn
To: Alexandra Vogel
Subject: Re: How is Academy?

Always is, kiddo. When will you be back?

From: Alexandra Vogel
To: Peter Dunn
Subject: Re: How is Academy?

Tonight!

From: Peter Dunn
To: Alexandra Vogel
Subject: Re: How is Academy?

That's the best news I've heard this month. We miss you!

I stared at my phone and couldn't keep the grin from spreading across my face. Feeling charitable, I finally opened the email from my parents that I had allowed to linger in my in-box for the past twenty-four hours, and agreed to meet them for dinner on the day I got back from LA. I knew they were anxious to see me, having both remarked at Christmas that I looked thin and tired. As soon as I hit send, I regretted it.

CHAPTER 19

“Hi!” I kissed my mother’s cheek outside the entrance to L’Artusi in the West Village. She lingered close to me, inhaling my scent the way she always did. “Where’s Dad?” I asked, looking past her.

“He’s not coming.”

“Oh no! Why?” I struggled to swallow as my mouth dried out. I needed my father’s hospital stories and corny jokes as a buffer from my mother’s interrogation.

“Because I asked him not to,” she said, and patted my shoulder gingerly. “I thought we could have some girl talk.”

Crap.

I followed the hostess robotically to our table, feeling that I was somehow in trouble.

“How are you?” she asked as soon as we sat, looking like she was expecting me to break down right there at the dinner table.

I met her gaze, but no words would come. Instead, I gulped down my water. Why did I always feel sad when my mom thinks I might be sad?

“Working too much. Can we get wine?” I scanned the list of bottles without registering any of them.

“Yes!” she said. “Wine is a great idea.”

I ordered a bottle of cabernet, and all of a sudden I had the sense of occupying a different role in the universe than I had even a few months before—an adult on equal footing with my mother. When the waiter returned to open the wine with a flourish and pour a taste, I swirled it in the glass and smelled it and took a sip. I thought for a moment. And another.

“I’m sorry, I think it’s off,” I said politely, as my mother’s eyes widened. “Can we try something similar?”

"Miss, I just opened it," the waiter said, stating the obvious.

"Maybe you could just have the sommelier come over," I said before my mother had a chance to speak. The waiter looked annoyed but turned on his heel obediently.

"Alexandra, that's a perfectly good seventy-five-dollar bottle of wine. When they ask you to taste it, they don't expect you to send it back." Her voice grated on my eardrums.

"It wasn't. And they do if it's not actually perfectly good." I put my hands to my temples, attempting to soothe the headache that had just come on.

"Are you okay?" My mother eyed me apprehensively.

I looked up at her. I don't know what it was about my parents' concern for me, but it always forced me to become somebody who warranted it. Their sympathy made me depressed, their worry made me anxious.

I sat up and forced cheeriness into my voice. "Just jet-lagged, I think."

"You're so thin. And—"

I was saved by the arrival of the sommelier.

"Bonsoir, mademoiselle," he said with a slight bow.

"Bonsoir, monsieur. I think this wine is off."

I saw him size me up, noticing my Alexander Wang boots, and soften. He took the glass he was holding and poured himself a bit. He smelled and paused and scowled.

"Of course it is, *chérie,*" he said, shaking his head, then shot a scornful look at the waiter. "If it's cabernet you're after, I have just the one. A real gem. And I'll charge you the price of this bottle. Which is just passable when it's at its best."

I looked back at my mother, who studied me as though I were a stranger, but I felt somehow steadier in my position from having been right about the wine.

"I'm so glad we did this. I never see you as just us," I said, breaking the silence.

"I know, me too. Tell me what's going on. How's Sam?" She leaned in as though I was about to tell her a secret.

I inhaled sharply. "He's good! He's the same! We're the same!" I raised my voice, trying to reassure her, but I detected a slump in her shoulders. Suddenly the image of the engagement ring surrounded by black velvet burst into my mind, and I felt nauseated. I hadn't thought about it in so long. Thank god work had been so busy.

"Oh honey. What's wrong?"

"Nothing! Is it hot in here?" I swatted at the air around my face.

"Well, if nothing's wrong, why are you 'the same'?" she asked, using air quotes. I hated when she used air quotes.

"We've always been happy. Why would being the same be bad?"

"Alexandra, Sam has spoken to your father and I about . . . wanting to move forward. Are you ready for that?"

"Your father and me," I muttered, staring down at the menu without focusing. Of course she knew the correct grammar. I didn't know why I felt the need to correct her. I felt her frustration emanating from her intertwined fingers, but the arrival of our wine was a helpful distraction.

I nodded as the sommelier moved his lips and I pretended to take note of the label. I thought for a moment about telling her I wanted to get another year at Klasko under my belt before I got engaged. Who knows, maybe that was the truth. It occurred to me that if I told her everything I was feeling, she might be able to snap me out of whatever was keeping me from being excited about marrying Sam. She could help me to stop whatever itch I'd been scratching when I slept with Peter.

I stuck my nose in the glass and inhaled.

"Is that asparagus?" I asked. The sommelier almost clapped, chatting so gleefully about the grapes and the fog that year that I bought myself another four minutes of mindless chatter before facing my mother.

When we were left alone, we clinked our glasses, and I thought I saw a look of pride in her eye at the sophisticated adult daughter.

"I taste asparagus for sure," she said after taking a sip. I inwardly sighed. She didn't taste asparagus, I would hope. She probably didn't even smell it. I suddenly felt an enormous gulf between us. It seemed like the life she had given me had spun off in a direction so different from her own that we had irreparably diverged. I decided against telling her what was going on with Sam and with Peter. What advice could she offer me, anyway?

"What is it, Bunny?" she said.

I opened my mouth but couldn't quite bring myself to speak as the tightness in my chest migrated upward to my nose. I wavered for a second, and then opted to change course.

"My life with Sam isn't exciting anymore. I don't think it's the life I want forever," I said softly.

"That's just intimacy, honey," she said with a slightly dismissive but knowing smile.

"It's boring," I said, staring at the table. "But you're right. Boring is part of intimacy. I'm not sure I want to get married. Ever."

I looked up, expecting to see disappointment on her face, but she just laughed. "That's just cold feet. Of course you want to get married."

"No, Mom. I think I'm just not the marrying kind. I don't really know what kind of person I am yet." My words were raw, the kind that escape your lips in a rare and precious moment. And they can really knock the wind out of you when you hear them aloud. I fought back tears.

"Alexandra, you act like a relationship owes you something. Like it's supposed to make you whole or better or more fulfilled or excited without working on it. You want a perfect marriage to appear the way you can order delivery for dinner—like it's sitting there waiting for somebody to bring it to you in neat packaging. It's not a thing you can order, it's a fluid state. A process."

I stared at her. "You're not even listening to me! I don't want to be served marriage at all! I want Aspen for the weekend and a vacation home and good wine! Maybe if I want kids down the line, I'll think about it. But right now, the idea of wedding rings and wedding plans and suburbs really doesn't appeal to me."

My mother straightened her spine against the back of her chair. "Do you not think we gave you a good life growing up?"

"Mom, this isn't about you. I promise."

My mother blamed herself for anything that ever went wrong in my life, and as a result, anything that went wrong in my life became about her. When I was young, she used to apologize for my asthma and my slight scoliosis, telling me she was sorry she "made" me that way. But my problems were harder to solve now, and I had no patience for this. I scratched at my forearm as I planned an exit strategy from this topic of conversation. "I do love Sam. I guess you might be right. It's probably cold feet. I just need time."

As I took a long drink of wine and watched her posture relax, I felt a hollowness in the pit of my stomach, an oblong shape with round edges that was so dark it was almost black.

***

On Friday the entire office vibrated with the rumor that Derrick had just gotten fired for his indiscretion at First-Year Academy, the stories spinning so fast it was impossible to tell fact from fiction.

I heard he got arrested in the hotel.

He had a huge party in his room with hookers and blow.

He's dating a stripper.

The firm is freaking out because he was their star black associate.

He's cleaning out his office right this second.

I didn't know what had precipitated his downward spiral, but I felt a blinding guilt for not sitting down with him earlier to figure it out, as well as for my role in his being caught. I shot him a quick note.

From: Alexandra Vogel
To: Derrick Stockton
Subject: Can I stop by?

From: KLASKO TECHNOLOGY SUPPORT
To: Alexandra Vogel
Subject: ERROR: Invalid email address

ERROR1209724 - derrick.stockton@klasko.com is not a valid email address

I typed his name into our firm database, only to find that his picture was no longer up on the website. It didn't surprise me that an institution as powerful as Klasko had a way of making people who reflected poorly upon the institution vanish into thin air. I opened my iPhone to send him a Facebook message but couldn't find any trace of his account. He must be mortified, I thought. He must want to disappear. I got up out of my chair and marched down the hallway. Maybe I could catch him before he left the building.

When I arrived at his office, the door was half open, but he wasn't alone. Lincoln stood watching him, arms folded and his expression stoic and tight-lipped. They both looked up as I entered.

"Hi," I said softly, and turned to Lincoln. "Um, can I have a moment with Derrick?"

"Afraid not," he said apologetically.

It took me a moment to realize that he wasn't joking. Derrick had stopped packing up the cardboard box on his desk and was looking at me expectantly.

"Can we sit a minute?" I asked Lincoln. He thought for a moment and nodded, as though making a concession. I took a seat in his guest chair.

"I just wanted to come by . . . I just wanted to say . . . I'm sorry this happened."

Derrick took the seat opposite mine. "Thanks. You're the only person who's come by." He watched me for a moment, then arched his spine backward, as though he had a pain in his rib. "I totally deserve this. I think sometimes I get so sick of this place treating me differently, even if it's better, because I'm black. I was sick of it. It's like being a show pony. I guess I just got carried away with testing the boundaries."

I paused before answering that. "I think I sometimes feel just a fraction of that as a woman." I didn't want him to think I was pretending to know exactly how he felt, or experiencing it at the same level. But I did feel some of it. And honestly, most of the time I was grateful for it. "I'll miss you. Can we stay in touch?"

Derrick nodded at me and then looked at Lincoln, as though weighing his next words. "Watch out for yourself here, Alex. You're one of the good ones."

I hugged him goodbye and headed back to my office, not realizing until I settled into my chair to start drafting a term sheet that Derrick had not given me his new number.

***

I spoke quickly as I watched Harold Gottlieb, my fellow first-year associate, scribble down every word I said. I should have been kind and spoken more slowly, but part of me took a twisted pleasure in challenging him. Harold had worked for the tax group for his first five months, and had only recently decided he wanted to make the switch to M&A, so Jordan and Matt had staffed him on a deal with me, and put me in the unusual position of supervising a peer.

Harold combed through his curly red hair and scanned the room, looking everywhere in my office except at me—he was awkward and unsure of himself. He was put together, though—his suit was perfectly tailored, and he wore a tie clip, which I thought gave him a charming and old-fashioned touch of flair—except for his fingernails, which he'd bitten down so far that they were simply small strips of keratin with bloodied borders, the equivalent of webbed feet paddling frantically below a glassy surface.

"I can never find your attachments. You attach them way at the bottom of the chain. It's like a treasure hunt," I said, scrolling down. Harold parted his lips to apologize, but I cut him off. I was trying to remember what it was like not to know anything, but annoyance trumped my sense of empathy. "So, after you read the minutes, you and I—" My phone rang. *Jordan.* I heard Anna pick it up. "—you and I can sit down and review any of the flags you raised on stock—"

I half heard Anna saying ". . . in with an associate. I'll give her the message." An instant message popped up on my screen.

JORDAN SELLAR: NEED YOU ASAP!!!! DEAD BODY IN MY OFFICE

I peered at my computer to confirm what I had just read. "I'm so sorry, Harold. I need to go. I'll call you as soon as I can to finish up our conversation. Feel free to stay in here and finish up notes," I said, already halfway out the door. Anna stood up in her cubicle as I exited.

"Make sure he doesn't touch anything," I whispered to her. She eyed the back of his head through my open door and raised an eyebrow.

I pushed the elevator button repeatedly, despite knowing it would do nothing to accelerate its arrival. When the doors opened on Jordan's floor, I ran down the hallway to Jordan's office to find his door closed and the sound of a frantic female voice coming from inside. I almost turned to leave before reminding myself that he had begged me to be there. Instead I knocked casually.

"Come in!" I heard him call, and I swung the door open to see a woman standing by the desk. Her eyelids were so swollen they drooped low, leaving only little slits. Her hair was piled into a messy bun, and the unforgiving fluorescent light of the office did no favors to her blotchy skin, a mosaic of tear stains. Was that what I looked like after I closed a deal?

I glanced at the wedding portrait behind Jordan's desk to confirm that she was the same bright-eyed, glowing bride I'd spotted across the ballroom at the Pierre in December.

"Hi, Jessica! I've heard so much about you!" I smiled and then allowed it to fade, pretending to just now notice the expression on her face. "Is this a bad time?" I asked innocently.

"Yes," she hissed.

"It is," Jordan began. He'd been pacing nervously. "But actually, it's good that you're here." His wife whipped her head around to him in disbelief. "Shut the door."

I obeyed.

"Jessica, Alex Vogel." Jordan pointed to his wife and then to me.

"It's so nice to finally meet you," I said, bending my legs at the knees just in front of Jordan's spare chair.

"Don't sit!" she snapped. I straightened up.

"Alex, I can't tell you what this is about, but . . . answer one question," Jordan said, then paused and looked at me squarely. "What do I think of Nancy?"

Jessica whipped her head at him, looking indignant, but then she turned to me, and I saw something softening her features—maybe hope.

In that moment, I threw out any sense of morality or girl code. There was only loyalty.

"Nancy who?" I asked. "Duval?"

Jordan nodded. I let out a small snort of laughter.

"She's fit for a straitjacket. She's the butt of all our jokes," I said. "Look, I don't really know that much about her, but I do know that she's totally unstable." Jessica looked at me, clearly latching on to my words. "I know it's not nice, but Jordan and I spend every waking work hour together, basically, so we need something to make fun of, and she's just such an easy target."

I saw Jordan's shoulders relaxing away from his ears as he took a seat at his desk.

"I'm so sorry," I said, touching Jessica's shoulder and furrowing my brow. "I don't understand. Are you friends with her? Sorry. I didn't mean to upset you. We're just mean and bored."

"No." Jessica shook her head and wiped her cheek with the

back of her hand. "You think she's crazy?" I nodded. "How do you know?"

"Oh, it's all rumors," I said with a dismissive wave of my hand. "But I heard she just gets really obsessed with guys. Like apparently she's even created fake boyfriends." I swirled my finger around my ear and crossed my eyes, my Oscar-worthy performance continuing.

"She texted me," Jessica whispered.

I looked up at Jordan, who gave me a small nod.

"Saying?" I asked, looking incredulous.

Jessica burst into tears again, and I suddenly understood that Jordan had called me, rather than Matt, to his office because she'd never ever have believed a man's answer. A surge of guilt went up my spine but instantly dissolved at the base of my skull.

"That she was having an affair with Jordan and had to tell me because the guilt was too much."

I watched Jessica in feigned disbelief for a moment before I burst out laughing. She stared back at me. I covered my mouth but continued to force the laughter.

"I'm sorry. I'm so sorry," I went on. "I get why it's so upsetting, but it's just so ludicrous. Look, I'm basically with Jordan every second he's not with you. I assure you, he doesn't have the time to even talk to Nancy, even if he wanted to. Which he doesn't. And if anything had happened, I'd know. And I'd tell you!" Jessica exhaled and wiped her cheeks. I leaned in more closely. "But you do need to be careful with her. She once spread a completely insane rumor that I was sleeping with a partner. It was nuts." I paused and pretended to think before widening my eyes. "How does she have your number? Does she know where you guys live?"

Jessica's eyes flashed nervously, and she looked over at Jordan.

"Babe, the doormen would never let her up to our place. It's fine," he reassured her. She nodded at him, and he looked like he might pass out from the release of tension.

"I actually have to get back to work—I've got an associate to train," I said with an eye roll. "But don't believe a word that girl says. Jordan would never. This place is like a shrine to you."

I gestured at the one picture of her on his wall as I headed toward the door. *He really should have more pictures up.*

She smiled gratefully, and Jordan gave me a wave of approval and dismissal.

"Will you please close the door, Alex?" he asked calmly. I lingered for a moment outside his door and was relieved by the calm tones of the voices emanating from within, then heard a throat clearing and turned to see Jordan's assistant watching me eavesdrop. I clenched my jaw and gave a small, sheepish laugh before disappearing down the hallway.

Hours later, when I'd finally gotten rid of Harold and was in the middle of drafting a letter of intent for the latest National acquisition, my phone rang.

"Hi," I said, cradling the phone to my ear and checking that my door was shut. "Is everything . . . copacetic?"

"Yes." He was quiet for another moment. "Thank you. I'm sorry to have put you in that—"

"You're welcome," I interrupted. "Anyway, you made me look super cool in front of this Harold character. I literally left him in my office in the middle of a sentence."

Jordan snorted. "Turns out, you're my phone call, Skip," he said, his tone turning sincere.

I didn't answer at first, relishing the words, not wanting to disturb them. I didn't regret doing him the favor of saving his marriage, even if it meant betraying the girl code that had been drilled into me since preschool. But I didn't want to think about it anymore. "I'm glad to hear it. Now let's never ever discuss this again."

CHAPTER 20

"I'm not sure that Sam fits into my life anymore now that I work here," I confessed to Jordan as we sat cross-legged on his office floor and half-heartedly tossed cheese balls from a huge clear plastic tub into each other's mouth. His only response was to shrug and toss another orange sphere toward me with his powdered fingers. I caught it in my mouth and grinned. It was three o'clock in the morning on closing day for the latest National acquisition, and we were waiting for final comments from the seller's counsel.

"I don't know how to talk to him about it. I don't even have time to talk to him about it," I continued. Jordan gave me a skeptical look. "What?"

"In my almost seven years here, I've found that this job is always a viable excuse. But it's an excuse. People who are busy have just enough time for what they want to have time for. No more. No less."

"So, you're saying I don't want to have time to talk to him?"

"Exactly." He stared at me for a moment as I contemplated arguing with him. "We spent two hours fucking around in my office before we ordered dinner. You know, if you asked me, I'd cover for you if you wanted to go home and have dinner with Sam. Not every night, but if it was important to you, every once in a while."

I nodded. He had a point. But I liked being here with Jordan. I liked being at work more than being at home. Was that so bad? Didn't lots of people do that?

"Okay, Skip. I'm going to try to catch a few hours. Can you

cover me?" We both stood up. I felt like my legs might not support me.

"Fuck! I'm so tired! Up! Please?"

Jordan took a vial out of his desk drawer. "You know, Skip, I think it's time you start buying your own."

My heart sank. Did I do coke often enough to have to buy my own? "That's what I have you for! I only do it with you anyway." I bent low to his desk as I snorted, trying to erase the feeling that I needed the white powder to make it through the night.

While Jordan took a nap in the restoration room, I cleaned every crevice of my office using a Q-tip dipped in Windex. I was taking an air duster to my computer keyboard at four o'clock in the morning when the draft from opposing counsel dinged into our in-boxes. With my knees bouncing wildly under my desk, I took a first stab at comments and turned in changes before Jordan woke up. I flipped the draft to Jordan by ten in the morning and tackled a few more mundane tasks for my other two active matters before losing steam around two in the afternoon, when I passed out, spread-eagle on my stomach, in the middle of my office floor. When Anna poked her head in at six that evening, she shook me awake to make sure I wasn't dead.

I never knew how I'd feel when I woke up from a nap. Sometimes I felt like I had gotten run over by a Mack truck, my thoughts creeping like sludge through my brain, but other times I was completely fine. I was lucky enough that day to wake up feeling like a million bucks. I dove right back into work.

"Hi, this is Alex," I said into the phone, grabbing a pencil and readying myself to take notes. Having finished another deal with

Peter, during which I noticed a few flirtatious comments from him but no actual overtures, I'd thrown myself into working furiously for Matt and Jordan. I had always enjoyed working for them, but now I also didn't trust Peter to give me a good review despite the fact that I had leverage over him. If he ever wanted me gone, a bad review would be the way to do it. I needed to be perfect for Matt and Jordan.

"Skippy!" Matt's voice rang through the receiver.

I put my pencil down.

"I'm here with Didier. You're on speaker."

"We missed you last night, Skippy!" Didier's French accent sounded especially heavy, meaning he was either drunk or hungover.

I looked at my clock. Eleven a.m. Hungover, I hoped.

"I was completely unaware you were going out! Thanks for the invite!" There was a pause, and I panicked that I might have overstepped before I heard Didier grunt in approval.

"Come up!" Matt commanded.

"On my way."

When I reached his office, I knocked once on the closed door before it swung open and Didier ushered me in with a dramatic bow and shut it behind me. Jordan's notebook was on the couch, but Jordan was not. Matt was at his desk, looking slightly green. Matt and Didier scrolled through their phones and then pulled the screens closer to their faces and burst out laughing.

"What?" I asked.

"Check your email," Didier told me.

"Check your sent mail!" Matt corrected him. I furrowed my brow and looked at my phone. The first email in my sent mail was marked urgent, but I didn't think I'd added the red exclamation mark to a recent message.

From: Alexandra Vogel
To: Salomine, Didier; Morris, Taylor; Rogers, KJ; Matt Jaskel; Sellar, Jordan
Subject: I need to cut loose tonight. I don't want to just go to a strip club, I want to dance at one!!!

I reread it three times, my eyes bugging out of my head. When Jordan entered Matt's office, hysterically laughing, I punched him in the arm. "You're an asshole," I announced.

"Just teaching you to lock your computer before you leave your office, Skip."

I didn't even bother to email Didier's team to explain that Jordan had actually written it—they would know it was par for the course. The three men, who'd sunk down in their seats, looked miserable. Matt had one finger to his temple, while Didier breathed in with a hand over his stomach as though he was trying to keep from vomiting.

I sniffed the room. "Jesus. You guys reek," I said, taking a seat on the opposite end of the couch from Jordan.

"Quite a night you missed, Skip," Matt said. "I slept on that couch because I was afraid to go home to my wife."

"Yikes."

"Tell her," Jordan said. He put his fist to his mouth as he let out a small burp, as though he was afraid vomit would escape.

"I saw that," I told him. "You are literally the most repulsive human on earth."

"Didier, tell Skippy what we did last night," Jordan demanded.

"No! Don't," Matt interjected.

"Skippy doesn't care. She's cool," Didier insisted. "She's one of us." He turned to me. "I blew coke up a stripper's ass."

I felt my jaw drop open. I looked from Didier, who was smiling broadly, to Matt, who was nervously gauging my reaction. I laughed nervously.

Jordan slapped his forehead. "Fuck, Didier! I meant tell her about the new deal we got!"

"What new deal?" I asked, eager for a new topic.

Matt started in on a story of how they were at dinner at Carbone next to the M&A team from our biggest private equity client, and as he rambled on, I picked up my phone pretending to see what messages had come in.

"Yo! Skip! What the fuck?" Didier said. I looked up from my phone. "What are you typing? Who are you emailing?"

"Nobody! I'm not." I put my phone down.

Jordan grabbed it out of my lap before I had a chance to lock the screen.

"Stop! Give it back!" I pleaded.

"What was she typing?" Matt asked anxiously.

"Don't worry, Matt, Skippy's not telling anybody. She's doing a Google search for 'cocaine up butt,' " Jordan said, doubling over. Didier and Matt burst out laughing.

"I don't understand! I didn't even know that was something people did!" I held my cheeks in my hands as I felt them grow hot.

"She's ze cutest," Didier said to Matt, then turned to me. "You should have seen this girl's asshole."

"Ugh! You people are pigs. So what deal did you get?" I asked.

"We're doing the Hustler acquisition!" Didier said.

"Like, the magazine?" I asked.

"We got it last night when we were doing coke with the private equity guys," Didier said proudly.

I took a moment, then shrugged. "There's no one way to bring in new clients," I said, leaning back. "Put that in your business development training, Matt. By the way, who did you staff as the junior associate?" I asked. They shot awkward glances at one another.

"Carmen," Matt said. "But only because we had to—she was there with us last night!"

My shoulders slumped. Going to a strip club with our clients? She was pulling out all the stops to get into M&A.

"You're getting good reviews with the partners you've been working for," Vivienne said matter-of-factly at lunch the following week. I gloated inwardly.

This lunch was going like all of our others had: she typed furiously on her phone, her elbows on the table, while I discreetly did the same on my lap. We ordered. We spoke about the weather—we were both so glad that we were having a warm spring.

"That's so nice to hear," I said. "I've been working hard."

Vivienne looked at me. "Are you happy here?"

The question took me by surprise. She and I had yet to speak about anything substantive—we had grown accustomed to pleasantries, not eating carbs, and keeping our phones on the table during these lunch meetings.

I looked at her, wondering whether she wanted a real answer. "Very," I said cheerfully.

"Good," she said. "I don't believe anybody ever asked me that when I was an associate. And it seems people would like you to stick around for a while, so I thought I'd ask." She took a piece of bread from the basket. "The first months here, before you match into a group, are the worst. It's all about politics. But soon it'll be all about the work." I watched her pluck out the soft interior of the roll and pop the crust into her mouth.

I wondered what had changed to make her eat carbs, and took a piece of bread as well. "I'm okay. I think that 'happy in my career' doesn't exactly look the way I thought it would," I said, chewing.

She looked up at me, something raw and honest passing between us. "Nothing looks the way I thought it would," she said wistfully, then caught herself immediately. "We're practicing corporate law at the biggest firm in the entire world. Whether we know it or not, we're blazing a trail for women in the future. The key to having it all is redefining what 'all' is. I wanted three kids. That means I have two nannies. I want them to eat home-cooked meals every night. That means I have a chef."

I squirmed in my seat. Was this what trailblazing for all women looked like? Doing coke with clients, betraying my gender by lying to a colleague's wife, and last but not least, having sex in my office with a partner?

"I can count the number of dirty diapers I've changed on my fingers. Not kidding," she continued, holding up her manicured hands to me.

"My idol." I brought my palms together in front of my chest and gave a slight bow of my head.

"Should we get wine?" She took her phone off the table and placed it in her gray Moreau, the same one I had eyed at Barneys on bonus day.

I nodded eagerly, and as she ordered a bottle, I had the fleeting thought that I was somehow becoming just like her. Despite our friendly chatter and the smile I kept plastered on my face, the feeling remained until I shoved it down to a comfortable distance with my first glass of wine.

***

I walked into the presentation late.

". . . and because of this volatility, our busted deal arrangements have become a crucial part of engagement arrangements."

I really didn't want to go, but I had to. First of all, it was a mandatory training for corporate associates. Second of all, I intended to support Jordan. Third, I still couldn't resist the opportunity to put myself in front of Peter, as though doing so would somehow remind him that he was attracted to me.

I took a seat next to Carmen, but she barely seemed to notice me as she stared up at Jordan with a slightly stupefied expression. I wondered exactly what was going on. I know Jordan had said that his ending things with Nancy was what had triggered her reaching out to Jessica, and that he regretted that anything had ever happened, but I found it difficult to believe that the infidelity I had caught him in was the one and only occurrence.

"You're so obvious," I whispered to her, testing my theory. She looked over at me with an alarmed expression, so I winked. She laughed and put a finger to her lips.

"Shhhh."

Jordan was standing at the front of the room in a perfectly tailored navy suit, one hand resting in his pocket while the other moved the clicker through the slides. Peter sat beside him, affording the younger attorney the spotlight, but then made a remark that precipitated an eruption of laughter, and I blinked myself back into the room.

"We're going to need to be perfect . . . PERFECT . . . from here on out. Which means I'm going to be leaning on all of you a lot, because my wife is honestly going to divorce me if I ruin another vacation, and I'm out of here next week," Jordan added.

The room burst out into laughter again. I looked out of the side of my eye at Carmen, expecting to see hurt on her face at the mention of Jordan's wife, but she appeared unruffled. I punched in my code and pulled up my email.

From: Peter Dunn
To: Alexandra Vogel
Subject: Tonight

Dinner at Cipriani?

At the end of the presentation, I watched as a crowd of male and female associates flocked to the front of the room to introduce themselves to Peter and Jordan and ask whatever questions they thought might make them stand out.

From: Alexandra Vogel
To: Peter Dunn
Subject: Re: Tonight

Early? Need to come back to the office after, I'm getting crushed.

I watched as Peter checked his email, taking twisted pleasure in the finger he held up to the young female associate speaking with him, signaling to her that my email was more pressing. He frowned slightly, and I worried for a moment that I had pushed my luck.

From: Peter Dunn
To: Alexandra Vogel
Subject: Re: Tonight

Done. 6:30. We're on.

A rush of nerves and adrenaline swept over me as I smiled down at my phone.

That evening, as Peter and I walked silently out of the elevator into the lobby, we ran into Carmen, who was exiting a different elevator bank.

"Hi!" I said, waving at her. When I looked back, Peter was already outside.

"Hey." She was pale, and focused her attention on a stray thread of her scarf.

"What's going on?" I asked, but she just shook her head.

"I'm just waiting in here until . . ." She looked over her shoulder. "I have a dinner. Are you going to dinner with Peter Dunn?"

I felt waves of judgment emanating from her. "Yeah," I said casually, "and four bankers. But yeah."

Why did I just lie about that? Peter and I worked together. We could go to dinner together.

She just looked at me.

"Are you okay?" I asked.

"Just boy stuff," she said, so softly I could barely hear her.

"Is the mystery man making you sad?" I asked. Carmen had never actually admitted to me that she was dating somebody at work, and she certainly hadn't admitted it was Jordan. But she had stopped denying it, too.

"He's just being a jerk," she said.

"Can we do lunch tomorrow?" I asked.

"Yes, please."

"Great!" I hugged her goodbye and walked quickly to meet Peter. When I reached his side, I looked back at the lobby. Jordan was exiting the elevator bank. I saw him head toward Carmen and greet her, their body language tense.

Ugh, what an asshole. Hadn't he learned his lesson with Nancy? I hope he didn't think I was going to clean up another of his messes. Then I thought about what I was doing that evening, and felt like a hypocrite.

The Quality Car driver opened the door for us, and Peter gave the driver an address on Fifth Avenue as he slipped into the Escalade behind me. We sat silently in the bucket seats, a few feet apart, the tension between us palpable. I looked out the window as the misty raindrops, flirting with the idea of coalescing into droplets, drifted downward through the prism of street light. Peter took my hand and led me back in a crouch to the third row, where he kissed me. I had craved his embrace more than I had even realized since we last slept together. I didn't dare play coy. We never did make it to the restaurant.

When I pushed through my apartment door around eleven, after I had returned from "dinner" with Peter only to order dinner at my desk to keep working, Sam was sitting on the couch, playing a video game with a headset on.

"Hey!" He leaned all the way down to one side as he steered into his virtual turn. "You motherfucker!" he yelled at whatever teenager in Singapore he was competing against.

I stared at him and felt a lump forming in my throat. "I'm going to shower."

He didn't hear me, or if he did, he didn't react.

I let the water rush over my face, then placed my hands in front of me on the cool tile and rested my head against them for support, afraid I'd lose my balance.

Q. It's clear that you formed friendships with both colleagues and clients. Did you ever feel that you were treated differently because you were a woman, not just because you were a friend or were good at your job?

A. Yes. I think Klasko works hard to promote diversity, and their emphasis includes gender diversity.

Q. How exactly did Klasko "promote" this diversity?

A. I think they aim to promote a diverse range of associates through the ranks, and that I was sometimes given opportunities to work on deals and attend social gatherings because I was female.

Q. Did you ever use your gender to manipulate a situation to your advantage?

A. What do you mean?

Q. Did you ever use your gender as a way to secure work from clients or manipulate your position at the firm?

A. I don't recall that being my intention at any stage, no.

CHAPTER 21

I fought the urge to lunge for my phone and let it ring twice before I answered.

"Hey, Peter," I answered cheerily, pointlessly rustling papers on my desk to sound as though I was in the middle of something.

"Hey, kiddo. What do you think of Vermont this weekend? We could both use a break . . . There's still snow on the mountain, believe it or not . . ."

I didn't hear much else, but again I forced myself to wait a beat before answering.

The trees bled into one another in brushstrokes of green and brown as we sped up the Taconic in Peter's black Range Rover. It was the first time I had ever seen him behind the wheel of a car, and I found it strangely erotic. As I stared out the window, I wondered how exactly I came to be sitting in the passenger seat next to Peter Dunn. I was giddy with the anticipation of a weekend tryst with the man I'd been imagining weekend trysts with since I'd first encountered him.

I needed this weekend. I deserved this weekend.

"Where did you tell your boyfriend you were going?" he asked, snapping me out of my reverie.

"To an M&A team-building retreat at your ski house," I answered, staring out the window. I wondered if he could sense the fact that I had had sex with Sam that morning. I hadn't really wanted to, but somehow the guilt of turning him down when it had already been so long was worse than the depravity of doing it. I felt Peter watching me. "What?" I looked over at him.

"Great call," he said with an approving nod. I knew it had been smart to tell the truth about my location and the fact that I was with Peter, but I hated that I was getting so good at lying.

I watched his large palm rest gently on the ball of the gear selector of the automatic car, sensing from his grip that he must have a stick shift back in his garage in Westchester. I wanted to know what kind of car it was. I wanted to know everything about him. I wanted to stop lying to Sam, and I wanted a weekend with Peter to turn into a full week with Peter. I took my finger and traced swirls around his scars, picturing him young, on the docks in Cape Cod. I imagined him still with the same wide, pure smile.

"I wasn't the most well-behaved kid."

"Hmm?" I turned my head to him lazily, still lost in my daydream.

"I used to have my hands slapped with a ruler every time I acted up in Catholic school."

I stared at him as my mental image of him as a child vanished. Why would he have told me the scars were from oyster shucking? What was it Vivienne had said? *Nobody is ever what they seem.* I checked the clock. We were only two hours into a four-and-a-half-hour drive, with a weekend and a drive back stretching before us. I wasn't about to press him on his inconsistent testimony. So I shoved it out of my mind.

We entered the house through the pristine garage, which smelled subtly of pine and peppermint, and the main floor was as lovely as I remembered it. The image of Sam and me playing drunk Scrabble and laughing popped into my head. I had a glimpse of us eating cold pizza in the hot tub. I thought of us making love on Peter's bed. Despite the cold mountain air, I felt my wool sweater constricting around my body, and when I freed myself from it, Peter mistook my guilty sweat for something else.

As soon as Peter's hands were on me, though, nothing else mattered. We spilled from his enormous rain shower to the plush carpeting of his bedroom; we tumbled from his bed straight into the hot tub. Tired and satisfied, we were both quiet as we pushed our backs up against the jets.

"We need dinner," he finally said. "There's a great gastropub in town. Great beers on tap, and they do the best Korean-style braised short rib I've ever had."

"It's five o'clock," I said, calling my phone to life. "Early-bird special."

"Honestly, Alex, I'm sick and tired of you always reminding me how old I am." Peter smiled, splashing the hot water up toward my neck. I laughed in delight as I slung my legs around his waist. "Okay, seriously, we really do need to eat."

By the time we walked into the restaurant at five thirty, we grabbed the last two seats at the bar. "Post-ski rush," he said knowingly.

It seemed bizarre to me that Peter wasn't more concerned about being seen in this small town with somebody who wasn't his wife, but I was enjoying it all the same. He ordered us pints of beer and lobster tacos and tuna tartare, and we split short ribs and creamy polenta for our entrees. I'd only gotten one bite into the soft, unctuous meat when Peter got a call and excused himself with an eye roll that let me know he had to take it. I was almost through my second beer when he came back to the bar, wireless headphones in his ears, and muted his phone.

"Do me a favor and call a car to Starlight. You can bill it to—"

"Got it," I told him. By this point, I called cars to the Starlight for Stag River almost weekly. I was glad to be useful to the client, however minorly, but in this moment my mind drifted to that night the driver had reprimanded me. "You know, the

Quality drivers hate making the Starlight Diner run. Isn't that so weird?"

Peter turned his entire body toward me as he stood beside me. "Why do you say that?"

"One of them told me so," I said, and shrugged. He stared at me as though expecting me to continue.

"That's beyond unprofessional. It's not up to the drivers to *like* a specific route. Can you send me the name of the person who said it?"

I nodded, knowing I wouldn't. However much my interaction with the driver unsettled me, I didn't want to get the guy fired.

Peter looked back down at his phone. "I've got to get back to this—Gary is really flipping out." He nodded in the direction of the short ribs and opened his mouth. I placed a forkful on his tongue. "Thanks for saving me that one bite," he joked.

"You snooze, you lose," I said, sipping my beer. He leaned in to me and gave me a brief kiss before heading back outside, and I sat basking in the glow of it until I noticed the bartender staring at me, stone-faced. *He knows*, I thought. *If he doesn't actually know Peter's wife personally, he knows this is an affair. I'm sure he's seen a million girls just like me in this town.* I picked up my phone and called a car to the diner.

We spent Saturday in the spa, and as far as I could tell, the only actual break Peter took from his phone was for his sixty-minute massage. I was bracing myself for the announcement that came around four o'clock that afternoon while we were in robes on his couch, each on our laptops.

"Alex, I'm so sorry, but I have to get back to the city. But I want to take you for dinner tonight. Can we just head out first thing tomorrow? I know we were planning to . . ."

"Of course. I expected this," I said, and smiled softly. I was surprised it had taken so long to suggest leaving early, and I was even more surprised he still wanted to spend Saturday night. We went to the local steakhouse for a decadent dinner and a bottle of red wine, and we were both peacefully asleep immediately upon our heads hitting the pillows, without so much as the suggestion of sex. We woke up at six on Sunday morning and headed back to the city just as dawn was breaking.

"I love that you get it." Peter kept his eyes on the road as he spoke.

"Hmm?" I answered, slowly sipping at the coffee we had stopped for.

"Leaving early would have been a fight with my wife. It's really nice for me that you get it." He placed his palm on my knee. I nodded, thinking the same was true from my perspective. We drove home alternating between work discussions, singing along to 1970s music on the radio, and me reading Peter's emails to him and him dictating his responses to me. I felt a new level of intimacy between us that came from sleeping next to but not with Peter.

I made Peter drop me a block from my apartment, just in case Sam was outside. As he pulled up to the corner of Twentieth and Eighth, he cleared his throat. "Hey. You know, Gary keeps telling me to remind you that we're his guests at the Private Equity Fights Hunger gala at the Met in a few weeks."

"I can't wait!" My cheeks flushed, and my mind raced with the anticipation of another backseat rendezvous, this time in black tie. I smiled back at Peter and gave him a small wave. He held up his palm to me as he drove away.

I was dragging my small rolling suitcase down the bumpy city sidewalk, replaying the amazing, though abbreviated, weekend over in my mind, when a baritone voice punctured my thoughts. "Looks like you could use a hand."

I looked up, prepared to stare straight through whatever asshole was bothering me, and saw two men, one of them beaming in my direction. He seemed much taller than I remembered, perhaps because I had only ever worn heels around him. He was wearing sweats, and his skin glowed, like he was coming from a tough workout.

"Derrick!" I took my hand off my suitcase and wrapped my arms around his neck as he bent low into me to return the embrace.

I turned to his friend. "I'm Alex."

"Sean," he said, stretching his hand out to me, his smooth pale skin almost glowing. I shook it as he turned to Derrick. "You two catch up. I'll meet you back—" He stopped his sentence short and took off down the street.

"It's good to see you. How are you? You look so good!" I gushed.

"I am good!" He nodded convincingly. "It took a minute to regain my footing, but now I'm good. Are you heading home? Can I help you to your door?"

I was too exhausted to protest, and he lifted my rolling suitcase effortlessly and fell into step alongside me.

"So believe it or not, I'm working for the Brady campaign on new gun-control policies to present to Congress," he told me. "I've never been happier. It's pretty amazing how people act dumb, make mistakes, and then we wind up in the exact position we need to be in. It's a subconscious life-saving technique, I guess."

"I'm so happy for you," I said, squeezing his forearm so he knew I meant it. We walked in silence a few more paces before I slowed my gait. "This is my block," I said, pointing east as we turned. "I wanted to call you so many times. And I tried to find you on social media . . ." I trailed off, covering my eyes to shield them from the sun's glare.

"Yeah, I just needed to disappear for a bit to recharge. And to figure out who I was again. I was so tired of being who everybody wanted me to be at Klasko. The black playboy, the token diversity seat at a table with clients, the voice for all minorities at the firm. It was exhausting. And I didn't feel like I fit the mold for any of them, but I think I tried so hard to be those things that I went overboard."

I nodded. "I get it."

"No offense, but you don't."

"You're right, I don't," I said, slumping. "But I do get being stereotyped . . . as the 'good girl.' And I get the urge to break out of it."

His expression invited me to continue.

"I just got back from a weekend with Peter Dunn at his ski house. I had him drop me off a block away in case my boyfriend was outside our building." I couldn't bring myself to look at Derrick as I spoke.

"Just you and Peter?"

I bit my lower lip to keep the tears at bay, and was only able to manage a small shrug.

"Must have been so terrible for you, playing the part of the good girl who got all the attention from clients and partners," Derrick said, his tone gently mocking me as his lips formed a half smile.

I felt a laugh escape my mouth even as tears spilled out the corners of my eyes. "I just blew up my entire life. I don't even know why I did it. It was a good life." I looked up at my building and imagined Sam inside, waiting for me. "I don't even know why I'm crying, because the most fucked-up thing is, I've never been happier. I'm the only person on earth who feels like she's living her best life while having an affair."

"Life is fucked up sometimes," Derrick said, then paused. "My life was super messy a few months ago, but things settle. They always do." He put a hand on my shoulder. "When I left Klasko, my dad got wind of what happened, and I could have denied it, but I came clean. You know his one and only question? He asked if the hooker they caught me with was a woman. I could see the relief in his eyes when I told him yes. So screwed up." I gave him a snort of sympathetic disgust. "The hooker was just . . . a show. That guy was my boyfriend," he continued, gesturing down the block.

I wiped my nose and smiled. "He's cute."

"You're not surprised?"

"I sort of always wondered if you were gay. But I didn't know until Carmen and I met your ex-boyfriend at Bergdorf's."

"James? Carmen met him, too? Fuck!" Derrick ran his palm over his head in annoyance. "Now I bet everybody knows. Whatever, it doesn't matter now." He sounded a bit like he was convincing himself. "I don't have to worry what those people think anymore. And I'm all about living a more authentic life now anyway." He seemed more certain of it in that moment.

There was so much I wanted to ask him. *Why didn't you want people to know? Are you sure your father wouldn't come around? Did you feel like Klasko wouldn't be okay with it?*

"She'd never say anything, Derrick. And I obviously wouldn't, either."

He shrugged. "By the way, Peter is super hot."

I put my hands over my heart, pumping my arms in and out, mocking my own schoolgirl crush, and we dissolved into laughter.

"You're the only person I've told."

He bowed his head. "I'm honored."

I hugged him close and held on for a few moments too long, but when I released him he looked at me for a moment before wrapping me up in his arms once again. I laughed and kissed his cheek and gave him my number and strict instructions to use it.

When I came into the apartment, Sam was sitting on the couch. "Hey! Sorry you needed to cut the retreat short. How was the drive?" he asked, without looking up from the papers spread out before him on the coffee table.

Because he wasn't really asking, I didn't really answer. "Hmm." I walked over to the couch, where he looked up at me with a smile. I gave him a kiss as I took in the mess of Excel printouts in front of him. "What is this?"

"We have interest from a private equity company, and they want to meet tomorrow, so I'm just making sure I know all of our financials cold."

"That's great!" I sat down next to him. "Which one?"

"High Tower Capital," he said, searching my face for recognition. I'd never heard of them. Which wasn't a good thing for Sam. I smiled and nodded enthusiastically but said nothing. He opted not to press my knowledge of them. "Actually, it's a four o'clock meeting. They want to go to dinner after. But I would rather go with you if you're free, since I haven't seen you enough lately." I saw uncertainty flash in his eyes and instantly recalled his nerves the first time he'd asked me out, in the sticky bar in Cambridge where we met. In New York, I should have wanted to have a celebratory dinner with him too. I should have been missing him all weekend. But I didn't. And I hadn't. I wanted to lock Peter's office door and screw him in his office chair. I wanted to go drinking with Jordan and the National guys, if they were around. I wanted to laugh too much, spend too much, stay out too late.

"I'm so happy for you! You should totally have dinner with those guys. It's a great opportunity. And I have to work late anyway. I didn't do any actual work this weekend," I told him, rolling my eyes.

Sam turned away from me and nodded. "Yeah, you're probably right. I should start putting my career first too."

His last word jabbed at my chest, and I had to bite my tongue not to say "*What career?*" I waited for him to register my reaction, but he was focused on the papers again, so I took my suitcase into the bedroom to unpack everything I'd brought for a weekend away with another man.

***

There were rare mornings peppered throughout my weeks when emails drifted into my in-box gradually, with little urgency, allowing me to ease myself into the day. That Monday morning wasn't one of them. I woke up to seventy-one fairly urgent emails from our Hong Kong office, with whom we were working on a merger for a Chinese company. I didn't shower and took a Quality car in to work so I didn't need to break from emailing while I didn't have service on the subway. Around two o'clock, I welcomed the first email that wasn't urgent or deal-related.

From: Jordan Sellar
To: Alexandra Vogel; Morris, Taylor; Rogers, KJ
Subject: Dinner

Want to get dinner tonight?

From: Rogers, KJ
To: Jordan Sellar; Alexandra Vogel; Morris, Taylor
Subject: Re: Dinner

Taylor and I are in. Craving steak.

From: Jordan Sellar
To: Rogers, KJ, Alexandra Vogel; Morris, Taylor
Subject: Re: Dinner

Strip House. 7pm. Alex, you in?

I stared at my computer for a prolonged moment, then allowed the memory of Sam accusing me of putting my career first to dispel any trace of guilt I might have felt.

From: Alexandra Vogel
To: Jordan Sellar; Rogers, KJ; Morris, Taylor
Subject: Re: Dinner

I'm in!

Strip House coaxed the most awful, delicious parts of humanity out into the open. I scanned framed pictures of full-figured strippers as I absentmindedly unbuttoned the top of my blouse for air. I rolled my neck as I released it from the grip of my collar. The thick white napkins with red figures of dancing women somehow encouraged me to take a goose-fat-fried potato with my fingers, if only to make use of the linen. The dark floors and red walls allowed my shoulders to relax after my long day and lean into the raunchy conversation swirling around me.

"She's absolutely insatiable. Honestly, I should never have started sleeping with her," KJ said.

"Dude, you definitely should not have started sleeping with her! On top of the ethical reasons, she has zero discretion. You're an idiot," Taylor told him.

I looked up from my phone. "Wait, what did I miss? You're sleeping with somebody at work?"

"His *analyst.* So fucking cliché," Jordan said with a sneer, getting out of his seat. "Jesus, I'm exhausted from this closing. Give me a minute to get myself together."

I grimaced at KJ as Jordan walked toward the men's room. "Your analyst? You're better than that."

"I can't help it. She's nuts. In a good way. She makes me finger her during meetings. With other people in the room. It's . . . it's wild." He looked exceedingly pleased with himself.

"Stop it. I don't believe you. Like, what, under the table? How does she *make* you do that?"

"Obviously, she doesn't," Taylor muttered.

"Whatever, she didn't make me, but she didn't stop me," KJ said, then signaled the waiter for a refill of scotch.

I stared at KJ, wishing Jordan were there to tell him that he was taking advantage of the girl who worked for him, that he was an abusive boss, that he could get fired. How demeaning it must be for that analyst, who was probably twenty-three at the most, to have her supervisor—a man she at best had feelings for and at worst was too worried to reject—touch her in front of other people. My blood pressure rose on her behalf, the back of my neck growing clammy as I pictured the scene, wondering if the other men around the conference table were blind to KJ's behavior, chose to ignore it, or actually encouraged it.

"Don't pretend to be so shocked," he went on, pounding his fist on the table. "Just because she is open about what she wants when the rest of you pretend to be so proper when you all really want us to dominate. You have one set of rules for the bedroom, and one for the boardroom, and *we're* supposed to keep it straight? Fuck that! I play by one set of rules, and this chick LOVES it." He was practically yelling.

"Easy," Taylor warned him, then turned to me. "He's kidding."

I squeezed my nails into my palms beneath the table, fighting the urge to punch him.

"I'm not shocked," I said instead. "I think it would explain why you're suddenly upping your suit game in the office. You usually look like a schlub." I relished KJ's confusion at which one of my statements to focus on as I gestured to his gray suit with threads of burgundy and navy running faintly throughout for emphasis.

KJ looked down, adjusting his lapels. "Zegna. You like?" he asked, ignoring my insult.

"Love," I stated flatly, then raised my glass, hoping to wash down the sour taste of disingenuousness in my mouth.

I felt my phone buzz in my purse, which was hanging from the back of my chair, as Jordan returned to the table, holding his nostrils together as discreetly as he could.

"Got any for me?" KJ asked him, and he reached into his breast pocket and handed him a vial from a downturned palm. As KJ excused himself, I looked at my phone, welcoming the distraction.

Sam: Are you stuck at work?

Alex: :(

Sam: Hope you're not going to be too late tonight. I should be home from dinner at a decent hour . . .

Alex: Me too! But I have no idea when I'll be out of here. It's a bit crazy today. Shouldn't be more than a few hours. See you at home. Can't wait to hear how your meeting went.

I watched the ellipses appear and then disappear, but no further text arrived. Taylor and Jordan talked about golf as I spooned thick creamed spinach onto my plate, vowing to work out in the morning, even though I knew deep down I'd be too hungover and too slammed at work to engage in any form of physical activity come daylight.

KJ plopped himself down in his seat, then sneezed loudly into his napkin.

"Fuck!" Jordan exclaimed, and I looked up to see thick red blood streaming out of KJ's nose, staining the white parts of the cloth.

Our waiter appeared out of nowhere, deftly took the bloody napkin from under KJ's nose and replaced it with a paper one, and gestured to the men's room.

"Watch it!" KJ growled as he made his way to the bathroom, disentangling himself from a passing diner he smashed into. "Fuck."

My heart skipped. I blinked hard and refocused on the back of the other man's head as he walked away, clearly disgusted by my coked-up colleague, before he turned and locked eyes with me.

Sam stared at me, his face stoic, then he shook his head almost imperceptibly before joining two men in suits by the door whom he followed out of the restaurant without so much as a word to me.

I heard Jordan and Taylor chatting somewhere in the background, then KJ settling down again, applying pressure under his nostril with a new napkin. But I sat there motionless, processing. Sam's life was so removed from mine—the start-up world seemed to be centered around happy hours in grimy bars, daytime meetings in coffee shops, and long hours in WeWork common spaces. Why was he suddenly there, in my world, in my expensive steakhouse that catered to corporate expense accounts and middle-aged hedge-fund portfolio managers trying to impress their twentysomething girlfriends?

"One more time . . . hello!" Taylor yelled at me. I blinked twice and coughed, then gulped down a glass of water along with its ice. I waited for the chips lodged in my throat to melt before I spoke, grateful that just then the waiter appeared with our dinners.

"Sorry," I said, and shook my head. "I spaced."

"You okay?" Taylor looked at me.

Jordan watched me closely, wondering what exactly I was doing and why I was ruining the mood at a dinner with his most important client. I nodded as convincingly as I could manage. It was time to push myself back into client development mode.

"Thank god this place is already red," I joked, touching the side of my nose and pointing to KJ.

Jordan seemed to relax his shoulders as the banter resumed. "Taylor, you have to try this veal!" He cut a piece and put it on a bread plate, shoving it in his direction.

"I don't know, man. Who orders veal? Very suspect. And don't even get me started on Alex with her tuna."

"It *kills* you that I don't eat steak, doesn't it?" I narrowed my eyes and leaned into him. Taylor nodded, knowing he was being toyed with. "How much will you give me to eat one?" I asked him, my voice low.

He leaned back, loving the negotiation. "A steak?" he asked. I nodded. "Five hundred."

"Six," I said, knowing he would enjoy proving to me that he could spare it.

"Five-fifty."

My mind bounced, calculating the angles I was toying with. "You're senior enough to choose counsel. Give us your next merger, and we'll call it even."

Taylor looked surprised for only a moment before smirking. "Done."

I raised my palm, and our waiter started in our direction immediately. Taylor clapped, and KJ laughed as he took a long sip of his drink. "I'll have the filet, medium rare. If you could rush it, that would be wonderful."

"Was the tuna not to your liking?" the waiter asked nervously, his white sport coat bunching at the waist as he leaned over me.

"Something like that."

I was halfway through my steak, with KJ and Taylor cheering me on for every bite and thoroughly enjoying the spectacle, when Jordan leaned over and whispered in my ear, "Matt and I created a monster."

I smiled in his direction but barely looked over. "I think we need another bottle." I swirled the last bit of red wine in my glass. I needed a lot more wine to wash down the revolting ball of flesh lodged in my throat.

***

As my eyes adjusted to the scene inside my apartment, I dropped my keys to the floor with a clatter. Sam was standing in the middle of the living room, hunched over a large box, sealing in its contents with duct tape, and a few more unassembled boxes were scattered around the room.

"What are you doing?" I asked, letting the door shut behind me without picking up my keys.

He stared back at me blankly. "We need to talk," he said, straightening his spine.

I took another step into the apartment. "I didn't lie to you. That was work. That's part of my job."

"Really, Alex? That's your story? Honestly . . ."

"What do you want from me? I have to entertain clients. It's how we get work. And for your information, I actually brought in a deal tonight."

"Alex, I don't give a shit about work or deals or anything! You chose your colleagues over me. You've been doing it for months now."

"I'm trying to build a career here!" Within seconds, I was crying. And I was drunk. I was hoping Sam couldn't tell the difference between just upset and upset and drunk. "You wouldn't understand," I mumbled.

Sam bowed his head. "I do understand. I just don't understand why you feel the need to make it a choice. Why don't you ever invite me to firm drinks or out with clients? Take dinner breaks with me, invite me to events—and not just the Christmas party. Am I that embarrassing?" He asked the question facetiously, but before I knew it, I had shrugged. He inhaled sharply. "You're fucking embarrassed of me? YOU? Are embarrassed. Of ME? Do you know how insane that is, Alex? Do you even know who you have become? I should be embarrassed of you! Coke nosebleeds at dinner in overpriced restaurants? I should be embarrassed by your obsession with money and clothes and your sense that you are better than everything and everyone. You are so out of touch with reality, it is completely insane!" He was so angry, he was practically hopping as he yelled.

I opened my mouth and closed it. I tried again. Finally, I shook my head and stormed into the bedroom, locking the door behind me. I paced the thin strip of floor between the bed and my dresser, fuming. *Incorporate* him *into my work world? Is he kidding me? He'd be eaten alive!*

Unable to sustain that level of indignation for long, I sat down on the bed, exhausted by the whole evening.

I was bound to get caught at some point, I thought. It could have been worse. I shuddered at the idea of him catching me with Peter, and a sense of relief replaced my fury. I looked at the locked door, wondering momentarily whether I should try to speak to Sam. But I opted to shower and climb into bed instead, thinking it would be best to have a civilized discussion in the morning. It wasn't lost on me that my having locked him out of the bedroom meant he wouldn't be able to finish packing, or use the bathroom, for that matter. I crawled under the covers and shut my eyes, but a few minutes later, a soft knock on the door forced them open. I stared up at the ceiling for a moment, mulling whether to get up, then finally shut them again.

I woke early, my heart racing from a combination of anxiety and last night's drinks. I opened the bedroom door quietly and stuck my head out, not wanting to wake Sam if he was sleeping, but he was sitting up on the couch, staring straight ahead at the blank TV. He looked at me with his large, kind eyes, and I was surprised to find myself feeling deeply sad to be ending my relationship with the man I had spent the entirety of my young adult life with. I leaned the side of my face into the door, my hand still around the knob, and tears silently poured down my cheeks.

Sam got up and made his way toward me.

"I'm sorry. I'm so sorry," I hiccuped through my tears.

He took my face in his hands and kissed my forehead. "Shhh. It's all okay. It's just. . . . We've just . . ."

"Grown apart," I finished, then cried harder into his chest. He led me to the couch, where I almost collapsed, weeping from the bottom of my stomach. I knew the tears weren't just over Sam leaving. They were about the person I had become, the left turn my neat little life had taken into a mess of cheating and partying. He steadied me with his arm, letting me cry while shedding a few tears himself, and when I calmed down a little, he brought me a glass of water. He then turned back to his boxes, and though I couldn't bring myself to help him pack, I watched him intently.

When he had sealed the last one, he sat next to me, placing a hand lightly on my upper thigh and smiling sadly. "It wasn't forever. But it was a great run, wasn't it?"

"Are you sure about this?" I asked, suddenly uncertain myself.

Sam nodded. "There was a point at Thanksgiving where I think we were either going to move forward or . . ." He trailed off. "And we didn't. I gave it a few months to see if we could get back on track, but it didn't happen. And we can blame your job and my company or any number of other things, but if this were right, we'd have made it work. Don't you think, Al?"

I felt an ache in my chest when he said my name, and I had to look away, but I nodded, knowing he was right.

"It's better this way. We're both going to be better this way," he assured me.

"Where will you go?" I asked quietly.

"My buddy Chris from work just had a roommate move out of his place in the East Village. I'm going to sublet the room." He glanced around the apartment. "I've been to his place before. It's not this. But it's really nice."

I felt stung by the speed of his answer. "You can stay as long as—"

"I'm going to go today," he said firmly. "It's the right thing. I'll have my stuff out before you get back tonight."

"I understand," I said, and I did.

I felt sad about the breakup, but only in a dull, detached sort of way. I realized that I'd been mentally preparing for a life without Sam for months, and the forefront of my brain was consumed with closing three deals. My heart, which might have otherwise ached, burst with the excitement of my affair with Peter. My days rolled forward with no regard for the fact that anything in my life had changed. As a result, it was easy enough to pretend it hadn't.

I put my palms on my forehead, drawing the skin tight and up; I found it helped to keep my eyelids from closing. I was nearly finished with the markup Jordan had given me and was on track to be home at five o'clock and asleep by six that evening, the earliest I would have been to bed in months. I grabbed at my ringing office phone and cradled it between my chin and shoulder as I continued to type.

"Hey, Matt."

"Hi. Are you able to come to my office now?"

My stomach lurched at the formality of his tone. "Sure. Be right there."

Matt's door was closed, but he called for me to enter before my knuckle hit the wood for the second time. He was on the phone but gestured for me to close the door and take a seat. *Yikes.* Closed-door meetings were never a good thing.

As I listened to the tail end of his conversation, I scanned the room for the trash can I'd need if my lunch climbed any higher in my throat.

"I appreciate your understanding. She's a wonderful associate, but she's still in her first year. I'll speak with her. Thanks for catching this . . . Okay . . . Okay . . . Thanks again." He hung up and turned to me, his eyes serious. "Alex, there was a reference to a change in employment agreements in the Hat Trick deal we closed a few months back. The company caught that we never raised a flag. Did you loop in our employment specialists on the deal? I can't believe they'd have been okay with it."

I stared at him, unable to speak. Of course I hadn't looped in our employment specialists. I was completely unaware that I was supposed to. Now I would have, but a few months ago, it was just not on my radar.

"Alex, in order to be a good lawyer, you need to know what you *don't* know. Neither you nor I know what is kosher in employment law. It's why we have employment specialists. It's why we have tax, and real estate, and every other group. It's why I'm part of this firm and don't just open up my own shop."

My mind raced. *Is this a fire-able offense? What are the repercussions to the company? And to Didier and his team? How can I undo this?* I crossed and recrossed my legs as I thought of what to say. I ran my hand through my hair. Then I paused. I breathed in and stuck my chest out a bit farther as I corrected my posture. I invited Matt to stare with large puppy-dog eyes. I reran my fingers through my long strands, flipping them messily to one side. I slithered my backside on the leather and uncrossed my legs slowly as I maintained a carefully thoughtful expression.

"I'm so sorry. It won't happen again. What can I do to fix this?" I forced a sultry tone into my voice. Matt stared back at me without speaking. *Crisis averted.* I whined a bit more. "It was my first closing. I would never do that now. Do I need to get on the phone with Didier?" I didn't feel as though I was about to cry, but I pouted my lower lip anyway.

He held up a palm. "Whatever is happening right now . . . stop." His eyes blazed furiously despite his calm tone. "I'm not like Peter. Don't get it twisted, Skippy."

I slumped my shoulders, my cheeks flushing. I felt like I'd been dealt an electric shock. I prayed he was speaking in generalities about Peter's personality and that he didn't suspect anything specific.

He shook his head to dispel the anger lodged in it and straightened his tie. "I've handled it. You need to send the minutes from the board meeting that discussed the new agreement to Bruce Shyer on the employment team, and explain to him we'd appreciate his review by COB. I've handled everything with the

National team. Didier is fine with us proceeding with opposing counsel and not bothering him further with this."

I straightened, utterly mortified and unable to speak. I nodded as he gestured to the door and stood to leave.

"Skip!" Matt called after me. I turned. "Don't forget you're actually good at your job. Go. Fix this. CC me and Jordan on everything. This will be cleared up within a few days." He gave me a short, forgiving smile. I nodded and blinked in apology before turning.

I walked slowly down the hallway, not trusting my feet beneath my wobbling knees, promising myself to never make the mistake of relying on my appearance over my intelligence again.

I cracked my neck as emails about what I had thought was a closed deal flooded my in-box. I stared at the number on my ringing phone.

"Hi, Mom."

"Dad's here too! We're just checking in."

Phone calls with my parents were the only points in my week when I actually remembered that I had broken up with Sam. I couldn't quite bring myself to tell them Sam had moved out, and my willful omission alerted me to a deep sense of failure over the relationship not working that was bubbling beneath my skin. And not telling them one thing made my brain skulk shamefully off to all the other things I'd never tell them, like my thing with Peter and my occasional drug use. Instead, I filled our conversation with chatter about my deals and the upcoming gala.

The Private Equity Fights Hunger gala was one of the most highly anticipated and popularly photographed charity events on the New York social calendar. It would be a veritable who's who of upper-echelon New Yorkers from every walk of life and line of work, and this year it would be sponsored by Stag River because Gary was chairing the event. I googled last year's event from my office, clicking wide-eyed through pictures of Anna Wintour, Oprah, and the Obamas. I had only one thought: *What am I going to wear?*

Practically, I wasn't going to spend thousands of dollars on a couture gown—less because of the money than because I would never have the time to tailor it properly, and it would be a total waste. I opted for Rent the Runway, borrowing a $12,000 Naeem Khan runway gown with a corseted bodice and black gossamer tulle skirt covered in deep violet silk flowers. It fit perfectly.

I knew I had made the right choice as soon as I arrived at the steps to the Met, trying desperately not to grin at the flashing cameras, knowing the photographers were mistaking me for somebody important. I didn't actually care what the random photographers thought, but I believe their reaction portended what Peter's might be when he saw me. My heart pulsated wildly as I posed for the press while standing in between the posters of Gary Kaplan shaking hands with the president of the Fight Against Hunger organization that flanked the step-and-repeat. I traded emails about my location with Peter until I finally spotted him in front of the oyster display, dashing in his perfectly tailored shawl-collar tux and classic bow tie. I watched him from a distance for a moment, plotting how we'd slip out together unnoticed at the end of the evening.

"Hey!" I tapped him playfully.

He spun around, flustered. "My wife is here. Just came. You look amazing." He said it all as one word.

I plastered a smile on my face as my chest tightened and my throat closed.

"Well . . . I'm going to get a martini." As I turned toward the bar, tears sprang to my eyes. I had somehow convinced myself in the past few weeks that his wife didn't exist—that she was just some beautiful figure who fed his kids while I played the romantic lead in Peter's life. It was more difficult to pretend she was a mere nanny when she was on his arm at a gala. I sniffled and steadied myself, missing Sam for the first time since I had watched him pack.

I twisted the clasp of my evening clutch anxiously as I waited for the elderly couple in front of me to get their club sodas.

"Somebody get this lady a drink." I recognized Gary's voice immediately. This just wasn't my night. I turned and greeted him with a smile, though I'd been hoping to make it through the evening without seeing the host.

"Hi, Gary. This event is lovely. Thanks for having me."

"Alex, I want you to meet my wife, Cynthia, and our daughter, Olivia." Gary turned his body diagonally in the crowd, and his wife and daughter leaned their heads forward into my view. His wife had a large, bright smile. She was conservatively dressed in a stately black gown. His daughter was wearing a sequined shift that was perfect for her gangly teenage frame and took the attention off her pink braces. I smiled broadly and sidestepped the older couple so I could stand in front of them. I was almost confused by the sight of them—they seemed the picture of a New York society family.

"Hi. It's such a pleasure to meet both of you. You must be so proud."

"We are." His wife beamed over at her husband. Maybe I'd misjudged him entirely. Had the Rainbow Room grope actually somehow been an accident or misunderstanding? Was that woman in the Nomad a friend? Did he have an arrangement with his doting wife?

"Alex is at Klasko. She works a lot with Peter Dunn," Gary announced to his wife, who seemed to recognize Peter's name.

And all of a sudden he knows my name. "She's really been integral to a few of our deals. She's going places."

I tried to wipe the look of confusion off my face.

"Honey, I want to catch Bill and Hillary before they leave. They never stay for dinner." Cynthia pulled gently at Gary's arm, and Gary nodded, putting his arm around his daughter as they all waved goodbye to me. I watched the happy family leave before shaking myself back into the moment.

I made certain to finish two martinis before taking my seat at the Klasko table across from Peter and Marcie. She wore a simple sleeveless black velvet sheath with a diamond brooch, and she'd swept her hair into an effortlessly loose knot, accentuating her impossibly long neck. I looked at the parade of fabric marching across my breast and had the sudden and overwhelming feeling that I was emphasizing my short frame and small chest with the busy gown. I only lasted twenty minutes across from her, forcing myself to wait until Gary's speech was over before excusing myself.

I ran my fingers angrily over the silk petals protruding from my gown as I made my way out of the dining area. Somebody opened the front door, and the unseasonably cold air was so inviting that I slipped outside, the night air stinging my lungs as though reminding me I was still breathing. *What a fucking disaster of an evening!* I looked at my watch. It wasn't even eight o'clock, and while the idea of hours alone in my empty apartment made me shiver, it was better than even a moment longer at the gala. I snapped myself out of the pathetic pity party, hiked up the bottom of my gown, and plunged down the long set of granite stairs leading to Fifth Avenue.

As I reached the bottom step, I saw the outline of two men fighting, arms locked around each other like two boxers who got knotted up.

"Alex! Hey! Can you give me a hand here?" Gary was struggling to keep another man vertical as he slipped down the stairs, missing whole bunches of the concrete plateaus as his feet spilled over them. Not fighting, I corrected myself. The man was wasted.

I rushed to the man's side and took his other arm, trying desperately not to get my gown caught on my heels as I did so. Gary and I practically carried him down the steps of the Met.

"I can walk! I'm not a fucking baby!" The man writhed as though in pain in an attempt to extricate himself from our hands. I moved to release him once we were on flat ground, but he was so unsteady on his feet, I grabbed for his arm again.

"Alex, this is my partner, Simon. Simon, Alex." Gary smiled at me over the man's drooping head.

"Shouldn't you be inside?" I asked Gary, who rolled his eyes.

"Fuck Alex," Simon slurred, laughing after with his lip curled up into the base of his nose.

"There." Gary threw his chin toward the black Escalade. "Help me." His driver opened the door as he saw us approaching, and I prepared to transfer Simon into his arms.

"Hop in and pull him up from inside, will you?" Gary asked.

I hoisted my gown over my knees and stepped up into the black SUV, turning and grabbing Simon's hand, then pulled it hard as Gary and the driver shoved him into the car. Gary hopped in after him, and the door shut behind him. I found myself huddled into one of the bucket seats with Simon practically on my lap.

"I'll drop you," Gary said to me. Simon was laughing at nothing in particular, leaning the full weight of his body on me.

"You're leaving your own gala?" I didn't know what else to say.

"Drop her? Let's go out! All of us." Simon rolled his head from side to side as he stared at the ceiling. The driver started the engine. "You are no fun anymore!"

Gary didn't react, but he pulled at the side of his bow tie until it released.

"I can get my own car," I offered, reaching for the door handle.

"Let's go," Gary ordered the driver. Before he'd finished speaking, the car lurched into drive, and I heard the doors locking automatically. I swallowed hard, trying desperately to figure out why I felt so panicked. I could barely see the trees from the park streaking by the tinted windows.

"Where are we going?" Gary demanded.

"Chelsea. Eighteenth and Eighth," I managed shakily.

I finally extricated myself from Simon's weight and slipped back into the third row's cool leather, where I shoved myself against the far window. My stomach churned as a feeling of dread spread over my entire body. Chill out, I told myself. The firm's biggest client knew me and was just being nice by giving me a ride home. I'd be there in a few minutes. Still, I couldn't shake the feeling that something was off. I grabbed for my phone and dialed my own work number, leaving it on and putting it back in my bag.

"So, you're the one who's fucking Peter," Simon slurred from the middle row. I whipped my head up, praying I had misheard. When I met Gary's gaze, he smiled sadistically and nodded. I couldn't believe Peter would tell people that. Not people, clients!

"Turn the music up!" Gary commanded the driver. The thudding of the bass from somewhere below my thighs rattled my bones against one another. The bile in my stomach rose as I felt the energy in the car shift. I wanted to disappear into the leather, to melt into the cool black seat and leave only my rented dress as evidence I had ever existed. I crossed my legs tightly and clasped my hands together over my knees. I wondered if they could see the tears welling in my eyes.

"This is just her act," Gary snarled. "She pretends to be so proper."

Simon burst out laughing and looked at me hungrily. "Really, she wants it," Gary whispered.

Despite the back of his chair shielding him from me, and the darkness of the car, I could tell Gary was getting excited. *I need to get out of this car.* The driver turned left and picked up speed. I looked outside and realized we were on the West Side Highway, going at least sixty miles an hour. With a sinking feeling, I noted that there was no door to my left. I had given up my ability to flee the vehicle when I moved to the back row.

I turned to face the front, only to find Gary now next to me.

"Please don't," I whispered. Simon leaned over the back of his chair as though watching a dogfight. My mind raced, and I grabbed onto my last hope. "I'm glad that NDA we drafted is working out for you. Do you keep track of who signs them? I never did."

Gary's eyes bulged, and a large vein running directly down the middle of his forehead pulsated.

"You don't have to sign one. You're my lawyer. What we do is confidential. You only have a job because I let you. Your firm only exists because I let it. This is MY fucking town. Do you hear me, you ungrateful little whore?"

As he screamed, I felt hot tears run down my face.

"Ungrateful!" Simon echoed, cackling.

Gary grabbed at the bottom of my dress and pushed it up toward my thighs. I became an animal in survival mode. I fought him with every ounce of my strength, with every limb and body part I could throw at him, but then I registered another set of hands on me. Simon had somehow gained enough muscular control to hold down my legs quite forcefully. I felt both sets of hands ripping down the top of my dress and shoving the bottom of it up. I could no longer fight and scream at the same time. I fell silent as I struggled to keep my waist pointed down and as far away from the predators as possible. *I'm going to die. They're going to kill me. They're going to rape me and then kill me.*

For just a moment, I felt less weight bearing down on me. Was it over? Were they tired? Had they decided not to do it? Then a primal fear unlike any I had ever experienced froze my body as I heard the unmistakable sound of a zipper being unzipped. They weren't tired; they were moving on to phase two. Taking advantage of Gary having to lean away to unzip his tux pants and Simon's inebriated state, I kicked as hard as I could in the direction of the zipping sound. I felt my heel hit something and then sink into it just as Gary let out a gut-wrenching scream.

The car screeched to a halt, and the lights turned on. I pulled back my foot, but my shoe slipped off, stuck on something. When Gary finally removed the revolting weight of his body from mine, Simon and I stared at Gary's ripped pant leg, revealing a thick red line of blood against his pale, hairy upper thigh. The door opened from behind Simon as the driver, apparently unaccustomed to the sound of male screams, came to see what the commotion was. With the car light illuminating the back seat, we all gawked at my Louboutin heel and Gary's thigh, his blood matching the color of my sole.

I pulled the top of my dress up and the bottom down and slipped out between Gary and the driver. I paused for a moment, knowing it was stupid. Nobody was paying attention to me. Were they just letting me go? I kicked off my other shoe and began to run, the ground slicing into my bare soles like an angry blessing.

"Let her go," I heard Gary yell. "She won't talk."

I don't remember much about the rest of the night. I have a vague recollection of the doorman eyeing my feet, more out of annoyance that I was leaving bloody footprints on our white marble lobby floor than out of any real concern for my well-being.

I remember taking great care to remove my dress, as though returning it in decent shape would allow me to ignore what had happened entirely. I remember crying in truncated bursts, but mostly because I felt as though I should. I wasn't actually sad. I was angry. And relieved. And scared.

For the bulk of the night, I shook. Sometimes gently, and sometimes more violently. And I had terrible nightmares, though I couldn't remember their substance. I'd find myself upright atop sweat-soaked sheets, my throat raw with the screams still ringing in the air. As the sun rose, I made my way out of bed, feeling dirty from the inside, knowing I should shower, but wanting nothing less than to be alone with my naked body, which suddenly seemed such a liability.

I emailed Anna that I had the flu and asked her to let anybody who called know as much before crawling under my covers for two days. I felt that the bottom, the reliable floor of my life, had been ripped out from under me. I was in free fall. Finally, I checked my phone for the first time in days. I apologized to Jordan and Matt for not answering emails, blaming my illness. I finally read the missed emails from the morning after the gala. The words made me feel as if my brain were in a vise, about to be squeezed to the point of permanent debilitation.

From: Peter Dunn
To: Gary Kaplan
Cc: Alexandra Vogel
Subject: Gala

Gary,

Thank you so much for having us. The event was spectacular. We're so proud to represent somebody who does so much good.

From: Gary Kaplan
To: Peter Dunn
Cc: Alexandra Vogel
Subject: Re: Gala

Alex and Peter,

You guys are the best! Thanks for being there and for all that you do for me and Stag River.

—GRK

I dropped my phone to the cushion beside me and stared at it for a moment, willing the pressure in my skull to subside just a little. I never once, not even for a moment, contemplated telling anybody what had happened. I could barely recount it to myself: *I left the gala early because I couldn't stand to be around the wife of the coworker I've been sleeping with . . .* I had to stop there.

I attempted to control the pain I was feeling by picturing myself floating on a cloud, conjuring the instructions from the one time in college I had tried meditating, but my mind raced with the sense that I'd somehow deserved the punishment, spliced with the actual feeling of my dress being pushed up and their hands all over me. I was unable to make sense of my thoughts or quell the anxiety numbing my limbs, but I did arrive at one conclusion: If I didn't talk about it and I didn't let it affect me, then it didn't happen. What *did* actually happen, anyway? Attempted assault? What was the punishment for that? A slap on the wrist? This was *Gary Kaplan*. Nobody would believe me. And he would destroy my career, and maybe even my family. I would just continue to live my life, and not let him affect me. That way, I would win.

PART VI

POSTBREAKUP MATTERS

The “cleanup” and adjustments made after a deal or breakup in order to ensure that each party to the transaction can successfully function.

Q. To be clear, you engaged in consensual sexual congress with Peter Dunn. And you did not consent to the alleged sexual advances made by Gary Kaplan.

A. Correct. You must realize that consenting to one man is not consenting to every man.

Q. There is no implication that it is. It's a yes or no question. Is it correct that you consented to sexual relations with Peter Dunn but not with Gary Kaplan?

A. Yes. It is.

Q. Did you benefit financially based on your claims of alleged sexual assault against Gary Kaplan?

A. No.

Q. You did not benefit monetarily, either directly or indirectly, from your accusations against Gary Kaplan?

CHAPTER 22

I walked into the office the Monday morning after the Stag River gala and stared at the blinking red light on my phone. I'd listened to and deleted all my messages from coworkers and clients, so I knew what I would hear if I listened to the last voice mail, the one I had left myself that night. The air around my head hummed, and I shoved my index fingers into my ears and shook hard in a futile attempt to dispel the ringing. Though I hadn't been thinking clearly when I'd lied about having the flu, it actually was the perfect excuse because I knew how ill I looked—my sunken cheeks had a greenish hue, and my hair was matted to my head from the constant beads of sweat bubbling up through my scalp.

I covered the blinking red light with a napkin and dove into my emails. Throwing myself into work distracted me from the mess that was my personal life, sucking all emotion out of me and leaving behind a calculating shell of a human. I spent the next hour tending to my Stag River messages, though none directly from Gary, and responded clearly and professionally. Starting at ten, I was in meetings all day, including three with Peter where I successfully avoided making eye contact with him even once. When I returned to my office at the end of the day, Anna was looking up at me expectantly from her cubicle. "I have Jordan for you."

I nodded and closed the door to my office behind me. "Hi," I said into the receiver.

His voice was warm. "How're you feeling?"

"Better. Yeah, better," I told him. In reality, I felt almost nothing but a nagging angst at my fingertips—making me type faster, speak more quickly, walk more swiftly.

"I'm getting a drink with some guys across the street. Are you still knocked out from the flu?"

"I need a drink tonight more than anybody has ever needed a drink."

"Is that a yes?" Jordan laughed. "Meet us there at seven."

I sat back in my chair and bit at a fingernail. For the moment, I had no unread emails and nothing pressing on my to-do list, and my brain drifted back to The Incident. I shook my head to steady myself and dialed the first three digits of Carmen's extension but couldn't press the last one. I leaned back in my chair and stared up at the ceiling, willing my hand to stop trembling. I shook it out, hung up, and dialed her full extension.

"Hey lady!" Carmen chirped. "What's cookin'?" I could hear impatience in her tone.

"Hey . . ." I had called her to make small talk, just to cancel the noise in my head, but hearing her voice, I realized how badly I needed to tell her about the gala. Whatever was going on between us at work, I had no doubt whatsoever she'd stand beside me as a loyal friend.

"Al, so sorry. Gotta take this. Call you right back." Carmen clicked onto her other line.

I cradled my head in my hands and heard a knock on the door. I took a moment to gather myself before speaking. "Come in!"

Peter opened the door, which let out a slow creak, and closed it behind him. I noticed that his usually smooth jawline was covered in stubble. It suited him—of course it did. I suddenly felt angry that everything was so easy for him. That I had been so easy for him.

"May I?" he asked, gesturing to a seat. I gave him a short nod.

"Are you avoiding me?" he asked, sounding uncharacteristically apprehensive. "I mean, I know you're avoiding me. I know you're mad about the gala."

I swallowed. "I'm not mad. Or avoiding you. I've responded to all your emails, haven't I?" He cocked his head to one side, indicating that he'd noticed that my responses had become short. And cold. No exclamation points or witty replies, no smiley faces or open-ended questions regarding anything other than deal terms. Granted, we had never been overtly flirtatious via email, but my tone toward him had undoubtedly shifted.

I stared at him, realizing that I blamed him for what had happened to me.

"I'm just confused because I thought we had a nice weekend together . . . I'd feel terrible if I did something to . . ."

"You didn't," I said. "But what we had, whatever that was, is over. I want to continue working on your deals. But we can only work together. No more . . . anything," I finished, and exhaled. Saying those words was much easier than I had thought it would be.

Peter met my gaze with a half smile and nodded a few times, slowly at first and then faster. "Fair enough," he said. Then we both froze as we heard a mechanical click from somewhere in my desk, a slight rustling, and the undeniable shift of the energy in the air. The hairs on the back of my neck stood up.

"I'm still on the line," Carmen said, her voice coming from the black grid, and then we heard the click as she hung up.

I dropped my head into my hands. "Shit."

"Was that—" Peter began.

"Please," I said, without looking up.

I heard him shut my door as I said "Shit" over and over to myself, head still in my hands. I finally swallowed down the bile that had made its way to the back of my throat, sat up, and dialed Carmen's extension. I heard her pick up the receiver, but the line went immediately dead. I tried again. Same thing.

Three more times. The same result. She had to be so disgusted with me—thinking this was how I'd gotten an edge over her in M&A.

"Fuck!" I yelled into the ether. Within thirty seconds, Anna poked her head in.

"Not now," I snapped at her. She darted back out and closed the door quickly, leaving me alone in a space that seemed to be closing in on me as my thoughts of shame ballooned out.

When I arrived at the bar, I was surprised to see Kevin sitting next to Jordan at a high-top table, two empty beers in front of them. "I didn't realize you two knew each other," I said in between hungry sips of my drink, eager to wash away the day I just had.

"Jealous?" Kevin said with a wink. I rolled my eyes and ordered a round of tequila shots. I barely paid attention to what they were saying as I focused on drinking enough to dull my racing thoughts and emotions. I replayed the conversation with Peter that Carmen had overheard over and over in my mind as Kevin and Jordan laughed about some story they heard from the Litigation team. I ordered another round of shots, ignoring Kevin's curious glance, and watched as the bartender slowly poured our shots and the waitress took an eternity to bring them over. I threw mine back before the guys did, without a "Cheers."

"Another!" I demanded, slamming my shot glass down.

Jordan shook his head and laughed. "I think you've had quite enough, Skip."

"I'll be the judge of that," I said, and sneered. "I'm not some, like, little woman." I couldn't come up with a better word.

Jordan held up his hands. "Fine, fine—have as much as you want."

As much as I hated to admit Jordan was right, I was drunk. Really drunk. I hadn't eaten a substantial meal in days, and between the shots and the drinks, I was four or five deep. And for the first time in my life, I was an angry drunk.

"Cigarette?" Jordan cocked his head to the side.

"I don't smoke. It's disgusting."

"Then just stand outside with me," he said curtly, pulling me by the arm. I ripped it out of his grip and spun around with my finger pointed at him, but I saw so much concern and kindness in his expression that I dropped my arm back to my side and turned toward the door. "We'll be back in two minutes," I heard him say to Kevin.

The fresh spring air forced my pores open, sobering me up for a moment. "I'll have one too," I said, as though I was doing him a favor.

Jordan shook his head. "I quit months ago. I don't have any on me." He folded his arms over his chest and stared at me. "What the fuck is going on with you, Skip?"

As I shook my head, the tears came almost immediately. "I feel like I'm coming apart," I coughed out, gasping for air.

"Shit," Jordan said. He took a step toward me and then retreated, not knowing how close to get. I thought for a moment of telling Jordan about Gary assaulting me, about my relationship with Peter, about Carmen finding out—maybe he'd be the one who could help me out of the mess I had made. But if somebody else knew everything that had happened, it would suddenly become real.

"How could you sleep with Carmen?" I said instead. "I won't cover for you the way I did with Nancy, you know."

His jaw dropped open. "Huh?"

"I know you guys are having a thing."

"You've lost your mind, Skip. Seriously, you're insane. I've never laid a finger on Carmen." He spoke slowly, as though I were holding hostages. "That's Peter's job," he said.

Everything stopped.

"Who?" My knees grew weak, and I bent slightly to rest my hands on my thighs.

"Peter! Shit!" Jordan said.

"Peter Peter? Peter Dunn?" I asked. I leaned backward against the wall, no longer trusting my legs. Carmen knows I slept with Peter, I thought. And Peter's the guy Carmen has been seeing? This was not good. Not good.

"Yes, Peter Dunn! How did you not know that? Everybody knows. Carmen is pretty obvious about it," he said with a smirk.

"Oh my god. This day is actually so much worse than I thought it was. And it was really fucking bad to begin with. My life is completely going to shit!" I yelled, stomping my foot in frustration.

"That's a bit dramatic, Skip. But yeah, he's fucking Carmen. And Peggy in recruiting. And Sarah in accounting. I mean, the man can't keep it in his pants."

I struggled to take a deep breath, with only minimal success.

"Did you *really* not know this?" Jordan said. "I actually feel like we've spoken about it." I shook my head, and my heart banged against my ribs. "Shit. Skip? Are you okay?" Jordan's hand was on my back. "You're freaking out. I mean, this doesn't even really involve you. You need to chill." As he spoke, he dug into his breast pocket, and I heard the rattling maraca of pills.

I watched his lips moving, and in a crystal-clear moment, I saw it: my cheating with a serial adulterer, my assault by a rich scumbag, my entire existence in corporate America, was just so . . . typical. I realized what I had always feared to be true, since the moment my world records were shattered. I wasn't special at all, I was just like every other pathetic person I knew. I bent down and puked between my shoes.

***

I stared at my bite marks in the pizza crust, taking one last small nibble at the corner, as we sat on a bench. I wiped the grease from my chin with the back of my hand and threw the rest of my slice into the trash, then leaned my head on Jordan's shoulder, which felt solid and warm against my cheek.

"I can't do this job anymore," I muttered into the foggy air.

"You're really fucking stressed. And you don't sleep. And you drank too much tonight. You can do this. You're so talented," he said calmly.

Images flew through my mind—Carmen's sideways glances during that presentation, the ones I'd thought were directed at Jordan; the locked restoration room door; her questions about where I was going with Peter; and finally, the conversation she'd overheard—until, like a gift, the Xanax Jordan had given me kicked in.

"Kevin. We left Kevin," I realized aloud.

"Kevin is fine. Let's get you home, Skip. It's Sam's turn to deal with you," he said, laughing. I burst into tears again at the mention of Sam's name, but allowed him to hail me a cab to take me home.

CHAPTER 23

"Sloppy," Peter muttered under his breath, and I cringed. In the forty-five minutes it took him to read the acquisition agreement I'd drafted, I sat in his office and alternated between watching him and reading my emails on my phone. He didn't say a single word to me as he took a pen to my draft with short, tight, angry marks.

I winced as I watched the red lines slash through the words I'd chosen carefully, and thought of how Carmen wouldn't return my phone calls. I watched Peter gnaw at his lower lip, and I wondered momentarily whether he was so angry because Carmen had stopped sleeping with him as well. But I couldn't quite bring myself to care—about anything, really. Except my deals.

I was throwing myself into work, gladly letting it consume all of my energy and waking hours. I almost managed to convince myself I was doing okay—until I drank. Liquor allowed all the vile bodily fluids to escape from my face—hot tears and yellow mucus and bubbles of saliva—as soon as my defenses were slightly weakened. A few days after my less-than-stellar showing at drinks with Kevin and Jordan, I tried a few glasses of wine alone on my couch when I got home from work. Even before I was through with my first glass, I found myself wailing and shaking my shoulders, the way I only ever did when I was certain everything was crumbling around me, and when I was positive nobody was within earshot.

But sober, I convinced myself that I felt somewhat calm about my personal life and the state of chaos it was in. Weekdays in the office somehow felt very much normal, aside from the fact that Peter was reviewing my work with a much harsher eye.

When he finally looked up and handed me the document, it was entirely covered in red. “Turn these changes by COB,” he said without any trace of warmth.

I nodded and turned to leave. “When did you start doing M&A?” he asked, looking at me as though we barely knew one another.

“October.”

“Hmm,” he snorted, and turned back to his computer.

He was going to write me a bad review. He was going to kill my career. I was so screwed. Klasko was sadly the only place that felt like home, where I felt like the competent adult I’d been, pre-affair, pre-breakup, pre-Incident. I needed the tailored business clothes to hold me together, the sterile lobby to make me feel sane, the superficial pleasantries and mundane deal work to keep my mind off everything that had happened.

When I woke the next day, I inhaled in disgust. *What was that smell?* I looked under my bed for remnants of food, then looked at my gym shoes to see if I had stepped in poop, before burying my head in my chest and breathing in. I had actually thought it was impossible to recognize one’s own stench, but I could tell I smelled rotten, in a way that indicated sickness rather than bad hygiene. I forced myself into the bathroom, where I painstakingly removed my clothes, breathing harder with panic as every article of clothing dropped onto the tile floor. I looked at my sunken eyes and matted hair and forced myself into the shower, where I remembered why I had been avoiding it. Being naked made the whole night rush in on me, the pulsing music in my ears, the anxiety in my veins. I mostly heard my own screams, my own struggle. My body didn’t feel like my own any longer. It felt like this unnecessary weakness following me around, and I didn't want to exist in it. *Snap out of it*, I told myself. *You're fine. At the end of the day, nothing even happened.* I scrubbed myself and toweled off as quickly as possible, then checked my email as I pulled on black pants and a silk blouse.

From: Carmen Greyson
To: Alexandra Vogel
Subject: Can we talk?

My office? Now? We really should talk . . .

From: Alexandra Vogel
To: Carmen Greyson
Subject: Re: Can we talk?

On my way in now. Will come straight to your office.

"Hey," I said after knocking on Carmen's doorframe forty minutes later. We looked at each other, both seeing a thinner, more hollowed-out version of our friend. I shut the door behind me and took a seat.

"So . . . ," she started, and her lip immediately began to quiver. "I have something to tell you." It was unnerving to watch her unwind, tears leaking out of her eyes and her hands shaking. "Peter Dunn and I also slept together."

I tried my best to look surprised, but my effort was wasted; she could barely make eye contact.

"I'm sorry," she whispered.

I gave her a moment before I responded. "Look, Carmen, I made a mistake with Peter too. It was brief, and now it's over."

She lifted her head and cocked it to the side, and I sensed that it had been more than a mistake for her. Of course, it had been more than that for me too.

"Alex, we have to go to management about this," she said. "The M&A group has pitted us against one another from day one. They make us fight for work, for offices, for acceptance. And one of the most important partners in the group has been sleeping with both of us, and god knows who else. It's a hostile work environment for women, and I, for one, will not stand for it. Let's fight for an equal place along with the men on the M&A team." Her words sounded rehearsed, as though she had run through them in the mirror.

I nodded slowly. I appreciated her willingness to act, but I felt too defeated to get fired up. "Look, to be honest, Peter Dunn is the least of my worries these days. He didn't force me to do anything."

"Alex, are you kidding me? First of all, partners can't just sleep with associates. Second, what does 'consent' even mean when the power dynamic is so screwed up? Did you ever consider what would happen if you turned him down? Or tried to end it? It's sexual harassment if you even need to think about those things. When I overheard your conversation with him, I never wanted to speak to him again—but I'm on an active matter with him, so I have to. I have to be deferential to him because he's my boss, in a way. It's all sorts of fucked up."

"I did end it with him. And he has been retaliating," I said aloud before I realized it, then shook my head. "I'm sorry, but this doesn't *feel* like harassment." Granted, my baseline had shifted wildly in the past few weeks. "But if you feel harassed, you should say something. Be careful, though. Think about what you want out of this, because—"

"I want Peter *gone*, and I want an equal playing field so I can try to make partner without being made to compete with my best friend at the firm, or feeling like I need to go to strip clubs just to get staffed on deals." She had raised her voice and was gesticulating wildly. I sat calmly, watching her, thinking that hers was the reaction I *should* have been having. Something was wrong with me. What had happened to me couldn't be undone. *I'm damaged goods*, I thought.

"I totally agree, Carm, but I think you need to consider that this is a business," I said. "And Peter Dunn has the most lucrative list of clients at the firm. They're not going to fire him. We're more disposable than he is. They'll offer you money to leave, and he'll stay."

"I'd never take it!" she hissed.

"Look, I've got a lot going on. Can I think about it?"

She'd gotten up and was pacing by her window. "Of course. But I'm going to management on Monday." It was Wednesday. "I can't stand it anymore." She stopped and placed her hands on her hips, her back to me, searching the city for answers.

"I understand," I said, and she turned around.

"I think we both have stories that need to be told," she said firmly, then approached me and flung her arms around me in an uncharacteristic display of physical affection. "I hope you do the right thing."

I nodded, and she loosened her embrace, freeing me for a hasty escape.

CHAPTER 24

Carmen lasted until nine o'clock on Thursday evening before calling my office, presumably to press me for an answer. I ignored her call, silencing the ringer and letting it go to voice mail, before heading out to work from home and avoid a potential drop-by from her. Though I'd been trying to weigh the pros and cons of her offer, I knew I had no real intention of reporting my affair with Peter. I had wanted him, had even initiated at least one of our encounters—but more importantly, it wasn't high on the list of battles I knew I should currently be fighting.

As soon as I stepped out into the marble lobby, the night sky cracked open with a bolt of lightning and the sound of a downpour reverberated through the walls. I looked back at the closing elevator doors and contemplated heading back upstairs to get an umbrella, but then I remembered that Lincoln always kept a few on hand. The security desk was empty, but I spotted him a few paces away, heading out of the building for a cigarette.

"Lincoln! I'm grabbing an umbrella, okay?" I shouted, and he threw me a thumbs-up as he stepped outside and under the awning. As I reached into the brown cardboard box under his desk for a Klasko-branded umbrella, I noticed a new column of moving images on one end of the screen, labeled "56th Floor." I leaned closer to the screen and noticed the bare floors and the scaffolding I'd seen the night of the keg party, plus the yellow caution tape around the exposed elevator shaft, and . . . I leaned in closer. She just stood there, looking down. She wasn't moving. I thought for a moment she might have been praying. I squinted at the grainy image, less clear than the ones on the other screens because of the lack of light on the floor. Shoes?

Were those shoes? My spine snapped into a straightened position. *Shit.* I dropped my bag at the security desk and ran to the elevator bank, where I pushed the up arrow five times fast then held it down. *C'mon c'mon,* I prayed silently.

When the elevator finally came, the ascent to 56 felt like an eternity as my thoughts raced. *Fuck. I don't have a plan. What am I supposed to say? I'm not qualified to handle this. Maybe I should make up a reason to be there so I don't embarrass her.* I ripped my pearl earring out of my ear and held it in my palm, my idea just beginning to take shape.

As the metal doors opened, I saw her before she saw me. She was standing in the darkened room, lit only by the city lights surrounding our building, peering out into the unfinished elevator shaft at the far end of the floor, her bare toes hovering at the edge of the precipice, and crying. I narrowed my eyes, hoping to find evidence that what I feared was happening wasn't actually happening. But instead, I saw her shoulders shake slightly, and I heard the echo of her soft weeping even from the other side of the room. *Calm. Calm. Be calm,* I told myself. *Don't make any sudden movements.* The last thing I wanted to do was make her lose her balance.

I felt her register my presence, and I immediately dropped to my hands and knees, focusing on the floor as I crawled toward her, my hands patting the ground in front of me as the concrete dug into my kneecaps.

I looked up slowly, as if I was just noticing her in that moment. "Nancy. I'm so glad you're here. I lost my earring earlier when some of us came up to scout office space. Can you help me? I'm sure it's here somewhere." She turned only partially to me before taking one more longing look fifty-six stories down into the dirt floor below Fifth Avenue. For a moment, I panicked that she would do it. "Please," I begged, "can you help me?" I stretched my arm out to her, my voice breaking.

As she took a step away from the edge and toward me, then sank onto her hands and knees, I let go of the earring in my fist. Leaving it on the ground, I continued past it. I snuck a few glances at Nancy's tearstained face as we inched past one another, moving like two toddlers.

"I got it!" she declared, sitting back on her calves.

"Oh my god! Nancy! You're amazing! You're a lifesaver!" I took the earring from her hand and hugged her close to my chest. The tension in my spine released, and I sank into her, realizing that tears were now streaming down my face too. "I'm so glad you're here," I said into her hair. "So glad," I repeated, barely above a whisper.

She began to cry again, covering her face with her hands as I sat cross-legged on the floor and rubbed her back.

"Do you want to talk about it?" I finally asked. There was a long pause, and Nancy looked everywhere but at me. Her gaze finally rested on her bare feet.

"Sometimes I don't want to be here," she said quietly. "I don't fit in here. I've never fit in—my whole life I've never fit in. Anywhere. You don't understand. Everything is so"—she lifted her eyes to mine and held out her palms, as though waiting for the correct words to fall into them—"easy for you."

I sat back for a moment, the concrete digging into my backside. "This year is hard for everybody. Even me." I shrugged, putting the earring back into my lobe. "I just wear the struggle differently. We all do. But we're all feeling the pressure. It will get better. Things always do. Nothing is forever." This was a horrible don't-kill-yourself speech. "I'm a disaster right now, by the way. Our clients are pigs, my closest friend at the firm and I slept with the same guy, and my boyfriend and I broke up a couple months ago and you're the first person I'm telling about it. We come to work in skirts and heels, but it's all just a costume to keep people from seeing how messed up we are."

Nancy stared at the floor as I spoke, then finally looked up.

"You should see somebody if you feel like you don't want to be here," I continued. "Will you do that?"

She looked over at her shoes and blushed, realizing that I knew what she had been doing on the vacant fifty-sixth floor. She nodded, locking her eyes with mine so I knew she took my request seriously.

"I really am so glad you're here," I reiterated, my voice and the meaning of the words in the broader, more mortal sense not lost on me. "This place can be super lonely. Which is weird, I know, because we're in an office surrounded by people. But we all feel alone. I'm always here for you. For whatever. Even if you just want to walk around the block."

"Maybe we could just . . . get dinner every once in a while?" she said sheepishly.

I brought Nancy down to my office, where I prattled on about how I'd gotten mixed up in a romantic relationship with somebody at work and how it ruined my relationship at home, how Sam had packed and left. It felt cathartic to share my mistakes with her, though I didn't feel like I could let her in on the dark pockets in my mind that Gary had left in his wake. And Nancy, while she was sympathetic, was clearly comforted by the knowledge that I was not remotely as together as she had thought.

"Jordan was my first boyfriend," she finally blurted out. I looked at her, slightly confused. "I know he's married. And that we weren't really conventionally *dating* . . ." She stopped and laughed nervously. "You wouldn't understand."

I took her hand from across my desk. “I might.”

“Why are you so nice to me? Even after you heard me say that awful stuff about you in the bathroom? I still feel terrible about that.”

I shrugged. “People say and do awful stuff all the time. I figured you were just doing it to fit in with those girls.”

“I was. But that’s no excuse.” She bit at a hangnail.

“I guess,” I said. “But don’t beat yourself up. This place is one big excuse for people to behave badly.”

An hour later, when I was sufficiently certain she had calmed down, and she had refused multiple offers to sleep over at my place or have me on her couch, I settled for calling her a car. We traded numbers, and she assured me she would be okay and that she would call me if she wasn’t. On my way home, I checked on her twice via text, and she called me to say good night. Though I felt racked with anxiety that I’d made a mistake in letting her go home alone, I could only watch the clock until, around four in the morning, exhaustion overtook me.

I woke on Friday to silence, allowing it to seep in for a moment before lunging toward my nightstand to see if Nancy had written me. She had. As I opened her message of thanks plus a promise that she’d stop by my office that day, I finally indulged in my tears, knowing they were coming from so many tender and painful places inside me.

I so badly didn’t want to need my family right then—but I did. I dialed their landline from my “Favorites” list and attempted a lighthearted “Hi!” when my dad picked up.

“Hi, sweet pea! What’s cookin’?” he boomed into my ear, oblivious to my emotional state.

"I was thinking of coming home tonight for the weekend. Just to get out of the city. Work has been really crazy. I need a break. If you and mom don't have plans . . ." I trailed off, wiping away my tears with the back of my hand.

"What a great idea! Your mother and I have no plans. I'll scoop you and Sam from the train whenever you give me the word. And guess what—our internet is fixed!"

"Sam can't come," I said quickly. "I'll call you as soon as I know which train I'm on."

I pushed a roasted carrot around my plate before pushing my fork prongs into it but making no movement to lift it to my lips. I felt both my parents watching me, expecting me to explain my dark mood and sunken cheeks, but I wasn't ready.

"How's the hospital?" I asked my father instead.

"Good! Good good. Busy," he said, shaking his head as if disagreeing with himself. My mother looked at him worriedly and turned to me with an empathetic frown. "Your father had a really sick patient today," she explained.

My dad put his elbows on the table. "My patients are all really sick. Otherwise they wouldn't need an oncologist," he said, as though reminding himself as much. I watched his eyes scan the table and linger at the bread basket before he opted for more salad.

"Sorry, Dad," I said. He shrugged and forced a smile. I attempted to recalibrate my own problems, but they somehow weighed just as heavily on me. I turned back to my food.

"How was your day, honey?" he asked my mother.

"Great!" she said brightly. "We finally raised enough money for the new children's wing at the library. I think it'll have a bunch of optional classes to offer as well. And we're going to have a whole room devoted to Legos and computers with virtual city software. So important for kids to be able to build things."

My father looked at me. "And who better to oversee that room than your mother?" he asked proudly.

"Why? Because you have an architecture license?" I said to her. *One she never used.* However dysfunctional, abusive, misogynistic, and unbalanced my short tenure in corporate America had been so far, I still disagreed with my mother's path, giving up her career to be a housewife.

My mother stared at me.

"Because she *is* an architect! Still certified," my father interjected.

"I don't need the license to do this. I just love the idea of children building something tangible." She placed a forkful of salmon in her mouth and chewed calmly, though I knew I was trying her patience.

"The salmon is especially good tonight, Mom," I said, and gestured to the platter. She smiled softly at me, accepting my apology.

At eleven o'clock, an hour after my parents had gone up to bed, I was halfway through *Terms of Endearment* on cable and two-thirds of the way through a box of Kleenex. I lay on the same couch on which I'd had my first kiss, and on which the recipient of that kiss had later broken up with me, proving to me that the fist-sized muscle in my chest could actually break. The cushion beneath the tan leather was still molded perfectly to my form, and the faux fur throw was just heavy enough to weigh me down comfortingly. When I heard a noise in the kitchen, I pressed pause and wrapped myself in the blanket to check it out. Only the refrigerator light illuminated my father's frame as he stood contemplating the contents of the Tupperware containers stacked on the lowest shelf while shoving a croissant in his mouth.

"Gotcha," I said with a laugh.

He jumped back as he covered the K&F symbol over his heart with his hand, croissant still shoved in his mouth. "You scared me!"

"Hungry?" I gave him a sideways smile.

He rolled his eyes. "I try to eat just a little out of every container so your mother can't tell that anything is missing. But I forgot I could blame the missing food on you this weekend," he said. "Sit with me for a second, sweet pea."

Still draped in tan fur, I took a seat at the kitchen table as my father stacked four containers of Tupperware in his hands and made his way over to me.

"Your mom is the best cook," he said, putting a slice of cold turkey on his plate and squeezing out a dollop of ketchup next to it. "You know, when I first married her, she couldn't boil water."

I nodded, allowing the familiar story to ease my mind.

"The first meal she cooked for me was lamb roast," he went on. "I swear I chewed my first bite for ten minutes, and it was still just sitting there in my mouth."

I giggled, and he leaned in closer to me, studying my face.

"Are you crying?" he asked, squinting into the dim light. I wiped at my cheeks.

"*Terms of Endearment,*" I explained, nodding toward the den.

"Ah, you love the tear-jerkers. You're just like your mother."

"I'm not," I whispered.

"You are," he said, not arguing so much as correcting me. A wave of sadness snuck in under my blanket. My father watched me patiently for a minute before reaching out and taking my hand in his, and I burst into tears.

The words tumbled out of my lips before I could stop them.

"Sam and I broke up. He moved out. And work is a mess right now. It's too much."

"Oh, sweet pea. Your mother and I thought that might be the case. I'm so sorry." He scooted his chair next to mine and put an arm over my shoulder. I threw my arms around him, and he rubbed my back over the blanket as I allowed myself the comfort of his embrace.

"You and Mom knew?" I asked, pulling back. "Why didn't you say anything?"

"We didn't know, but we wondered. Sometimes people need to share things in their own time."

I sobbed harder. "Mom must be so mad. She loves Sam," I managed to say.

My father stared at me. "Your mother loves *you,* Alex. You should talk to her about this."

"I can't. She doesn't understand my life at all!" I cried. "She quit her job when she had me. I broke up with my boyfriend mostly because I work too much and don't have time for him. And my stress is all . . . work-related. She wouldn't understand at all." I was wiping my tears away with my palms now.

"Enough, Alexandra. Enough is enough." His voice was harsh.

I looked at him, shocked at his rare angry tone.

"Do you remember any of your nannies?" he continued.

I blew my nose and nodded, indulging him, though I had no idea where he was going.

"What about Ada? Remember her?" he prodded.

"Of course." The memory of a large bosom and the smell of pierogis wafted over me, and I smiled despite myself.

"Do you remember why she left?"

I squinted to bring the scene into focus. There was a storm. I was in a tree with an umbrella, trying to fly. Then there was a white bone jutting out of my right leg as I lay, crumpled and crying, on the ground. I didn't quite understand why he was reminding me of a time I'd misbehaved. "Was I a bad kid?"

He shook his head vigorously. "You were the most amazing child. Everybody loved you. All of your nannies. They loved you so much that they couldn't take it."

"Take what?" I suddenly felt warm, and let the blanket slip off my shoulders.

"When you had to do exactly what you wanted to do when you wanted to do it. It's served you well. You were a champion swimmer, got into the best schools, and now you're at the best firm. You simply . . . will your life to happen, it seems. But Ada left after you jumped out of that tree and broke your leg. Farrah left after we took her skiing with us and you took off down the black diamond without so much as a word to any of us. Cynthia left once you went on a hunger strike in an attempt to force us to get you a puppy. They all loved you so much they couldn't stand to take care of you when you didn't follow the rules."

"I ate when everybody was asleep," I mumbled. I pulled my sleeves down over my hands self-consciously and rubbed my right forearm. "What's your point? That I scare off everybody who gets close to me?" I could hear my voice becoming shrill.

"No no no, sweetheart," he said, and rubbed at my back again. "The point is . . . well, two things. First, you always created your own path, your own rules. I'm sure you will do the same at Klasko. And second, why would we have nannies if your mother was home, taking care of you?"

I squinted to see the glaringly obvious. "Mom worked when I was young?"

"Your mother was at Dunns & Simons in the city until you were six."

I furrowed my brow as he continued. "She stopped being a full-time architect to be a full-time mother. It's what she wanted, but she also worried you were too much to leave with anybody else. And she was the only one you ever really listened to. She wanted to be a better mother, and that meant not being an architect. She was absolutely a career woman. But it never meant as much to her as you do."

My lower jaw hung loosely. The tears had stopped, replaced by a sense of anxious dread that I had somehow misjudged the people who had raised me.

"She worried about me?" I knew she had, of course. But it was oddly comforting to say out loud. It dispelled my feeling that I was a cheap, disposable surplus commodity in the world.

"She worried about you because she saw herself in you! The way mothers do. The way parents do. We worry about you all the time, even now. Whether the subways are safe. Whether you're sleeping enough. Whether you're eating enough." He shoved a container of noodles at me. I laughed and sniffled. "Whether you're happy," he finished softly.

I rested my head on his shoulder and stared up at the water stain in the ceiling, a reminder of the leak it had sprouted when I was in eighth grade. I was having a sleepover with Sandy Cranswell when we were in a "best friends" phase, and rather than having pancakes and watching television on a lazy Sunday morning, we were carrying buckets up from the basement to catch the water and dumping them out the back door before they overflowed.

"I can't believe I kept Mom from working. And you guys would have had a second income . . . you might have been able to retire by now," I said, sniffling, still staring at the ceiling.

I felt him sigh. "Alexandra, we did just fine. We have more than enough. I love my work. We're happy." I held my father's gaze and finally nodded. Satisfied, he exhaled. "Now I'm going back to bed. I have rounds at seven tomorrow."

"Night, Dad."

I watched him meticulously cover the Tupperware and place it back exactly where it had come from, the refrigerator light illuminating the Klasko & Fitch shirt he wore so proudly.

"You're one of my two favorite people in the world," he said as he closed the fridge door. "You should get to know my other favorite one. She likely has a better idea of what you're going through than you think."

He smiled as he walked back toward me, kissing the top of my head before disappearing up the stairs.

The sun was just coming up as I heard my father's car engine start in the driveway. I peeked out of my curtains and made my way down the hall to my parents' bedroom.

Low voices were wafting from the television into the hallway. I opened the door slowly to find the shades still tightly drawn. The beige carpeting was as soft as ever under my feet, and the light-blue chaise where I used to lie to watch my mother apply makeup looked just as inviting as it had back then.

My mother, who was propped up on her pillows in bed, reached for the remote and clicked off the TV. "Good morning, Bunny! Did the TV wake you?"

I shook my head. "No. I was up."

She patted the mattress, and a deep sense of comfort washed over me as I hopped into the bed and settled into my father's still-warm imprint.

"I broke up with Sam." My lips quivered as I rested my head on my father's pillow and turned toward my mother. "Well, he broke up with me."

She nodded. "Are you okay?"

"Dad told you?"

"Are you okay?" she asked me again.

"I wanted to tell you . . ." My voice was unsteady.

My mother reached out and touched my cheek with her palm. "Sometimes we don't say things out loud because we don't want them to be true." She contemplated my face. "You will be okay."

"I'm so sad," I admitted, mostly to myself, and blotted the stream of tears spilling from my eyes.

"Breakups are sad." Her obvious words were oddly comforting.

"Are you mad that I couldn't make it work? I know how much you love Sam."

My mother stared at me for a long moment. "I love you, Bunny. And whoever makes you happy, but only because he makes you happy and only for as long as he makes you happy."

"You wanted me to marry Sam. You said it was just cold feet."

She shook her head. "One day, if you want, you will have a child of your own. And you'll understand that her health and happiness is the thing that matters most in the world. You have always been so . . . restless—so resistant to the idea of becoming too comfortable, too normal. What did you want me to say, Alex? Yes! Run away! Break up with him! No." She shook her head. "No, my job was to give you a calm baseline. You've always done exactly as you wanted to, anyway."

I recalled her seemingly offhand response when we had dinner, understanding how much thought she'd put into it. I finally nodded, my eyes locking with hers, a palpable connection that I hadn't felt in years passing between us.

"I don't think I can make it at Klasko," I blurted out. "I feel like . . . it's breaking me."

"Shhhhhh. Don't be absurd. My beautiful, bold girl." She patted my hair as I cried. "You are far stronger than you think.

Maybe Klasko is not the place for you. Maybe it's just a stepping stone on your way to your next adventure. But you're not broken. You just need some time. You're still new there!" She spoke with her lips flush against my forehead, so I could feel her words. I closed my eyes and allowed them to resonate.

CHAPTER 25

That Monday morning, a tease of summer weather momentarily fooled me into thinking I had hibernated away the remainder of the bad dream that would be my first seven months at Klasko. In reality, I had yet to match into a practice group, and the temperature was expected to cool again the following day. But my weekend at home with my parents had quelled the anxiety that had been building in me since the gala. I walked the length of the marble lobby surer of myself than when I'd wobbled out on Friday.

When I got to the forty-first floor, Kevin was leaning against the wall outside my door, scrolling through his phone.

"Hey, sorry—were you waiting for me?"

"Hey," he said, his face brightening. "Yeah. Didn't want to go in there without you."

"Next time, you should feel free." I beckoned him into my office, where I dropped my bag and hung up my coat. He closed the door behind him and then took a seat. "So, what's up?"

"Nothing. I just . . . nothing. I just wanted to say hi. See how you were," he said, then looked above my head and out my window.

"Good. I'm good. What about you?" I asked, forcing enthusiasm into my voice.

"No, I'm really asking." His eyes met mine. "You seemed . . . off . . . that night at the bar with Jordan."

"It was just a bad day," I assured him. "It's a bad few months before we match. Anyway, we're in the final weeks now. Come the end of April, we'll all know where we belong."

"It didn't have to be that stressful. This place makes you think you need to—"

"No offense, but M&A isn't like other groups," I told him, calling my computer to life. "I don't expect you to understand, but trust me, it actually is more stressful in M&A."

"I disagree," he stated plainly. I turned my gaze back to him as he continued. "I do M&A too. Almost exclusively. That night I saw you, Jordan was taking me out to celebrate a really rough deal we had just closed."

I stared at him, feeling betrayed. "Why didn't you ever mention this?" *And why didn't Jordan or Matt?*

"I didn't not mention it on purpose. Or maybe it was on purpose, I don't know." He smoothed his hair behind his ears, looking more and more like Jordan with every motion. "I like you, and I want to be your friend. I saw how you and Carmen treated each other, and I didn't want any part of it."

My cheeks flushed. "Carmen is my best friend in our class!"

"Really? When you got an invite to Miami, she told the whole class you got it because you were sleeping with Jaskel. With friends like that . . ."

I sat there stunned for a moment before forcing out a short laugh. Part of me had always known she was the source of the rumor. But the other part of me was crushed. I wondered how many more lessons in the ugliness of human nature I'd be forced to endure.

"Alex, you know how much work the group has. They have room to take on at least five new associates a year. And they do want associates who will go out and party with them. But they need associates who are good lawyers."

I stared back at him, recalling the countless times Didier, Matt, and Jordan had told me that all that mattered was my work. "You should have told me you were ranking M&A," I grumbled. I needed to be angry at something other than my own behavior.

"Maybe you're right. But we're both going to match, so who cares?" He coughed, then changed the subject. "More importantly, how are you doing?"

"I'm okay. Really. Just going through some personal stuff right now, but I'm hanging in."

Kevin nodded, seeming to accept my brush-off. "Yeah. Okay. Good. We all feel the pressure. I mean, I took the not-so-subtle free gym membership as a hint and gained thirty pounds of muscle. I changed my hair. And my clothes—"

My phone rang. "*Peter Dunn*" flashed on the screen. "I have to grab this," I said apologetically, and Kevin stood to go. "For what it's worth, you look good," I called after him.

"Hi, Peter," I said, feeling a new sense of calm and control after my conversation with Kevin and a weekend with my parents. I wondered if Carmen had gone to management about him. Maybe I should go. Start putting up my own boundaries. Making my own rules.

"Hi. I'm swamped, but can you send a few NDAs to Gary? I just updated them for the year and made some changes. They're saved on the system. And can you call Quality to make a pickup at Starlight?"

He sounded like business as usual. I guess Carmen either hadn't talked to anyone yet or no longer planned to. In the past two weeks I had performed all associate tasks on my Stag River deals flawlessly. But I knew I would have to speak up eventually if I was asked to do any work directly for Gary. I closed my eyes, readying myself for the speech I had rehearsed on the train back from my parents' house. *I would prefer to no longer work for Gary Kaplan directly in any capacity. Though I'd like to continue working on Stag River matters he's not involved with. If this means I can no longer work on Stag River deals more generally, so be it. I will find replacements on all my active matters. I . . .*

"Sure," I said hesitantly, still playing out an idea that had started percolating in my mind.

"Great. Thanks." He hung up, and I stared at the phone for a moment before deciding not to call Quality. Instead, I grabbed my coat.

"Anna!" I called, and she popped her head up. "I have some appointments uptown this morning. I'll be on email."

I hailed a cab as I wriggled into my thin trench coat and slid into the back seat. "Seventy-Second between Park and Madison, please," I instructed the driver, then leaned back, the edges of the duct tape covering the leather's tears sticking to my back. Anxiety coursed through me, and my rational brain insisted I'd see Gary Kaplan waiting outside his building. But every instinct I had told me I'd find something different.

The Starlight Diner awning was a well-worn navy canvas, with faded gold stars dotting the background. As soon as I entered the small restaurant, I saw a rotating cylinder displaying a carrot cake dotted with walnuts and the obligatory carrot made of frosting, pillows of meringue atop a bright yellow gelatin filling, and a variety of chocolate-based confections. A stocky gentleman with his neck draped in a large gold chain and cross and a thick black mustache greeted me.

"I'm meeting somebody," I told him. *I'm just not sure who.* I smiled politely and scanned the restaurant. A few of the red leather booths were filled; I saw an older couple bent low to their soup bowls, two young moms tending to their children while struggling to carry on a conversation, a beautiful young woman with soft, strawberry-blond waves, and three teenage boys huddled around one of their phones, laughing. But Gary Kaplan was nowhere to be seen.

I looked back at the young woman, who sat wrapped in a pale-blue oversize pashmina as she stared out the window. Her face was placid, but the fingers on her right hand picked nervously at a cuticle on her left. I focused in on her and noticed that her posture was awful—she was hunched over the table in a way somebody dressed that expensively would have been taught not to be—and she seemed to be fighting tears. I watched as she grabbed for her water glass, which shook so wildly in her hand that she placed it down again without taking a sip.

I nodded to the host and made my way to her, then stood next to her booth for a moment as she looked up at me expectantly. She was radiant, with delicate features and the clearest blue eyes I'd ever seen.

"Are you waiting for a Quality car?" I asked softly. I prayed she would have no idea what I was talking about, but I saw a muted terror behind her eyes before her expression went studiously neutral. *Shit.* It was her. I didn't know who she was or what she was doing. But this was who I was looking for. To bring myself to eye level with her, and hopefully reassure her, I took my coat off and slid into the booth opposite her.

She stared at my waist rather than my face as I sat, craning her neck over the table as her face filled with panic, her eyes darting wildly.

"It's okay," I said, and held my hands up. I had never in my life elicited such fear in another human. "I'm not here to hurt you, I promise."

"I wasn't going to say anything. I'm just waiting for a car." She looked off into the distance, her legs still on the seat.

"I'm just . . . say anything about what?"

"You're with Klasko," she said accusingly.

I quickly realized what had frightened her and ripped my Klasko security badge from the waist of my skirt before tossing it into my purse.

"No," I said quietly. "No. I'm not . . . Not right now. I'm here . . . I want to help."

She allowed a sarcastic laugh to escape her lips. "I'm sure you do," she hissed, rising out of her seat. "Klasko! That name is all over those fucking NDAs I sign."

I slid across my seat and took a step toward her. When I placed a hand on her shoulder, though, she visibly winced, and I instantly pulled it back. She opened her pashmina quickly to rewrap herself, and I spotted an angry red bruise with purple borders peeking out from the top of her shirt. It was the kind of mark that made me swallow hard and lose my breath—the kind that would be black in a week and green the next and yellow the one after.

She saw me notice it and retreated deeper inside the plush blue cashmere, sitting again. I slid slowly into the seat next to her.

"I'm Alex," I said, not knowing where else to begin.

"I'm just waiting for my car," she said, and I gave a small shake of my head to communicate that her car wasn't coming. Her shoulders slumped.

"What did he do to you?" I whispered.

She smoothed a few red-gold strands away from her perspiring brow and looked me dead in the eyes for a long, pregnant moment. "I can't," she finally whispered, taking out the personal NDA for Gary R. Kaplan with which I was all too familiar, the firm's red letterhead shouting from the top of the page.

"NDAs can't prevent somebody from reporting a crime," I assured her. "They're null."

She straightened slightly. "I'm not sure it is a crime. I go willingly. I sign up for it."

"Well, you can tell me. Consider it attorney-client privilege," I told her. *Please don't point out that Gary is actually my client in this scenario.*

She doubled over again in a wave of pain, and I placed my hand over hers. She flipped her palm and squeezed mine tightly until it passed.

"I think I need a doctor," she said quietly. Her eyes focused and unfocused, and before I even knew what was happening, I was in a cab with her to Lenox Hill Hospital.

I had never taken somebody to the emergency room before, and though I tried my best to fill out the forms, she was so delirious with pain that I didn't trust most of her answers. According to her Miami driver's license, she was Kristen Molloy. According to her, she was allergic to all pain meds. "Except morphine," she added with a laugh. I erred on the side of caution and wrote "might be allergic to pain meds." I felt like I was watching myself from outer space as I argued with the nurse at the front desk, then moved on to a physician's assistant, who took one look at her and ushered us into a room with a promise he'd be back with a doctor as soon as possible. I propped Kristen up in front of me and gently removed her blue wrap from her shoulders and began to undo her white button-down so she could put on the robe the PA had provided. As her shirt fell slowly open, her alabaster skin darkened down her torso into angry shades of red and black. I felt tears spilling out over my cheeks despite my attempt to be stoic.

As soon as her top was off, she turned her back to me, and I had to shut my eyes for a moment. Her back was a collage of patchwork violence. I couldn't imagine which instruments made most of the marks, but there had to have been belts or whips involved. I took in the scratch marks, bloody and raw, and the bite marks up by her shoulder. I held open the robe as she eased her arms through the armholes, and she turned back to me as she pulled the two sides of the robe across her chest.

"I don't have insurance," she said.

"Don't worry. I got it." I could barely get the words out through my tears.

The PA returned with a tall, balding physician, both of their expressions serious.

"Are you family?" the doctor asked.

I shook my head, and they politely asked me to wait outside, though I could still make out most of what they were saying through the thin curtain forming her ER "room." She adamantly refused a rape kit. Her breast implant had somehow been flipped. "He kicked it," she kept repeating. There was a flutter of movement, and from what I could gather from the whispers, she had tried to stand and fallen slightly. I could hear her yelling for them to take their hands off her, when I assumed they were trying to help. Then there was silence. Then crying. I plugged my ears with my fingers and sank to the floor.

As soon as the doctor left, I slipped back in to find Kristen getting dressed.

"You're finished?" I asked, though I knew she couldn't have been.

"Thanks so much," she said, avoiding my eyes as she did.

"Where are you headed now?" I asked.

"Home," she said with a shrug. "I just email his assistant to say when I want the plane to be ready. And I guess they ask you to get us the car. But *that* didn't happen this time. So, I'll cab it to LaGuardia." She sounded angry with me, rather than with the man who'd beaten her black and blue.

"You've done this before?" I asked, looking at her in disbelief.

Her sharp gaze pierced through any notion I'd had of being a hero. "Don't look at me like some victim. He pays us twenty-five g's to beat the shit out of us. He just got out of control this time. No matter how many times I screamed our safe word, he just kept hitting and hitting and hitting . . ." Her voice trailed off as her brain seemed to go to some dark place, and then retreat from it. "It happens. I'll definitely pay you back for the hospital bill. I just need a little time."

I shook my head. "Us?"

"He flies us up from Miami. Because we don't know people here, I guess."

"But . . . how? I mean . . . where? Where is his wife during all of this?"

"I don't know. I assume somewhere else? Not like we hang out at his apartment. He has a whole separate entrance for us. A separate space. Just four walls and some beds and . . . contraptions." She shuddered, seeing something in her mind that terrified her. "Look, I have a kid. I'm too old to model anymore. I do what I have to. We all do."

"So you're just going to let him do this? You're going to let him get away with it?" I couldn't believe I was yelling at her, a woman who had just taken the beating of her life, but the words came before I knew it.

She took a few cautious steps toward me and bent her impossibly long legs to bring her face level with mine. "You don't get it. He is a monster," she hissed at me before taking a step back, menace in her tone. "This is nothing compared to what he *could* do to me. To my family."

Her words were an echo of what Gary had said the night of The Incident. *She won't talk.* The Incident flooded back to me. I heard their laughter and my screams. I recalled how I had trusted his words, his power to ruin me. I nodded at her slowly, empathetically.

I stepped to the side to leave her to fill out her discharge paperwork. What other option did I have?

Still standing in the emergency room, I took out my cell phone and called Carmen's office line. She picked it up right away with a "Hey."

"Hey. Did you go to management?"

"Yeah," she said, her tone hard to read.

"And?" I asked.

"And . . . I think I'm going to take some time away from Klasko. From BigLaw, actually," she said quietly. They offered her money to sign an NDA, I thought. Those assholes. And Peter was just going about his business, enabling Gary Kaplan's monstrous violence.

"Did you sign anything yet?"

"Alex . . . I can't talk about it."

"Carmen! Did you? Don't say anything if you haven't signed it yet." I waited a full five seconds. "Good. Don't sign anything. I have a plan."

I walked back into the lobby just as my colleagues were returning from their long lunches at Wolfgang's and The Grill. As soon as I sat down at my desk, I immediately emailed Matt and Jordan and asked them to come to my office. I sat in my chair and stared at the open door, biting at the callus on my thumb as the unread emails stacked up in my in-box. When they appeared in my doorway, I motioned for them to close my door.

"I've got a dead-body situation," I said to them as soon as they sat, taking a tissue and wrapping my thumb in it, now bloody from where I'd bitten my cuticle. "I think I need help." I wasn't fully certain I'd ever uttered that phrase before.

"What have you gotten yourself into, Skippy?" Matt's tone was calm, measured, and I understood immediately why people wanted him as their attorney.

I stopped fighting the tears that streamed down my cheeks. "There is a laundry list of very screwed-up shit happening to women at this firm. Peter Dunn, who is not even the worst part, has had sex with both Carmen and with me," I said, spitting the words out as though they were poison. I tried to ignore their facial expressions, which seemed to freeze in shock and then melt in disappointment, and forced myself to continue. "The most egregious, possibly criminal act with which the firm is involved is the facilitation of Gary Kaplan beating women half to death by arming him with airtight NDAs prior to engaging in such activity. We then call cars for the bruised and beaten women, from our own car service, to take them to the airport. I just met one of the women. She was all messed up."

I paused. They were staring at me, looking uncertain whether I was serious.

Finally Jordan cleared his throat and forced a half smile. "I had my money on you being way too deep into a coke habit."

Matt ignored him as he squinted, trying to make sense of it all. "I assume you can prove this Gary thing?"

I shrugged. "Well, I guess there's enough evidence with the cars. And I'm not trying to prove this in a court of law. I just want the firm to stop it. I have enough to prove to Mike Baccard that it's happening."

"And Carmen? Is she willing to speak?" Matt asked.

"She already did."

Matt leaned back in his chair and clasped his hands behind his head, ready to analyze all the angles of the situation, then dropped his hands and straightened his tie, preparing for battle. "Okay, Skip. What do you need from me?"

"Come with me to a meeting with Mike Baccard?"

He nodded. "Of course. And I know it's not worth much, but for what it's worth, I'm really sorry. . . . I wish I could have shielded you from this."

"Yeah, Skip. You're our girl. I'm so sorry this happened to you, that we didn't protect you," Jordan added.

I nodded in gratitude as I fought the urge to correct them. I didn't need their protection. Not any longer. I could protect myself.

I shifted my weight in my seat as I forced myself to recount the mistakes I had made with Peter and what I had discovered about Gary Kaplan to Mike Baccard. I heard my own words in my ears, but my brain was focused on the brittle hairs of whatever hide Mike's designer chairs were made out of digging uncomfortably into the back of my thighs. Only when I had finished speaking did I notice the thudding in my chest. I immediately regretted saying anything at all. What was I thinking, telling the chair of my firm that I'd had an affair with a senior partner? This was the dumbest thing I could have done. My career was over. I breathed in deeply and exhaled slowly, calming my pressured breaths, and then turned to Matt. He gave me an encouraging nod of approval before we both looked back at Mike, who nodded deliberately, leaning his balding head back in his plush leather chair in his massive office.

"I'm so sorry that this has been your experience thus far at Klasko. I'm terribly displeased," he said, transforming from an attorney into a politician. His face somehow revealed nothing at all about what he was thinking, making my effort to determine whether he already knew any of what I had told him entirely futile. "And I cannot speak to the situation with Carmen Greyson, but we would very much like to make you whole after this experience."

I glared at him. "I don't want money. I want things to change. Are you going to address the situation with Stag River and Gary Kaplan?"

Matt spoke up from next to me. "Mike, we need to do something about it."

"I'm sure your information is accurate," Mike said slickly. "But we have no proof."

"I have proof that Gary Kaplan's a sexual predator," I said, and they both snapped to attention.

"What did you say, dear?" Mike asked me. *Did he just call me "dear"?*

"I have a recording of Gary attempting to sexually assault me. I left myself a voice-mail message of the entire thing. It's fuzzy, but his voice is clear enough that you would know it's him. A jury might, too." In reality, I knew that the message was probably an indiscernible blur of noise, but at this moment it was the only leverage I seemed to have.

"Gary Kaplan sexually assaulted you?" Mike leaned in toward me.

"He did," I said as calmly as I could manage.

The two of them stared at me with slack jaws. Matt put his hand on my shoulder, and then took it away, as if suddenly thinking it was inappropriate.

"If you don't want money, what do you want?" Mike asked measuredly.

"I do want money. Just not for myself. Sorry if that wasn't clear. I want an annual budget. A women's initiative budget of two million dollars. That's the amount of our legal fees on one or two deals every year for Stag River. We must do thirty of them each year."

"Two million? Annually?" Matt clarified.

I nodded.

Mike grunted. "You couldn't possibly spend that in a year."

"We can. I'm thinking globally. I want to start a BigLaw women's initiative, with events throughout the year and one large global event annually in New York or London with guest speakers, breakout sessions, empowerment and self-defense seminars, the whole nine yards. It will be free for all women in BigLaw. Klasko will graciously offer to finance it. At least for the first few years. I'd imagine other firms will want to sponsor going forward." I looked down for a moment before continuing. "The only way I'm ever going to feel normal again after what happened is if I use it to make a difference."

Matt puffed out his chest. "We have to make sure this kind of thing never happens again."

"It will happen again," I said, stopping just shy of snapping at him. "Many times, I'm sure. My goal is to teach people how to deal with it. And to create a system of accountability and repercussions and support."

Matt and Mike looked at each other, and Mike's expression grayed over as he opened his mouth to speak. My mind clicked through a montage of the countless occasions in which I had watched Matt and Peter negotiate terms in their favor. I saw before me a series of choices: Speak or listen? Firm or friendly? Lowball or overshoot?

I cut Mike off. "If I'm not given the funds, I'll forward that email of the recording to every contact I have. *Below the Belt* would eat it up. I'll ruin Stag River. Can you really survive without them as a client?" I narrowed my eyes. "Thank god for digital voice mail, right?"

Mike stared at me, looking defensive. "You'd take down Gary Kaplan. Not Stag River."

I raised an eyebrow at him. "Are you so sure?" I saw Matt trying not to smile as he recognized his own signature move on my face.

"Young lady, I know you'd like to join the ranks of the M&A team, and destroying their largest client is not the way—"

I almost leapt across the table at his use of the diminutive, but Matt felt the change in my energy and intervened before I could.

"Give her the funds, Mike," he said, cutting him off. "You don't really have a choice."

Mike stared him down for a protracted moment as I squirmed in my seat, then blinked first. "I'll need to convince the executive team. This will come out of the global budget."

I exhaled and allowed my shoulders to drop below my earlobes. It was essentially a yes.

As we left Mike Baccard's office together, Matt's eyes were glistening. I gave him a smile and shook my head as if to tell him, *Don't be sad for me.*

"I'm proud of you, Skippy. And a little scared of you, to be honest." He gave a small laugh as he walked down the hallway.

I'd sent Carmen and Nancy a cryptic email asking them both to stop by my office, and recounted the story of the assault, the diner, and the budget I'd secured for the women's initiative, barely stopping for a breath. "So?" I finally asked. "What do you say?"

They sat staring at me, which I hadn't anticipated. I'd expected excitement, even gratitude, given what we'd all been through.

"Say something," I said, my tone almost pleading.

"It's so awful" was all Carmen could manage.

Nancy nodded. "I can't believe that happened to you."

"No! I mean about being VP and secretary of the Women's Initiative." They were focusing on entirely the wrong part of my story. "I need you guys."

Nancy seemed to process it, and began to nod. "I'm in. Whatever you need. I think we can make it really great. We can—"

"I can't," Carmen blurted out. Nancy and I watched her with bated breath, hoping that she'd change her mind. "I just need to get out of here. Make a clean break." She crossed her hands and pulled them apart like an umpire calling somebody safe.

She'd rather take the money. I started to leap to judgment, but stopped myself. However disappointed I was, I couldn't fault her for taking it and starting a new life. I almost wondered if I'd have done the same if I had seen whatever they were willing to offer me in black and white, a check waiting to be deposited.

A few days later I rose with the sun and made my way to midtown to handle some paperwork before my lunch with Mike Baccard and the global chair of the firm. They'd signed the papers guaranteeing to sponsor the annual seminar for posterity in an amount not to exceed $2 million per annum, with a minimum of 1 percent of Stag River billings to be donated to the Klasko Women's Initiative budget. We were meeting to discuss my experience, my goals for the initiative. I wondered whether they would ask me to sign an NDA. I never would, of course. They could either give me what I wanted and hope I never spoke up, or they could not give me what I wanted and be certain I'd go to the press. I assumed they were smart enough to proceed with the former.

As I approached my office, Anna stood to greet me. "Vivienne White is waiting for you in your office," she said nervously.

I pushed through my door, and Vivienne glanced up briefly from my guest chair and gave a tight smile. Her gray Moreau bag was tossed carelessly on the floor beside her. I held my breath as I made my way to sit behind my desk.

She stared at me for a protracted moment. *She's heard about The Incident. She's going to want to talk about it.* My legs bounced, and when I pressed down on my knees, my palm bounced too.

"I heard about what you're doing. The women's initiative," she said. I looked up at her, hoping I wouldn't need to tell her what had precipitated the initiative. I could use her help, after all. I'd accept it graciously, crediting her mentorship for all the work I'd done; I'd figure out a large role for her to play—maybe even VP.

She cleared her throat. "I understand the inclination, but first off, this place won't change. This industry won't change. And second, you need to be careful not to undo the hard work that women in my generation did to get things to where they are now."

I pushed my spine up against the back of my chair, lifting my chin. "I appreciate the advice," I managed.

Vivienne's eyes narrowed. She uncrossed her legs and recrossed them, then enmeshed her fingers together in her lap. We stared at one another, anger boiling underneath our perfect posture and designer blouses.

She broke first, to my delight. Her tone was low and angry. "I gave everything I have so this place would invest in female associates. I swallowed my pride and fetched coffee so you'd get invited to board meetings and charity balls. I let clients sweat on me and drool over me so you could be here now and walk into Mike Baccard's office and ask for firm funds to be allocated to the betterment of women in the workplace and he wouldn't laugh you the fuck out of there." She leaned back and smoothed her beige silk blouse into her navy pleated skirt, then readjusted her diamond drop necklace so it lay back in the center of her chest.

She has no idea why Mike didn't laugh me out of his office, I thought. *Not because she made great strides for women. It was because I almost got raped by a client.* I tried to view her reaction more rationally. She was right, of course. I owed her and her generation a debt of gratitude for making the firm care about its diversity statistics and its ratio of female to male partners. But BigLaw, big business, had gotten off course somewhere, missing the mark entirely.

"I appreciate what you've done. But you must know things aren't right around here. They're better—in large part due to you. But they're not good." I watched her carefully and added, "And women like you and I would never settle for good enough."

Her lip curled as she shrugged and plastered a small smile on her face, then grabbed her Moreau and rose from her seat. "Good luck to you, Alexandra. I mean it."

"Oh, by the way, I always meant to tell you—I love your bag," I said, standing to show her out. *I hope everything you did to be able to afford it was worth it.*

I arched my back, folded my arms, and turned to stare down at all the people scurrying about on the street below my window like ants. I heard a faint knock on my door.

"Come in!"

Anna poked her head in and stepped over the threshold. "If you need anything today, let me know," she stammered. "I don't mean to pry, but are you okay?"

"I am," I told her with a small smile, appreciating her concern.

Anna pushed the door against the frame without shutting it all the way. "I've seen thousands of associates start here. Everybody gets tired. Everybody starts dressing better. Some get fat. Some get skinny. But you . . . you have a lunch with Mike Baccard on your calendar today." She paused. "I've never seen somebody with so many important partners in her office in her first year." I didn't know what to say. It didn't exactly feel like a compliment. Or a question. "You're doing something right."

"Or very wrong!" I looked at the ceiling and laughed.

Anna nodded, apparently having said what she came to say, and slipped back out to the hallway.

I turned back to my window, trying to work out what my view would be like from the fifty-sixth floor. I mentally placed myself in the office and oriented my mental image. It would be totally different. I'd be looking uptown.

EPILOGUE

Q. Do you currently represent Stag River or Gary Kaplan in any capacity?

A. My firm did until recently. I have not personally worked on a Stag River matter or for Gary Kaplan since my first year as an associate.

Q. Thank you, Ms. Vogel. That concludes our questions regarding your experience at Klasko & Fitch. Thank you for your candor. One last question, for the record: Do you know or have any relationship with the plaintiff, Sheila Platt?

A. No. Well, I understand she is Gary Kaplan's longtime assistant, so it's possible that at some point I spoke with her when I was working for Stag River. But no, no relationship I am aware of.

Q. Thank you, Ms. Vogel. That concludes our deposition. The questions and answers today will be typed up by the court reporter into a deposition transcript. You have the right to read the deposition and review the answers prior to signing a statement as to their accuracy.

A. Thank you.

Q. Trial is slated to begin on October 1st. We will be in touch about the day of your witness testimony. It is at the judge's discretion whether you will be permitted to attend the entire trial. Do you have any further questions at this time?

A. No. Thank you.

I heard nothing except a tinny ringing in my ears as the judge banged her gavel. Her lips moved resolutely above the collar of her robe, but when they stopped, I thought I could detect disappointment in their slope. I inhaled sharply and looked at Gary, wishing I could hear anything at all. He hugged his attorney close before falling into a tearful embrace with his wife. His wife looked grave, as if she'd aged twenty years in the past few since I'd seen her at the Met. His daughter, now a young woman with long dark hair and an elegant long neck, hung back slightly, seeming to wrestle with something in her head, before leaning in and hugging her father. I wished desperately that they were saying goodbye to one another. But their tears were decidedly happy ones. They were celebrating.

Suddenly the courtroom cacophony rushed in on me—uproarious joy from some pockets and the silent endurance of agony from others. I was now painfully aware of the wooden bench digging into my backside, which was less padded than usual after a week of a stomach in knots and intermittent vomiting.

"Excuse me," the couple to my right said, making their way into the aisle. They looked pleased. The woman was the female version of Gary. *Must be his sister and her husband.* Her calf-length mink coat brushed my legs, and her perfume pervaded the air around me, perverting it further, choking me.

I forced myself to stand and make my way out of the large, dark wooden doors and into the marble-floored hallway, staring straight ahead as people filed past me. I pushed my feet forward and into step with the crowd.

It had been futile. All of it. There'd been no purpose to my public recounting of that night, and the nights that led up to it, and the aftermath. No sweet end to reliving the bitter nightmare aloud to a room full of stoic strangers and unfeeling recording devices. Gary Kaplan's poor secretary, who had accused him of rape, who had relied on me to provide convincing witness testimony, would have to live with the fact that he'd simply gotten away with it. He was innocent under the law. And in my world, the law was the only thing that mattered. I felt that the system had somehow failed me, and attempted to mollify my racing thoughts with the soothing idea of the women's initiative, now successfully celebrating its third anniversary, but it did little to help.

I continued down the marble steps, avoiding the sideways glances and whispers from the people who'd seen me testify, and filed out of the double doors with the crowd, allowing the hibernal air to rouse me out of my trance. I moved off to the side of the courthouse steps, the sun forcing me to squint, and I suddenly felt, saw, and heard everything, as I began to process what had just happened in the courtroom. I had the sense of a bottomless black hole appearing below me, of being in free fall. I doubled over and pressed my palms into my bent knees to steady myself. I could hear my heart thudding.

I'm having a heart attack. I'm dying. This is it.

When death didn't arrive, I wiggled my fingers to confirm I was still among the living, then straightened my spine. As I did, I locked eyes with a woman who stood a few steps below me, her light red waves of hair spilling out from beneath a powder-blue hat as she contemplated me with an unsmiling expression. My stomach flipped as I recalled her bruised, slashed back. She continued to stare at me, but then she suddenly dipped her head forward from the tip of her long neck in an almost imperceptible bow of gratitude, before turning away and descending the stairs.

I remained frozen in place as my breathing slowed, then craned my neck to the sky and let the sun warm my face for a prolonged moment before heading down the steps, into the subway, and back to my office on the fifty-sixth floor. I held on to the metal bar above my head for balance as the 4 train jerked its way uptown, scanning the faces of those on the train with me, wondering how many of the women around me had been victims of unwanted advances, unwelcome touching, and assault.

I hurried out of the elevator and into my office, eager to dive into work and put the trial out of my mind. I'd spoken the truth, I reminded myself. But Gary Kaplan wouldn't be going to jail, and he could always accurately claim he was an innocent man. Still, Klasko had fired Stag River and Gary as a client as soon as the alleged extent of the abuses came to light when charges were filed, unwilling to be publicly affiliated with such a scandal in any capacity. Whether of his own volition or a not-so-gentle urging from the partnership, Peter left the firm even before the trial had begun. He had already joined Pennybaker & Neff, another top-ten firm, and I knew he would have a whole host of associates working for him who had no awareness of his past. I knew he might be replaced at Klasko by new transgressors. But I had to reassure myself that in speaking the truth, there is a kind of victory. Though I wanted nothing more than to see Gary put away for a long time, I had to find a bit of peace in the justice inherent in the process, more than in the verdict.

As I rushed by Anna, the phone on her desk rang. "Alex Vogel's office . . . I'm sorry, she's not in right now." I paused to listen. "I'll give her the message." Anna hung up and stared at me without saying anything. *Reporters.* I pushed through the glass door into my office and slipped out of my coat. Before I even sat, there was a knock on my doorframe, even though the door was open.

"Hey!" I sank into my desk chair as I looked up to see Nancy. She measured me with her eyes for a moment, and I knew from the way she cocked her head to the side that she had heard the verdict. "Not my best day," I sighed, admitting it so she didn't have to ask.

Nancy gave me a small smile. "I'm so sorry, Alex. Is there anything I can do to help?"

I nodded, because there was. "Let's get to work. We've got a lot ahead of us."

ACKNOWLEDGMENTS

To Michael, Risa, Mindy, and Greg, thank you for tempering the lows and heightening the highs of this publishing process. Thank you to Jude and Liv for giving me the extra hugs and kisses I needed while editing. One day when you're older, I'll show you this Acknowledgments page and let you read this book. And to Liv in particular, and all little girls, may the working world be more level for your generation than it was for mine.

To Allison Hunter, I do not know where I would be were it not for your faith, friendship, and guidance. This book would not be without you. And if somehow it were, it would certainly be titled something else.

To Emily Griffin, thank you for making my book the best book it could be, for your meticulous attention to detail, for your patience, and your support.

To Debbee Klein, Sally Willcox, and Valarie Phillips, thank you for seeing the movie this book could be before it was ever even a book.

To Carey and Courtney, who yelled a resounding "Do it! Start today!" when I said I was thinking of writing a book.

To my dear friends, for always asking me how my writing was going, for never making me feel silly for trying to write a novel in my minimal free time, for knowing when I needed your encouragement, and for knowing when I just needed your company . . . and some wine.

To Jennifer and Brendan, for the keen and gentle eyes with which you read.

To Peter Gethers, thank you for telling me to "keep going" and for telling me I was so close when you knew just how far I was.

To the young man on West Twenty-third Street who stood in my path and told me to smile when I was taking one of my nightly walks to contemplate my book, get out of my way. I wasn't thinking happy thoughts. I was thinking big thoughts.

To everyone who sees the ugly parts of themselves in these characters and wonders if I'm writing about them, I'm not. (But I am . . .)

ABOUT THE AUTHOR

ERICA KATZ is the pseudonym for a graduate of the University of Michigan, Ann Arbor, and Columbia Law School who began her career at a major Manhattan law firm. A native of New Jersey, she now lives in New York City, where she's employed at another large law firm. *The Boys' Club* is her first novel.